## The stellar science fiction of
## RICK SHELLEY

## The Buchanan Campaign

For years the planet Buchanan was a peaceful place
where hardworking citizens could carve a life for
themselves far removed from the battle raging between the Federation and the Second Commonwealth.
Until now . . .

*Now comes Shelley's newest adventure of*
*interplanetary warfare . . .*

## The Fires of Coventry

*Ace Books by Rick Shelley*

UNTIL RELIEVED
SIDE SHOW
JUMP PAY
THE BUCHANAN CAMPAIGN
THE FIRES OF COVENTRY

# THE
# FIRES OF
# COVENTRY

# RICK SHELLEY

ACE BOOKS, NEW YORK

This book is an Ace original edition,
and has never been previously published.

THE FIRES OF COVENTRY

An Ace Book / published by arrangement with
the author

PRINTING HISTORY
Ace edition / November 1996

The Putnam Berkley World Wide Web site address is
http://www.berkley.com/berkley

ISBN: 0-441-00385-0

ACE®
Ace Books are published by The Berkley Publishing Group,
200 Madison Avenue, New York, NY 10016.
ACE and the "A" design are trademarks
belonging to Charter Communications, Inc.

PRINTED IN THE UNITED STATES OF AMERICA

10  9  8  7  6  5  4  3  2  1

To Stan Schmidt
For starting it all

and

To Chloie Airoldi
and the whole gang at
The Knoxville Area Science Fiction Association
For keeping the fires stoked

# THE
# FIRES OF
# COVENTRY

## COURT NEWS TODAY

**The following exchange** is reliably reported to have taken place during a Commonwealth Day reception at St. James Palace in Westminster. The earl of Bath, one of our most noted military strategists until his retirement before the start of the current war, was speaking prior to the arrival of His Majesty.

"There is only one thing wrong with war," the earl said.

"There is everything wrong with war," Prince William, duke of Haven, said, interrupting. "The difficulty is that sometimes every conceivable alternative is even worse. Anyone who thinks otherwise has no business being involved in decisions relating to war or the conduct of it."

From *The Westminster Court Intelligencer*

## DISASTER ON REUNION

**The Seventh and** Ninth Territorial Armies, with attached units of Fifth Army Corps, Thirty-first Armored Brigade, Second Home Guard Regiment of Lorenzo, and Sixth Pioneer Regiment (Provisional) under the overall command of Field Marshal Sir Edmund Raleigh Manchester, have been virtually wiped out on the new colony world of Reunion.

No precise casualty count has been released yet, but unconfirmed reports state that no more than 1200 survivors have been located. The total manpower of the army group was estimated at 250,000 prior to the unexpected Federation attack. There were also substantial civilian casualties, although the full extent of those has not yet been determined.

The raid, apparently by two frigates from the Confederation of Human Worlds, introduced a new and very disturbing weapon into their ongoing war against the Second Commonwealth. A series of large and extremely powerful incendiary devices ignited a firestorm which literally consumed the entire area where the Commonwealth Army was staging training maneuvers.

Reunion, far removed from any Federation world and from any area where hostilities have taken place, was considered to be an exceptionally safe site for training purposes. The world had been colonized only within the past thirty years. The fact that military exercises were being conducted there was thought to be secret. The Federation raid came without warning.

A spokesperson for the Ministry of War states that preparations are already under way for an official Board of Inquiry into the tragedy.

From *The Times of Westminster*

## April 19, FY 562

**The Chancellor of** the Exchequer today presented me with rather dismal figures concerning the cost of defending ourselves against the Confederation of Human Worlds. The complete report is quite extensive and detailed, but the summary in the introduction is depressing enough. The first forty-two months of warfare, dating from the Federation's declaration of war, have not only entirely consumed the surplus revenue of His Majesty's Government, but they have taxed to the limit our ability to raise funds. Even with the higher tax rates approved by Parliament for Buckingham, and the additional funds subscribed by other member worlds of the Commonwealth, we are not keeping pace with the costs of this war. In fact, the Chancellor estimates that each year that hostilities continue will require seventeen years of peacetime prosperity to retire the debt. And that, he notes, is making the most generous estimates of future revenues, and the quickest conceivable end to the war. The longer that hostilities continue, the longer the payback ratio will become, entailing higher interest rates and so forth. The Chancellor's most startling conclusion is that if this war should—God forbid—last another six years, the debt will be so huge as to be self-perpetuating, an eternal drain on the finances of His Majesty's Government unless substantial changes are made to the Constitution of the Second Commonwealth, which is politically unthinkable.

From *The Secret Wartime Diaries of*
*Prime Minister Sir Wallace Telford*

# Part 1

**Reggie Bailey leaned** back in his chair at the head of the dining room table and smiled in deep satisfaction. No one noticed. The rest of the family was staring at the birthday display in the center of the table. The centerpiece was magnificent, and his twin girls, Angel and Ariel, were obviously overjoyed. They kept squealing in delight, pointing at each new convolution of the four-foot bubble that had risen from the narrow power base.

The skin of the bubble shimmered and trembled as if it were no more than the iridescent soap film it appeared to be. Inside, two smaller bubbles orbited each other at increasing speeds. Each of the smaller spheres enclosed a display of eight sparklers that spun and twirled, cycling through a rainbow of colors.

The birthday girls, now eight years old, sat along one side of the table. Their twelve-year-old brother Al sat across from them, trying not to show that he was as delighted as the girls. Reggie's wife Ida sat at the far end of the table from her husband. The expression on her face, halfway between a smile and a smirk, resulted from more than the joy of her daughters or the magnificent birthday surprise that Reggie had come up with. She had just that afternoon learned something that none of the others knew yet, not even Reggie.

After ten minutes, the show went into its climax. The sparklers in one balloon turned an intense blue and brightened. Those in the other small sphere cycled through to a brilliant red. The lights seemed to expand to completely fill the smaller globes, which in turn grew in size until they pressed into each other and deformed, filling the largest sphere. The intensity of the light grew until it was almost, but not quite, painful to watch. Then the bubbles all burst simultaneously, spreading a shower of very tiny confetti, red and blue, over the table and the people sitting around it. The confetti would evaporate in less than an hour, leaving nothing to clean up.

Angel and Ariel launched into a storm of excited applause and cheering. Their faces were both red with the force of delight and excitement. Then they were talking, both at once, sometimes in unison but more often at cross purposes.

"It was the best ever, Daddy," Ariel managed to get out during a short pause by her sister.

"Wonderful!" Angel said. "Wonderful, wonderful!"

"Delightful," Ida contributed. Her voice remained low, but the word did penetrate the renewed cacophony of the twins.

"I didn't know anybody could do anything like that," Al said. He had taken his time deciding what to say. He didn't want to sound *too* impressed for something given to his sisters.

"I wasn't sure myself that Eric could pull it off," Reggie said. Eric Knowles, a close friend and neighbor, had long claimed to be the best specialty nanotech designer on Coventry. Reggie decided that he would no longer contest Eric's claim, even if the town of Hawthorne was far from being all of the world. Reggie had been prepared to settle for something more modest, but he had talked about the fanciest display he could imagine, and Eric had kept assuring him, "I can do that." Reggie had taken him at his word. Now he was glad that he had.

"I'll get the cake and ice cream," Ida said, getting up from the table. It would be much later, she decided, after the children were in bed, before she would tell her husband that they were going to have another child.

The children were all in bed. Ida was in the bathroom of the master suite getting ready. Reggie sat on his side of the bed, turned on the complink, and dialed up the late news summary, part of his nightly ritual. He started to lean back to listen in comfort, but the first news item stopped his movement instantly.

"Naval vessels of the Confederation of Human Worlds have emerged from Q-space over Coventry and appear to be launching large numbers of small craft. They have not contacted planetary authorities or replied to queries from local space traffic control in Coventry City. There has been no response to attempts to find out what this enemy fleet is doing here. Home Defense Force units are being alerted."

"An invasion?" Reggie asked softly. "How can they be invading *us*?" His initial reaction was a mild skepticism, and greater curiosity. But that was quickly followed by a tightening in his chest, a constriction that seemed to make it hard to breathe.

"It can't be," he whispered, already not certain that he could believe his denial. He turned up the volume on the complink, but the news recap went on into other items, headlines that had been inserted before the important story had come up. Reggie flipped to the terminal menu and switched to the full-service news link from the capital, Coventry City.

"We no longer have any video feed from our communications satellites," the announcer said. "We would be off the air ourselves if not for the ground-based backup systems. In those remote areas where we do not have that backup, I fear that we are already off the air."

Reggie noted, with some relief, that there was no sign of panic in the announcer's voice or face, no gloom-and-doom histrionics. It eased, minimally, his own growing tension, the tightness in his chest, the way that blood appeared to be draining from his face. It must be true, whatever the reason. Incredible, perhaps, but . . . It *couldn't* be true, not on Coventry, not so close to the heart of the Second Commonwealth. It just wasn't possible.

"Ida, come out and listen to this!" Reggie glanced toward the bathroom door only briefly. "It looks as if we're being invaded." *That sounds totally ridiculous,* he thought.

There was no response from Ida. Reggie realized that there was water running. She was in the shower.

"Let me recapitulate what we know to this point," the news reader said as Reggie stood and took one step toward the bathroom. He stopped, looking back toward the screen, waiting to hear if there was any more than what he had heard on the summary channel—hoping to hear that it was all some dreadful mistake. Thirty seconds of listening convinced him that he had heard everything that was known on Coventry, so he continued across the room and opened the bathroom door.

"Ida!"

"What?" She stuck her head out around the shower curtain.

"Federation ships overhead. It looks like an invasion." His voice was nowhere near as measured as the words. Reggie felt as if he had lost control over the tone and timbre of his voice.

Ida's face went blank. Then she showed a confusion of expressions, as if she could not decide whether Reggie was serious—as impossible as the idea of an invasion sounded— or if he was playing some sort of bizarre joke. "Are you serious?"

"I'm afraid so. It's all over the news."

"I'll be out in a minute."

By the time Ida joined her husband, still toweling herself dry, the first reports of landings had been received.

"Apparently," the news reader said, "none of the Space-hawks of our Home Defense Force have managed to get off of the ground to contest the landings. It does appear that our forces would be hopelessly outmatched in any case. The situation seems very confused. That may be largely due to the difficulties we are having in collecting accurate information." The news reader's professionalism started to slip. The comforting monotone broke. His voice started to climb in pitch, and the hand holding his copy trembled a little. He paused for a moment to collect himself, then resumed after taking a deep breath and glancing at someone or something off camera.

"We are still attempting to contact officials from the governor's office to learn more definitive details, as well as to find out what course of action the citizens of Coventry should take. For the moment, all we can do is suggest a commonsense response, to urge everyone to remain calm and to remain inside your homes. If you are elsewhere, it would most likely be advisable for you to remain where you are until we get clarification of the situation from the government. If you are outside, seek shelter and remain tuned in. We will bring you the news, and any information from the government, as quickly as it becomes available, for as long as we are able to."

"This simply cannot be happening," Ida said, sitting on the edge of the bed. Her eyes were open wide. Her mouth sagged open. She looked from her husband to the complink and back. "This can't be real."

"They wouldn't dare broadcast this if it weren't real," Reggie said with a helpless shrug of his arms.

"But what can we do?"

Reggie felt more powerless than he possibly could have looked. "I don't have the foggiest idea, dear. I'm no soldier. And I don't think we have enough soldiers to do any good. You heard what he said. None of our Spacehawk fighters have got off the ground even."

A soldier? Reggie Bailey was far from that. If asked for his occupation, he might say "architect" or "gentleman farmer" depending on his mood and what he was doing at the moment. He worked at both, but not with any great intensity. Like most people, he did a little farming, and, occasionally, he did design a building on commission, and saw those projects through to completion. It brought in enough money to give his family the extras that normal maintenance did not provide.

"An invasion?" Ida still could not accept the idea.

"An invasion," Reggie repeated. He felt almost numb. The concept was, or had been, unthinkable. Coventry was one of the core worlds of the Second Commonwealth, less than eight light-years from Buckingham, the capital world of the Commonwealth, with dozens of planets, and dozens of light-years, separating them from any of the worlds controlled by the Confederation of Human Worlds. *It just can't be,* Reggie thought.

Ida stood, careless of the bath towel that fell to the floor. For a moment, she stood in the middle of the bedroom, naked, undecided what she should do next—put on her nightgown or get fully dressed again.

"What do we do?" she asked, turning toward her husband, who was still sitting on the bed staring at the monitor.

He gestured at the complink. "Do what he said, I guess. Stay inside and wait for the government to tell us what to do." *Wait for the government to tell us what to do. They'll know. They'll . . .*

"What if they can't?"

"Who can't what? The net can't tell us what the government says, or the government can't tell us what we should do?"

"Either! Both! What do *we* do, you and I? What about the children? We have to decide what we're going to do if we don't hear from the government soon enough. Or what we'll do if the government's advice doesn't sound . . . proper."

Reggie stood slowly and moved to his wife. His thoughts seemed mired, unable to travel beyond what he heard, looping back through the same data over and over. Absentmindedly, he put his arms around Ida. "The only gun we have is my old shotgun, and I don't think we've got more than a single box of shells for that."

Ida pushed away from him. "What the devil are you talking about? What do you think you're going to do, stand off an entire army? Listen to what you're saying."

"What do you *want* me to say? I don't know what to do about this any more than fifty million other people on Coventry." He stared at her, not even noticing that she was naked. "Who ever thought something like this could happen? I mean, here. I'll check downstairs, make sure the doors and windows are locked. See if you can get anything local on the link. Maybe they aren't anywhere near Hawthorne."

"But what are we going to do if the Federation takes over Coventry?" Ida asked, finally lowering her voice. "What are we going to do if we're prisoners for the rest of the war . . . or forever?"

Reggie took a deep breath. "It's too soon to think about that. Maybe it won't make any difference at all to us. Prisoners? How could they lock up fifty million of us? What good would it do if they could? We'll just have to wait and see what happens."

"What do you mean, wait and see what happens? What kind of answer is that?"

"Ida." Reggie stopped, not certain what to say. He took a deep breath and let it out, trying to think, trying to find some order in what was happening. "Just see if you can get any local news. I'll be right back."

Before he got to the bedroom door, and before Ida had finished pulling on the robe she had reached for as he moved, "God Save the King" started to play on the complink, very loud.

Delbert Montcalm, the governor of Coventry, was standing at a table. The governor was clearly shaken, sweating mightily. He stared at the camera as the volume of the anthem was gradually lowered. Once Montcalm started to speak, the music faded to just a hint, background to his remarks.

"My fellow Coventrians, an evil night has come to us. I order all members of the Home Defense Force to report to your emergency rendezvous locations. Assemble as best you can. Do whatever is possible. Leave now, immediately." He paused, as if waiting for some sign that those people had left the rooms where they might be watching.

"For the rest of you, I fear that I have little substantive to offer," Montcalm said after taking a gulp of water. "The situation is not very clear yet. We do know that our world has been invaded by military forces of the Confederation of Human Worlds. They have landed in or near all of our major cities. There may be other landings as well that we do not know about yet because the Federation forces have apparently destroyed all of our communications satellites. There has been no contact between the invaders and your government. They have made no demands, and have not responded to our inquiries.

"We can only advise citizens to remain inside, to do no traveling that is not absolutely essential. Report anything pertinent that you see or hear to your local authorities. If you are confronted by soldiers of the Federation, do not make any foolish attempts at resistance. Leave the defense of Coventry to its Home Defense Force. Remain calm.

"We will continue to provide you with all of the information we can. God save the king!"

As the governor's image was replaced by the Commonwealth and Coventry flags, the sounds of the anthem came up again, and "God Save the King" played through to the end before the news reader appeared on camera again.

"As Governor Montcalm stated, there have been reports of Federation landings in or near every major city. Airports appear to be primary targets. The Coventry Information Network has been unable to make contact with the invaders. We have reports of minor skirmishes in Coventry City, The Dales, South York, and elsewhere. We have no details, nor do we have confirmation from the government. Over the next few minutes, we will attempt to bring you live reports from our studios around the continent."

"I'll check downstairs," Reggie said, still staring at the screen. He blinked several times. "You check on the children. Make sure that their windows are closed and locked, then leave their doors open a crack. I'll be right back."

There had been no reports of enemy landings near Hawthorne. The children were asleep. The house was as secure as it could be—safe against common intruders, the home-grown variety, but doors and windows would not stop soldiers if they chose to break in.

Like most single-family houses on Coventry, the Bailey home had been built to the oldest colonial tradition, centered on a courtyard that gave the residents a chance to go outdoors without hazarding any dangerous native animals, even though those were rare near the towns and cities. There were few windows facing outward on the ground floor, and those windows were mostly high and small. The larger windows, and all but one door, faced the courtyard, which could be closed off by a heavy gate. Even the garage where they parked the family floater—ground-effect motorcar—was inside the courtyard. But the shutters on the windows which faced out were ornamental now, not functional.

Reggie turned the bedroom light down until it was little more than a luminous glow when he returned from his tour of the house. Reggie and Ida sat together on the bed and watched the news on into the night. At first, the thought of sleep would have been alien to either of them, but both had had a long, full day. They were tired, and not all of the fear and uncertainty in the galaxy could hold that off indefinitely. One or the other would doze for a few minutes, somehow never both asleep at the same time.

The news remained spotty. There were reports of minor fighting, more reports of enemy landings. Several of the network's bureaus went off the air—one by one, usually without warning. The assumption—never confirmed—was that they had been taken by the invaders.

Thirty minutes before sunrise in Hawthorne, when Reggie and Ida both slipped into sleep, there had still been no reports of any fighting or landings around Hawthorne.

It was past eight o'clock when Ida woke, not much later than she did on any normal morning, after a full night of sleep. She woke feeling groggy, disoriented. That was not normal. The loginess meant that it was a moment before she recalled the frightening news reports in the night and glanced toward the complink. The set was still on, but there was only a cyan background on the screen and a message from the terminal: INCOMING SIGNAL HAS BEEN LOST.

"Reg!" She reached across the bed to shake his shoulder, keeping at it until he responded.

"Huh . . . ? Wha—?" A touch of fear was obvious even in Reggie's half-awake reply. Then, as he too remembered what they had seen and heard during the night, he sat up quickly.

"It wasn't a dream," Reggie said. He squeezed his eyes shut for a moment, a futile bulwark against the return of fear, a renewed constriction to his chest.

"Nothing's coming in from the net." Ida pointed at the stark message on the monitor.

"Let's check on the kids."

"I'll do that. You look back and see what we missed before the link went out."

Reggie nodded as Ida got out of bed. The house's central complink would have stored everything coming in. That was standard, giving the Baileys a chance to select anything they might want to keep from news or entertainment channels. The complink's buffer memory could hold six days worth of incoming signals from all seventeen available channels until overflow caused it to erase the oldest data.

He played back the feed. As more net bureaus went off, the announcer in Hawthorne grew visibly more agitated. He kept looking around the studio, as if waiting for the appearance of armed men. At twelve minutes before seven o'clock, the local signal was lost, abruptly, while the news reader was in the middle of a sentence. The last few minutes of news, before first the signal from The Dales and then the local signal were lost, was especially troubling.

"There was no report of landings here," Reggie said when Ida returned. "But that's the only thing that could have forced them off here in town."

"The girls are in their bathroom, getting ready for the day. Al's still sleeping," Ida reported.

"Did you tell the girls anything?"

"I didn't know what to say. They're only eight years old. I couldn't just say, 'Oh, by the way, we've been invaded.'"

"I guess not. We'll have to explain. We'll have to say something. Everything is off the net, even the school channels."

"Explain? I wish somebody would explain it to me."

"Look at the last report that came in from The Dales."

Reggie replayed the last news that had come in from outside.

"We have been receiving scattered reports of burning in a number of locales," the news reader said. The night had taken its toll on his appearance. He was beginning to look quite bedraggled.

"There are definitely Federation troops in The Dales. We have this video." As the images replaced the announcer's face, he continued, "Federation forces used loudspeakers to order residents out of apartments and houses in the East Beach area and then set fire to the buildings. The residents were forced to head east, away from other populated areas. Before our video feed suddenly ended, we saw, as you are seeing now, Federation forces ordering still more residents from their homes, near the center of The Dales. You can also see some of the fires. More than three dozen buildings, that we know of, had been put to the torch before we lost our video feed."

After a few seconds, the Hawthorne announcer came on screen, his voice plaintive and worn now. He spoke slowly, as if having difficulty summoning energy. "We have lost the signal from The Dales. At present, we are receiving no feed from any other bureau on Coventry. All communications are out with the rest of our world. It is impossible to tell what is going on outside Hawthorne, and we have only sketchy information locally. All I can say now is—"

Then he too was gone.

"Forcing people out of their homes in the middle of the night, and then setting fire to them?" Ida stared at her husband, seeing her own fear reflected in his face.

"Maybe it was just in that one area. Maybe something happened there to make the invaders mad. Or . . . I don't know."

"But what if they burn *our* house?"

Reggie's shrug showed how helpless he felt. "What *can* we do? If they tell us to get out, we won't have any choice."

"We've got to do *something*."

Reggie did his best to think of options, but after a moment he shook his head. "All I can think of to do is to fix up small survival packs for all of us. A change of clothes for everyone and as much food as we might be able to carry.''

Ida nodded while he was talking. "We'd better do it in a hurry. And dress in warm outdoor clothes, just in case.''

Doing something, *anything*, felt better than doing nothing—even if those measures turned out to be useless.

# 2

**Noel Wittington did** not hear the governor's speech. Nearly thirty minutes before Delbert Montcalm came on the public net to call out the Coventry Home Defense Force, Noel's commander had, on his own initiative, ordered his people—Company A, First Battalion, South York Rifles— to their emergency rendezvous location.

The South York contingent of Coventry's HDF was organized as two infantry battalions. Even though South York was Coventry's third largest city, neither battalion had ever approached anything close to its authorized strength. They were generally lucky to include enough members to fill half of the slots in their tables of organization. And getting all of the individuals who were carried on the muster sheets to training sessions had always been nearly impossible. Traditionally, a turnout of fifty percent was considered a success. The HDF had never been a high priority for most Coventrians, even its members. Since the start of the war a few more people had joined and gone through basic training; a few more "veterans" had started to meet their training obligations. But the war was far away, something for professionals to handle. Few people had foreseen the possibility that it might actually come to Coventry.

Noel loaded his alert bag in his floater, then set his rifle, and his allotment of one hundred rounds of ammunition, and a box of field rations—designed to last one person for five days—in the car. The bottle of whisky and the dozen beers were his own addition to the prescribed call-out kit, a habit formed during monthly training meets.

Twenty years old and single, Noel had spent the evening

with his fiancée, watching a performance of *A Comedy of Errors* put on by a local repertory company that included several of Noel's college friends. Noel had taken his fiancée home long before the mobilization order, and the invasion, came.

He had even anticipated Captain Stanley's call by nearly fifteen minutes. Hearing a lot of shuttles overhead, he had turned on the complink. Multiple shuttles, too noisy to be civilian, meant that something was drastically wrong. Noel was gathering his call-out kit even before the local news reader had reported the arrival of the enemy fleet and the landings. If the alert call had not come, Noel was prepared to head out to the emergency rendezvous site without orders. He had had plenty of time to follow the war news, and he retained his full share of youthful imagination.

With a population exceeding two million, there was always traffic on the streets of South York, even late at night—private vehicles, trucks, busses, and the I-Rail, the monorail public transportation line.

Noel lived fairly close to the center of South York, in what was usually termed the old city. It was an area with plenty of bachelors and a few unmarried young women, close to the centers for social life in the city, and close to the university that Noel attended fitfully.

He was not the slowest driver under normal circumstances, and the call from Captain Hubert Stanley had made it clear that these were not normal circumstances. Federation troops were invading Coventry. Some were in or near South York. Their orders had been simple: get to the rendezvous as quickly as possible. Noel had a long way to drive, nearly eight miles across the center of South York and out to the northwest.

He worried that he might run into the invaders. The captain had not been able to say where they had landed, or where they might have gone since. Noel had no idea what he might be able to do if he did run into Federation troops before he reached his unit. He thought that he might simply try to break through any roadblock, or try to go around it. He had his rifle on the seat next to him, loaded, with the safety off. If nothing else, perhaps he could shoot his way through any roadblock.

Noel had never been on the wrong end of a gunshot. In his eighteen months in the Coventry HDF, he had fired only 120 rounds from his rifle, all at stationary targets on the practice range north of the city. Those targets had never fired back.

No Federation troops blocked Noel's race across South York. He made the drive in fourteen minutes, turning off of the road and following the unmarked grassy lane back to the rendezvous. It wasn't until he was almost there that he thought to wonder why he had not seen anyone else from his HDF company on the road. There were only two other civilian floaters, and one of the company's ground-effect trucks, at the rendezvous. The vehicles were all properly dispersed around the perimeter, under trees.

Noel parked his floater, turned off the lights, and got out with his rifle. He stood next to the car and looked around in the almost total darkness. No one called out a greeting. He heard nothing. He saw no one approaching.

*I can't be the only one here,* he thought. There were those few other vehicles. Some of the others had made it.

*Or have they been bagged already?* That possibility made him really nervous for the first time since he had heard, and then seen, the shuttles passing overhead. If the others had already been captured, there might be Federation soldiers waiting to add him to their catch as well. Noel brought up his rifle in both hands and moved farther away from his floater, sliding one foot along the ground and then the other, being careful not to trip over anything in the dark.

Time seemed suspended. Noel thought that five, maybe ten minutes passed with nothing but the normal sounds of the night, insects and small animals that could be heard but not seen. As his eyes adapted to the dark, he saw shapes that would have been familiar, reassuring, in the light but which were menacing hulks now, perhaps hiding dozens, hundreds, of enemy soldiers.

Noel whistled softly, a rising tone, a questioning sound. A moment later, he tried to whistle again, but his throat was too dry. *Anybody here?* For an instant, Noel thought that he had actually spoken. After that, he simply wasn't sure.

A light caught him in the face, blinding him, pulling panic out of his core like magma reaching for a vent on the surface. Before that panic could erupt, before his finger could spasm across the trigger of his rifle, he heard a familiar voice.

"Wittington, over here. Straight ahead."

Noel recognized Captain Stanley's voice and obeyed his directions as the light went out. A galaxy of stars seemed to orbit just in front of his eyes. Noel kept one hand out in front of him, feeling for obstructions, as he slid one foot in front of the other. He blinked furiously, trying to get his eyes to adapt to the dark once more. He had taken only a couple of steps before the flashlight came on again. This time it was directed at the ground, several paces in front of Noel.

"You're staggering like a drunk," Captain Stanley said.

"It's the torch. You blinded me," Noel replied.

"Here, slip a helmet on." The captain handed him a battle helmet. Those were not routinely taken home by the members of the HDF, as maintaining the electronics took some expertise. The helmets, and the few mapboards that the South York Rifles possessed, were normally stored at the armory and brought out only for drills and maneuvers.

Noel put the helmet on, lowered the visor, and switched on the electronics and night-vision circuits as the captain turned off his flashlight again. The helmet was not the latest model. All of the HDF's helmets were nearly obsolete, replaced in the Army and Combined Space Forces more than a decade before. The Coventry HDF did not even possess field skins, part of the normal gear for any full-time soldier or Marine for a generation. But the helmets did function, giving the wearer relatively decent vision at night. Coventry's Parliament had never taken its HDF seriously, always making it one of the lowest priorities when the annual budget debate was held. Even after the start of the war, too many members of Parliament had held to the notion that the Home Defense Force was a vanity. The borders of the Commonwealth were too far away, and the military might of the central government too vast for part-time soldiers to have any effect.

There were only six men present besides Noel and Captain Stanley. Noel looked around, as if he hoped to spot more of the company lurking at a distance.

"We're it, so far," Stanley said. Then, as if he were afraid that he sounded too negative, he added, "But it's early days yet. Some of the men might need another thirty minutes to get here." He didn't want to scare off the few men who *had* rallied to his call.

"What about the Federation?" Noel asked. "Where are they?"

Captain Stanley shook his head. "No idea yet, except that there are some in the vicinity of South York. I couldn't find anyone who saw where they landed." He shrugged. "I couldn't waste the whole night ringing people up, except for our lads."

"My kit's in the floater. Should I bring it out?"

"What you can carry. As soon as we collect everyone who's coming, we're going to move away from here. The vehicles are too easy to spot from the air."

"What are we going to do?" Noel asked.

This time Stanley hesitated for thirty seconds before he shook his head. "I really don't know. There hasn't been time to give it proper thought. Whatever we *can* do. Maybe we'll get enough turnout to make some difference." He did not really believe that, but Hubert Stanley would try, just as long as he was able.

Forty-five minutes later, Captain Stanley had twenty-seven men dispersed around the rendezvous area—twenty-seven including himself, of the fifty-two carried on the company's muster sheet. It had been eight minutes since the last arrivals, and there was no sign of any other vehicles approaching.

*There should be more than this,* he told himself. *Barely half?* It was depressing. Some of the men might have been captured, or been unable to get past Federation troops to the rendezvous. Stanley tried to tell himself that more would have come if they could . . . but he was having difficulty believing that. He knew his people. Those who had come were mostly the oldest and the youngest, those whose children had grown up and moved out on their own, and those who were not yet married, or at least had no children yet.

The last two men to arrive told of seeing fires being started near the center of South York, near the river, not far from where Noel lived. But they had heard no gunfire, seen no enemy soldiers.

Captain Stanley looked at the time line on the head-up display of his helmet visor. He had promised himself when he arrived that he would wait no more than an hour before taking whatever men had shown up away from the rendezvous. But it had already been an hour and a quarter, and he was still reluctant to give up on more of his people coming. He watched the seconds tick off to the next minute. Conversation around him had stopped again. His men were waiting for their leader to lead them. Stanley squeezed his eyes shut for a moment.

"We can't lollygag around here any longer," he said softly. "Gather your gear. The more distance we put between ourselves and our vehicles, the better our chances. I want each of you to carry an extra helmet, just in case some of the others manage to catch up with us later." He would leave a sign, a particular assortment of rocks that would look random to casual passersby but which would tell anyone who knew what to look for where they were going—if they recalled the codes.

"Let's cache the rest of the gear away from the vehicles," Stanley said, making that decision as the others were walking toward the truck that had the helmets and much of the other gear. "Any of the others show up, they'll know where to look, and maybe the Feddies won't."

They had made this hike before, but always in daylight. In training, it had been an undemanding walk—three miles through fairly open forest, on land that was level to gently rolling, nothing to tax strength or endurance. At the end

there had always been beer to replenish liquids sweat out
by their efforts, and the company trucks to carry them back
to their cars. Discipline on those training hikes had never
been especially rigorous. Volunteer part-time soldiers could
not be treated too harshly, not when it was impossible to
get enough warm bodies to train in the first place. The men
had talked more than they should have on those training
hikes, joking around. Sometimes the beer started to flow
early on. Sometimes a few of the volunteers would be more
than half drunk before they started.

Captain Stanley had been in the Coventry HDF for fifteen
years, as long as he had been teaching—he lectured in Gov-
ernmental and Political Studies at South York University—
working up to captain from the ranks, as much because of
his perseverance as any special talent for soldiering. He had
marched this route at least a dozen times a year, once a
month. Not one of those hikes could be compared to this
one, made at night in almost perfect silence by men who
had to be feeling some fear. Their homeworld had been
invaded. They might be the only armed force available to
fight for Coventry, for their families and neighbors.

*And there aren't enough of us to begin to matter,* Stanley
thought, a sour feeling growing in his stomach.

"We can't stay here very long," Captain Stanley told his
men when they arrived at their destination. "We'll take
thirty minutes to rest. Get something to eat if you're hungry.
If any of the other lads gets caught and questioned, this will
be the second place the Feddies come looking. We're going
to head off away from any of the locations we've used during training, and we've got to be well away from here before
first light. We'll find someplace farther out to hole up for
the day. That'll give us time to try to figure out what we're
going to do."

"Just what the hell do you think we can do?" somebody
asked.

"I won't lie to you. I don't know. I'm still hoping that
some of the other companies got men out, that there'll be
somebody from battalion or higher to tell us what to do. If
not, we'll just have to fend for ourselves. We can't let the

Feddies just slide in and take over our world, now, can we?''

None of the men suggested that they should do just that, but Stanley had few illusions. He guessed that some of his men might vote that way if they were given a chance. He would not put the matter to a vote.

Daylight. Captain Stanley wanted to be somewhere they had never gone before as a unit, but he was determined to stay close enough to the city to confront the invaders. He hoped that there was still a chance of linking up with other units. On the march, he had attempted to contact the other companies of the South York Rifles, and battalion head-quarters, by radio, but he had not dared spend much time at that for fear that the Federation troops might have direction finders working. And once his company came to rest for the day, he dared do nothing but listen on the command chan-nels, waiting for someone to come on to find out what forces were available, to give orders—any orders.

But there was only silence.

Make camp. Stand watches. Set up listening devices far enough out to give warning if anyone approached. No one had much confidence in the latter devices. They had only seemed to work about half of the time in training exercises.

Noel went through the motions with the others. The nor-mally garrulous part-time soldiers had turned unnaturally si-lent. Captain Stanley had not needed to mention sound discipline. Silence came on its own. The men looked at each other, searched faces for clues, for some echo of what they themselves were feeling.

*What are we going to do?* Noel had asked himself that question at least thirty times since reaching the rendezvous area. He had hoped that Captain Stanley would have a quick, and easy, answer. But the captain obviously had no more idea than he did.

*Just stay out here and hide?* That made no sense. *Go back in and try to fight?* That thought was beginning to terrify Noel. Twenty-seven men with little training and no real experience to take on who-knew-how-many professional soldiers.

*What the devil am I doing here? Why are any of us here? All we can do is get ourselves killed to no good end. We might as well cut our own throats and have done with it.* He had joined the HDF because of a talk Captain—Professor—Stanley had given during Noel's first week at the university. Because of the talk and the small training stipend; earning a little extra money had been important to Noel.

Noel finished one of his turns as sentry, then returned to where he had spread his bedroll. He sat under an evergreen tree—a native variety with thick, glossy leaves that hung in such a way that the area around its base remained dry in almost any weather—and looked at the few of his comrades he could see.

*The smart thing would be to forget all this and just go home. If we're going to be saved, it's going to take help from outside.* Noel stared at the ground and thought about going home. He could dump anything that might call attention to his membership in the HDF, go home and wait for whatever happened, wait with the overwhelming majority of Coventrians.

*All but the few misguided fools like us, sitting out here, trying to convince ourselves that we're doing something right and noble, that we can do anything at all.* He suspected that if one man among the twenty-seven decided to head for home, many—perhaps most—of the others would follow the example.

But that first man would not be Noel Wittington.

Shortly after midday, Captain Stanley signaled to one of the men who was awake and led him away from camp, south, toward higher ground. Stanley had slept no more than thirty minutes. He was tired, but the demands of command kept him awake.

*I've either got to find an intelligent way to use the lads I've got, or take them home,* he had decided. One or the other. Indecision was dangerous in a military leader, and

Stanley knew enough about his responsibilities to recognize that.

"I'm going to climb this tree and see if I can spot anything back toward the city," Stanley explained to his companion, Michael Polyard. "Maybe I can get some idea what's going on."

It had been a lot of years since Stanley had done any tree climbing, but he worked his way up this one as quickly as he could. He was twenty-five feet off of the ground before he found an opening in the branches that let him see back toward South York. What he saw was smoke. The fires were scattered about in several areas, and he saw two new ones start. After fifteen minutes of watching, he came down the tree more slowly than he had gone up.

"Well?" Michael asked.

"It looks as if a quarter of the city is on fire. Smoke in every section."

"Fires?"

"The Feddies must be setting them intentionally, burning for the hell of it. There couldn't have been fighting in that many places for the fires to start accidentally."

"We've got to go back, see to our families," Polyard said.

"We're going back. We've got to give the Feddies something to think about besides arson."

"You mean fight?"

"That is what we're supposed to be about, in case you've forgotten. Let's get back to the others. We've got a lot of walking ahead of us."

There had been some discussion of Captain Stanley's decision, but no one had refused, no one had deserted the rest. Company A hiked back toward the city, taking an almost direct route. The march did not start until sunset, and the men stayed near cover at all times.

Stanley still had no solid plan. His only intent was to find some of the troops who were doing the burning and start shooting at them. "If they're scattered all over the city, the way it looks," he told the others, "then they must have broken up into small units. If we can find a small group, maybe one with fewer men than we have, we can hit them hard, show people that it is possible to fight the invaders and win.''

He used their last rest stop for a pep talk. ''Remember,'' he said after he had given them what vague plans he could make without knowing what they would find, ''we'll be attacking, coming out of the night while they're at their business. We should have surprise on our side, and the first shots. It gives us a real chance. We'll hit, take any weapons or other gear we can from the Feddies we put down, then get out fast.'' He had almost convinced himself that they could do it.

They headed toward the nearest area of fires. There was no sign of any new blazes being set, had not been in some time. The Federation troops had apparently finished their work for the night. Somewhere, probably near the last fires, there would be enemy soldiers camped, sleeping, with only a few sentries.

''That's even better,'' Stanley said. ''We hit them while they're asleep. They won't be fully awake until it's too late.''

Finding a Federation camp proved to be more difficult than he had anticipated. The Feddies had moved back into an area that had already been burned out.

Seeing the fires, and the ashes from fires that had already burned themselves out, affected every man in Company A. So had seeing Coventrians walking away from the ashes of their homes, heading into the night with only what they could carry.

''I need a couple of scouts,'' Stanley said when they got close to the burned out area. ''Noel, Michael. Go out there.'' He pointed directions to both of them. ''See what you can find, then get back here at the double. Don't use your radios. There's too much chance they'll pick up on it. And be careful not to be seen. The Feddies will have night-vision gear too, probably better than what we have.''

• • •

Noel blinked when the captain chose him. He never would have volunteered for the duty, but neither would he refuse it. *I guess I can sneak about as well as the next bloke.* He got to his feet and glanced at Polyard. They nodded at each other, then started out on their separate courses.

It was almost like being a boy again, playing games with his friends. Noel moved with exaggerated caution, always looking where he placed his feet, staying in the shadows as much as possible, trying to become a shadow himself. Darkness gave him a sense of security. Looking through his visor, using the helmet's night-vision capability, made Noel feel as if he had an advantage, as if he might be the only one who could see in a world of the blind. That the Federation troops would also have night-vision gear did not intrude on his thoughts. He had yet to see an enemy, and they possessed only a limited reality for him. There were no lights in any of the buildings that had not yet been burned. None of the public lights were on either.

Noel stopped frequently, searching as far as he could reliably see to either side, checking around corners and down lanes. Nothing appeared to be moving. There were certainly no soldiers marching sentry tours.

He hesitated for more than a minute before entering an area that had been burned more thoroughly. Even the grass here had been charred black. Three nearby buildings were blackened rubble, still warm, with a few tendrils of residual smoke rising from nothing. Before he moved on, Noel used his radio to tell Captain Stanley how far he had come without seeing anything, completely forgetting the instructions not to use it.

"Keep going," Stanley said. "And stay off the air, damn it."

Noel kept his rifle at the ready, and moved more slowly than ever. He passed the three burned out buildings, treading over grass that had been turned into soft ash that crumbled silently under foot. Beyond those buildings there was an area where the fire had not spread, where the grass was still green. Ahead, he could see the wreckage of several more burned buildings, but those fires had not disturbed the greenery around them.

He headed toward a grove of trees, angling close to the corner of a building. Noel was as careful as he knew how to be, looking, listening, pausing before every pace, desperate to hear or see any enemy before they could spot him.

It was not enough. Noel had no warning of the Federation soldier who came up behind him. He did not recognize the sensation of being clubbed by the butt end of a rifle. Something hit his head, knocking the helmet off, but all Noel felt was an instant of blinding pain and a sensation of bright lights exploding inside his eyes. He was unconscious before he fell.

Captain Stanley had been biting his lips, so hard that they were both bleeding. After a time, he disregarded his own orders and used the radio to call Wittington and Polyard, but he did not raise either of them. He waited, his nervousness growing almost exponentially, until he couldn't stand it any longer.

"They've found something," he whispered to the others. *Or someone found them,* he thought. "Let's go." There had been a noise on Wittington's channel, just an awkward bleep. Stanley guessed that something had happened. Noel couldn't tell him what, but at least he had an idea of where.

"Two skirmish lines, thirty yards apart," Stanley said. If the first line walked into something, the second would be there to bail them out. Wittington and Polyard had not enjoyed that safety measure.

Stanley positioned himself in the center of the second line to make sure that he had the best possible view of whatever developed. As the lines moved forward, his mouth and throat felt so dry that he was uncertain if he would be able to talk; he wanted, *needed,* a drink. At the same time, his bladder was signaling an urgent need to empty itself. He did not address either need. *Later,* he told himself.

The skirmish lines moved slowly. The men in the first line looked at the men on either side of them, almost as much as they looked out front, wanting to keep the line fairly straight, not wanting to get much ahead of or behind their neighbors.

Someone saw something and whistled a warning over the company's radio channel. The men went to the ground. Several men in the first line started shooting at the figure they had seen. By the time that Captain Stanley got that shooting stopped—afraid that the target might be one of the scouts—it was too late for stealth. It was too late for anything except a brief, desperate fight.

Enemy rifles returned the fire. Some of the men from the South York Rifles thought that there were a couple of hundred Feddies shooting at them. The actual number was under thirty. In two minutes, a third of Captain Stanley's men were casualties, dead or wounded. New gunfire started off to their right, directed into both lines.

Then the Federation rifles went silent. In response, Stanley ordered his men to cease fire. A voice shouted for them to surrender, or else. Stanley hesitated no more than five seconds. It was obvious that the "or else" could be implemented all too easily.

"Lay down your weapons, lads," he told his men. He was the first to stand, with his arms raised to show that he was unarmed.

Six of Captain Stanley's men were dead. A dozen were wounded. His missing scouts were brought in, both conscious but groggy, both suffering from concussion. The Federation soldiers gave the wounded first aid. Then all of the survivors were searched. They had already been stripped of weapons and helmets. Now they were left with nothing but the clothes they were wearing. Afterward, they were herded together, out in the open, away from any cover. Each had been marked on the forehead with a small device that left what appeared to be a tattoo—or a brand—of a stylized *F*. Federation soldiers stood around them, watching, their weapons held at the ready. Only three of the invading soldiers had been wounded, and none killed, in the fight.

Company A, First Battalion, South York Rifles were left to brood for an hour or more, not allowed to talk among themselves. Then a Federation officer came and gestured for Captain Stanley to approach him.

"Go home while you can," the officer said. "If you try any more foolish stunts, you will be killed. You have been marked. Any of our troops will know that you have already received a first warning. There will be no second chance."

The officer formed up his men and marched them away, leaving the South York Rifles with their dead—and with a feeling of humiliation that would fade more slowly than the marks on their foreheads. They might be part-time soldiers, little more than amateurs, but it hurt to lose so quickly—and to be dismissed so cavalierly.

# 3

**The men of** the Second Regiment of Royal Marines marched from their barracks on the main Combined Space Forces base on the outskirts of Westminster, Buckingham, to the shuttles that were waiting to carry them up to their transport, HMS *Victoria*. The regiment's baggage as well as the equipment of the engineers and the heavy weapons battalion had already been loaded.

For the first time in memory, the regiment was almost at full strength, with only a handful of slots in its table of organization remaining vacant. Five months of garrison duty and hard training had given time for replacements to arrive and be assimilated. Even though the men of the Second knew that they were heading for combat, many of them were relieved to be escaping the discipline and work of their training regimen.

Only the most senior officers in the regiment knew the name of the world they were scheduled to go to. But the training had been very specific. Even the rawest recruit could draw some conclusions about the type of campaign expected—including building-to-building urban fighting, the most deadly kind for an infantryman. "And every Marine is an infantryman, first, last, and at every point in between," a drill instructor might have thundered. "Every Marine from the regimental commander down to the cooks' helpers carries a rifle and has to qualify with it every year."

Parading the regiment was mostly for the benefit of the civilian population of Buckingham, and the rest of the Second Commonwealth. Cameras recorded the event. Westminster's public complink net carried the proceedings live, along with vague announcements that the Marines were leaving to carry the war to the enemy. There was, of course, no announcement of the Second Regiment's destination, nothing that might provide even a vague hint in the unlikely event that the Confederation of Human Worlds had espionage devices near Buckingham that could get intelligence to the Federation capital on Union in time to do them any good.

Headquarters and Service (H&S) Company of the First Battalion was one of the first units to reach its shuttles. The men formed up in ranks twenty yards away to wait for the rest of the regiment. There would be one last parade formation before the order to board shuttles was given. Noncoms and officers would go through the routine reports. This time it would be "All present," not "All present or accounted for." No one was staying behind.

After Captain McAuliffe put H&S Company at ease, Lead Sergeant David Spencer walked along the front rank, behind the junior officers—platoon leaders—who stood in front of their men. The tour was only partly a casual inspection. David kept up a soft monologue, general remarks mostly. Only a couple of his observations were targeted toward individuals.

"We're just putting on a show for the people. The colonel wants us to look sharp for the cameras, so see that you do." Spencer was a career Marine, with nearly seventeen years in uniform. He was one of the smallest men in the company. Having come out of the intelligence and reconnaissance (I&R) platoon, which normally drew most of the small men in any Marine battalion, he seemed almost tiny against many of the others. But he could hold his own against any of them in unarmed combat drills. He worked hard at his own conditioning, holding himself to even higher standards than he did the young recruits and the almost-as-young veterans of the regiment's previous campaigns.

"You lot know the drill. Hurry up and wait. Stand out here in the sun and bake. It gives you something to remember while we're locked in aboard ship going to wherever they're sending us this time." Spencer could rattle off that sort of talk in an endless monotone, scarcely thinking about what he was saying. But while he walked and talked, his eyes remained busy, looking at every man in the company, inventorying, comparing what he saw now with what he had seen on other occasions, assuring himself that there were no new problems that he might have to deal with. A company lead sergeant in the Royal Marines did not spend all of his time behind a desk processing bureaucratic fodder. Even in H&S Company he took an active part in the routine training of garrison life—as did every officer. Especially since the start of the war with the Confederation of Human Worlds some three and a half years earlier.

David Spencer knew every man in his company, their strengths and weaknesses. He even knew a lot about the officers. That could be as important as anything else. Now he looked over the lieutenants as closely as he did the other ranks. After he finished his tour, Spencer went to where the captain was standing.

"They're all ready to go, sir," he reported softly. "We're in good shape, better than we've been since before the war."

Captain Hector McAuliffe nodded very slightly. "You've done a good job with them, Spencer." The two men had served together, in various capacities, for more than eight years. McAuliffe had been a green lieutenant when he first came to the company, and Spencer had been a squad leader. Promotion had come slowly in the peacetime Royal Marines. It wasn't like that now, with a war on, and casualties to open up slots in the table of organization. This might well be McAuliffe's last tour as company commander. He would likely be promoted to major, and move to a staff position, soon after this mission ended.

"They might have at least brought around a couple of tea carts," Spencer said. The captain almost laughed at the jest.

"It won't be long now, David. We're just waiting on the engineers again."

Spencer turned to look at the last units forming up. The engineering battalion was something of a sour joke to the rest of the regiment—except when they were desperately needed. "This war goes on long enough, sir, we might actually turn some of them into proper Marines.''

"Don't hold your breath.''

"Not me, sir.'' David nodded toward the left. "Looks like we're about due. The colonel and his staff are coming out.''

"Right. Best get into position, Sergeant.'' The use of rank informed Spencer that the informal interlude was over. It was time for both of them to get back to duty.

A full regimental formation could last anywhere between five minutes and two or more hours. The expectation this day was for a moderately short ordeal. Once the inevitable manpower reports were demanded and delivered, the colonel was expected to have a few remarks prior to embarkation— a pep talk full of clichés that many of the men could anticipate before they were delivered.

The regiment was called to attention. The ritual of reporting was performed. The order, "Report!'' went down the tree from Colonel Arkady Laplace, the regimental commander, and the reply, "All present, sir!'' came back up it—the age-old military glissando. But the order to "Stand easy'' did not follow, as it would have if the colonel were going to address the men. Instead, orders were given to embark, "At the double.''

There were no sidelong glances in ranks. The men of the Second Regiment were too disciplined for that. The commanders of each battalion and company relayed the command and started their units toward their assigned shuttles.

"Lively, now,'' Spencer said as his men trotted up the ramps into their shuttles. A company required three shuttles, fitting two platoons into each. Spencer rode with the service and I&R platoons. Captain McAuliffe was with the headquarters and supply people, and the executive officer rode in the third shuttle.

"We'll be taking off straightaway,'' the shuttle's pilot informed Spencer over a private radio link. The Marines were wearing battle helmets, with the wealth of communications channels those provided. "Get your lads strapped in.'' Not even the two lieutenants in the passenger bay questioned the fact that the pilot had relayed the message through

Lead Sergeant Spencer rather than through them.

"Will do," Spencer replied. He switched to the channel that put him in the ear of everyone in the two platoons. "Get to your seats and strap in. We're going straight out."

The ramp was already coming up. No sooner did it stop moving when Spencer felt the slight vibration under foot that told him that the shuttle's engines had fired up. He moved to his seat, the one nearest the ramp, and sat as soon as he saw that everyone else was in position and working at their lap straps—including the officers. There was no artificial gravity in a shuttle, nor did they have Q-space capability. A Nilssen generator, necessary for both, would have been a foolish luxury in a combat shuttle.

"We're ready back here," Spencer told the pilot.

"We'll be off in less than a minute, right behind regimental HQ," the pilot said. "We're going up in a flock, like a combat landing in reverse."

David raised an eyebrow but didn't reply. It took ninety shuttles, passenger and equipment, to move the regiment—seventy-five just to move the men. *Victoria* had gone through a major refit that had added more hangars and facilities to handle that many craft at once. Before, a regimental move would have been a more leisurely affair, with fewer shuttles making several round trips to get everyone moved. Even though *Victoria* now had the capacity to move the entire regiment simultaneously, throwing the whole lot up at once was unusual, irregular . . . and almost peculiar. It created traffic problems at both ends of the short flights.

The shuttle was in the air pulling more than two g's before Spencer decided that he would learn soon enough what the rush was. High acceleration was also unusual for a lift up from home port. The Navy was normally more cost-conscious.

*Some sort of drill?* Spencer wondered as he felt his apparent weight increase even more. The pilot was really pushing the engines. There had to be *some* reason.

"What the hell's going on?" Tory Kepner, the I&R platoon sergeant, asked Spencer. "Where's the bloody fire?"

"Nobody's told me anything, Kep." Kepner had been an

assistant squad leader while Spencer was I&R platoon sergeant, and had moved into the top position in the platoon when David made company lead sergeant. "Maybe it's just part of the show for the civvies."

"Makes me nervous with the whole lot in the air at once. Got no control over anything." Just twenty-four years old, Kepner had made sergeant in less than half the time it had taken Spencer. That was the difference war made.

"I'll tell the colonel you're unhappy with the travel arrangements if you like," David offered, smiling.

Tory just snorted.

Video monitors along the shuttle bulkheads showed *Victoria* as the fleet of landers approached their ship. *Victoria* was five miles long, and as much as 800 yards in diameter in places. The ship was constructed of tubular segments, five of them bundled together, with the main drive pod and its Nilssen generators at the rear. Multiple gastight hulls were a safety measure. Each tube had independent life-support systems and several gastight divisions. Survivability had been a major concern in the design and construction of the troop ship and its sisters. It was armed as well, with particle and light beam weapons, and with missiles that could be targeted against enemy fighters or missiles. Troop ships were almost always accompanied by other ships, frigates and battlecruisers, to provide even more defensive—and offensive—power.

Fifteen shuttles could dock at once, moving into hangars that were spaced along and around *Victoria*. The ship needed a minimum of three minutes between each set of dockings, forcing shuttles to maintain station and move in by turn. The men in the first shuttles taken aboard had to wait inside their landers until the process was complete. Not until the last craft had been secured and the hangars pressurized could the ramps be lowered to allow the men to move through to their barracks bays.

Forty-five hundred men disembarked and started to march toward their assigned compartments. It was not nearly as chaotic as it might have been, or as it might have appeared.

Each platoon was always assigned the same compartment, and *Victoria* was *the* ship of the Second Regiment. Many of the men had made other voyages aboard her, and everyone had studied plans of the ship, and gone through embarkation and debarkation drills since the ship's overhaul. No one got misplaced during the maneuver.

"Okay, lads, get your kits sorted out and find your bunks," Spencer said as the company reached its compartments. The men's field bags had been delivered in advance. Each platoon's bags were piled in the center of its living area. "Get squared away as quickly as you can, before they sound 'mess call.' "

Spencer left the men to their platoon sergeants and squad leaders. He went down the corridor to his stateroom. Lead sergeants and above were quartered two to a room, while platoon, staff, and squad sergeants were put in four to a room.

David's duffel bag was on the floor between the room's two bunks, along with the bag of Hal Avriel, Alpha Company's lead sergeant. It was the work of no more than three minutes for David to transfer his things from the bag to the cupboard and footlocker. The bag itself was folded with Spencer's name and service number showing, and placed in the bottom of the cupboard, ready for an inspection that would probably never come.

"Some good from the quicker trips now," David mumbled, smiling. A trip out used to take as many as fourteen days—five days in normal space before the ship made its first Q-space transit, three days after each of the three transits necessary to get from one star system to another. The war had changed that. Now, it rarely took more than three days, and on occasion, less than one, depending on how urgent the mission was.

The door opened and Hal Avriel came in. "I don't think I'm going to bother to unpack," he said as David turned toward him. "I wouldn't even count on getting to use the bunk."

"What are you blithering about?" David asked. "We're

supposed to have close to three days, last I heard.''

"I just saw Colonel Zacharia running up a passageway," Hal said. Lt. Colonel Zacharia was the battalion commander. "He said something about a meeting with Laplace as he went by. I guess my jaw had dropped when I saw him moving at the double."

"So?"

"What's the big hurry? Why the race up here with all of the gnats swarming at once? Why was Zacharia running like a recruit in his first week of training camp? There's something out of the ordinary afoot, I think."

"I think you've let your imagination go racing too far from your brain, is what I think. This lark has been laid on for at least five months, hasn't it? You don't spend that much time training for a mission, then have to run around at the last minute to find out which leg to stick in your knickers first."

Avriel shook his head. "I tell you, something's up that wasn't on the schedule. I've got an itch that . . . I don't know. Just *something*."

"Maybe the First lord of the Admiralty decided to come up to wish them well." David sat on his bunk and leaned back against the bulkhead. Baiting Hal Avriel was one of David's minor pleasures, in garrison or aboard ship.

"You're proper hopeless, you are." Avriel shoved his field bag into his clothes cupboard without unpacking, as he had said.

"You'd best hope we don't get an inspection. Fine example you're setting for your lads," David said.

"Bilge, as the Navy chaps say. Tell you what. I'll bet you a night's ale that we're not aboard *Old Vic* more than twenty-four hours."

David grinned. "I'll take that bet. And I'll make sure I'm proper thirsty when I collect."

Alfie Edwards wore his corporal's chevrons lightly. He had received them a year before, and had come close to losing them a half dozen times. "They're not sewn on, just held in place with sticky tape," he was wont to tell his

comrades in the I&R platoon. "That way I can take them
off in a hurry when the time comes I get busted back to
private." His hair was a rusty color, and he wore it cut
nearly to the scalp. The shortest man in first squad, he was
the assistant squad leader, heading the squad's second fire
team. Each squad was divided into two four-man fire teams,
able to operate as part of the squad or independently.

Leadership did not come easily to Alfie. Leadership
meant responsibility for other men, and being responsible
just for himself had always been a difficult chore. As a private he had only needed to follow orders and be the best
fighter he could be. He had taken the fighting part of that
role seriously, though following orders had not always come
easily in garrison. Even before enlisting in the Royal Marines he had been a dangerous fighter. In the neighborhood
he had grown up in, that had been an essential survival skill.
The Marines had honed his skills and given him more self-
discipline. But his leadership duties still required conscious
thought. He tried to be conscientious, and worked hard to
get everything right. Mostly, he succeeded.

"Get yourselves straightened out quickly, lads," he said.
Tory Kepner had gone on to his cabin, leaving Alfie in
charge of the squad. "I don't want to be late for mess call."
The "tired" voice was only partly artifice. It was this part
of the assistant squad leader job that he hated the most.

The three privates in his fire team were William Hathaway, John McGregor, and Eugene Wegener.

Hathaway, known as "Wee Willie" or "the Hat" to his
mates, was the only one of the three who had never been
in combat, despite eighteen months in the Royal Marines.
He had missed the Second Regiment's short mission to Dun-
dee because he had been in civilian custody over a charge
of causing grievous bodily harm to four men, civilians, in a
pub fight. The fact that the charges had eventually been
dropped had been all that had saved him from court-martial
for missing shipment. Keeping Hathaway in check was almost a full-time job for Alfie and for Tory Kepner. Wee
Willie would never have been tolerated in the peacetime
Marines. With a war on, though, he might be just the ticket

in combat—as long as he remembered who he was supposed to be fighting.

John McGregor was almost too true to his Scottish heritage to be real. Born on the world of Bannockburn, Gaelic was his first language, and his accent was so thick that his English was barely intelligible. He was large for an I&R man, but McGregor had proved to be so proficient in the necessary skills that he had gone to the platoon straight out of training.

Matched with his more fiery squad mates, Eugene Wegener could almost disappear from thought. Quiet and retiring when not on duty, he was the sort of person often overlooked. He talked little, and almost never about himself. The others in the squad knew little about his background or family. Any of them would have needed time to recall that they had even heard that he came from the German-speaking world of Hanau. Wegener showed almost no trace of accent. Perhaps he would have had he spoken more, or more rapidly. Like everyone assigned to I&R duties, he was an extremely qualified Marine. He carried the squad's needle rifle, a short-range weapon that could fire sixty short needles a second, shredding enemies or the underbrush that might conceal them.

"Get settled in quick-like, because we won't be aboard long," Alfie told the others as he stretched out on his berth. As a corporal, he rated a bottom rack in a stack of three. "It's not like the old days when we'd have a couple of weeks for drills and fatigue work along the way. Now it's out and in before you know what's what. We won't hardly have time for more than a field skin drill, most like."

*Out and in, and in and out, if you're lucky,* he thought. The shiver that came over him was entirely in his mind. He closed his eyes briefly, thinking of lost comrades, and times when he had thought that his own time had come. *You're pushing the odds now, Alfie-boy. This'll be your third time in. Nobody lives forever.*

By the time that mess call sounded, *Victoria* was already two hours out from her parking orbit over Buckingham. Ac-

companied by two battlecruisers, HMS *Sheffield* and HMS
*Hull*, four frigates, a scout ship, and two supply vessels,
*Victoria* was at nearly its maximum rated acceleration, pushing for its transit to Q-space. Galleys for the lower ranks
were scattered throughout the living areas of the ship. Officers and sergeants each had two mess halls (another change
made during the ship's refit), located so that no one had to
make too long a trek for his meals.

An officers' call had already been held. A sergeants' call
was announced during the meal, for immediately after it, in
the forward sergeants' mess.

"This is where we get the news," Hal Avriel said as he
and David Spencer made their way from their mess hall to
the other. "This is where they tell us that we're going in
someplace by tomorrow morning, and probably not the
place we've been training for all these months."

Spencer didn't respond. The quick meeting almost convinced him that Hal was right. It wasn't unusual for the
colonel to give his noncoms a pep talk, but this was too
soon.

"It can't be good news, that's for sure," David finally
allowed. "But it doesn't necessarily mean a change of
plans."

There was standing room only in the forward sergeants'
mess. It was ten minutes after Avriel and Spencer arrived
before Regimental Sergeant Major Alan Dockery spotted officers at the door and called, "Attention." Colonel Arkady
Laplace and several members of his staff came in and
moved to the front of the room.

"As you were," the colonel said when his people were
all in place around him.

"There hasn't been much time for rumors to get started,"
the colonel continued, "but I've already heard a few." At
the rear of the room, Hal nudged David.

"I am here to tell you that there has been a change of
plans." He paused and let his eyes scan the room. Laplace
had taken the King's shilling more than four decades before.
He was a line officer, a combat veteran, and totally at ease
with himself. If he had started looking forward to finally

making brigadier, it never showed in his words or actions.

"As you know, our training the last several months has been aimed at a specific target, even though none of you have known where that target was. Even now, I cannot tell you the name of the world we were scheduled to attack. We won't be going there, at least not on this trip, but someone will, at a later date, so there's no cause to create additional security worries for whoever draws that assignment." Laplace had the undivided attention of every sergeant in the room, even Sergeant Major Dockery, who already knew what he had to say.

"The Federation have forced our hand. They have attacked a Commonwealth world, and we have to respond immediately. That world is Coventry, part of the core of the Commonwealth, and far too near Buckingham for us to fail to contest the Federation invasion just as quickly as we can possibly get there."

An undercurrent of murmuring moved across the room when he named the world. Only Lorenzo was closer to Buckingham. Some of the men in the room had been to Coventry. There might even be two or three who had been born there.

"That's right, Coventry, one of the founding worlds of our Commonwealth, not quite eight light-years from where we are right this minute. Federation forces have entered every city on the planet, and the reports we had were that they had started doing large-scale burning in at least a few of the urban areas. The locals managed to get off several message rockets in the early hours of the invasion, not yet a week past.

"It's up to us to go there and kick the Federation back off of Coventry, with as many casualties as we can inflict on them. At first, it will be just us. For perhaps more than a week. But we will be reinforced as quickly as the Fourth Regiment can be assembled from its current deployment and rushed in if required. And, if needs be, units of the Second Territorial Army will be brought in as well, though organizing and transporting them could well take more than a fortnight. It is up to us to determine the situation and make the call for whatever reinforcements we need. With a fair amount of luck, we might be able to do the job ourselves, or with just the help of the Fourth. I would be loath to call on the Army to help us, unless that is absolutely necessary." He received a scattering of nervous laughter for that, then quickly squelched it.

"After the recent catastrophe on Reunion, the Commonwealth Army needs time to recover, in more ways than one, lads. The worst one-day disaster in recorded history. A quarter-million people wiped out like that." He snapped his fingers. There was not so much as a smile left in the room.

"Here's the drill. We'll make our first two Q-space transits in fairly short order, no more than an hour between them, then lay to for twenty-four hours before we make the third. During that interval, we'll provide what we can in the way of revised plans for our landings on Coventry and our initial objectives there. We anticipate a rendezvous with a scout ship during that layover as well, with the latest intelligence from Coventry. We'll be playing this one by ear, so take care with the one day you'll have to get your people ready. Your officers will provide the latest information for you, as we get it. Remember, we're Marines. We'll get the job done."

He glanced at the sergeant major, who jumped to his feet and called, "Attention," again. As the noncoms stood, the colonel and his staff filed out of the mess hall.

"More than twenty-four hours," David said, turning to Hal. "That makes one good night of drinking you owe me."

# 4

**Five days had** passed on Coventry since the Federation landings. Somehow, Hawthorne had earned a respite. No one that Reggie Bailey talked to had seen a Federation soldier, although there were second-and thirdhand reports of a small unit in Hawthorne the night of the initial landings. One neighborhood, near the airport four miles from the Bailey house, had been torched, its residents given five minutes' warning to clear out. But since then, there had been nothing—in Hawthorne.

The public service nets remained off. None of the news or entertainment channels were functioning. But, on occasion, private links were still available. The automatic machinery that controlled the communications nets was still working, at least sporadically. Bit by bit, some news—or rumors—did reach Hawthorne. None of the reports were encouraging.

The Bailey house was located just over two miles out from the ring road that encircled the center of Hawthorne. The neighborhood was moderately old for Coventry, having been settled 350 years before, which made it only a little more than half as old as the first cities on the world. The original settlement was a circular area a mile and a quarter in diameter, with Black Sloe Creek marking nearly a third of the circumference. For a long time, that had been all there had been to Hawthorne. Now it radiated out from the core of the original settlement in a half dozen tendrils, widely separated, with houses outside the core occupying rather large tracts of ground, often as much as several acres.

Despite this, Hawthorne still numbered no more than 25,000 residents.

The Baileys had three acres of land, backed by untouched forest that spread into the foothills east and south of town. There were neighbors fairly close at hand, but the houses along this stretch of Sherwood Pike were, on average, about one hundred yards apart. Like most people on Coventry— at least outside the proper cities—the Baileys gardened, using nearly a quarter of their land for vegetables and flowers. Winter was never too harsh, although they could count on perhaps six significant snowfalls each year. Mild winters left lengthy growing seasons.

"They could show up here any minute," Reggie told his wife after they had seen the children to bed on the fifth evening. "We've got to use every bit of time we have to get ready."

"I can't help it," Ida said. "I worry myself sick when you go out at night. If soldiers come around, they're apt to shoot you on sight if they catch you skulking about like a thief."

"It's the only chance we've got." Reggie was dressed in black and dark gray. As soon as he left the house, he would smear mud on his face to make himself even less visible. "They're burning people out of their homes, chasing them off into the woods. Caching supplies now, while we've got the time, is our only hope."

Every night but the first, Reggie and a few neighbors had gone out into the forest, carrying whatever they could—a few valuables to be buried, but mostly food, clothing, and other articles that would be worth more than gold if they were forced out into the wilderness.

"I still don't like it," Ida said, resignation in her voice. After the news of the landings, it had been the next night before she had remembered to tell Reggie that she was pregnant. And, if the stories were true about the soldiers forcing people out into the wild, that pregnancy was a terrible complication to think about.

"I don't like any of it," Reggie said, "but we've got to do whatever we can. This might be the last time we go out.

There's not much more we can take. We wouldn't be able to carry everything we've stashed out there now if we had to.'' Each night, fewer people had made the trek, a mile or more into the native forest that bordered the community. "I think it's just Eric and me tonight. We can move as quietly as red mice. Nobody's going to catch us."

"Soldiers don't need to hear you, they might see you. Anna says that soldiers have night-vision gear that lets them see as well in the dark as in the day.'' Anna Knowles was Eric's wife. "All this playacting is useless."

"They won't be out in the forest anyway. There's nothing out there for them to do. I've got to go. Eric will be waiting.''

Reggie stepped out from the kitchen into the courtyard, then moved along the side of the house toward the gate in front. Before he opened that, just enough to slip through, he stood quietly for several minutes, listening and looking. There was little light. No one in the neighborhood had been burning outside lights since the invasion. There were no public streetlights along Sherwood Pike either. And Coventry's only moon was so small that it scarcely showed a noticeable disk. The fullest starfields were on the daylight side of the world just now, not that the sky was anything approaching empty. In the heart of the Commonwealth, there were plenty of stars.

When Reggie finally left the courtyard, he took the path across the garden toward the Knowles house. Eric was waiting at the property line, crouched low next to a tree. His neighbor had a flashlight switched on, the lens covered with tape so that only an eighth of an inch opening was left, and he kept that near the ground, moving it occasionally until Reggie arrived.

"I was getting nervous," Eric whispered.

"Ida," Reggie said, as if that were all of the explanation needed. He shifted the backpacks he was carrying, one over each shoulder. A few nights of lugging heavy loads for two or three hours was not enough to overcome a lifetime of minimal exertion. Reggie was only in his early forties, not even approaching middle age by the standards of a developed world like Coventry, but those years had been overwhelmingly sedentary.

"Anna's not very happy about our expeditions either," Eric said. He was ten years younger than Reggie. Eric and Anna had two sons, ages ten and seven. Anna was pregnant, within a month of her expected delivery date, and Eric's preparations had something of a grim determination to them. Winter was coming, and mild though it might be around Hawthorne, it could be too much for a mother and infant to survive easily in the wild.

"We're wasting time," Reggie said. "The sooner we get there, the sooner we'll get back so they can stop worrying."

They followed well-defined paths. Near the houses, the paths had been made by humans and their animals, pets and livestock. Farther off, the paths had been made and kept open by native animals. Wildlife still flourished. Some species were more numerous now than they had been when the world was first settled, their predators thinned out or chased away. Many residents did some hunting, to provide treats for the dinner table, but there was little "sport" hunting. Animals were hunted for food, or because they posed an immediate threat to people.

"I've been thinking," Eric said after they had covered two thirds of the distance to their cache. "If we *are* forced away from our homes, people are going to get desperate in a hurry. All of the goodwill in the world might evaporate over a chilly night as soon as folks start getting a little hungry."

"What are you getting at?"

"I think maybe we should take a little more care with what we've brought out than we have so far."

"Come on, say it."

"I think we should move our stuff someplace else, farther off, away from where the rest have put their things, someplace only you and I will know about. At least part of our caches. We can leave a little where it is, move the rest to where we can get to it when we need it. If we need it."

"I don't know. Showing the others that we don't trust

them might make things just as difficult as leaving everything where it is and taking our chances along with the rest.''

''We've both got kids and pregnant wives to think about.''

''Let me think on it a little, at least until we get to the caches. We'd best both think on it—a chance that our neighbors might take advantage of us, or a chance that they might resent the fact that we don't trust them, and show it. Whichever we do, we'll have to live with it.''

Away from the houses, they remained as nervous as the animals they disturbed. Twice, one of the two-foot-tall grazers that Coventrians called deer started and bounded away. The sounds stopped both men and slapped a tightness on their chests until they recognized the sounds of the animal. The only animal that might pose a threat to them was a wild grey, the felinelike predator that fed on the deer. But there were no confirmed reports of wild greys attacking humans.

The closer they got to their destination, the tenser Reggie and Eric became. They worried that Federation soldiers might have found the caches and have them staked out to nab whoever came. They stopped thirty yards from their goal. A dry gully ran along a slight incline toward a creek. Erosion had exposed the roots of several trees along one side of the gully. Two trees that had been toppled in storms formed temporary bridges. The people from the neighborhood had used the exposed roots systems of those trees to store food and other necessities. Those who had buried valuables had done it a little beyond the gully—or in different locations altogether—taking whatever measurements they could to recall just where they had left their treasures.

The two men went down on their stomachs and listened for several minutes, hoping to hear if anyone was waiting for them. Dozens, perhaps hundreds, of soldiers could have lain in wait in the gully. Eric was the first to move, long before Reggie would have felt safe to advance those last few yards.

''What do you think?'' Eric asked when they reached the gully.

"I don't know."

"Better to be safe than starve. And starvation is a more immediate threat than ostracism." Eric had made his decision, but he wanted to persuade Reggie as well. Two families could face the displeasure of their neighbors more easily than one.

Reggie hesitated before venturing a reluctant, "Okay. Where do we move our stuff?"

"You know where that rocky area is, southeast of here?"

"What rocky area? This is as far as I've come this way."

"It's a mile or so from here, a limestone protrusion of some sort, breaking right up in the middle of a patch of trees. There are some small caves, just little holes really. It shouldn't be hard to find room for our things. And there's a lot of loose rock lying about as well."

"If we're going to take everything we've brought out, it's going to take several trips. Have we got time?"

"We'll have to make time. If we don't get it done tonight, we might not get another chance."

Although the temperature was fifty degrees Fahrenheit, both men were sweating long before they finished. They needed three trips. The first time, they had searched for twenty minutes before finding a suitable place to hide their stores.

"I came out here several times, some years back, looking for good caves to explore," Eric said. "I didn't find what I wanted, but there are several we can use." After those years, his recollection had been slightly deficient—the rocky area was farther off than he had thought and the caves even smaller than he recalled—but they did find one hole that was suitable. The entrance was under a sloping slab of limestone, just barely large enough for one of them to slide through at a time. Four feet down, it opened up onto a dry shelf eighteen inches high, three feet wide, and six feet deep. The main hole went down another six feet before it became too narrow for anything larger than a malnourished rat.

"None of the caves I found were big enough to shelter people," Eric said after they finished storing their last load. "This must be the biggest I ever found."

Reggie was trying to recover his breath after their exertions. He looked toward the eastern sky and shook his head. "We'd better hurry. It's going to be light before we get home." After a pause, he added, "Ida's going to be frantic."

"We can save a few minutes if we cut directly across toward home instead of going back to the other place first."

"You sure you can find your way without getting us lost?"

Eric hesitated, then said, "Not sure enough, I guess."

Although he panted with effort through most of the return trip, Reggie did not stop for a break, and he managed to keep Eric moving as well. They did not move nearly as quietly as they had coming out. Reggie was more worried about Ida than any danger of noise. She would be almost beyond panic at the length of time he had been gone.

Eric and Reggie could see their houses in silhouette as soon as they emerged from the forested area behind their tracts. The black of night had muted into the grays that preceded dawn. The men angled toward their homes directly instead of going along the property line between them and turning away from each other only at the end.

Reggie was out in the open, feeling much too visible, when he heard the noise in the sky. He dropped to the ground instantly, before he looked up. Just to the northwest, no more than a half mile away, the dark shape of a military shuttle was heading in, dropping at a steep angle, obviously ready to land near the center of Hawthorne. Two more shuttles followed, coming out of the north, from the direction of The Dales. They circled around, almost as far south as Reggie's house, before angling back toward the oldest part of town.

After a moment of nearly paralytic fear, Reggie got to his feet and sprinted for the house. Ida was at the door. She pulled it open before Reggie reached it, and almost pulled him through the opening.

"What was that noise?" she demanded.

Out of breath again, Reggie had difficulty answering her question, but did finally manage.

"Where have you been?" Ida asked next. "You were gone so long I was sure you were dead, or too hurt to move."

Reggie collapsed on the nearest chair and leaned forward, resting his arms on his thighs, while he tried to suck in air. It took more than a minute before he could talk without excessive difficulty, or the feeling that he might vomit. He told her what he and Eric had done that had taken so long.

"He's afraid some of the others might take what we've got if we do get turned out." Reggie looked at the wall, roughly in the direction of the center of town. "If those shuttles mean what I think they mean, that time might come awfully soon."

"You really think we might lose our home?" Even after five days of hearing stories—and not hearing any official reassurances that the rumors were false—Ida Bailey still could not fully accept the possibility. She didn't *want* to believe.

"If they want to destroy the house, there's not a damn thing we can do to stop them," Reggie said.

That wasn't the answer that Ida had hoped to hear. She turned away from her husband, not wanting him to see how his words affected her. But he didn't need to see her face to know. He felt the same things. Reggie had put as much of himself into building the house as anyone could have. And there were all the years of memories, the years of *living* that they had put into the place. It was the only home the children had ever known.

"You've been up all night. You'd better get a little sleep while you can," Ida said. She sucked in a deep breath. "If those shuttles did land in town, this could be the day."

Reggie stared blankly at the back of his wife's head. *Yes, it could be,* he thought. *Probably is.* But he didn't want to say that. Ida had sounded fragile, as if she were about to burst into tears. Reggie wasn't certain what he should, or could, say—certainly nothing that would make her feel any better.

"Ida . . ." Reggie stopped, and she turned to face him, strain visible in her face, more than he had ever seen before.

"I guess I had better try for a little sleep," he said when nothing else occurred to him. "You've still got the packs for us to carry if . . ."

"Yes. I ran fresh food supplies through the replicator after you left, enough for a couple of days."

"I think I should eat before I go to bed." Reggie had just realized that he was hungry. "It's been a long night."

When he finally collapsed across the bed, after a meal and a shower, he fell asleep almost instantly. There was no need for the rest of the family to be quiet while Reggie slept. It would have taken extraordinary noise to wake him. He had dressed before flopping on the bed, all but his shoes. If the Federation troops came before he woke on his own, he didn't want to waste time putting on clothing. There would be more important claims on that time. If . . .

The children knew what was happening, even if they did not fully comprehend it. They had spent too much time on the complink before not to notice that nothing new was on it, and that they couldn't be certain of contacting their friends. The girls were frightened, and could not understand why soldiers would come to take over their world, or why they might turn people out and burn their homes. Tears came easily to them, and questions that their parents could not begin to answer. Twelve-year-old Al was torn between his fear and not wanting to show that fear. He wanted reassurances, but he talked of fighting the invaders. Like his sisters, he had been suffering nightmares for the last several nights, waking at the most frightening scenes.

Ida had been making her own preparations during the days, and at night while Reggie was out on his treks. There was a small compartment in the cellar, a three-foot cube built out under the courtyard, waterproof and lined with insulating plascrete that might keep the contents safe against fire. The first items that Ida had put inside were data chips—photographs and letters, important documents, the keepsakes of her family. Maybe they would survive in the underground vault. And, the biggest maybe of all, maybe the family would someday get to come home and reclaim them. If they were forced to leave.

Ida did her crying when there was no one around to see. Silent tears never stopped her from working. At times, the crying seemed uncontrollable, yet if another member of the family came into the room, it stopped instantly.

*Whatever happens, we will survive,* Ida told herself every time she started thinking of all of the terrible things that the war might bring. *Somehow, we'll make it.*

She spent as much of the daylight hours as she could staring out windows, wondering how much warning they might have before Federation soldiers came down the street and ordered them out. After the shuttles had come over and headed toward the center of Hawthorne, Ida concentrated on looking in that direction. The children got up and dressed, then ate breakfast. Ida urged them to have seconds, without saying why. Even sweets, usually forbidden in the morning, were there for the children.

*Eat while you can,* Ida thought. Then she had to leave the kitchen to make certain that the children would not see tears come to her face. She went upstairs and looked out the window in the girls' room that faced the center of Hawthorne.

It had been two hours since the shuttles had passed overhead and Reggie had returned from his night out in the forest. Almost anything could happen in two hours, in imagination, at least. Ida searched as much of the horizon as she could see, expecting, fearing, to see plumes of smoke rising, perhaps the start of a huge conflagration that would span the horizon like a forest fire out of control in late summer. Three years earlier, a wildfire had come within two miles of the house before nature, aided by local residents, had finally beat it out.

It was past noon when Ida finally saw the smoke.

''Go wake your father,'' Ida told Al. The boy had come into the room a few minutes before. He took one look out of the window, then ran for his parents' bedroom.

It was less than two minutes later when Al returned, followed closely by his father. Reggie crossed to the window and put an arm around his wife's waist, pulling her close to him as he looked at the three columns of smoke he could see—while he tried to estimate where the fires were, how far away.

"Almost to the center of town, I think," Ida said.

"It might be a long time before they get to us," Reggie said. "Have you heard any more shuttles coming in?"

"Nothing."

Al squeezed in next to his father so that he could see out the window too. "They're really burning people's homes?"

"They're burning something," Reggie said. "I wonder if we can get through to anyone on the net."

"There's been nothing all morning," Al said. "I've been trying to link to some of my friends. Nothing's going through."

"Not even next door?" Reggie asked. "The Knowles boys?"

"Nothing. I ran over there a little while ago to see if maybe it was just our system that was out, but they can't get anything either."

The three were all staring out the window when two more pillars of smoke started to rise.

"It looks like they're working toward Royal Oaks Pike," Reggie said.

"That's just the next road over!" Al said.

Reggie pulled away from the others. "I'm going up on the roof to get a better look. If there's just one group doing the burning, it could be days before they get to us."

"Or maybe just tonight," Ida said.

A narrow stairway led to the roof over the main wing of the house. A low parapet surrounded the flat roof. Now and then, the Baileys had spent evenings up there, eating or just enjoying cool breezes in the summer after the sun set. The last time they had eaten on the roof had been a couple of months before. Late in autumn, it would be too cool, especially if the wind came out of the northeast, carrying a polar chill inland.

Ida went to see to the girls, wanting to reassure herself that Angel and Ariel were still safe, that the distant smoke had not somehow hurt the twins. Al followed his father. When the two of them got to the roof, they could see more smoke, farther away and off to the left.

"That looks like it's clear out on the other side of town," Al said, pointing.

Reggie nodded. "It means that there's more than one group working."

"Why are they burning things?" Al stared at his father until he answered.

"I don't know. I don't even know why they came here in the first place. It's not like we had an army on Coventry."

Al needed a moment before he thought of another question. "What will it be like if we have to go live in the woods?"

"I'm not sure. Like camping, I guess, but we've never done any of that. I guess it'll be cold at night, uncomfortable, dirty. If it goes on for very long, it might be hard to find enough food to fill our stomachs every day. We'll have to hunt for animals, look for berries and other plants we can eat."

"Like in the adventure vids?"

"Something like that, I guess."

"Dad," Al said after they had been silent for nearly ten minutes, watching more fires start up along Royal Oaks Pike—no more than four miles away.

"What?" Reggie turned toward his son, then sat on the edge of the parapet, which put their eyes almost at the same level.

"I don't want to die." There was a tremor behind the words, and fear in the boy's eyes.

"Nobody wants to," his father said. "We'll make out okay, I think, even if they drive us off into the woods. We'll just have to use our wits and keep going until the Commonwealth comes to drive the Federation off."

"*Will* anyone come?"

"Of course they will." Reggie hoped that he sounded more confident of that than he felt. "The government got message rockets out before the Feddies could stop them.

We're an important part of the Commonwealth. They won't let the Federation stay here for long.''

*How long?* he asked himself. *Will we be able to hold out until they get here and free us?*

Part **2**

# 5

**"This video has** been magnified considerably, but little detail is visible," Colonel Laplace told the second gathering of all of the sergeants during the voyage out from Buckingham. *Victoria* and her escorts had made their second Q-space transit and were halfway through the twenty-four-hour layover that the colonel had promised before making the final jump to Coventry.

"The scout ship was unable to approach the planet close enough to get anything better. The Feddies were prepared, and knocked out each of the drones within ninety seconds of launch." Laplace turned sideways so that he could see the pictures on the bulkhead monitor. For thirty seconds he remained silent, watching.

"In addition, more Federation ships arrived in-system while our scout ship was on the scene, forcing it to break off surveillance. To the best of our knowledge, the initial invasion was carried out by a single regiment. Since Coventry had negligible defensive capability, that would have been more than sufficient." Laplace hesitated. The invasion of Coventry would force some new thinking on Buckingham. Every world in the Second Commonwealth would have to be defended now—every important world, at least, and with membership in the Commonwealth voluntary, every world was important. The prospect seemed impossible to Laplace; troops and money both would be lacking for that enterprise. But it was plainly no longer enough to garrison only "frontline" worlds. After Coventry and Reunion, fighting could touch any world in the Commonwealth.

"Our official intelligence estimate—for whatever that

might be worth—is that total Federation manpower on Coventry cannot total as much as three regiments, with naval assets in orbit to protect them from chaps like us. But we have direct knowledge of no more than the initial invasion force. This''—he gestured at the screen—''poses questions for which we have no satisfactory answers. The fires. There are too many for us to assume that they result merely from military action, that they represent places where the local inhabitants defended themselves. There appear to be fires in virtually every city and town on the planet, growing numbers of fires. Our tentative analysis suggests that the fires are being deliberately set. We have no idea what purpose there is to that, why the Federation might be doing it . . . and the chance that the locals might be starting the fires can't even be eliminated. The only possibilities that we have been able to come up with to explain the phenomenon strain credulity almost to the breaking point.'' He paused again, staring at the video replay.

''We'll know more when we arrive over Coventry and can get new video showing what has happened in the interim, and perhaps make contact with the planetary government or residents.'' The colonel turned away from the screen and looked at his sergeants, most of whom were still staring intently at the video.

''We haven't identified any concentrations of Federation troops. To the extent that our scout was able to determine, those troops have been widely dispersed, covering every settled portion of Coventry. Dispersed as occupation troops would be if no military counterstroke was anticipated.'' Laplace did not have to emphasize that statement. Any sergeant in the Royal Marines could leap to the thought: *How could they possibly think that we wouldn't come?*

''For those of you who might not have looked at the database yet, Coventry has only the one major continent, and that contains virtually all of the population. The greatest concentration of people is in the northwestern region of that continent, in three major cities, that is, cities with more than a million population, and a score of smaller cities and large towns, with even smaller communities scattered along the seacoast, several major river systems, and along routes connecting the larger population centers. There are lesser concentrations elsewhere on the continent, decreasing in number and size the farther one gets from the capital at Coventry City.

"We won't be able to determine our landing pattern and initial objectives until we see what the situation is when we arrive. Regimental operations has several possible scenarios for you to study and go over with your men. We will likely not have a final plan of action until we're ready to board shuttles for the landing. That means that we will rely on the basic skills of a Marine even more than we do in most circumstances—basic skills and the intelligence to improvise as needed.

"That's all for now, gentlemen. Take the next three hours for training. After evening mess call, get your men settled in for the night as quickly as possible. I anticipate the call to board shuttles in under twelve hours, at 0300 hours ship's time."

"We're going in blind, without any idea what the hell we might find," David Spencer told the noncoms of H&S company. "We've got two and a half hours of training time left, with no idea what to train for. We might not have our assignments until we're in the boats heading down."

"So what do we do, teach the lads to knit?" Alfie asked.

"Might as well, for all the good we can do in a couple of hours," Tory Kepner said.

"Run a drill on field skins. That sort of thing, basic drills. Hand-to-hand combat. Remind them about urban tactics. We may have to root the Feddies out building by building, if they don't burn them all down first."

"I really don't get that, Sarge," Alfie said. "What the hell's the point of taking a world just to burn the buildings?"

"We don't know that that's what they're doing," Spencer said. "We can't even guess yet why they're doing widespread burning. They might be burning selectively to make a point and keep the locals docile. We'll know when we get there."

"Hell of a way to run a war, if you ask me," Alfie said.

"I don't recall anyone asking you. Now, back to your men and back to work. I want squad leaders to inspect all combat gear, especially helmets and field skins. Make sure we don't jump in with defective equipment."

Everyone in H&S Company drilled for combat, even the cooks and clerks, who routinely griped whenever they were called upon to do any training outside of their specialties. Since Spencer had become company lead sergeant, that training had been more frequent and more intense. "Maybe I can't turn you all into I&R lads, but we're going to do our damnedest," he had told them on the day he received his promotion. "Every Marine is a rifleman first. Everything else comes second, a distant second." For the first several months, he had personally overseen the training of the "other" platoons in the company, all but I&R. Even now, he gave those others more of his attention than he did I&R. He had trained Tory Kepner and trusted him to keep that platoon in top shape. Tory pushed the men as far as they needed to be pushed, and often close to as far as they could be pushed without diminishing returns. Spencer was certain that the I&R platoon still met the standards he had set when he was its platoon sergeant.

David took a few minutes in the gymnasium to see that the platoons all got into their last training session before Coventry, then went looking for Captain McAuliffe.

"This looks dicey as hell, sir," he said when he found the captain. "Not knowing what to expect and all that."

"I know." McAuliffe sighed. "Sit down, David. Take a load off. Nobody's happy about this all the way up to Colonel Laplace and the admiral—probably all the way up to the War Cabinet. We've simply got no choice. We can't let the Feddies set up shop so close to Buckingham without challenging them fast and hard. Let them get a toehold on Coventry and they could be on Buckingham next, or Lorenzo, or Hanau, or Jersey, or any other world in the Commonwealth core. If we let them hold Coventry, the entire Commonwealth could unravel almost overnight.''

"If it's so bloody vital, why wasn't it protected better?''

McAuliffe shook his head slowly. It was a question he had asked himself a number of times. And others. Not even Colonel Laplace had found a satisfactory answer. "I guess what it boils down to is that nobody saw this coming. A minimal invasion force, in before anybody suspected that anything was up. It's easy to second-guess now. But we're all still learning how to deal with a real war. After the war is over and the skull-jockeys have had a few years to pick at everything, then maybe we'll know how to fight this war.''

"After it's too late to do us any good,'' Spencer said.

"I guess that's the way it's always been.''

"As long as the Feddies are in the same shape, I suppose it evens out.'' There was no conviction in David's voice.

"The aggressor always has the edge going in. We're still playing catch-up. When we were supposed to be going over to the offensive.'' He frowned. The officers of the regiment had been given a much more thorough briefing on the disaster on Reunion than the noncoms and other ranks had—more detailed information than had been made public on Buckingham.

Spencer got to his feet. "When does it all end, sir?''

All McAuliffe could do was shake his head again. "When one side hasn't the strength or the money to keep fighting. Or when one side beats the other so badly that they lose the will to keep going. The news about Field Marshal Manchester's army being destroyed with one blow could have done it to us. If we come a cropper on Coventry on top of that . . .''

"You get face-to-face with an enemy, if you hesitate, you die. It's that simple.'' Tory had the platoon sitting on the gym floor. They had gone through one long workout. As soon as this break ended, he intended to put them through another.

"The only rule is 'There are no rules.' No referee is going

to blow a whistle for a foul. No linesman is going to raise his flag to say you're offside. You kill as fast as you can, any way you can. If you get a chance to put him down by kicking him in the balls, do it. Stomp on his windpipe. Break his bleeding neck. Gouge out his eyes. Do anything you have to. I repeat, *anything*.'' He paused for just a beat. ''Of course, the preferred method is not to let it get face-to-face, and if it does, you'll have a bayonet on the end of your rifle. Just hope it isn't smeared sticky with marmalade.

''We're going to break down into fire teams. I want each man in the team to fight each of his mates, one right after the other. The only way you get a rest is to beat your man before the other two finish their fight. Let's go. On your feet.''

As I&R platoon sergeant, Kepner was also first squad's leader and head of that squad's first fire team. The three privates in the first fire team were all new to the platoon since the battalion's first combat.

Ramsey Duncan had been the first assigned. ''The Ram'' was an extremely methodical Marine on duty, and an absolute mess away from it. ''When I let go, I let go,'' he had explained, over and over, until his mates tired of ragging him about his habits.

Patrick Baker managed to be eternally adequate to any situation—but never rose above mere adequacy. He did what was required, but only by the minimal margin to make certain that his superiors could never fault his work. It wasn't that he enjoyed the frustration he caused those superiors. He never seemed to notice that. It was just the way he was.

Geoffrey Dayle was a hard worker. I&R skills did not come easily to him, but he was determined, and he had always managed to rise above mediocre talent with exceptional diligence. Earnest and intense, he had picked up the nickname ''the Thinker'' within a week of reporting to the platoon. Dayle had one other mark of distinction that no one had noted before. He had been born and raised on Coventry. His family still lived there. Since hearing that his home-world had been invaded, and that the regiment was moving there to contest the invasion, the Thinker had not said one word that was not absolutely required.

"Come on, Dayle. I'll take you on first," Kepner said, facing the private directly. "Give it all you've got." Tory moved into a ready stance, balancing his weight equally on both feet, crouching slightly, arms out and a little to each side.

Tory had fought every man in the platoon in training, and he had spent more time watching the men in action. He knew how each man fought, what to expect. Dayle was always careful about his opening moves, anxious not to make an early mistake, when it could be most dangerous. Always. But this time, Dayle dropped into his ready stance, then lunged quickly, putting his head into Kepner's stomach as he tipped the sergeant over onto his back, hard. Before Tory could react, Dayle had twisted around and dropped a knee across Kepner's throat, with just enough pressure to show that he could finish the job in a real fight.

"Okay, you caught me," Tory said. *My own damn fault,* he thought as Dayle released the pressure and let him up. *Looking for what I expect instead of looking for anything. That can get you dead in combat.*

"You caught me for fair," he said, rubbing at his throat. Dayle nodded and looked at the continuing fight between Duncan and Baker. They had scarcely made contact yet.

"It's not a dance," Kepner said. "Get at it!" Yelling at the others made his own quick defeat slightly easier to bear.

HMS *Hull* was the newest Cardiff-class battlecruiser in the fleet. As a result of incremental improvements made over the twenty years since the first had been designed, no two Cardiff-class ships were identical. Any naval officer who had been in service in those two decades would know the basics of the type, but protocol in the Royal Navy required extensive formal study, and testing, before a senior officer could be posted to a new ship—except under emergency conditions.

Captain Ian Shrikes had taken command of the *Hull* while it was still in the construction docks, after a nine-month tour as skipper of a frigate, and two months of training for the new battlecruiser. He had welcomed the formal training. The Cardiffs were the largest and most powerful weapons platforms in the Commonwealth arsenal. Only the Federation's Empire-class dreadnoughts were larger. The step up from frigate to battlecruiser was more than just a matter of degree. A frigate had only its own weapons. A battlecruiser also carried a fighter squadron—sixteen Spacehawks—and a full company of Marines. There were more weapons and a more complex infrastructure.

Coventry would be the first time that Ian had taken *Hull* into a combat situation. He was nervous about that. Four hours before the scheduled time for the fleet's last Q-space transit going in to Coventry, Ian woke, and made his way to the bridge.

"The ship is in normal space," the officer of the deck reported. He gave the $x$, $y$, and $z$ coordinates to three decimal places—figures that meant little to Ian without reference to a chart. "The time remaining until scheduled insertion into Q-space is three hours, fifty-seven minutes. All stations report nominal readiness. There have been no action dispatches from the flagship."

"Very good, Lieutenant Zileski. Carry on." The forms had to be maintained, even though had anything out of strict routine happened, Ian would have been wakened. He spent another ten minutes on the bridge checking things that did not need checking, and finding nothing amiss.

"I'll be in the wardroom having breakfast," he told Zileski. "Be sure to have the next watch wakened in time for them to have breakfast before we go to action stations."

"Aye, aye, sir."

In the privacy of an empty passageway leading away from the bridge, Ian permitted himself a thin, brief smile. *I handled that fairly well,* he thought. *Admiral Truscott couldn't have looked or sounded any calmer. Nothing to give the watch anything to talk about.* Ian had served as Admiral Truscott's aide before getting his captain's stripes and a ship of his own. The admiral was quite the consummate showman, inordinately calm in front of subordinates even during the most trying of circumstances.

Captain Shrikes lingered over his breakfast longer than he normally did, chatting with the mess stewards, going back into the galley for a third cup of tea after he finally finished eating, continuing to put on a show of assurance, knowing that rumors would quickly spread that "the old man" was not at all worried about the coming action. Once he left the wardroom, Ian made his way back to the secondary control center, nearly a mile aft of the bridge, to make certain that all was well there. 2CC was always manned, ready to take over control of the ship should disaster strike the bridge. By the time Ian returned to the bridge, only two hours remained until the scheduled Q-space transit to Coventry.

"Admiral Greene has requested a conference with all ships' captains in twenty-seven minutes," Lieutenant Zileski informed the captain as soon as he had gone through the routine report.

"I'll be in my day cabin," Ian said. That was just off of the bridge. Until the end of the Coventry operation, Ian expected to spend more time in that cabin—a two-room suite—than in his other quarters, a deck below and forty yards aft of the bridge. "Ask the steward to bring a tea cart around, will you?"

Rear Admiral Paul Greene had commanded HMS *Sheffield*'s battle group for two years. *Hull* and the two frigates of her escort had been seconded to Greene's command for this operation. Hence, the *Hull* had no flag officer aboard, as she would have if her battle group were operating independently.

Greene had spent thirty years in the Royal Navy before the outbreak of war. That past, and the politics of the peacetime Combined Space Forces, had made him methodical and thorough. He had served in varied capacities, mostly administrative. His first wartime campaign had been as second-in-command to Stasys Truscott, the architect of the Navy's new tactical operations manual. This would be Greene's first time in combat as commander of a task force.

"I wish I could say that we know exactly what the situation is on Coventry, and that we have detailed plans on how to execute our mission," he said once the meeting started. The conference was holographic. Only Greene and the skipper of *Sheffield* were actually in the same room, although it appeared that the other captains were also gathered around the admiral's chart table.

"The truth is otherwise. We don't know a lick more than we did twelve hours ago, and won't until we emerge over Coventry. We will stick to the initial deployment I outlined before. Tell Captain Naughton that I want her to have *Victoria*'s Marines in their boats ready to launch before we make the transit. I also want all of the Spacehawks of both *Sheffield* and *Hull* in their cockpits ready for launch.

"The first minutes, the first hours, after we emerge from Q-space over Coventry are going to be dicey, and our greatest enemy might prove to be confusion. We'll have to gather and analyze what information we can immediately upon our arrival, and be ready to meet any quick response from the Federation fleet. Since we can't be certain how we will find them deployed, battle might come on us literally within seconds. In circumstances like that, confusion would be doubly dangerous. You'll have to rely on your division chiefs to keep it from getting out of hand."

Speakers in every troop bay aboard *Victoria* sounded the three-note signal that the Marines had been waiting for. It was time to move to their shuttles, to wait—for an unknown length of time—for orders to head down to Coventry. The ship was in normal space. The final Q-space transit, in and out, had not yet been made. For the first time ever, the Marines would make that transit already in their landing craft.

There was no disorder. The regiment had drilled at this maneuver as they drilled at everything. There was little congestion in the passageways leading to the shuttle hangars. The hangars were widely dispersed, and there were sufficient routes. By battalion and company, the Second Regiment moved to its landing craft, with weapons and field packs. The guns of the heavy weapons units and the machinery of the engineering battalion remained in their larger shuttles during the voyage, ready for deployment as soon as the men to operate them took their places.

David Spencer stood next to the ramp leading into the shuttle that service and I&R platoons would ride to the surface, doing a quick inspection of the men as they trotted past him, up the ramp and into the lander. He had his visor up so that everyone filing into the shuttle would be able to see his face clearly. There was no dawdling, no idle chat. The idle chat might come later, while they were waiting, locked up in the shuttle, perhaps with the hangar partially depressurized in case they had to be ejected immediately upon arrival over Coventry. The chat would come only if the wait were prolonged beyond the point where human nerves could tolerate continued silence.

It was unnecessary, but David also maintained a silent count, making certain that every man in the two platoons boarded the shuttle. The possibility that someone might try to avoid going into combat at this point never entered David's mind, but nevertheless he did the count, as he did even on routine movements during training maneuvers.

H&S Company boarded its three shuttles in little more than a minute. For a moment, only three men remained on the hangar floor, one at the ramp of each shuttle—Spencer, Captain McAuliffe, and Lieutenant Ezra Franklyn, headquarters platoon leader and assistant battalion operations officer. Lieutenant Frank Nuchol, company executive officer and I&R platoon leader, waited for Spencer at the top of their shuttle's ramp. Nuchol had come into H&S Company after a longish stint as a company commander and I&R tactics instructor in the Marine Training Brigade on Buckingham. His assignment to a combat unit now was to make him eligible for promotion to captain. If he survived.

The three men on the floor looked at each other in turn. Spencer and Franklyn nodded to the captain, who nodded back, then made a gesture up the ramp of his shuttle. All three boarded their craft at the same time.

David looked around from the top of the ramp before he moved to his seat. A navy petty officer, the shuttle crew chief, hit the control to close the ramp and seal the lander. As David strapped himself into position, he felt a slight change in the air pressure on his eardrums. The shuttle was using its own air now, cut off from the hangar and *Victoria*'s life-support systems.

He took in a deep breath and let it out slowly. *Now we wait,* he told himself. For all of the practice he had had at waiting in his career, waiting to go into combat still did not come easily.

# 6

**The word** *confusion* lingered in Ian Shrikes's mind, repeating itself as if it were his personal mantra, while the countdown toward Q-space insertion ticked through its final minutes. He sat at the command console, slightly elevated over the rest of the bridge, scanning the half dozen monitors and the ranks of lights that showed the readiness of weapons and power systems throughout the vast ship. Ian had spoken privately with his division chiefs and a few key junior officers, impressing on them the need to remain calm and professional, no matter what they stumbled into when they entered Coventry's system. He had done what he could. The rest would depend on how well everyone had been trained—including himself.

*Sheffield* transmitted the order for Q-space insertion. *Hull* executed it simultaneously with the rest of the battle group. For the next three and one half minutes, HMS *Hull* was effectively alone in a bubble universe of its own, separated from the rest of creation by the distortions forced on the fabric of space-time by its Nilssen generators. Initially, the bubble was just a little larger than the long dimension of the ship. The navigational computers determined the direction and amount of pressure that the ship had to exert on the bubble to exit Q-space at the proper location. The generators then reversed the polarity of the Nilssen field and the ship emerged above Coventry. After that, Ian was far too busy to even recall the word *confusion*.

The battle group did not emerge in formation. The need to gather intelligence quickly, as much as the fear of disaster, had convinced Admiral Greene to order a wide dispersal so that there would immediately be video available of all of the planet's land areas. None of the ships emerged from Q-space more than 12,000 miles above the surface. Two of the frigates came in only 400 miles above sea level, accelerating to attack speed, aiming for the horizon in front of them—the line dividing space from atmosphere rather than the ground horizon—ready to make quick passes as their cameras and other sensors took in every available bit of data, both from the ground and from space around them. In addition, they also had to locate all enemy vessels currently in the system.

It was entirely chance that put all of the Commonwealth ships into positions where none of the Federation ships could strike at them immediately. In the first forty-five seconds, the battle group spotted four Federation troop ships, three of them the Cutter-class ships that each held one battalion of ground troops and the other a Beamer-class ship of approximately the capacity of *Victoria*. There were also three Federation frigates visible.

"No battlecruisers or dreadnoughts?" Ian asked himself. It was too good to believe. "Almost two regiments of soldiers and only three frigates to protect them and the troop ships?" That meant no fighters, no air cover for the Feddie soldiers, no long-range defenses for any of the ships. Louder, Ian said, "CIC, I want another sweep for capital ships. Check with the rest of the fleet as well. There have to be more Feddie ships around than we're seeing." The Combat Intelligence Center was deep inside *Hull*, and linked to CICs on each of the other ships.

"We're looking," came the immediate reply. "There is nothing else within range of our sensors. We are starting to get video from the surface, sir."

"Give me the feed on my number two and three monitors," Ian instructed. He turned his attention to those screens. The video was being relayed from the two frigates that had come out of Q-space closest to the surface. Their cameras had targeted The Dales and Coventry City. Little detail was visible in the raw video—the resolution was only enough to show objects that were at least eight feet in diameter—but that was enough to show the large number of fires, and the larger areas that had already been burned out, leaving only ashes and scorched remains.

*Hundreds of fires,* Ian thought, shocked at the extent, even in what was visible in the first passes. *What are they doing?*

The Federation frigates were leaving their parking orbits, accelerating toward the nearest Commonwealth vessels. The Federation troop ships started accelerating away from the planet, preparatory—Ian guessed—to jumping into Q-space. Escape was the only sane alternative for transports that were not adequately protected.

It took ten minutes for Admiral Greene's staff to gather enough information to decide which of the scenarios that the operations staff had concocted they would recommend. CIC was coordinating the response to the Federation frigates. Those were outnumbered, outgunned. *Sheffield* launched its Spacehawk fighters. *Sheffield* and *Hull* both launched missiles toward the enemy frigates. The Commonwealth frigates were also maneuvering to close with the enemy ships. The transports were allowed to flee, even though they might take news of the Commonwealth battle group back to the Federation capital on Union.

"We take care of the folks on Coventry," Admiral Greene said when CIC asked about the transports. "That's our mission. Transports only make worthwhile targets if they're loaded."

Watching video of the fires caused him to grit his teeth. After a few minutes, his jaw began to hurt. He had to consciously relax, and that was not easy.

"If those transports represent the entire Federation force on the surface, they must be spread awfully thin," came the estimate from CIC. A dozen satellites had already been launched to provide continuous surveillance of the populated areas, but it would be some time before they could start returning useful information—if they survived; those satellites would likely be targeted by the Federation frigates as soon as they could get around to them. "It appears as if they have units in or near almost every concentration of people on the planet.''

Greene shook his head, a minute gesture that was only noticeable to those few officers who happened to be looking directly at him. *What kind of lunacy?* . . . He cleared his throat.

''We'll have to leave some areas to them for now,'' he said, holding open his link to CIC. ''For our initial landings, we'll try to deal with whatever is going on around the largest cities. I don't want any units smaller than battalion size split off until we've got a better idea of what we're up against.''

''That limits our options, sir,'' the officer in CIC said.

''Of course it limits our options!'' Greene snapped. ''That's the entire purpose of gathering intelligence, so we can limit our options to the best course available.'' He had raised his voice and come half out of his seat, his hands gripping the arms of the chair. He was afraid that his hands would be seen to tremble if he let go too soon.

''Sorry about that, Carl,'' he said, addressing the CIC man. ''We'll hold the heavy weapons battalion aboard ship until we figure out where they might be most effective. Put Third and Fourth Battalions, and the engineers, close enough to Coventry City to get into action quickly. Send First and Second to The Dales. I want them all on their way in thirty minutes. Have *Hull* move to give the landings fighter cover. I want the frigates to keep working at improving our intelligence. We might be outnumbered five to two on the ground. We'll need any edge we can get to counter that.''

''Air and heavy weapons ought to do it, sir, unless the Feddies have more ships lurking where we can't see them.''

Greene leaned back. ''That's possible. The Feddies might be sitting in Q-space and just coming out periodically to have a look-see. Keep me informed on what you're doing, Carl. Remember, I want the first landers out in no more than thirty minutes.'' He cut the audio on his link to CIC and paged the flag communications officer.

''I want an MR ready to go to Buckingham in fifteen minutes. Program it to make the trip with only one Q-space transit, insertion as soon as it's safely away from our ships, exit as close as practical to Buckingham.'' Radio communications were limited by the speed of light—years between star systems. A message rocket—basically a Nilssen generator tied to a single rocket, with limited fuel and limited room for data—was faster. ''I'll get my message written now. Include all of the video and other telemetry we've picked up.'' *It's time to bring the other regiment in, as fast as possible. We've got to stop the Feddies from destroying everything on Coventry.*

The men in the shuttles aboard *Victoria* had video to watch while they waited. Before orders came for their launch, each battalion received video on the areas to which they would be going. Officers and noncoms started to go over charts of those areas on their mapboards—specialized complinks that were flat, folded in thirds, and could provide a wealth of mapping information on demand.

Geoffrey Dayle had pulled the faceplate down on his helmet as soon as the video started to show. That was his world burning. He didn't want his mates to see the tears on his cheeks.

# 7

**After the Baileys** saw the first fires burning along Royal Oaks Pike, they had one more day of nervous waiting before Federation soldiers came marching out Sherwood Pike. Reggie had been spending most of the daylight hours on the roof, watching. Even after sunset the evening before, he had hesitated before leaving his vigil, retiring inside only after the evening got too dark for him to see. All of that afternoon and evening the fires had moved farther out along Royal Oaks Pike. Some of the blazes died out after an hour or less. Others smouldered on into the night. Where Hawthorne was most heavily built-up the fires appeared fiercest, and lasted the longest.

It was not long after dawn the next morning that Reggie thought that the fires had started to move out from the center of town along Sherwood Pike as well. He watched for a few minutes longer, then went downstairs.

"Get everything ready," he said after he told Ida about the newest fires. "I'll move our packs out to the back of our land."

"What if they make us go the other way, out the pike?"

"Then we'll change direction as soon as we can. But I don't think they'll force us out along the road. We haven't seen anyone come out from town. There haven't been any floaters driving past, on the road or out in back."

Like nearly every family, except some in the old town, the Baileys had a ground-effect motorcar, but even at the start Reggie had given little thought to taking that along when, if, they were forced to leave. There had been considerable debate in the neighborhood. Some favored moving their cars into the woods, away from the houses, on the chance that they might be able to get to them when they had to. The argument that had carried the day, though, was that if all of the floaters were missing, the Feddies might go looking for them, and might destroy or confiscate everything that the families had managed to cache.

"I'm scared, Reg, terrified."

He blinked, twice. "I'm a little scared myself. We'll just have to make do. We'll keep the kids safe and fed the best we can, whatever it takes."

"Will it be enough?" There were always the same questions, and the same vague, uncertain answers. Inertia, and an almost complete ignorance of what to expect, had kept them home. They worried about what the soldiers might do when they came, but they worried even more about abandoning their home to hide in the wild. They had made their preparations, but they would not leave until they were forced to. If they were forced to. Even now, they found the prospect hard to believe.

"I'd better get back upstairs," Reggie said. "Get the kids ready, and try to keep them calm."

"Keep *them* calm? I'm having trouble keeping *myself* calm."

"As long as we keep *our* heads, the kids will be okay."

Over the next four hours, Reggie detected a clear pattern in the start of new fires. Four to six would start at once. Then there would be a pause of as much as forty-five minutes before the next batch. Then, finally, not long before midday, Reggie saw men in camouflage dress, too far away for them to display any individuality, only briefly visible along the road in a narrow gap before Sherwood Pike curved slightly to the right. Trees blocked anything more.

Ida brought up a tray with almost double the amount of food that Reggie normally ate for lunch.

"It won't be long now," he said. "I don't think it will be more than an hour and a half before they get here."

She stared at the nearest fires. The Baileys knew, at least casually, most of the people along Sherwood Pike for a mile in either direction. Already, friends and acquaintances were being burned out of their homes. Ida did not try to hide her tears now.

"All along, part of me didn't really believe that it was happening," she said. "I thought, prayed, that it was all some bizarre nightmare, that I'd wake and find that it really wasn't so."

"Where is our militia, the HDF?" Reggie asked. "Why haven't they stopped this?" There was no bitterness, only sadness, and the knowledge that he had also tried to believe that none of this was really happening. That delusion was no longer possible.

"You'd best eat while you can," Ida said. "I've got to get back downstairs before the kids notice I'm gone."

Reggie scarcely looked at the food that he methodically lifted to his mouth, chewed, and swallowed. He forced himself to eat every bite, long past the point when he felt stuffed to capacity. Every meal had been like that since the invaders had come to Coventry. *Laying in fat for the winter.* He ate, and he drank the coffee and juice that Ida had brought, but he continued to watch the fires. The breeze shifted from west to north-northwest and brought the smell of fire with it, burning wood and memories.

*I had my chances to join the HDF,* he reminded himself, as he had often since the start of the invasion. There had always been notices on the net asking people to do their patriotic duty and sign up for the Coventry Home Defense Force, to train against . . . just such a possibility as this. Reggie shook his head. *It wouldn't have worked. I was never cut out to be a soldier.* He tried to think of other things, but a nagging voice in his mind kept telling him that he was rationalizing his failure to do something for his world—and for his family.

After a time, it became easy to escape those thoughts. The Federation troops moved closer. Reggie could hear shouting, though he could not make out the words. People just two houses away—less than a quarter mile—were being rousted from their homes at gunpoint. A few minutes later, there were new fires, blazes he could see from their onset.

"We'll be in the next group." Reggie stood and watched. He could see soldiers going from point to point, using flame-throwers and incendiary devices to start several fires in each house. Then Reggie went downstairs. He wanted to be with his family when the soldiers came for them.

Ida and the children were gathered in the parlor. That had a window that gave them some view of the road going toward the center of Hawthorne. The twins were at either side of their mother, holding on to her with all of their strength. Al stood close as well, his fists clenched at his sides, his arms trembling with the effort.

"They're almost here, aren't they?" Al asked when he noticed his father.

Reggie nodded. "I could see them starting fires three houses down. It won't be long before they get to us."

"Why?" Al asked.

"I don't have any idea."

"What do we do?" Ida asked. "Do we go outside, or wait for them to break in?"

"I think we should be in plain sight," Reggie said. "That might be safer. They won't have to be nervous about an ambush." He hadn't heard any gunfire—except maybe once, early, a long way off—but he didn't want to take chances. He had seen videos of soldiers at war, throwing grenades into buildings before they went in shooting. All he could do now was try to minimize the risk to his family.

"Out front?" Ida asked.

"Might as well. They must expect people to know what's coming, expect people to be watching them."

"I packed a little more food. It's on the kitchen table."

"Let's get it and move out on the front lawn." Reggie led the way. The rest of what they had to carry away with them was already away from the house, out at the rear of their property, near the path that Reggie and Eric had taken out to where they had cached things in the woods. There were packs for all of them, very light ones for the girls, somewhat heavier for Al and Ida, and the heaviest one for Reggie himself.

The family floater was parked in the driveway by the courtyard gate. Reggie led his family through the gate and a little closer to the road. They could see the fires down the road. The smoke was heavy. The light breeze carrying it was hot.

Fifteen minutes later, thirty soldiers marched down the road in two columns, rifles and other weapons carried at the ready. The soldiers were anonymous figures in camouflage battledress, expressions hidden by tinted helmet visors. No insignia of rank or unit were visible, only the crest of the Confederation of Human Worlds in camouflage colors on the sides of the helmets.

An order stopped the soldiers just before they reached the Bailey driveway. More orders sent smaller groups off to their next six houses, three on either side of the road. The Knowles house, just south of the Baileys', was the last on the east side of the road to draw soldiers this time. One squad, five men, came a few steps up the driveway toward the Baileys. The leader raised the faceplate of his helmet.

"You have five minutes to gather whatever you can carry and leave," he said. The accent was unfamiliar, harsh to the ears of the Baileys.

"Where do we go?" Reggie asked.

"Away from town. Anywhere."

"Can we take our floater?"

"No vehicles. You can take whatever you can carry, nothing else."

"Why are you doing this?" Al demanded, starting forward. His father grabbed his shoulder to stop him. "Why are you doing this to us?"

The soldier stared at the boy for an instant but did not answer his question. He looked to Reggie again. "Five minutes. And don't try to come back later. Any civilians found around here after today will be shot." Then he lowered his visor and started giving hand signals to his men. He apparently gave no more thought to the civilians he was displacing.

"Come on," Reggie said, fighting to keep his voice calm. He kept a hand on his son's shoulder, turning him, moving him toward the side of the house. The others followed, staying close. At every step, Reggie feared that the soldier would yell for them to go the other way, away from where their other belongings were—those back near the rear of their property, and those that had been cached in the woods. But the only interest any of the soldiers seemed to take in the Baileys was to make certain that they did not go back inside their house.

The Baileys moved away from their house as the soldiers moved into position around it. Seventy yards away, they could see the Knowles family also moving away from their house, carrying what they could.

Anna Knowles could carry little more than herself. She moved slowly, awkwardly. Eric stayed at her side, one hand on her arm, helping to support her weight, helping her keep her balance. Their sons were in front of them, though the boys kept looking back at their home. Ida looked toward Anna, but had to look away. Unless a miracle happened, Ida knew that she would be in the same condition as Anna in little more than six months, ready to give birth with nowhere to do it safely. Six months: even if the Federation burned everything and then left immediately, six months would not give the people of Coventry time to rebuild, even with help from the outside.

The Knowles family needed longer than the Baileys to reach the edge of the forest, at the corner where their properties met. Toward town, the Watersons were moving toward them as well, but stopped before leaving their own property, turning to watch the destruction of their house.

It was the first of the latest six to be put to the torch. Windows were broken out on the ground floor. A soldier with a flamethrower went from one to the next and sprayed gelatinous fire through each broken window. Two other men attached small packets of explosives after quickly boring holes into the walls near ground level at each corner. Once the primers were set, the soldiers ran to a safe distance.

When the soldiers started to set fires in the Bailey house, Ida gripped her husband's arm so hard that he flinched in pain. Her fingernails seemed to stab through the sleeve of his shirt and into the flesh beneath. Long tongues of fire leaped out from the flamethrowers. The blazes spread quickly. In less than three minutes, the flames were visible through the upstairs windows as well, and smoke was pouring out through the openings on the ground floor.

The charges on the Waterson house went off first, and the building seemed to rise a little off the ground before settling down into itself. Dust and smoke billowed out to the sides and then rose in a dense cloud. For a moment, it looked as if the explosives had extinguished the fires, but then new tongues of dirty flames rose through the smoke.

The subsequent explosion of their own house took all of the Baileys by surprise except Al. He had not taken his eyes off of his home, not even when the blasts sounded at the Watersons'. His parents and sisters all jumped, and looked at their house as it exploded in a similar cloud of dust and smoke. A few seconds later, an incendiary device placed in their floater went off, engulfing the vehicle in orange flames.

Ida started to cry silently, the girls with more sound. Reggie swallowed hard and blinked several times, fighting to keep tears from his eyes. Al remained absolutely motionless, his fists still clenched at his sides, no emotion at all on his face. Gradually, his eyes narrowed a little. *They'll pay. I'll make them pay,* he promised himself, *if it takes the rest of my life.*

The soldiers remained only long enough to make certain that none of the houses would remain habitable, that nothing of value could be salvaged from them. The explosions at the Knowles house did seem to put out the fire. Two of the soldiers went close enough to toss in incendiary bombs in order to rekindle the blaze. Then the soldiers moved on to the next set of houses.

"You'd think we were no more than gnats, safe to ignore," Eric Knowles said. "Doesn't bother them a bit to turn their backs on us. They didn't even check to make sure that none of us had weapons."

"We might as well *be* gnats," Reggie said. "Less than gnats. Even they can bite hard enough to get themselves swatted."

"Don't start talking like that," Ida said. "You know there was nothing we could do."

"There should have been," Reggie said, almost viciously. "We should have been ready to defend ourselves."

"It's too late for should have been's," Ida said. "All we can do is face whatever comes and make the best of it. Let's get away from here. I don't want to watch my home burn the rest of the way. It'll be better when I can't see what's happening." *I hope,* she thought, without any great confidence.

Mason and Elizabeth Waterson had finally joined the other families with their children, three boys and a girl ranging from three to ten years of age. Their four, the three Bailey children, and the two Knowles boys all stayed close to their own parents.

Everyone's attention was diverted from the fires then by a series of sonic booms that seemed to come from the east. At first they could see nothing. Then a flotilla of shuttles went over from east to west, heading in the direction of Coventry City.

"Dozens of them," Al said. "They're bringing in more soldiers."

Another half dozen came in separately, seconds behind the first. These were lower, and banked into a turn to the right.

"More coming here," Eric said. "Guess these bastards weren't doing the job fast enough."

# 8

**The three families** watched until the last shuttle disappeared. For the most part, that vigil let them forget—for just those few seconds—what was happening to their homes.

"We've got a long way to go," Elizabeth Waterson said then, glancing at Anna Knowles. "And we can't travel all that fast." Her voice was hoarse, cracking, scarcely under control.

The group turned and moved off into the forest, away from the burning wreckage of their homes. The other families that had cached supplies with them would undoubtedly be along soon. Their homes would be in the next batch destroyed. They walked slowly, accommodating their pace to Anna's, stopping frequently for a minute or two to let her sit and catch her breath. Her face remained pale, bloodless. The effort to walk the rough trail was obviously taxing her almost to the limit. Eric suggested that the others go ahead, but the Baileys and Watersons both declined—to Eric's obvious relief.

"You may need us," Reggie said. Anna's face seemed to go even whiter at his words. She knew that they were worried that she might go into premature labor. This was her third child, and labor might be short; she might have her baby very quickly once the first contraction came.

"I haven't been getting much exercise lately," Anna said, her voice weak and reedy. "If I'd known something like this was going to happen...."

"We'll manage," Ida said. "We've had plenty of experience among us. We'll cope."

"Don't try to pass it off like sprinkles on a picnic," Anna

said. "I know how bad it's going to be. If there are any problems with the delivery, there's nothing any of us can do."

"Nothing is going to go wrong," Eric said, helping Anna to her feet. "With the baby or anything else. We've all got our nanobugs to keep us healthy, no matter what." Molecular health maintenance automatons, agents that coursed through the system to keep people healthy, were routine parts of life on a civilized planet like Coventry.

During the next stage of the trek, Reggie and Eric told the Watersons that they had moved part of their supplies. "The last time we came out, after everyone else quit coming," Reggie said. "We got nervous about leaving everything in one place."

"I don't blame you," Mason said. "I thought about it myself that night. I figured the two of you had already left by then, so I didn't do anything. I just hope our stuff's still there."

"It should be," Eric said. "The one thing we haven't had to worry about is neighbors stealing." *Yet,* he thought glumly.

"It hardly matters how much we stashed," Mason said. "It can't be enough. If only we could have hauled out a few food replicators and solar panels to power them, we might have had a better chance to make it through the winter."

"There's plenty of game," Reggie said. "I know you're not much of a hunter, but Eric and I have done some. And for at least the next few weeks we'll be able to pick nuts and berries. There should be nuts available all winter. One thing working for us, anything that looks edible is, you know that."

"How long will the game last with everyone hunting?" Mason asked. "The animals will leave, those that aren't killed."

"Then we'll follow the animals, wherever they go," Reggie said. "It's either that or just lie down and give up." *Give up now, or give up later?* Reggie shook his head, then looked at his wife and children. He would not give up. No matter what it took, he would provide. As long as he could breathe and move.

Before they reached the dry gully, they were resting more than they were moving. Anna seemed to lose strength with each pace. The next group of families caught up with them and went on. It was mid-afternoon before the Baileys and their companions were within sight of the gully and the trees that concealed the supplies.

"We'd better plan on staying here all afternoon," Reggie whispered to Eric when the latter finally let himself be drawn away from his wife. Anna was lying down, next to the gully. Two folded blankets were under her, and another covered her. Her eyes were closed, but her husband wasn't certain that she was asleep.

"I sure don't want to try to move her in the dark," Eric replied. "I didn't think it would be so hard on her this soon."

"Part of it must be the shock," Reggie said. "I know how hard it was on me, seeing our home destroyed." The medical nanobugs would—unless there were an almost unheard-of malfunction—protect Anna against any *physical* illness, but they could not cope with emotional or mental distress that did not result from physical imbalances. They also could not completely cope with the lack of muscle tone Anna admitted to. She simply had not been getting enough exercise during her pregnancy. In normal circumstances, that would have made little or no difference.

"Maybe. I'm going to have to figure some way to provide shelter for Anna right away. When the baby comes, it could be a week or more before we'll be able to move on. They'll both need more than a blanket to roll up in, even if nothing goes wrong."

"We'll help, as much as we can. You know that. Over where we put the rest of our stuff, it should be easier than here. All that loose rock. We can stack up enough for walls, then we just have to rig some kind of roof."

"And hope it doesn't rain too hard, or too soon." Eric looked at the sky. About a third of the trees in this area were deciduous, and many of those had already shed their leaves.

"I haven't heard a weather forecast since the landings," Reggie said. It was the first time he had thought of that lack. "I don't think it'll rain tonight, though. The sky's been as clear as glass. But we're getting pretty well into autumn. We usually get a lot of rainy days in the fall."

"I know. I've got one waterproof tarp, over at the other place, but it's only eight by twelve."

"It'll be enough to keep Anna dry."

"If she's up to it, maybe we can move around sunset, maybe a little before to give us time to get there before it's full dark. Or we can wait for morning. I'm having trouble thinking. My mind's more than half numb from it all."

"We're going to try to find a better place for Anna," Eric told the other families as sunset approached. She had slept for a time, uneasily, but had wakened and claimed to feel better than she had all day. "Someplace where we can build a shelter without too much trouble."

Eric and Reggie had told the others about their second cache. After they had told the Watersons, not telling the others might have left hard feelings. But neither Eric nor Reggie felt any compulsion to draw a map.

The two families left the others, weighted down by taking everything they had left at the first cache along with the things they had brought that day. There were no farewells among the adults, and few among the children. Reggie and Eric both helped Anna, one walking on either side of her when that was possible, supporting some of her weight. They made slightly better time than they had earlier, but even so it was almost too dark to see by the time they reached the rocky area where Eric and Reggie had cached most of their supplies.

Anna sat on a rock while the others started a small fire, then started putting together what little shelter they could for the first night. There wasn't so much as a two-man tent in their supplies. Neither family had ever gone in for camping. A day's excursion, with a picnic in the middle, was all of the "back to nature" that they had cared to assay.

The children sat around the fire when they were not helping to arrange things for the first night. All of them were
subdued. They had watched their homes burning. They were
out in the "jungle." Night had come. It was chilly, and they
had not yet eaten supper. Even the youngest knew that this
was serious.

Clothing that had seemed far too warm during the day
was not warm enough now. The men had made the best
arrangements they could for Anna, spreading the tarp from
a rock wall and weighting the other side down with stones,
then turned to unpacking the lightweight thermal blankets
that had been cached.

"We'll just have something light to eat tonight," Ida Bailey told her daughters. "We ate so much earlier." She kept
her voice light, not to give away that she was already worried about how soon they might run short of food.

"I'm not *real* hungry anyhow," Ariel said, and her twin
nodded agreement.

Anna was already asleep, but restless. Eric kept a worried
watch. He no longer worked to keep the worry from his
face, as he had while she was awake. Their sons, Walter
and William, also spent much of their time watching their
mother. Their father was worried; they were frightened.
Walter was ten, William seven.

Supper was cold, sandwiches and vegetable crisps. There
was only water to wash it down. No one complained. After
the meal, the children rolled up in their blankets. Even with
fear and cold noses, the youngest refugees quickly escaped
into sleep.

Only Al Bailey did not sleep. He stared at the campfire,
hardly blinking. His thoughts were filled with grandiose, and
expanding, fantasies of the vengeance he would take on the
Federation soldiers who had burned his home, and then on
those faceless people on some distant world who had ordered the crime. It took an hour or more for those fantasies
to finally carry Al into sleep.

Ida and the men were still up. After doing a rough check
to make sure that everything they had stored in the cave was

still there, Eric was pacing. Ida and Reggie sat close together, where they could watch the children as well as Anna.

After he was certain that Al was finally asleep, Reggie stood and stretched. He walked away from the campsite. He was tired, more exhausted than simple exertion could account for, but he did not want to risk sleep yet—though he could not have explained why. For the past hour, he had been doing little thinking of any kind, allowing himself to be lulled into almost a trance by staring at the fire. It was so much easier to put off all thought for as long as possible.

*I've got to think,* he told himself. *We can't just drift along without trying to find ways to do things smarter. We'll die if we drift along like that.* Death would be the ultimate escape. He closed his eyes for a moment. *Don't even start thinking like that. You've got a family to think about.*

Make preparations. They had cached everything they could, but it would not be enough. Within days it would be necessary to start hunting for game, meat to help the mostly dehydrated vegetables of their stores last longer. And the sooner they started hunting, the better it would be.

*But will gunfire bring those soldiers back?* That had not occurred to him before. Hearing shooting might draw curious soldiers, or worried soldiers.

*It doesn't matter. We've got to hunt no matter what. Maybe they won't be close enough to hear. Or maybe they'll realize that the odd shot now and then is no more than what it will be, people trying to get food, and not worry about it.*

There were other questions. Should they stay where they were or move on, look for better shelter farther from the enemy soldiers and the ruins of their homes? *Could* they move any farther with Anna obviously frail and perhaps about to give birth within days, if not hours? Reggie had no idea how long he had been standing alone, thinking, when Eric joined him.

"We're going to have to stay here, I think," Reggie said, very softly. "At least until Anna has her baby and feels up to moving. As long as it takes."

"We'd be safer moving farther away," Eric said, glancing back to where his wife was sleeping, "but I think you're right. We'd have to carry Anna, and leave too much of our stuff unguarded while we made however many trips it would take to get all of our things moved. You can take your family on, though, and we'll try to catch up later. When we can."

"Don't talk nonsense. We won't leave you here. It's not even an option. We'll stick together. It's the only chance we've all got."

"I figure to build a better shelter for Anna in the morning," Eric said, and Reggie nodded.

"We'd better try to get some sleep," Reggie said a moment later. "We'll need whatever we can get."

"Maybe we should take turns watching," Eric said. "Keep the fire burning, make sure nobody sneaks in to . . . do anything."

"You go sleep. I'm not tired yet."

In the morning, there was coffee and soup, the latter made from dehydrated packets that the women had stocked in considerable quantity added to water from a nearby stream. Only the children seemed rested by their sleep. Ida, Reggie, and Eric had all taken turns standing guard, watching Anna and keeping the fire burning. Even after sunrise, Anna only got up for a few minutes to take care of the most essential needs, with the help of her husband, in the latrine that the men had just dug some distance away from the campsite and their water supply. Then she lay down again, so exhausted that she scarcely had the strength to eat her breakfast.

The men worked as quickly as they could to construct a more substantial shelter for Anna and the rest of them, and for their supplies. Six hours of steady labor produced a redoubt that would keep out all but the most ferocious of rains, and most of the wind. Hauling flat rocks and stacking them against the side of a rocky outcrop provided strong walls on three sides, with a door opening covered by a small tarp. The larger tarp that Eric had packed was stretched over cut saplings to provide a roof, weighted down along the edges by more rocks, and covered with layers of leaves and smaller branches to give it a little insulation. Anna almost had to be carried inside. The entrance to the cave where Eric and Reggie had stored their supplies was also inside, back in the far corner.

The two families were undisturbed through the day. None of the other refugees, even the few who had some idea where the Baileys and Knowleses were, came around.

Near sunset, a small native deer happened to come close to the camp. Reggie got his shotgun and stalked the animal as silently as he could. His efforts were not particularly credible, but he got within thirty yards before the deer turned its head to stare, and thirty yards was close enough for Reggie to hit a motionless target. He had no difficulty carrying the carcass back to camp. It might provide no more than ten or twelve pounds of meat, but that would serve the families for two meals. Reggie felt proud of his efforts.

"One shot," he boasted when he set the carcass down at the edge of camp. One shot was all he could afford for a small kill. He had only a limited supply of ammunition, even though he had managed to find two extra boxes of shells the morning after the invasion. He hoped it would be enough to see them through the winter—if help hadn't arrived before then.

No one felt like eating raw meat, and the fire the families had been maintaining was not enough. The men built a second fire, on the downwind side of camp. Reggie cleaned the kill.

"We should have thought about tanning hides," he told Eric. "We might need to make moccasins or clothes."

"Leave it. I'll scrape the hide down and stretch it to dry by the fire," Eric said. "That's the best we can do."

The stone shelter was large enough for all of the women and girls to sleep in, though barely. The men and boys slept outside. As long as no rain came and the nights did not get too cold, that would be enough.

Their second night out, Al Bailey shared the watches with his father and Eric. "I'm twelve years old. I can watch and wake everyone if something happens." *Maybe I'll get a chance to* do *something if anyone comes,* he thought. He spent the two hours of his first watch pacing, far enough from the others that he did not disturb their sleep.

It was much cooler than it had been the night before, partly because there was a strong breeze blowing out of the north. Al thought that he could smell the smoke of burning houses on the air, but was not entirely certain. It might be nothing more than their own campfire . . . or his imagination.

The feverish fantasies of vengeance had burned their way out of Al's mind. He had not forgotten his vows, but he realized that there was nothing he could do now but work to survive, and help his family survive. Later, he was certain that he would find opportunities.

*I'll take any chance that comes,* he promised himself, fingering his closed pocketknife. If he could find one soldier alone and careless, that would give him a rifle, and maybe other things. From there . . . He smiled at the possibilities.

Eric followed Al, and Reggie got up for his second tour of the night after Eric. Reggie had been up for an hour when he heard a sharp groan from inside the shelter. He had scarcely turned and taken a single step in that direction before he heard a louder sound, pain clear in it. Eric came awake quickly, sitting up and starting to his feet. Before either of the men got to the shelter, Ida stuck her head out.

"She's gone into labor."

Eric pushed past her. Angel and Ariel came out, their blankets wrapped around them.

"Find the girls someplace to sleep out here," Ida said as she brought out the rest of their sleeping gear.

Reggie arranged new beds for the girls as close to the fire as he thought safe and got them settled in. Ida went back inside to help Anna. Eric might have been able to manage on his own if necessary, but Ida knew what to expect, what to do, and she was not as near the edge of panic as Anna's husband was.

Reggie paced about, looking more often at the shelter door than away from camp. Anna made no further outcries for nearly an hour, except for an occasional soft grunt. At other times, Reggie could hear her breathing hard and fast. Inside, Ida and Eric had two flashlights burning, as well as a small fire. Even so, they were in deep shadows most of the time, waiting.

Finally, after little more than an hour, Anna gave another cry of pain. A moment later, her third child gave its own first cry. Outside, Reggie relaxed when he heard the baby. Whatever else happened, they had at least crossed one hurdle. But another ten minutes passed before Ida came out, sweating despite the chill.

"They're both okay, for now," she said. "It's a boy."

# Part 3

# 9

**Troop shuttles were** inviting targets, fat, slow, and not very maneuverable. They were helpless pigeons for any birds of prey, not only enemy fighters and ships, but even infantrymen with small surface-to-air missiles. The vulnerability of the shuttles was felt by the Marines who rode them. They could not fight back or defend themselves until they were on solid ground, out of the landers. Between ship and shore, they might die without even knowing that an enemy was near.

A message from Admiral Greene had assured the men of the Second Regiment that there were no enemy fighters around, nor were any of the Federation ships in position to attack them. And the landers would have fighter escorts on the way down. That did little to calm anyone's nerves.

A strong majority of the men in the shuttles felt themselves to be absolutely alone during a combat descent, as isolated as if they were in their own private Q-space bubbles, separated from the rest of creation by an impenetrable space-time barrier. They sat elbow to elbow with their mates, but most kept the visors of their helmets down, tinted faceplates hiding their expressions. Weapons were held in both hands and supported between their legs, a totem to cling to. Those men with religious inclinations—and even some who normally showed no interest in religion—took the time to put credits to their prayer accounts. Others distracted, or tortured, themselves with memories of loved ones. Some fought to deal with their fear, steeling themselves against the unavoidable inner turmoil and the outer chaos of battle. *Don't let me let my mates down,* was a common wish.

Heading for their landing on Coventry, the officers and noncoms of the Second Regiment did not have the luxury of solitary vigil. They studied mapboards, trying to memorize terrain and the improvised plans displayed for them. Initial orders came through after the shuttles had separated from *Victoria,* and those were expanded and altered as the shuttles raced in for "hot" landings—accelerating toward the ground to decelerate only at the last possible moment, exposing themselves to ground fire for as brief a period as possible.

"One thing looks good," Captain McAuliffe told his officers and noncoms. "We haven't spotted any major defensive formations. The Feddies are spread out to hell and around the corner, burning as if they didn't know that we were coming. We should be able to get down and out without opposition. Nothing more than scattered sniping, if that."

The men were scattered about in three shuttles, conferring over the radio links in their helmets, unified by watching mapboards slaved to the captain's. He showed them their projected landing zone and indicated how he wanted the platoons dispersed, where the first defensive perimeter would be. The battalion would land and take time to organize—and to gather more information about the location of Federation troops in The Dales—before their next steps were decided on.

"They have to know that we're coming in, sir," David Spencer said. "They can't be so blind to what's going on."

"We're not assuming that they are," McAuliffe replied. "This is no drill. We go in, organize quickly, and move to stop this bloody scorched-earth campaign the Feddies are waging."

The burning had not stopped. Even as McAuliffe and the others stared at their mapboards, currently zoomed out to show all of The Dales and the surrounding countryside, they could see new blossoms of smoke as the computers of Combat Intelligence Center updated the information being fed to all of the mapboards. It looked as if half of The Dales was on fire. Buildings and grasslands, commercial and residential neighborhoods. Some of the fires were obviously burning out of control, moving into areas that had been left wild.

It was the same at Coventry City, South York, and most of the smaller cities and towns. In some areas the burning was farther along. In some it had barely started. Only a few of the smallest towns and villages showed no fires at all. No one in the Second Commonwealth force knew yet whether only buildings were being torched, or what might be happening to the people who had lived and worked in them. Mass murder did not seem impossible for people who appeared to be doing everything they could to destroy all signs of human habitation on an entire world.

Spencer's attention was diverted when the shuttle pilot announced that they would be grounding in ninety seconds. David glanced at the nearest monitor as he put the mapboard away. The bulkhead monitor was displaying video of their landing zone.

"Get ready to ground," Captain McAuliffe instructed on an all-hands channel. "Check your weapons. Lock and load."

David checked his rifle and pistol, then felt for the grenades on his pack harness.

The pilot gave a thirty-seconds-to-landing warning.

"Brace yourselves, lads," David told the men in his shuttle. "Be ready to move out smartly when the ramp drops."

The shuttle grounded with enough of a shock for everyone to feel it. The ramp dropped open. Men released lap straps and stood. In many ways, this was their most vulnerable time, the last seconds when they were unable to defend themselves. Two platoons of Marines trotted down the ramp and away from the shuttle, taking less than thirty seconds to clear the lander and start forming their section of the defensive circle.

The landing zones for the First and Second Battalions were in the southern part of The Dales, close enough together for the battalions to support each other from the beginning. The area had already been burned over. Ruins of a dozen buildings were visible to the west, along the edge of what had apparently been a vast municipal park. The grass and bushes were ashes. Few trees remained standing, and only a couple showed signs of life above charred lower trunks. South and east of the LZs, a mile or more distant, the smoke of still-burning fires could be seen as the Marines formed their defensive perimeter.

In H&S Company, First Battalion, cooks, clerks, and mechanics went into the perimeter along with the I&R platoon and everyone else. H&S Company of the Second Battalion was similarly deployed. With regimental headquarters on the ground near Coventry City, five hundred miles distant, First Battalion's Lieutenant Colonel Emile Zacharia was in tactical command of operations around The Dales, although he was never out of contact with Colonel Laplace or with CIC aboard *Sheffield*.

As soon as their passengers were clear, the shuttles lifted off, pulling for orbit and rendezvous with *Victoria*. The Spacehawk fighters remained close until the last shuttles had started up, then pulled out as well. A second flight of Spacehawks was on call if the Marines needed close-air support. Until and unless they were needed for that, the fighters would continue to gather intelligence.

"Keep your eyes open," Spencer told H&S Company when he had a few seconds free of information coming in from Colonel Zacharia and Captain McAuliffe. "We won't be here long." The battalion was deployed on a wide, flat area with no natural cover.

The odor of ashes was almost overpowering, blotting out anything else. It was not an unfamiliar smell. Spencer could recall fighting wildfires on Buchanan when they threatened settled areas. The region southwest of Westminster was notorious for wildfires as well. By the beginning of August, the plains stretching off in that direction could get so dry that almost anything could start a fire. Hot southwesterly winds fanned the flames. It didn't matter that the battalion had not been called on for that duty in four years. Smelling the ashes brought back old memories with stark immediacy.

"Form the company up, Spencer," Captain McAuliffe

said after they had been on the ground for ten minutes. "We're moving out in five. I'll give Lieutenant Nuchol his instructions. I&R goes out in front, as usual. They need to get moving right away. I'll get back to you with the rest."

Each battalion formed a skirmish line two companies wide, with the rest following, each subsequent line fifty yards behind the one ahead. Weapons were carried at the ready, and there was constant communication between battalion commanders and the I&R platoons that were scouting ahead of the rest.

"We're going to intercept what appears to be two companies of Feddies," McAuliffe explained to his platoon leaders and platoon sergeants. "Try to prevent them from burning anything more. They're spread out, working their way south along three parallel streets. They must know we're here, so assume that they'll consolidate and move into position to meet us. Both I&R platoons, ours and the Seconds, are out looking to see what they can do. If possible, they'll engage the Feddies, try to keep them occupied until we arrive."


The camouflage battle dress of Lieutenant Frank Nuchol's I&R platoon had a new look. Blotches of soot obscured much of the greens and tans of the original, and visors were smudged. Nuchol had never led troops in combat before, but he had been a Marine long enough to learn the most basic lesson any junior officer needed to know—to rely on the veterans under his command. Nuchol and his platoon sergeant, Tory Kepner, worked well together. Neither managed to totally frustrate the other.

"You see any problems with what the captain wants?" Nuchol asked Kepner on their private link.

"Not up front, Lieutenant. The problems will come when the Feddies decide to take exception to our presence."

"Then let's get the lads moving."

Tory's men needed five minutes to get past the first burned area, but even beyond that there was evidence of other fires. Few of the torched buildings amounted to much now. Tory soon realized that there had been more to the work than just lighting matches. Explosives had been used to insure that no building shells survived to permit quick repair. Construction to replace them would have to start from scratch, *after* the debris of the original buildings had been cleared away.

*Deliberate destruction,* Tory thought. He had fourth squad take a quick look into the rubble of the first few buildings, to see if they could spot bodies, or survivors. The reports were negative. If there were bodies, they were buried beyond casual observation. If there were survivors, they were making no sounds that the sensitive microphones built into the men's helmets could hear. Tory relayed that news to Nuchol and Captain McAuliffe.

"We've also spotted several piles of goods near the buildings," Tory said. "It looks as if the Feddies cleared some things out of the buildings before they torched them."

"Don't waste time with that," McAuliffe said. "Our job is to stop them from destroying any more buildings. If the Feddies are looting, we'll worry about that later."

Tory kept his men dispersed along the sides of the street, with wide intervals between men. The lieutenant left operational details to Tory. Nuchol was across the street from Tory, and farther back, so that it would be unlikely for both to be taken out simultaneously.

Kepner had to consciously think about little things, like remembering to breathe normally. It was too easy, almost instinctive, to hold his breath, partly because of the stench, partly in anticipation of the first gunshots, the first blast of a grenade. It was often I&R's lot to go out to draw enemy fire. This time, they might be tempting odds of ten to one, or worse. Engage the enemy, keep them too busy to start more fires, hold their attention until the rest of the two battalions could arrive to finish the job.

*Bait, that's all we are,* Tory told himself. He tried to swallow, but his throat was too dry. *Staked out to give the Feddies someone to shoot at.*

First squad was on the right side of the street, third on the left. Second and fourth squads trailed behind, occasionally sending a fire team wide on either flank. Fifteen minutes after leaving the LZ, Nuchol and Kepner got a message, relayed from one of the Spacehawk pilots. "You're five hundred yards from the nearest Feddies. South-southwest of you. About company strength."

"What about the rest of them?" Nuchol asked after bringing the platoon to a halt and putting them down in defensive posture.

"It looks like they're still setting fires. Two more just started."

Nuchol and Kepner looked at the latest information on their mapboards. Blips showed Federation helmets with active electronics. The Feddies were making no attempt to hide their location by turning off radios and sensors.

"At least they're finally showing that they know we're here," Tory said. "I was just beginning to wonder if they were all blind and deaf."

"They know we're here, all right," Captain McAuliffe said, joining the conference. "I'm more concerned about why they're so damn confident that they don't have to worry about us. What's their secret edge?"

*I wish he hadn't said that,* Tory thought. *If the Feddies know we're here, why do they act as if we don't matter?* Tory prided himself on being a careful Marine. He had a wife and young son on Buckingham, and he had every intention of returning to them. That needed caution, talent, and luck. The first two Tory could take care of himself. The last . . . all he could do was minimize the need for it by being the best Marine he could be.

He switched channels on his radio to talk to the squad and fire team leaders. He relayed the intelligence he had received, gave the others a chance to see it on their mapboards.

"They might have something up their sleeves we haven't guessed at," Tory said. "We'll play this as tight as we can. Our job is to keep the Feddies occupied until the rest of our chaps get up here. We don't have to wipe them out ourselves."

He waited for comments, particularly from Alfie Edwards. Even as a corporal, Alfie remained the platoon comedian.

But this time Alfie simply acknowledged the message and asked, "So what do we do?" without the sarcasm that Tory half expected.

"Come out of the smoke behind them. The second they start shooting, we go to ground and play sharpshooter. Put all that training His Majesty's Government have paid for to good use. And we keep our eyes open all around; don't let them sneak up on us while we think we're sneaking up on them."

"Put out a squad on the wing?" Alfie suggested.

"You volunteering your fire team?"

"At least I'll know it's being done right that way."

Tory checked with Lieutenant Nuchol before he answered Alfie. "Work around to the right, but don't get in the middle of things. Mind where you're at, and keep in contact. This could get dicey in a hurry."

"I always know where I'm at. It's the why that gives me trouble now and then."

"You'd best start your flanking maneuver now, before we get close enough for the Feddies to watch you waltzing."

Alfie motioned to the three privates of his fire team, and took the point. Behind him, the others fell into their usual order—Willie Hathaway, John McGregor, and Eugene Wegener. It never bothered them when others laughed and said that they didn't know any better than to do things alphabetically. It worked for them. Wegener, as silent as a sleeping ghost, was the perfect rear guard. The Hat was audacious enough to spring to Alfie's assistance at need, and McGregor was the steady pivot in the middle, able to pay attention to what was going on behind as well as in front.

Alfie wanted plenty of room, so he went well wide of the Feddies before he turned south again. The fire team had plenty of cover between it and the enemy, even one building that had not been burned and blown up yet. In good cover, under a pair of trees and behind a thick hedge, Alfie brought his men together and lifted his helmet visor.

"Let's see if we can get inside that building. Find windows we can open to have decent shots at the Feddies.''

"Aren't you forgetting something?" Wegener asked. "Such as what it might feel like to be in that building when the Feddies put the burn and bang to it?"

"They're using flamethrowers to set the fires. Since they've got no artillery that we know of, they must be planting explosives by hand. That means they'd have to get right in our faces. Our rifles can keep even the flamethrowers out of reach. I'm not about to sit still and let them cook me without a fight."

"If we're sneaking in the back when they torch the front, what good can we do?" the Hat asked.

"We don't visit the loo first," Alfie said. "Once we're inside, we get into position fast enough they can't catch us by surprise. Any other objections?" His tone made it clear that there had better not be.

"Let's move." Alfie slapped his visor down and started forward, staying low, and doing what he could to keep some cover between him and the gaps on either side of the building, where enemy troops seemed most likely to appear. When they reached the building, a square three-story structure that appeared to be designed for offices, the I&R men flattened themselves against the outside wall on either side of the entrance.

Alfie signaled for Wegener and Hathaway to check the nearest windows on either side of the doorway. It was a stretch for both men, but they chinned themselves on the sills and pulled themselves high enough to see inside. Both shook their heads when they dropped to the ground: no one visible inside.

*If we weren't on the hush-hush, proper drill would be to toss in a couple of grenades first,* Alfie thought. Proper drill. The RM had a proper drill for almost any situation a Marine might conceivably find himself in.

"Okay, lads, in and down behind me. Be ready for anything."

It never would have occurred to Alfie to lead from behind and send one of the others in first. That might be "proper drill," but it was not Alfie Edwards's way. He took a deep breath and slid closer to the door. He reached for the handle as if it were a venomous snake, and hesitated before he grasped it in his left hand. Then he took another deep breath and let it out.

*One, two, three.* He counted silently, then twisted the handle and pushed the door open as rapidly as he could. He hit the door with his shoulder as he brought both hands to his rifle and dived through the doorway and off to the left. He slid along a polished tile floor and had his rifle in firing position before he realized that there were no targets in sight. The corridor spanned the building to a similar entrance on the far side.

Alfie got back to his feet quickly after the rest of the fire team came in. The muzzle of his rifle tracked back and forth from one side of the corridor to the other. There were three doorways on the right, two on the left. All were closed.

*No time to check them all,* Alfie thought. Within minutes, the rest of the two I&R platoons would start shooting at the Feddies to keep them preoccupied.

"We'll go into the last rooms on either side," Alfie told the other three. "Two and two. Wait for my signal to do anything, and be careful about showing yourselves. We want to see what's going on out there, but we don't want to be seen."

Alfie took Wegener to the left. Hathaway and McGregor took the other side.

The room Alfie entered had three desks and chairs. But there was nothing else, no complinks or office machines. It looked as if everything but the furniture had been moved. There had been no sign on the door to indicate what the office had been used for. It did have two windows looking out on the side of the building where Alfie expected to find Federation soldiers.

"Careful now," Alfie whispered. "Stay down. You take that window. I take the other. We wait until both of us are in position before anyone takes a peek."

It was only then that Alfie thought to check that the windows could actually be opened. *Nearly stepped in it there,* he chided himself when he saw that they could be. On some worlds, that would have been unlikely. And, anywhere, it was doubtful that small arms fire would shatter window-panes. Even on primitive colony worlds, window "glass" as strong as plate steel would be available, formed by nano-tech assemblers.

Alfie moved to the side of the window and raised up slowly, his back against the wall, allowing himself just a glimpse at a sharp angle across the terrain east of the build-ing. At first, he didn't see anyone. It was only when he moved closer that he spotted people, a hundred yards away. Some of them were near an assemblage of items that had to have been removed from this building and the others around the area.

"Civilians," he said. He radioed Lieutenant Nuchol to report where they were. "We've got Feddies in sight, but we've also got civvies out here. Looks like they've been cleared out of the next few buildings. They're just standing around, with a few Feddies who seem to be guarding them."

"Hang on," Nuchol said. "Don't start anything until you get the go-ahead from me. If you're attacked, defend your-selves, but be as careful as you can about hitting civilians."

Alfie passed those orders on to the others in his fire team, then settled in to wait. He spotted Federation soldiers drill-ing holes at strategic places around the base of one of the other undamaged buildings. *Getting ready to plant the ex-plosives,* he guessed. Then: *They must already have them planted on this one.* That started an itch at the back of his neck. He told the others. "Any Feddies head in this direc-tion, we may have to get the hell out in a hurry."

"How about right now?" McGregor asked. "Seems they don't need to head this way to set off any packets they've already placed. Wouldn't want to come too close, now, would they?"

"Just keep your eyes open," Alfie said. "If we can, we'll stay put at least until we hear back from the lieutenant."

It was nearly five minutes before Nuchol came back on line. "We still have to do our job, Edwards. The word is to be as careful as possible to avoid hitting civilians, but we have to stop the Feddies. You understand that?"

"Aye, sir. We do our job, taking what care we can to avoid civilian casualties. One thing, sir. It seems likely that this building we're in has already been prepared for demolition. The civvies and Feddies are well away from here, and we can see them planting the explosives on the next structure."

"Use your own judgement. If you think it's too dangerous to stay where you are, and you can find an acceptable alternative position, go ahead."

"I think we'll try sticking with this, at least for now, sir. It's a rare good spot for what we need to do."

"Fine. Just remember that you're no good to the RM dead. The rest of the platoon is just about ready to start the attack. Ninety seconds."

*I'm no good to myself dead, either,* Alfie thought as he turned his full attention to the situation outside his window.

"Just a minute now, lads," he told the fire team. "As soon as the rest of the platoon starts shooting, so do we. The object is to hit Feddies but not the local blokes. Do your best, but the order is we do our job." If there were a full firefight, civilians would die. There was little hope of avoiding that, especially once the rest of the two battalions joined the fray.

*Maybe the Feddies will surrender quick-like.* He did not put much faith in that hope. *Odds are better I could flap my arms and fly.*

The news that there were civilians close to the Federation soldiers had occasioned a quick realignment of the two I&R platoons. Frank Nuchol took the rest of his platoon more to the left, hoping to get a better angle on the enemy, one that would put as many of the Coventrians as possible off to the side, at least partially out of the direct line of fire.

"Mind what you're shooting at," Tory told the platoon. "No careless spraying." He had never been in a situation where civilians might be in the way. It made him think of his wife and son on Buckingham. *The war goes poorly, they could be in the same position someday.* That brought such a knot to his stomach that he grimaced in real discomfort.

The enemy troops came in sight. So did the civilians. The I&R platoon crawled into position, trying to stay undetected for as long as possible, looking for the best cover for the coming fight. There were no trenches or foxholes, no ready-made barricades they could shelter behind.

"We're in position," Nuchol reported to Captain Mc-Auliffe.

The captain paused just long enough to make certain that Second Battalion's I&R platoon was also in position before he gave the order. "Fire."

## 10

**While the two** I&R platoons engaged the Federation soldiers, three companies from each of the two battalions moved to envelop the enemy. First Battalion's companies moved around the right flank. Second's moved on the left. In the center, the remainder of the two H&S companies reinforced their I&R platoons. The rest of the two battalions moved close enough to join in the fight if necessary, but would remain in reserve unless needed.

After seventeen months as company lead sergeant, David Spencer was no longer as leery of the combat qualifications of the clerks, cooks, and others in H&S Company as he had been when he got the job. At least they were no longer hazards to themselves in combat. Once they could hear gunfire, the men of H&S moved with extreme caution, with none of the grumbling that had marked much of their training.

David directed the platoons into position, guided by radio. Tory Kepner had looked over the terrain and made suggestions. Spencer accepted them without question. He himself moved toward Kepner and Lieutenant Nuchol, and dropped to the ground between them, closer to Tory.

"What have you got, Kep?" David asked.

"From what Alfie said, there might only be about a hundred and twenty Feddies up ahead, but close to that many civilians as well." Tory didn't take his eye from his gunsight. "Alfie's fire team is in that building to the right, on the ground floor."

"Lieutenant?" Spencer turned his head toward Nuchol, who was twenty yards away. He kept his helmet radio on a channel that would keep Tory in the conversation as well. As company lead sergeant, Spencer's relations with the junior officers sometimes became very ambiguous. The position required extreme diplomacy. The lieutenants outranked him, but Spencer most often spoke with the authority of Captain McAuliffe behind him.

"We're ready," Nuchol said.

"Now that the rest of us are here, the captain wants you to slide the rest of your platoon off toward Alfie's fire team. Cover the angle between here and there. The rest of the troops are moving wide, going to try to get beyond, up past that building. You get set, have Alfie pull out and rejoin you as soon as possible. I heard what he said, that the building is probably packed with explosives."

Nuchol nodded.

"I know I wouldn't want to be sitting in there," Tory said.

For two minutes, Alfie's fire team might almost have been on the firing range on Buckingham, only a few miles from the pubs and pool halls of Cheapside, popping silhouette targets. With the rest of the platoon firing from Alfie's left, the Federation troops didn't notice that some of the incoming fire was coming from their flank, and from a considerably shorter range. Alfie's men were able to pick their targets and make sure of them.

Alfie saw the Feddie who spotted them. The man pointed, just before he became a casualty. An entire squad of Feddies turned their rifles toward the building, and the four Marines had to be more cautious.

"Get ready to move," Alfie said as he pulled away from the window, off to the side. *Maybe we should have gone higher to start with. We'd have had a better angle from the top floor.* But he quickly dismissed the idea. Going higher would not have been smart in a building that was likely set with explosives.

He flipped the selector switch on his rifle to automatic, then moved back to the edge of the window to spray a short burst toward the Feddies. Then he pulled back again.

"Let's not push our luck," he told his team. "We'll duck out the way we came in."

There was time for one more burst, from the opposite side of the window. The Marines met in the central corridor and ran for the door on the west side of the building. They went through the doorway at full speed, jumping from the small terrace to the ground, rolling away in case any of the enemy had managed to move around and get them in his sights. But Alfie didn't notice any shots whizzing past. The gunfire all seemed to be on the other side of the building yet.

"Time to get back to the rest of our blokes," Alfie said after Tory gave him new orders.

They did not move in a straight line toward the rendezvous. That would have exposed them to enemy fire at too close a range. Alfie instead led his fire team toward a clump of trees eighty yards off of the direct line, farther from the Feddies.

"We'll park it here for a few minutes," he told the others. "This puts us back in the fight." They could see Feddies, but at a range of more than two hundred yards. That wasn't excessive for a good marksman. Only the needle gun was past its limits. But the angle meant that they had to be more cautious than ever with their shots. From this angle, the civilians were behind the Feddies, but flat on the ground now.

"Keep your shots in the dirt at the faces of the Feddies if you can, away from the civilians," Alfie said. "We keep their heads down, we're doing our job proper. Let the others finish them off."

The building they had been in exploded. At least four separate blasts, perhaps more, cut too many structural members at the base for the building to continue to stand. It collapsed into itself, spreading a dense cloud of dust and debris. The Marines could see nothing of the Federation soldiers through it.

"Let's move again," Alfie said as soon as the first rain of debris had fallen. "We can't see them, they can't see us."

They were on their feet and moving when the second set

of explosions came, from farther off, apparently in the building they had seen the Feddies working on. Then there was a smaller blast, close. Wegener went down hard. The others all felt the sting of shrapnel that had traveled beyond its killing radius.

"Down!" Alfie shouted, an unnecessary order because he and the others were already on the ground. Visibility was still poor. The smoke and dust of the larger explosions had not completely settled out. Alfie touched his arm and side, where he had felt the stings. His fingers came away bloody.

"Willie, Mac—what shape you in?" Alfie asked. He was already crawling toward Wegener, who had stopped moving and was lying on his side.

"Just scratches, I think," Willie said through clenched teeth. "I think I've got a bit of metal left inside. It burns."

"I'm okay," McGregor said. "Where'd that come from?"

"Either Wegener tripped a mine or somebody set it off by remote and got lucky," Alfie said. "Slap med-patches on your cuts." He turned Wegener onto his back. Eugene's vital signs were still showing on the readout on the head-up display of Alfie's faceplate, but they were depressed.

"It hurts," Wegener said as Alfie turned him. "Dear God, it hurts." There were tears rolling down his cheeks. "Don't let me die. Please don't let me die."

"Just lie easy, lad," Alfie said softly. He tried to evaluate Wegener's wounds. He had taken at least a dozen pieces of shrapnel. Pools of blood had merged on his battledress top, making it impossible to determine exactly how many separate wounds there were. Alfie pulled Wegener's helmet off, then slapped an analgesic patch on his neck, right over the artery. Then he started slapping patches over the entrance wounds, ripping the uniform and field skin away as needed. When he could spare the time, he called Tory to let him know what had happened.

"We'll have help there in a minute or two," Alfie told Wegener. "You'll be fine. You won't even be 'excused duty' for more than a few hours." He wasn't nearly as confident of that as he tried to sound. There was no telling how much internal damage the shrapnel might have done. Wegener might be in worse condition than he looked. But if he stayed alive until he reached a trauma tube, he would almost certainly survive.

The rest of the platoon arrived and moved into position between the wounded men and the enemy. A medic was almost as quick to get there. He moved Alfie away from Wegener.

"Take care of those cuts you've got, Corp," the medic said, pointing to the wounds on Alfie's right arm and side. "I'll look after this one."

Wee Willie was already tugging at Alfie from the other side. "Let me get those," he said. He already had med-patches out, ready to apply. Alfie sat back and let the private do the work. He only needed a few seconds.

"Nothing too bad there," Hathaway said when he had finished. "Looks like we came off lucky."

Alfie glanced at Wegener before he mumbled, "Yeah, lucky. Let's get organized."

Tory slid in next to them, going flat. "What's the story?"

Alfie told him, gesturing around, as if Kepner ought to be able to see for himself. "We'll be a man short for a while, but the rest of us are fit for duty. It was a mine that did for us."

"We're going to slide around the far side of that building you were in, try to end this quick-like."

"The quicker the better," Alfie said.

"Gather up your lads and stay with the rest of the squad."

The building where Alfie and his men had been before was rubble now, a jumble of large chunks of plascrete, with windows, trim, and furniture scattered through the mess. The pile was less than ten feet high, from a building that had stood more than thirty feet above the surrounding land.

"Up the hill," Tory said. That was one thing about such destruction; the remnants provided excellent cover.

The I&R platoon scrambled up the rubble. Alfie and the two men remaining to him moved with the van of the platoon and found places at the very peak of the mound.

"Settle in and get your innings," Alfie told Willie and

John. "A little payback while you can still feel what you're paying them back for."

Some of the civilians had managed to edge farther away from the Feddies, but others were being held by force as human shields. That did the Feddies no good though.

Alfie went back to firing single shots, as did virtually all of the I&R platoon, picking their targets carefully, scoring more hits than misses. With the advantage of elevation, they had the better of the fight. The Federation troops held their ground for a few minutes more, then started trying to retreat south, along the one line that was—apparently—still free of Commonwealth forces. The civilians still within reach of Feddies were forced to move with them.

A few civilians fell in the continuing firefight, but more of their captors went down. A shorthanded company of Federation troops could not hope to stand against the eight hundred Commonwealth Marines ringing them in. But the Federation soldiers never offered to surrender, and no one asked them to.

No more than a dozen Feddies were taken prisoner uninjured. Another forty wounded soldiers were captured. There were seventeen dead civilians and thirty-two wounded. Some forty others had either escaped the fight or survived without injury. Marine casualties were light, two dead, a dozen men wounded seriously enough to need treatment beyond battlefield first aid.

Many of the civilians were interviewed. For the first time, the Commonwealth Marines learned some details of the Federation invasion and occupation. Feddie prisoners were interviewed as well, but little was learned from them immediately.

"It's as bad as we feared," Lieutenant Colonel Zacharia said over a link that included Admiral Greene, Colonel Laplace, and a number of staff officers. "The policy seems to have been one of total destruction. Turn the locals out and destroy every building and any possessions that the residents had to leave behind. Well, not everything. They've been gathering what they could from the public buildings for their own use, ferrying some of it up to their transports. But it doesn't appear as if they've done any stealing from private residences.''

Aboard *Sheffield*, Admiral Greene listened with a growing feeling of despair. Coventry had fifty million residents. So far, it looked as if half of the buildings on the planet had been destroyed, and Federation forces were still burning, still blowing buildings up, wherever they were not directly confronted by the second Regiment. The conference ended, and Greene shifted to a private channel to speak with Colonel Laplace.

"We've got to do more, faster," the admiral said. "We're not equipped to deal with the number of refugees that must be looking for help. We've got to keep the Feddies from burning out many more. We've got to go after every group we can, get between the Feddies and areas that haven't been burned yet."

"I've already got my ops people working with CIC, Admiral," Laplace said. "We'll do what we can, but there are limits, and we're going to hit them in a hurry. We can break into smaller units, use shuttles with fighter cover to move them from place to place, but we can't run everyone around the clock, not for long."

Greene hesitated. "Let me know what you come up with. I'll try to figure out what we can do for the people who have already been left homeless. They'll be needing food, shelter, probably medical aid, whatever we can get to them. We'll run all of the replicators in the fleet full out, but we can't supply millions of people for even a single day without getting something working on the ground, and getting raw materials for our replicators as well. I'll get back to you as soon as I can, Arkady. I just hope we get that other regiment in as soon as possible."

"You send an update back to Buckingham yet?"

"It'll be going out within the next ten minutes, telling them just what we're up against, Feddies and refugees."

*The cost,* Greene thought when he switched off. *It's like they're trying a stunt like this just to bankrupt the Commonwealth.*

# 11

**Reggie Bailey tried** to tell himself that it was only his imagination, that the Knowles baby, named Winston, did not really cry all that much more than most babies. But the youngest member of the group did complain a lot, in the only way he could. *He's got reason enough, I guess,* Reggie thought as he paced around the perimeter of the camp. *It's cold and drafty. If the lad knew what was going on, he'd really have something to squall about.*

The baby was a week old. It had been two weeks since the first Federation landings. The Bailey and Knowles families remained where they had been since before the baby was born. Winston appeared to be healthy, despite the crying. The problem was with his mother.

Anna Knowles could not be suffering any of the complications of childbirth that had plagued women through most of recorded history. The medical nanobots in her system would respond instantly to infection, hemorrhaging, or any other identifiable medical condition. Nor had she been particularly "delicate" before the pregnancy, or through most of that term. She had only felt significant strain during the last few weeks, beginning before the invasion. But even seven days after Winston's birth, Anna found it difficult to stay on her feet for more than a few minutes at a time. She was perpetually tired, no matter how much sleep she got, or how little she exerted herself while she was awake. She nursed the baby—an inescapable necessity with no food replicators handy to provide a suitable substitute—and held him while she was awake, trying to ensure the normal bonding of mother and infant. But the effort drained her energy far too quickly.

Two more shelters had been raised in the rocky clearing, flanking the first, sharing connecting walls. The new shelters were lower and narrower, just high enough for adults to sit under cover and wide enough to let everyone sleep almost dry. The roofs of the new shelters were not completely waterproof, but they kept off most of the rain. There had been rain, almost every day since Winston's birth. Generally, the showers were brief, light, but there had been one long stretch of moderate to heavy rain, close to eighteen hours without a break.

A whistle from Al, who had taken over as sentry, brought his father out of his shelter, no more than an hour after sunrise. Someone was coming.

Reggie carried his shotgun at his side. People had come past with some regularity in the last few days. The last holdouts were finally moving farther away from their homes. The Watersons and the others who had cached goods with the Baileys and Knowleses had gone past two days earlier, looking for . . . anything. But some of the people coming through had been from nearer the center of Hawthorne, or even from along the other roads that radiated from it. Some were simply wandering, not knowing what to do or where to go, often with a glazed look to their eyes.

Eric came out from the shelter where his wife and baby were. He had a rifle with him. Neither man had had any occasion to use their weapons on anything except food, but—without really discussing it—they had decided that it was better to be prepared for the worst. Some of the people they had seen had already been far along in hunger.

Ida went into the center shelter to sit with Anna. The children, except for the infant, were out, doing what passed for chores in camp. Al's chore was to serve as lookout. That job seemed to please him.

The strangers did not approach the camp directly, though they must have been guiding themselves by the thin trail of smoke rising from the campfire that was kept burning constantly. Walking directly toward the camp might have appeared too threatening. It had not taken most people long to stumble into new forms of etiquette to suit the new conditions.

"I say there," a voice called from thirty feet away. The newcomers had halted that far out. "Do you mind if we stop by for a moment?"

"Not at all," Reggie called back. "Come on in."

Al was nowhere to be seen. Once he was sure that his father had heard his signal, he had moved away from camp, away from the strangers. "They might be playing tricks," he had explained to his father and Eric after the first time he had done that. "A couple of folks come into camp to keep our attention while more of them sneak around behind to get us while we're not looking. If I'm out there sneaking around first, they won't be able to do that." It was something that neither of the men had thought of.

Reggie did not recognize these people, a man and woman with one child, a girl who appeared to be five or six years old. The adults were both carrying backpacks, but those bags hung as if they were less than half full. All three of the strangers showed the effects of being out in the weather. Their hair was wet and bedraggled-looking, their clothing only partially dry. And they had a hungry look, sniffing at the air as if seeking food. The little girl's clothes hung on her as if they were hand-me-downs, or as if she had lost considerable weight already.

"My name's Ted Brix," the man said, stopping at the edge of the camp. He might have been thirty, or less, though he looked a lot older. His cheeks were hollow. There were dark circles around his eyes. His clothes also hung as if he had lost considerable weight. "My wife Lorna, our daughter Helene." He gestured as he introduced each of the others, as if he thought that Reggie and Eric would not be able to decide who was who.

Reggie introduced himself and Eric, and made a sweeping gesture to include the visible children. The name Brix meant nothing to Reggie.

"I thought just about everyone had gotten farther out than this," Eric said. "How far did you come?"

"I'm not quite sure, actually," Ted said, looking over his shoulder. "I'm afraid we've done some wandering, lost our course more than once, don't you know. We live—lived— a mile east of the Downs." The Downs was a park, a gathering place for local residents since the founding of Hawthorne.

"I guess you *have* done some wandering," Eric said. "That's got to be nine, ten miles from here."

"You must have crossed, what, three roads?" Reggie asked.

The look that came over Ted's face might have suggested that he was about to get extremely ill. "Maybe three different roads, three matching lines of burned out houses and other buildings, but as I said, we've been wandering about quite a bit. We've crossed roads at least a half dozen times. We thought that we would run into other people closer in to town, thought maybe the government would have set up places for us to go to."

"You didn't find any?" Reggie knew that it was an unnecessary question—the Brixes wouldn't be there if they had found organized refugee centers—but it had to be asked.

"Not a glimmer of anything," Ted said. His wife and daughter remained silent, showing no interest in the talk. The girl stayed at her mother's side, hanging on to her as if she were a lifeline, sniffling occasionally. Her face was dirty and tear-streaked. "Just ashes, rubble, and bodies."

"Bodies? You mean the Feddies have started killing people?" Eric asked.

Brix shrugged. "Some had gunshot wounds, but I can't say who fired the shots. We never actually saw anyone get shot. But more of the blokes looked as if they had been beaten to death, or stabbed. Ghastly."

*It's too soon for people to starve to death,* Reggie thought, blinking once. Their health maintenance systems would carry them through until their bodies had absolutely no reserves left. But medical nanobugs would not stop hunger, or the quest for nourishment. *Fighting over food, most likely. I guess it had to come, sooner or later.*

"I imagine there'll be a lot more deaths before things start to get better," he said, speaking slowly, watching Ted Brix's eyes carefully. *Two weeks and killings. I thought it would take longer than that.*

Brix showed no reaction at all. "I daresay." There was no inflection to his voice, as if he were too exhausted, or too hungry, to waste energy beyond what was absolutely needed to get the words out.

"Do you mind if we sit for a spell before we move on?" he asked. It was clear that he wanted to ask for something to eat, but would not. That was another of the new rules of etiquette. Food could be accepted if offered, but it would not do to beg for a handout from other refugees.

"Not at all." Reggie glanced at Eric and raised an eyebrow as a question. He hadn't decided whether or not to offer. They had plenty of food, for the moment. The evening before, each man had managed to bring down game. So far, they had always been able to find meat, and that helped stretch the supplies they had carried out from their homes. Eric's nod, given while the Brixes were moving in closer, was almost invisible, but Reggie saw it.

"If you'd like something to eat, we've got meat and broth," Reggie said. Stewing the meat in water with a scant helping of their dehydrated vegetables seemed the best way to make everything last longer.

"Much obliged. Rations have been rather slim for us the past few days," Ted said. His wife blinked. Their daughter looked up at her mother but didn't speak. Her stare seemed to ask, *Are we really going to eat?*

Ida came out of the center shelter after she heard the invitation and acceptance. Reggie made the introductions, and Ida helped serve food to the strangers, making certain that there was plenty of meat in the bowls. The Brixes had hardly started to eat when Al came in, signaling an all clear.

Helene, the child, ate greedily, slurping down half of the broth at once, then picking chunks of meat out with her fingers. She did not look up from the bowl until it was empty. Then she turned to look at her mother, and it was impossible to miss the question in her expression.

"Have some more," Ida offered. Helene extended the bowl, her face suddenly beaming with a mix of emotions—relief, happiness, and gratitude. Ida had to look away, as soon as she had refilled the bowl. It was either look away or cry.

A few moments later, when the girl's parents were almost finished with their servings—they had eaten more slowly, to make it last—Reggie offered them seconds. Watching the child had hurt him as well. He turned to Eric then, and lifted an eyebrow again. Eric shrugged.

"You're going to find it a rough go if you haven't a gun to hunt with, or some way to set traps," Reggie said.

"I've never fired a gun, nor even held one," Ted admitted. "I don't know much about this living in the wild at all but what I've seen on vids. That's not much help, I fear. Those blokes always seem to come up with just what they need—in the nick, as it were."

Reggie tried to look at Ted, but Brix kept looking at his daughter, drawing Reggie's eyes to her as well. The logical side of Reggie's mind, normally dominant, told him not to do what he was thinking of doing. Dozens of couples had come by the camp, most with children. He had not made the offer before, had never really considered it. But he knew that, for whatever reason, this time was going to be different.

"Things are like to get rough for everyone before there's any chance of them getting better," he said, still temporizing even though he realized that it was unlikely to change his mind.

Brix nodded, moving his gaze to his wife. She was staring at him now, though their daughter continued to eat, more slowly now that she had her second helping.

"Winter's coming on," Reggie continued. "Nobody knows what's going to happen, how long it might be before Commonwealth forces come to rescue us, or how long the Feddies will stay."

"We figure, the way the Feddies are burning everything in sight, they can't plan to stay long," Eric said. "If they planned to occupy Coventry, they'd be leaving places for themselves to live in. But if, when, they leave, it may be up to us to get ourselves back together. If we can.''

"The government had to get word off to Buckingham about the invasion," Reggie said, hoping more than believing, even though two of the news readers that first night had said that message rockets had been dispatched. "The Commonwealth will send an army to kick the Feddies off and help us. Once our blokes come in, things will get better.''

"But there's no way to know how long that might be, now, is there?'' Ted said, his head drooping. He was talking more to himself than to his hosts.

"Exactly,'' Reggie said. He glanced at Ida, then at Eric—both of whom gave him minuscule nods—before he looked at the Brixes again. "For now, at least, we're going to have to do for ourselves.'' He gave himself one last pause, took in a deep breath, and held it for a moment.

"Look, we don't have all that much ourselves, but we do have guns. As long as our ammunition holds out, we should be able to keep getting game. And Eric and I know most of the edible berries and nuts. Those won't be gone for a few more weeks. If you'd care to, you could stay with us, help out as you can, that sort of thing.''

Reggie had to look away. As soon as the Brixes realized that they were actually going to be invited to stay, the expressions on all three faces changed. They suggested adulation to Reggie, and he wanted none of that.

"Things won't be easy, not after a while,'' he said, "but we can give it a good go.''

There was no chance that the Brix family would refuse.

Most of the men of Company A, First Battalion, South York Rifles who had been captured with Captain Stanley were still with him sixteen days later. *Only because they can't think of anything better to do,* he told himself. At first, they had gone back to their homes as their captors had ordered. But some of the men had found their homes already burned. The rest were chased out within the next two days. It had been, perhaps, logical for them to return to their rendezvous location. Surprisingly, the vehicles they had left were still there. Many still had supplies in them, and the buried caches were intact.

The men had come with their families, those who had families. Mostly, they brought wives; almost none had minor children. The ones with children had not answered the initial mobilization call, and those were not the ones who thought to head to the rendezvous point when they were dispossessed. The poor turnout for mobilization still left a sour taste in Hubert Stanley's mouth each time he thought about it.

During the first few days after the group started to congregate again, they had remained at the rendezvous location. More people happened by, including—eventually—a few of the volunteers who had not shown up for mobilization. Those latter kept moving. Their erstwhile comrades made it clear that they were not welcome. Other refugees were allowed to remain with the group. After six days the total number—men, women, and children—was considerably over a hundred.

That was when Stanley proposed that they move on to a better, or at least different, location. There was no game left nearby. Some of the volunteers had had extra weapons in the vehicles they had left at the rendezvous, or they had managed to bring them along when they were chased out of their homes. A few were experienced hunters. They had been able to bring in enough meat to make sure that no one in the group went completely hungry, but it was taking longer each day. And the nearby stock of wild fruits and domestic crops that had not been burned by the invaders was also becoming depleted. It was time to move farther away from South York, out to where game and other edibles might be more plentiful for a time.

After that? It was difficult to think very far ahead.

The group had moved only a few miles a day, looking for a place where they might stay longer, a place with water, materials to build shelters, and meat on the hoof. As much by default as choice, Captain Stanley became the leader of the entire group. He made decisions and people accepted them.

They kept the vehicles that the volunteers had originally abandoned at the rendezvous location. The floaters converted water into hydrogen and oxygen. As long as there was sunlight to recharge the floater batteries, the only fuel needed was water, and that could always be found. The trucks and cars allowed the refugees to carry more, not only the few possessions they had salvaged when they were chased out of their homes but also some of what they had made or found along the way.

After a week of moving from one camp to another, the group had finally found a place where they might be able to stay longer. There was plenty of game and the nearby stream had fish. Each day the new camp started to look a little more livable, and each day they stayed made it less likely that they would move on voluntarily—as long as they could still find food. Rough shacks were built. Routines were established. The adults, and this group remained overwhelmingly adult, had regular chores to help the community survive.

Once the routines were established, Stanley found little work for himself. It was only the exceptions that required leadership decisions, and disputes between individuals. He had plenty of time to think, to remember, and his memories were not pleasant. He found it difficult to think of anything but what he saw as his personal failure, and about the men who had been killed because he had not been a smart enough leader.

He tried diligently to get rid of the most visible reminder of that failure, the mark put on his forehead by the Feddies who had captured his company. That was work he shared with most of the others who bore the brand. Everyone wanted to remove the mark as quickly as they could, but Stanley had become fixated by the *need* to erase it. He had puzzled over its composition. Any foreign object should have been eradicated in short order by his body's medical nanobots. Those would erase even tattoos. But not this. He had scrubbed at his forehead with abrasive cloths until he drew blood. The scrapes healed, but when they did, the Federation brand was still visible. After sixteen days, it had faded a little, but it might have been a neon light as far as Stanley was concerned. It seemed unnaturally bright, a beacon signaling his shame to anyone who came within a hundred yards.

*Day sixteen of my shame,* Stanley thought. He was sitting in the lean-to that was the only shelter he permitted himself. It might have been easier if his wife were with him, but she had been away from home the night of the invasion, visiting their oldest son and his family near Coventry City. She had not been able to get home, had not even been able to call home.

Stanley's lean-to was situated so that the open side faced away from the rest of camp, looking back toward South York. He could hear the routine daytime sounds behind him, but they rarely registered. He stared off toward his lost home, his thoughts louder and more insistent than any noises the people with him might make.

*Sixteen days.* He had been idly honing the blade of his hunting knife. The blade was razor-sharp all along its seven-inch length. Stanley had shaved with it a couple of times, before he had decided that there was no longer any point to shaving. All he used it for now was to cut meat. He did some of the butchering when the hunters brought game in. He also used it to cut meat when he ate.

He stopped running the blade against the stone and held the knife close to his face. He stared at the blade, twisting it from side to side, watching light reflect off of it, and the tiny scratches near the edge. Other thoughts returned, routine thoughts of late. Mostly, they came in the night, when he could not sleep. Sometimes they also came during the day, like now, when he had too long to think without interruption.

*I'll never be able to live down the shame.* He let out his breath in a long sigh. "Why prolong the pain?" he asked softly, looking at his reflection in the knife blade.

With his left hand, he touched the side of his neck, feeling for the pulse in his carotid artery. Suicide was not a simple matter. The nanobots designed to keep people healthy would work quickly to repair any damage. The wound had to be massive, something that his system could not mend in time. Destroying the heart or brain was the surest method, but Stanley did not have the means to do that. The next best way was to slice open a major artery, lose blood faster than it could be replaced, lose a critical volume before the cut could be stopped.

There was never a moment of conscious decision. Stanley brought the knife around and plunged the blade deeply into his neck. His last conscious thought was an awareness of the hot fluid—blood—gushing out over his hands.

# 12

**Noel Wittington had** been away from camp, scouting in the direction of South York, starting back only after hearing military shuttles overhead. Military craft were the only ones flying since the invasion. Coventry's cities and towns had long been linked by a shuttle service, but those aircraft had been destroyed by the Federation.

The shuttles Noel heard this morning seemed to be aiming for the coast, possibly Coventry City, about two hundred miles away. Although Noel could not see them, the sound was (or seemed to be) different from any he had heard before, civilian or military. Coventry's civilian aircraft had been nearly silent, audible only during takeoff and landing. The Federation's military landers had not been designed for silence. They had a distinct harsh sound even several thousand feet up. Noel could not have explained just how these latest shuttles sounded different, but he was certain that they were. His imagination made the immediate leap: *Maybe the Commonwealth has come!*

Excitement had spurred him back toward camp as quickly as he could move, careless of what might be in his way, intent on reporting what he had heard, first to Captain Stanley, then to the rest of the people in camp. The trip out had taken two hours. He made the return in less than thirty minutes.

Out of breath but buoyed by the prospect that, perhaps, help had arrived, Noel stopped for a moment at the edge of camp. He had to lean forward and support himself with hands on thighs as he dragged in breath. Excitement and exertion combined were nearly more than he could handle.

He couldn't very well talk until he could stop panting out of control.

Preoccupied, Noel didn't notice anything out of the ordinary. There were a few people standing around. That was normal. But they did nothing but stare. It wasn't until Noel brought his head up, his breathing beginning to return to normal, that any of the others moved closer. The first two hesitated to speak, fearing that Wittington was bringing more bad news. *Good news crawls; bad news has wings* was the Coventrian proverb.

"What is it?" one of the men finally asked.

Noel shook his head, then dragged in another deep breath. "Good news, maybe. I've got to tell the captain."

"He's dead."

Noel stared at the man—he didn't recall the name. "What?"

"Captain Stanley killed himself. They found him an hour ago, in his shelter."

Noel ran toward the captain's lean-to, thirty yards from where he had been standing. Captain Stanley's body was no longer there, but Noel saw the blood soaking into the ground. The man who had given Noel the news, and several other people, came after him, more slowly, and stopped a short distance away.

"He cut his own throat," the same man said.

Noel turned and stared at him. Noel frowned as he tried to recall the man's name. It took a moment: Ned Asbury, a civilian, not one of the South York Rifles. "What happened, Ned?"

"I don't think anyone actually saw it," Asbury said. He looked around. Several of the others shook their heads. "Becky Meares found him, the knife still in his hand—that big hunting knife of his. He just shoved it right in here." Asbury put his hand to the side of his own neck. "We took the body out, away from camp, when we saw that he was really dead."

"Did you bury him properly?" Noel didn't need to hear the negative. The way the people looked around at each other gave him the answer before Asbury confirmed it.

"We just took him away from camp." He pointed vaguely toward the east.

"We can't just leave him lying around for wild cats to eat," Noel said. "We've got shovels. Let's get a few. Show me where you took him."

It wasn't until after they had buried the captain that Noel remembered the news he had run back to share. He told the few who had gone with him to dig the grave about the shuttles that sounded different and his guess about what it might mean. When they got back to camp, the news spread quickly. People started gathering, talking more than they had in a fortnight.

"Can we go back to town now?" several asked. Captain Stanley was gone. Two of his sergeants remained with the group, but both had already made it clear that they did not consider themselves potential leaders. The South York Rifles were no more. They were no different from anyone else. But no one else seemed to want to make decisions either.

"Can we go home now?" People started to direct the question to Noel. He had brought the news of the shuttle flight. He had directed them to bury Captain Stanley properly. No one seemed to think of his age, despite his being one of the youngest adults in camp.

"I don't know." Noel looked around. At least half, perhaps two thirds, of the camp had gathered around, all looking to him for an answer. *How did I get to be a leader?* he wondered. *I don't know what the hell to do.*

"Give me time to think." He pushed through the circle of people and walked out of camp, toward South York. A few of the others followed him, but none went more than a few yards past the edge of the encampment. Noel kept going until he couldn't hear or see anyone behind him.

*Let me think.* But thinking was hard, and painful. Noel had difficulty getting past the fact of Captain Stanley's death. Noel had seen the deep gash in the captain's throat, the exposed muscle and flesh inside the wound, the sightless gaze of the captain's eyes. The men who had carried him out of camp had removed the captain's belongings before dumping his body in a crevice, but no one had tried to keep those few things. They had been delivered to Noel as soon as the group came back from burying Stanley. Tokens of leadership, it seemed.

*I heard something. I thought it was a different sound than Feddie shuttles make. I assumed that it must be Common- wealth shuttles.* One by one, he went through the steps. He could almost replay the sounds he had heard in his memory.

"It's not enough to go on," he whispered after a few minutes. "I could have been hearing things. I could have been mistaken. We need to know for sure."

The next idea came easily enough. They would have to send scouts back toward the city, hope that they would be able to find out, one way or another, and get back with the news without being intercepted by Feddies.

*We need to stay where we are for now. Get the hunters busy stocking up extra food. Even if the Commonwealth has come, that doesn't mean that things will get better right away, and they certainly won't get back to normal anytime soon. When the scouts get back, then we can make our de- cision.*

He let out his breath. Maybe the rest of the people would not accept that, but as long as they wanted his opinion, he would give it. Waiting might be difficult, but the alternative could prove much worse. He turned and headed back toward camp.

Noel was almost finished with his explanation of what he thought they should do when Michael Polyard came running into camp, as out of breath as Noel had been earlier. Both had left on their scouting missions at the same time that morning. Polyard had obviously gone farther. The circle of people around Noel opened up between the two men. Wit- tington moved toward Polyard, wondering what he had seen or heard to send him running back. Michael sank to the ground and leaned forward, head between his knees, arms clutching his stomach.

"What is it?" Noel asked, kneeling next to Michael. "Did you hear the shuttles too? Or see them?"

Polyard had difficulty raising his head. "What shuttles?" came out as a gasp.

"Then what is it?"

Michael shook his head. He needed a moment longer before he could speak coherently. "Federation soldiers, hundreds of them, moving this way. They're no more than a mile and a half off, coming straight toward us." The speech exhausted his resources. He let his head droop forward again, still fighting to suck in air, oblivious to the panic that his words had launched.

Dozens of people started talking at once, some in private conversation, others trying to make everyone hear what they had to say. After about twenty seconds of that, Noel raised his voice.

"Shut up! Quiet!" It took time to restore some semblance of quiet. "We don't have time for chin wagging. Keep it calm, but gather everything you can, quickly. We'll load the floaters and move. There's not time for much. If we're not out of here in five minutes, it could be too late."

"Where will we go?" someone asked.

"Does it matter? Away from the Feddies. We'll worry about where when we can quit worrying about them. Move! There's no time for argument."

The floaters were loaded with whatever came to hand first. People gathered as much of their belongings as they could carry. Noel scattered the two fires that were burning, doing what he could to extinguish the flames and cover the embers. Even in a hurry, he didn't want to leave a fire that might get out of hand. The Federation troopers were doing more than enough burning. Noel needed little time to gather his own few belongings. Most of what he had was already in his floater.

"We'll head due east," Noel said, no more than three minutes after he had first said that they should leave. He stood on the rear deck of his floater, taking items from people, trying to wedge them in among the things already tied on. "Those of you who are ready to move, start now. The rest of us will be right behind you. Move as fast as you can. Hurry!"

Few needed Noel's injunction to hurry. Some had already left, grabbing what they could on the run. Later, when there was time to think, some refugees might regret racing heedless into the wilderness, but there was an edge of panic to the exodus.

Michael Polyard finally recovered enough to gather his possessions. He went to Noel's floater.

"Do you think this will do any good?" he asked.

"Give me that bag. I'll find room for it up here." Michael passed the canvas carryall up. "Do any good? I don't know. You heard that Captain Stanley killed himself?"

"Three different people told me while you were getting folks organized."

"We either do whatever we can to save ourselves, and keep clear of the Feddies, or we might as well take the same out the captain did. And I'm not ready to cut my own throat."

"If those Feddies want to catch us, they will. You think maybe a few of us should stay behind and try to slow them down?"

Noel snorted. "Have that turn out like our last encounter? Just make yourself room and climb aboard here. Let's move."

Noel sent the other floaters ahead of the people on foot, with as much of their goods and people as they could carry. He stayed with the rest, though, despite his itch to get as far from the Feddies as fast as possible.

*I might not be the best man to lead this mob, but nobody else seems to want the job. They sure as hell won't listen to me if I run off and leave them to fend for themselves. And if I'm back here, maybe it will stop a few folks from giving up and letting the Feddies take them.*

After a time, Noel moved up along the line, slowly, urging people on. He drove to the front of the main body then stopped to wait for everyone to move past him. After trailing the exodus for a time again, he repeated the sequence, making sure that everyone had a chance to see and hear him. For a few minutes now and then he got down from the floater and walked, leaving Polyard to drive the vehicle, hoping that Michael would not panic and race off. Staying active, encouraging the others, helped Noel minimize his own doubts. And fears.

Whenever he was at the tail end, Noel stood silently, straining to hear any sounds of pursuit. *I could go back a bit and have a look,* he would tell himself. He knew that it was a foolish impulse, but that did not lessen the attraction. The need to see for himself that there were, or were not, Feddies coming up behind became almost overpowering.

"You'll know far too soon if there are," he muttered during one moment of temptation.

Even before the end of the first hour, there were stragglers, people who simply moved aside and sank to the ground. Each time, Noel would stop to urge them on. If they were too exhausted, they might earn a ride for a few minutes. But there was no way that Noel could carry a tenth of the people, not even if they abandoned their supplies.

They had been moving for three hours before Noel started to nurture some hope that they might escape—or that the Feddies had not really been coming for them. Three hours: marching soldiers would move faster than tired and hungry civilians, some of whom were well into, or beyond, their sixties.

"We'll have to stop before much longer," Polyard said. With an absence of competition for the position, he had become de facto second-in-command. "Some of them can't take much more. And sunset can't be more than twenty minutes off."

"I know. I just want every yard of distance we can get before we stop, just in case. You take the floater up ahead. Try to catch the others. Tell them to find a good spot and wait for us. When we catch them up, we'll camp for the night. I'll stay at this end until you get back." Noel stopped the floater and got out. "I have no idea how far ahead the other floaters might be, if you'll even be able to catch them up."

Michael shook his head. "They're no more than a mile

or so ahead. I buzzed up to them the last time you got out
to walk and told them to ease off.''

There was little pretense of making camp when they
stopped. Fear and exhaustion left few with energy to do
anything more than the absolute minimum. Some could not
even manage to eat cold food. They found places under trees
and wrapped themselves in blankets, as close to where they
had been when Noel called a halt as possible. Even the
people who had driven the floaters, or ridden much of the
distance, seemed to have little energy. But Noel gathered
those he thought should be in the best shape.

"We need to post sentries tonight," he said. "It's going
to be up to us, payback for riding on our arses all afternoon.''

"What the hell good could we do?" one of the drivers
asked.

"Maybe not much, but we still need to do it. If we get
five minutes' warning of Feddies coming, maybe we can get
away again, at least some of us.''

"Get away for what?''

"If nothing else, just to make it harder for the Feddies to
bag us all. Remember, there may be Commonwealth troops
on Coventry now. And if they aren't here already, they will
be soon. The more we can do to spread out the Feddies, the
easier time our blokes will have trying to pick up the pieces
for us.'' He waited, but the complainer did not add any other
objections.

"Two of us at a time, one hour on, three off. That'll give
each of us two tours and nobody will lose that much sleep.
Thurston, you and I will take the first watch.'' Emery Thurston was the complainer. Noel watched to see where the others bedded down before he took Thurston off and placed
him where he wanted him.

"Just keep your eyes open and sing out if you see or hear
anything that doesn't belong," Noel said. They both had
helmets, so they would be able to see, and the sound pickups
would let them hear things a little farther off. "I'll come
back to collect you when our hour's over.''

"I still don't see what good it's going to do."

"You don't like the idea of doing sentry turns, walk tomorrow and we'll give someone else the option."

Thurston did not reply.

Noel moved farther back along the trail that they had been following. The temptation to hike back for a mile or so was easier to fight off now. Noel was tired, and he now knew better than to count on his ability to sneak up on Federation soldiers. The lump on his head from his first attempt was gone but not forgotten.

The refugees and their vehicles had left a track through the woods that a blind man could follow. Noel moved away from it and found a place where he was sheltered overhead by a broad-leaved evergreen and on three sides by dense shrubbery.

An hour with nothing to do but think. It had been hard to concentrate on the run. There had been too many distractions. Now Noel thought while he watched and listened. *How far can we run? Where should we go? Is there any purpose to it?*

*Questions. I've got more than enough questions. What I need is answers.*

When Noel returned to his floater, Michael was still awake, sitting up, leaning back against the vehicle's skirt.

"Anything?" Polyard asked.

"No sign of Feddies. I got some thinking done though."

"And?"

"In the morning, if we make it through the night, I think we ought to head a little more toward the northeast."

"You mean toward Hawthorne?"

"I see you've been doing some thinking too."

"No way to escape it. Hawthorne's fairly small. Maybe the Feddies haven't hit it. Maybe they'll only send a few troops there, few enough that we can make a difference if we get a chance. Anywhere but back to South York, and Hawthorne's the closest real town on this side of Danbury River."

"We know things are a mess in South York. We don't know that about Hawthorne," Noel said. "If nothing else, we might at least find some help."

# Part 4

# 13

**It was the** sixth time aboard the shuttles in as many days for the Marines of the First Battalion, Second Regiment. The entire battalion was moving again, but for the first time they were not all heading to the same destination. H&S, Alpha, and Delta companies were traveling together toward the next town along the main road south of The Dales. The battalion had been clearing one town at a time. Now the plan was for the two halves of the battalion to leapfrog each other from one town to the next.

"The Feddies are still burning everything they can," Captain McAuliffe told H&S before the men boarded their shuttles after less than five hours of rest. "Colonel Laplace and the admiral want us to stop it double-quick. That means going in piecemeal."

The six days of fighting had been brutal, not so much because of the fierceness of the opposition but just from short sleep and the frantic pace. Combat was always like that, but there was something about this operation that seemed to exacerbate the usual numbing of body and mind. H&S Company had paid its share of the price, eight dead and more than a dozen wounded severely enough to need several hours in a trauma tube. Four hours in a tube could handle all but the most severe injuries—neurological damage or traumatic amputation. Even Eugene Wegener, with multiple shrapnel wounds, had been back on duty in three hours. But no easy way had ever been found to cure the mental confusion, even damage, that combat could inflict on even the most hardened Marine.

"It's a crazy way to run a war," Tory Kepner said on his private link to David Spencer.

"They catch the Feddies who ordered this, they ought to roast them slow, over an open fire," David replied as he fastened his lap strap. Six days had given the Marines plenty of chances to see what the Federation plan had been: burn everything and turn out all of the locals to live or die in the wild.

"Dayle suggested slicing them up with a pair of fingernail scissors, one bloody joint at a time."

"Captain says they might try the Feddie officers and non-coms as common criminals instead of holding them as prisoners of war," Spencer said. The shuttle was accelerating rapidly, on a short arc to its next landing zone. Talking helped minimize the discomfort of the flight. There wasn't enough time for sleep.

"Might do for the officers," Tory said. "Can't say as I'm all that keen on doing the noncoms. When did a sergeant or corporal ever have a choice about his orders?"

David permitted himself a tight smile. "Officers would say the same thing, no doubt. 'Just following orders like every other bloke.'"

"They could say that all the way to the top, and that's the chap who never pays for his sins."

There was no en route operational briefing. Each of these excursions started like the rest. The Marines were landed just out of range of the enemy, then moved in on foot. If necessary, Spacehawks came in to keep the Feddies occupied until the men on the ground were ready to take over. There would be a fight. After the first day, the Feddies had been less reluctant to surrender, often after only a few shots had been fired. Afterward, the Marines would make contact with any refugees who were near, set them to looking for their compatriots. The real work of providing relief for the refugees had not yet begun. Small-scale assistance was all that had been possible.

This time, the opposition was estimated to be a single company of Federation soldiers, perhaps not at full strength. That would give the Commonwealth force an advantage of three to one or better. The burning of Hawthorne, observed by the fleet and by spy satellites, had been going too slowly for there to be more enemy troops involved. But more than half of the town and outlying houses had already been destroyed.

Ritual: the pilot gave her passengers a ninety-second warning. Captain McAuliffe gave the order to "lock and load" weapons. Officers and noncoms talked to their men. *Keep their minds occupied in those last seconds,* was the drill. *Don't give them a chance to think about getting scared.*

The drill for a combat landing for the Marines was to get out of the shuttle as fast as humanly possible, out of the box and into the open where they could defend themselves.

Spencer popped the release on his lap strap and lurched to his feet as the shuttle touched down, before the amber light over the ramp showed that it was being lowered. He turned to his men and gestured them up as he gave the same order over his helmet radio.

"Move it, lads!" he shouted as the ramp swung down. David's concern was the noncoms and other ranks. The officers knew what they had to do. If *they* screwed up, it would be between them and Captain McAuliffe.

I&R platoon was first out. They were the "true" fighters of H&S, the men best prepared for whatever might be waiting. They ran down the ramp in two files, Tory Kepner with one and Lieutenant Nuchol with the other. The squads separated as soon as they were outside, and moved to either side, ready to hit the dirt and lay down covering fire if needed. It made no difference that they had been told that there would be no enemy troops close enough to take them under fire. Long-range spy-eyes might miss troops that did not want to be seen, especially if they were not actively using their electronics.

As soon as I&R was out, Spencer led headquarters platoon out. After seventeen months under him, they moved out into the initial perimeter almost as smartly as I&R.

There was no gunfire. David glanced around as he ran to

his position. The other two shuttles were spaced around the clearing, no less than a hundred yards apart. The landers did not stay on the ground a second longer than necessary. As soon as their passengers were clear, they boosted for friendlier sky, out of range of portable surface-to-air missiles.

As the shuttles lifted off, Nuchol and Kepner led I&R platoon out of the initial perimeter. They had the positions of some enemy helmets. The closest was nearly two miles away, but they did not assume that all of the enemy had been pinpointed.

"Shut down everything you don't need," Tory told his men. "I don't want any transmissions that might give us away. It's time to play ghost and get up their armpits before they know we're around. Third squad, right flank, a hundred yards out. Fourth, you're next in. I'll be on your left with first. Second that puts you on the left flank, a hundred yards out."

Once away from the LZ, the Marines moved slowly. Each squad formed two skirmish lines, one fire team in front of the other by forty yards. Tory stayed with first squad. Lieutenant Nuchol moved with the rear fire team of fourth squad.

Alfie Edwards had his fire team in front. Looking around, he thought that the wooded area they were walking through had to be a park. The trees were too far apart and placed too regularly for the layout to be natural. There was no undergrowth, and little evidence of old leaves or the other debris that normally cluttered the ground in a forest. Too many trees seemed to be the same age, no mixture of young and old. *Good-sized town. No reason they shouldn't put in a park,* he thought. His speculations did not detract from his alertness; they were part of it. He kept his eyes moving, his head turning, looking and listening for anything. The trees were in the midst of shedding their leaves for winter, but the leaves had not been on the ground long enough to get dry and brittle.

Beyond the wooded stretch was another open space, almost the twin of the one the shuttles had set down in. Past that there were buildings running along both sides of a wide street. These buildings were larger than private homes—

blocks of flats or commercial space, Alfie thought. The important thing was that they had not been destroyed.

Once more, I&R's mission was to take the enemy under fire as soon as possible, put an end to their arson, and hold them long enough for the rest of the force to arrive and finish them off.

*Supposed to be odds-on again,* Alfie reminded himself. They would have a clear numerical superiority—if the intelligence was right.

There would be no sneaking about in buildings this time. After the first episode, the I&R people were under orders not to tempt fate that way again. "You got away with it once. Don't count on being lucky a second time," Alfie had been told by Captain McAuliffe in what was nearly a formal reprimand.

"We split up here," Lieutenant Nuchol told his noncoms. "Third and fourth bend around to the right. First and second to the left." There was burned out rubble to the right, wilder woodlands to the left. Another ten minutes of movement would put them in good positions, give them angles on the Federation soldiers that would leave the Feddies with little chance to hide.

That was the way the Marines wanted it.

As they moved around the open space, the squads moved from skirmish lines to single file, with ten yards between men. Alfie found himself at the tail of the two squads moving to the left. "Tail-end Charley" was almost as important as the point man. It was up to the man at the rear to make sure that no one overtook them from behind, or moved in to close off their retreat before an ambush struck in front.

When the squads reached their attack position, Alfie moved from the end of the line to put himself in the middle of his fire team. He led them forward toward the edge of the wood, snaking forward on their stomachs. When he got as far forward as he could, Alfie adjusted his position to get comfortable, as if he were preparing to spend hours there. There was a thick tree trunk just in front of him, with a little ground cover around it—knotted little vines no more than six or eight inches high. He slid his rifle through the vines, then looked through the gunsights, traversing the barrel slowly, checking his field of fire. When he was satisfied, Alfie looked to see that the others in his fire team were ready for action.

Unless they were spotted by the Feddies and taken under fire, it would be some time before Tory or the lieutenant gave the order to start shooting. The I&R platoon was to wait until the rest of the three companies got into position.

Either way, Alfie was ready. He reached down to his side to make certain that the pouch with his extra ammunition magazines was where it was supposed to be. He spent most of his time looking at targets, sometimes through his gunsights, sometimes over them. The sights had electronic enhancements that could be linked to his helmet to provide targets even in conditions of extremely poor visibility.

Alfie hummed silently, an old drinking song that always came to mind whenever he anticipated fighting, either in combat or during a liberty pub crawl. He was scarcely aware of the humming. It was a subconscious habit whose origins he would not have been able to guess at. In other circumstances, the humming might have been audible. When he had been drinking, it could get loud. But not now, when silence was important.

Seconds and minutes ticked away on Alfie's visor display. The red dots showing enemy helmets with active electronics were barely visible, not enough of a glow to interfere with aim. It could be confusing to a rookie, but sorting out everything was as unconscious as the humming for Alfie.

Eight minutes. *What's keeping them?* Alfie wondered. It was just a vague curiosity. If necessary, he could wait all day and half of the night without fidgeting. But he preferred to get the necessary over with as quickly as possible. *Better soon than late, but best not at all.*

Three more minutes passed before Tory came on the line. "Another five minutes, at least. Spencer saw something he wants checked out before we start this donnybrook."

*What kind of something?* Alfie wondered, but did not ask. If it was important, he would be told.

●　　●　　●

THE FIRES OF COVENTRY

Company lead sergeants did not go wandering off alone for a recce in a combat situation, not according to "The Book," but David Spencer gave that tome no more than pragmatic attention. He wasn't certain what he thought he might have seen, but *something* was not quite right. He brought the rest of H&S Company to a halt while he went to look. Alpha and Delta companies continued to move around on the flanks, as they had farther to go. David let Captain McAuliffe worry about passing the word that H&S had stopped for a moment. The sooner he got out, the sooner he would get back.

Spencer moved from tree to tree in a low crouch, heading for a point fifty yards from the line of march. He was still in the tended wooded area, not the wild woodland that half of I&R platoon had entered. He moved carefully, stopping to look around, scanning, still asking himself what he had seen, or what he thought he had seen. *Something that didn't belong,* was as close as he could come. It was instinct, a feeling that there was something in these woods that shouldn't be—or something missing that should have been present. He trusted his instincts.

David put the rest of the company, and the main mission, out of mind and focused totally on what he was doing. All he wanted was an answer to a nagging question, assurance that all was right with the area, or some tag so that he would know what was wrong.

By the time he reached the point he had been working toward, David's thinking had progressed to, *It can't be something on the ground.* That was too open. Anything out of the ordinary on the ground would have stuck out like a twelve-inch thumb. So he concentrated on searching the foliage overhead. David was no botanist, but he could see that there were two primary types of tree in the grove. The evergreens would give little cover to anyone attempting to hide in them. Some of the deciduous trees might, even though most of those were in the process of shedding their leaves for the winter.

*A sniper?* That was the obvious guess, but it did not feel right. Why would the Feddies have a sniper sitting up in a tree, well away from the rest of them? Supposedly, they hadn't had time to make any preparations. *But what else could it be?* David shook his head, a minimal gesture that scarcely moved his helmet. *I'll know whenever I find whatever it was I saw.*

He scanned the lower reaches of the canopy around him, letting his gaze move from the tree trunks out along the major branches, looking for anything that did not seem appropriate. Although he took pains to be thorough, he still scanned quickly, letting "normal" things pass almost without notice.

He was no more than eight yards away, laterally, when he finally spotted the anomaly that had caught his subconscious attention. The object was fifteen feet up in a tree, wedged between the lowest branch and the trunk, a camouflaged lump about a foot in diameter, almost a cube. The camouflage pattern did not quite fit the surroundings. David stopped where he was still mostly sheltered by another tree trunk, and stared at the object, wondering what it might be and why it was there.

"Captain?" he whispered. The radio circuits were sensitive enough that McAuliffe would have heard even a subvocal call.

"What?" McAuliffe asked.

David described what he had found. "It's far too large to be a snoop, and if it's a mine, it's like none I've ever seen, wrapped in a camouflage cloth."

McAuliffe scarcely hesitated. "Tag the location so we can find it later, and get back here at the double. As long as it's nothing that threatens what we're doing now."

"I don't see how it could."

Another building imploded as it burned. Three others followed in quick succession. None appeared to be single-family dwellings, but they were small buildings. One had a sign on the front that indicated that it had been a pub. There were no civilians in sight of the I&R platoon.

Tory Kepner listened to a flurry of conversation that included McAuliffe and Spencer. They were talking about other conversations, so Tory and the other platoon sergeants could only follow part of it. Delta had spotted a couple of dozen civilians, farther down the road, beyond the burned out stretch. They were being guarded by a squad of Feddies, but were far enough off that those soldiers should not be a factor in the fight.

"Apart from that squad, the rough count we have shows ninety-seven Feddies," McAuliffe continued. "Maybe a dozen doing the burning, the rest in defensive positions."

Tory frowned. That was new. In each of the other instances, there had been no protective perimeter. *I guess they're finally learning,* he thought. But the number was much lower than the estimate they had been given coming in.

Switching to his platoon channel, he said, "Wait for the command. Don't get antsy."

He started to track a target, the muzzle of his rifle moving just enough to keep the Feddie in the crosshairs of his sights. Tory kept his breathing even and shallow. It was too easy to let combat, or the anticipation of combat, screw up the body's rhythms. Adrenaline was necessary, but it could get out of hand, reach a level where it did more harm than good. Even a veteran could get carried away.

"Commence firing."

Tory pulled the trigger before the last syllable was out of Captain McAuliffe's mouth, and saw his target pitch forward. That was the only easy mark though. The rest of the Feddies were quick to take cover, almost as quick to return fire.

The I&R platoon had about thirty seconds in which it was the only Commonwealth unit engaging the enemy. Then the rest of H&S Company, as well as Alpha and Delta, joined in. The Federation unit had little chance of holding out, and none of escaping. They weren't dug in, and few of the Feddies had cover on every side. In each of the last few engagements, the Feddies had needed very little time to realize their plight and surrender.

This time was different.

The I&R platoon did not realize that new fire had entered

the fight at first. With the rest of their company behind them, they weren't directly taking fire from behind. Both Alpha and Delta found themselves in cross fires, though, with the preponderance coming from their rear. Within minutes, all three companies knew that they were being attacked from the rear. Some platoons took heavy casualties, caught with no cover on what they had thought was the safe side.

"Tory!" Spencer's call was almost a shout in Kepner's ear. "You concentrate on our original target. The other companies are each leaving one platoon to help you. The rest of us have our hands full."

"Any idea how many of them there are?"

"Not a clue. So many red blips came on close together that we can't get a good count. You concentrate on what's in front of you. Move in as you can and put the heat to them."

Tory could not put the new threat out of mind, but he did not let that persistent itch detract from the job. It wasn't possible for his men to move much closer without going into the open where they would be easy targets, but he did move those men who could get even a few feet closer.

"Pick up the fire," he told his men. "We've got to sweat these birds out fast."

Farther back, Spencer had gotten his clerks, cooks, and others turned to face the new threat. "Come on, lads. It's time to play the hero. Fire and maneuver." He had identified two concentrations of enemy electronics two hundred yards behind the company and a hundred yards apart. The idea was for H&S to move close enough that the Feddies wouldn't be able to link up, without getting so close that the company would be in a cross fire.

One platoon stayed put. The others started to move, one squad from each platoon rushing to the next cover while the rest laid down covering fire. After that first move, the rest was crawling. Getting any higher off of the ground would have been suicidal. David moved with his clerks. Even after all of the training he had put them through, most were still awkward at this business. For some of them, it was the first time that they had been at serious risk. But they gave it everything they had. And once they were in position, the volume of fire they put out—if not their accuracy—would have done credit to any line platoon.

"We just need to keep them pinned," Spencer told his men. "If we can hold these, Alpha and Delta can do the real work."

The Federation soldiers showed no inclination to move forward, or to try to link up, merely holding position. Nor were they putting out any great volume of fire at H&S Company. David frowned. *What's the point? It's as if they're just trying to hold us in position too.*

"Captain, can we get one of the Spacehawks to do a low flyby? I've got the feeling there's more to this than we've seen. These Feddies are playing it too cozy. There must be something else hanging over us."

"Hold on. I'll check." McAuliffe talked to the other company commanders first, then called CIC. He did not get a chance to make his request though. Before he could do more than identify himself, the radio talker had news.

"A Feddie fleet has just popped out of Q-space, in close. You'll have to hang on until we get this under control." Then the link was broken as *Sheffield* jumped into Q-space.

McAuliffe started to switch back to his link with Spencer, but before he did, the package that David had spotted—and four similar packages that had not been seen—exploded. They were incendiary devices that spewed shards of white-hot shrapnel and white phosphorus out in a circle around them, reaching as much as fifty yards away directly and setting scores of trees on fire.

# 14

**The attack showed** remarkable coordination between the Federation fleet and the troops on the ground. The two could not have communicated before the fleet emerged from Q-space over Coventry, and there was scarcely time for any extended planning between that event and the sequel. On the ground, Commonwealth forces in a half dozen different locations were attacked virtually simultaneously. At the same time, eight frigates appeared in near space, racing in on attack headings, managing to bring all of the Commonwealth ships under fire within thirty seconds.

There was nothing that Admiral Greene could do but order his fleet to make a tactical withdrawal through Q-space to a planned rendezvous while CIC sorted through the new data and came up with a more aggressive response. There wasn't even time for *Sheffield* and *Hull* to retrieve the fighters they had out on reconnaissance and ground support missions. Those Spacehawks that did not have fuel to wait for their ships to return had to land—near Commonwealth Marines, if they had a choice. And, while the fleet was gone, the Marines were on their own.

The movement of First Battalion's H&S Company was hardly a retreat. There were Feddies in front and in back of them. But David Spencer's men had to move—those who were still alive. The fires started by the incendiary devices in the trees gave them no other option. Those who were unharmed, or only slightly injured, helped those who were hurt more seriously. When possible, even the dead were dragged clear of the flames. The Royal Marines did not like to abandon any of their men. They moved in the least dangerous direction, toward the I&R platoon. That had not been affected by the fire bombs. While his men scrambled away from the flames, Spencer struggled to keep some sense of organization and tried to tote up the losses. It was hard to get full reports in the first minutes, and Spencer could hardly take time to examine each man's vitals on his visor display—not while he was dragging one of his clerks to medical help.

It took time before David even realized exactly what had happened. *I knew there was something wrong about that packet in the tree,* was a bitter thought. Leave it till later, the captain had said. It's no threat now. Hah. Then they had moved almost directly under the devices without taking notice.

"Remind me to trust your hunches after this," McAuliffe said when he and Spencer came face-to-face. "They had the place booby-trapped."

"It's easy to look smart after the fact, sir," David said. "Truth is, I wasn't thinking hard enough back then."

"First things first. Let's see to our wounded, find out how many dead we've got, then get reorganized."

"Aye, sir. I know we've got at least three dead, men right under one of the bombs."

"What about you? How's that arm and shoulder?"

David looked where the captain was pointing. The left sleeve of his battledress was burned through, and the field skin under showed the marks of being seared. It was starting to curl in, a sure sign that the organisms of the skin were dying. Field skins were one of the high points of molecular engineering. Fitting like a body stocking, a field skin was a colony animal that covered everything but face and hands— an artificial symbiont, drawing nourishment from its wearer's wastes, providing insulation and even some help in minimizing injuries.

"I hadn't felt it," David said. "Still don't. I guess the field skin kept the fire off."

"You'll need a new one as soon as we get the chance."

"Aye, sir. Too bad they couldn't save everyone."

"There's a limit. Come on. Let's get busy. We've got to get back in this fight."

Tory Kepner had no objection to being called the most cautious man in I&R. Caution was important to him. He did what he had to do, but tried to maximize his chances of getting home to his wife and son. Still there were times when a Marine had to make choices, and sometimes the properly cautious method was not a real option.

"We can't take all day. There's big trouble behind us," he told his squad and fire team leaders. "The rest of the company walked into some sort of trap. They're trying to sort things out now. We've got to finish here and get back to help."

He took a moment more to think. Lieutenant Nuchol had been less helpful than usual. "You've had more combat experience than I have," Nuchol had told him. "I trust your judgment." There were times when that response was appropriate. This was not one of them. Tory forced himself to step through the situation in his head. There were two buildings close enough to shelter Feddies, and most of the rest of the enemy had gotten into better cover than they had had before, at the edge of the next area of trees. Anything the platoon could do was going to be risky.

"Get the grenade launchers busy," was his first decision. "Keep popping them in until I say different." Each squad had one launcher, two other men carrying extra clips of rocket-propelled grenades for it. But the supply was limited. A full load for a squad was only six five-grenade clips.

"Fix bayonets," was Tory's next order, followed by, "I want maximum covering fire when we move. One team moving, three teams supporting, on each side. Spread out on the move, and let's set some speed records. At my order."

The lieutenant said nothing to contradict or amend Tory's orders. Kepner waited, giving the grenadiers time to lay in three more shots apiece before he gave the order to move. Tory took his fire team out first, angling to the left, stopping at the last vestige of cover from the trees. Alfie's fire team was next, then the teams from second squad, one at a time, each moving a little farther out. After the first move, there was no cover but short grass. The men angled themselves toward the enemy, hiding behind their helmets as much as they could.

Over to the right, third and fourth squads moved in the same fashion. For a time, they had a little more cover, but then they too moved out into the open.

Lieutenant Nuchol moved with fourth squad, keeping his rifle busy. For the moment, an extra gun was more important than trying to exercise any leadership but that of example. He recognized fear in himself, a thumping heart and a tightness in his face, but there was no time for it. Fire and move. Cover the other teams. Move with your own. Keep shooting—short bursts. Six days of minor skirmishes had not made him an expert, or that much of a combat veteran, but Frank Nuchol knew all of the moves, and he didn't forget any of them.

The grenade that bounced ten feet in front of Nuchol killed two privates from fourth squad instantly. The lieutenant felt an instant of intense pain before he lost consciousness.

"Hey, Kep!" Will Cordamon, third squad's sergeant, shouted over the noncoms' channel. "The lieutenant's down, and two men from fourth squad. I think all three of them have had it."

Tory could only spare a brief glance in that direction. Sorting out casualties would have to wait until after the fight.

*Get up and run, firing almost blindly. Drop to the ground and fire with more precision, but worry more about volume of fire than accuracy. Make the other fellow duck, spoil his aim, give your mates a chance to get closer.*

Only one man in I&R was not satisfied with suppressing enemy fire. Geoffrey Dayle tried to make every shot count. The Feddies were on *his* world, burning out *his* people. It wasn't enough to keep their head down. Dayle wanted to take them off.

A few Feddies tried to run as the I&R platoon closed in

on them, but they had no place to go except into the sights of other Commonwealth Marines. Most of the Feddies held their positions and continued to fire. It looked as if the fight would end in hand-to-hand combat, with the Feddies still holding a slight advantage in numbers. But they were surrounded, and all the Commonwealth Marines really needed to do was continue to pare down the numbers of the Feddies. Finally, the Feddies dropped their weapons and raised their hands. A few started to stand.

Tory was a little slow ordering his men to stop firing. Geoffrey Dayle shot two more Federation soldiers as they stood with raised hands. Kepner shouted at Dayle to stop.

"What the hell are you doing? They're surrendering."

Dayle brought his rifle down slowly, his hands gripping it so tightly that his knuckles shone white. "They ain't proper soldiers. They're murderers, arsonists," he said.

"Proper or not, you're out of line. Back off!" Tory moved toward Dayle quickly. This had to be stopped in a hurry, before it could get further out of hand . . . and before the wrong person saw what was happening.

Dayle took a single step back but did not turn his attention away from the Federation soldiers. Some forty were on their feet. Another dozen were on the ground, wounded. Most of them watched the Marine who had continued shooting after the surrender. Dayle stared back, his frown changing into a look of deep concentration. *Something's not right here,* he thought, but it took time for it to surface through the intense emotions that were battering his head.

"Sarge!" He barked the word in his helmet.

Tory had started to move away. He turned back toward Dayle. "What is it?"

"We're missing a bunch of these bastards. We had, what, ninety-seven helmets tagged before we started. A short company, you said. Even with the dead, there must be almost a platoon of them gone."

"Keep your eyes open, all of you," Kepner said on the platoon channel. "Spread out and watch all the way around." He scanned the Federation soldiers he could see, dead and alive, trying for a quick count. Then he linked to the sergeants from the platoons that Alpha and Delta had sent in to help, trying to account for the rest of the enemy helmets. It was nearly a minute before he heard enough to let him start to relax.

"It's okay, Dayle," he said. "We've got them all. It's the other lot that we've got to worry about next. As soon as we get these separated from their weapons and helmets."

With the platoon from Alpha standing guard around the perimeter—Delta's platoon was already on its way to rejoin their company—the I&R men went among the prisoners and dead, removing weapons, ammunition, and helmets. Until helmets were taken away, the prisoners had radios. The confiscated gear was piled up some distance from the prisoners. Two medics started treating the wounded from both sides, tagging those who would need extended treatment from the battalion's medical team.

"Turn the prisoners over to Alpha," Captain McAuliffe told Tory. "We need your platoon back here."

"On our way, sir," Tory replied. "The lieutenant's dead."

By the time that I&R rejoined their company, H&S had pulled into a tight defensive arc. Several trees had been brought down with beamers to provide better cover against the continuing fire from the other Federation unit. On either flank, Alpha and Delta were moving to close the gaps between them and H&S.

"What are we facing?" Tory asked as he slid to the ground next to Spencer.

David shook his head. "Nobody knows for sure, but it looks as if a full battalion crept in around us. There's trouble skyside too; a Feddie fleet popped in just as this mess started. Captain says the rest of the battalion got hit the same way, where they are. Maybe some of the other battalions also. I'm not sure about that. News is a little scarce."

"How bad was the company hit?"

"Bad enough, but we're not out of action. Right now, we're just trying to hold on until the fleet comes back and we can get some air support. If we can get any."

• • •

Even the shortest Q-space transit required a minimum of ninety seconds. It took that long for the Nilssen generators to cycle for the next jump, either going into or coming out of Q-space. On the bridges and in the CICs of the Commonwealth ships that jumped into Q-space after the arrival of the new Federation battle group, the first ninety seconds were a controlled confusion. No new information could be gathered in the gray limbo of Q-space, but the CIC computers continued to digest data that had been collected prior to transit. Admiral Greene and his staff immersed themselves in the flood of information almost to the point of drowning, trying to glean enough clues to allow the most intelligent decisions possible under the circumstances.

"We have to get back over Coventry as quickly as we can," Greene told his staff. "I don't want to leave the Marines or our Spacehawks hanging a second longer than we absolutely must. And while we're in normal space before jumping back to Coventry, I want an MR to go to Buckingham with the latest information."

As the fleet prepared to exit Q-space for its rendezvous twenty light-minutes away from Coventry, on the far side of the system's sun, information started to come out of the processors, summaries of the last action reports from the surface and the sensory input of all of the ships and surveillance satellites.

Admiral Greene scanned screens of data. The first time he looked from the screens to the three members of his staff who were gathered around, he said, "It's still just frigates. Not a battlecruiser or dreadnought in sight before we jumped."

*Sheffield* and the rest of the ships emerged from Q-space at the rendezvous a short time later, close enough together that there was no significant lag in communications. A holographic conference with all of the skippers and operations officers was set up as quickly as CIC summaries could be relayed to the other ships.

"We'll come out behind those frigates, if they haven't jumped back to Q-space, far enough back to retrieve as many Spacehawks as possible first. Get the last squadrons we have aboard *Sheffield* and *Hull* out to join in the attack on the frigates. I want liaison on to Colonel Laplace and the commanders of the various detached units as quickly as possible. Some of those units hadn't reported in before we bounced. And we need to get a handle on how many more Feddies there are on Coventry. It's clear they've got a lot more than we figured, at least double the number we allowed for, hidden away for all the days we've been here." He paused and shrugged.

"We'll have to puzzle out later how they managed to stay concealed for six days. And we need to get our own situation squared away a little before we can think of dispatching Spacehawks for ground cover operations. The Marines will simply have to hold out in the meantime. At least the Feddies didn't bring in any aircraft to make that more difficult."

He looked around at the people in the room with him and at the holographic projections of the others. "Eight frigates can't match our firepower, but it's enough of a force that they can do us considerable damage if we're not smart and careful." Greene glanced at one of his monitors. "The MR to Buckingham is being released now. We'll jump to Q-space heading to Coventry in two minutes. By that time CIC will have your navigational instructions ready.

"Good hunting, and good luck."

After the holographs faded, Greene looked at his staff and shook his head. "We'll need the luck, I think. This could get sticky." Then he blinked furiously several times and straightened up. "We've got jobs to do. Let's do them."

# 15

**There were only** finite amounts of ammunition available to the units of the Second Regiment, and no one knew when the fleet would be able to get more supplies down. Every officer and noncom had to start worrying about his men running out, and balance that possibility against the more immediate chance that the Federation soldiers they faced would overrun their positions if they cut back too drastically on their shooting.

In Hawthorne, Captain McAuliffe conferred with the leaders of Alpha and Delta. The three companies started to shrink their perimeter, pulling in, looking for more defensible positions.

"This is still no good, Spencer," McAuliffe said after he had finished coordinating with the other commanders. "It's ground the Feddies chose, and that's bad enough. There's no telling how many more surprises they've got waiting for us."

"I've been thinking about that, sir," Spencer replied. "But they're making it hard for us to spring loose, even if we knew which way to go."

"We're going to try to break east, then south," McAuliffe said. "Alpha will try to poke a hole in the Feddie lines. We'll move in behind them, and Delta will bring up the rear."

"That's dicey as hell, sir. We've got wounded to carry, quite a few."

"I know, David, but it can't be helped. We'll move our casualties the best we can. The fleet is in and out overhead. They've got at least eight enemy frigates to deal with before they can turn their attention back to us. We've got to do for ourselves for a while. I'm going to use Kepner's platoon to provide a little distraction for the move.''

''That's part of their job description, isn't it? You going to tell Tory or should I?''

''I'll handle it. You get your lads ready. When it starts, we'll be on the go in a hurry. Up and down a couple of times to get in position, then straight out . . . if this works.''

''Aye, sir. We'll be ready.''

''About five minutes. We'll give the I&R lads a chance to go to ground. When the rest of us move, they'll stay in place, hidden, then move again once we pull the Feddies past their position. When Kepner's platoon get to where they can distract the Feddies, Alpha will try to punch a hole in their front.''

*Hide? Where the blazes are they going to hide here?* David asked himself.

''Beautiful mess they left us, ain't it?'' Alfie asked Tory.

''Write up your complaints after we get back aboard *Old Vic*,'' Kepner said. ''Just get your lads in the best you can. We've got a chance. That's all any Marine can ask.''

''It's not all I could ask, mate,'' Alfie said before he started moving his fire team into position.

Tory was not at all thrilled with the chance himself, but no one had asked his opinion. *It could be worse,* he told himself. The platoon had moved into the middle of the area that had been burned. Several trees had come down in the blasts, but not lost all of their foliage, not been burned too badly in the fires that had caught the rest of H&S Company. If the Feddies went through in a hurry, there was a chance that the I&R platoon, its uniforms covered with soot and the odd piece of natural camouflage, would escape notice. Captain McAuliffe had assured Tory that the rest of the company would do everything they could to keep the Feddies from having the leisure to search carefully.

''I want everyone to get in position and then freeze,'' Tory whispered over the platoon circuit. ''I mean go as rigid as if you were already dead and cold. If you aren't, you will be, and maybe a lot of your mates with you. We'll have both sides firing over our heads for a time. Then we'll have Feddies closer than you ever want them. We've got to lie doggo until they get far enough past us that they won't notice when we slip out and move on to our real job.''

*Intelligence and reconnaissance.* I&R Marines were supposed to be able to move past an enemy, or hide from him.

*We're just not trained to let them crawl right up our arses,* Alfie thought as he slid into the position he had selected for himself. The others in his fire team were already in place. Alfie had added the finishing touches to their camouflage before moving in himself. He wedged himself between a trunk and a large branch that had bent and then snapped. He had to lift the branch a little to slide under it. When the branch moved back into place, Alfie was wedged in. Getting out would take time, even if he didn't have to do it silently.

*Now we wait,* he told himself.

Captain McAuliffe provided updates on a channel the entire platoon could hear, whispered notes and assurances that it would not be long before the new action started.

The increase in the volume of gunfire would have been clue enough for most of the hiding men. Then the focus of that fire started to shift. The sounds of Commonwealth guns moved farther away. The sounds of Federation weapons moved closer. H&S was making its first move, back toward Alpha and Delta, trying to draw the Feddies after them—and past the hiding I&R platoon.

Alfie found himself holding his breath, and consciously forced himself to resume breathing, quietly and shallowly. He focused hard on his breathing. That gave him something to occupy his mind that was more productive than wondering if he would notice being killed.

Ten yards away, Geoffrey Dayle felt a different itch. Lying silent to let the Federation invaders walk past him unmolested was almost more than he could bear. He knew that he could not surrender to his urge to start spraying bullets as soon as the enemy came within easy range. That would be stupid. It could do no more than get him and his mates killed to little purpose. But the urge was almost overwhelming. *I hope the wait's not too long,* was almost a prayer. *I don't know how long I can stand this.*

Each man was alone. The situation was similar to the ride in from ship to shore before battle. If the isolation was not as physically absolute as being alone in Q-space, it provided a near analogy for infantrymen in the middle of a fight—a fight they could only listen to for now. It made little difference if the man were a veteran or a rookie. Not even the few who had been in the battalion's every campaign in the war had ever been asked to perform quite this feat before.

"The Feddies are moving again," McAuliffe's soft whisper said over the I&R channel. "Their skirmish line is almost on top of you now." Then he went silent, worried that even his whisper in insulated helmets might give the platoon away. From two hundred yards away, he tried to watch, but he could not show too much interest, or expose himself to the fire of the advancing Feddies just to satisfy an almost ghoulish curiosity.

Tory Kepner had one of the more exposed, less protected hiding places, near the edge of his platoon. He heard the footsteps of at least one Feddie, steps that crushed charred grass and twigs. Tory held his breath, waiting for the sound of those footsteps to move by. But they seemed to stop, almost next to his head. Tory felt the need to urinate, almost certain that the Feddie had spotted something, that his concealment was not sufficient. Tory's hand was in position on his rifle, the right index finger on the side of the trigger guard. He fought the urge to move that finger to the trigger, not wanting to make even that small movement, in case he had not yet been seen.

*He would have fired by now if he had seen me,* Tory thought, not certain whether or not he believed that. Were the Feddies just gathering forces to take all of them at once? He squeezed his eyes shut. Under the tinted visor of his helmet, in deep shadow, there had been little chance that anyone could see even the whites of his eyes. The faceplate was totally non-reflective, even without the smudges of soot.

There was a flurry of shooting, too close. But there were no sounds of people hit or crying out in pain nearby. The

Feddies still had to be firing at the other platoons of H&S company, not at I&R. The noise started to recede then, moving south, past Tory. After what seemed like hours, he let out the breath he had been holding and sucked in another deep one.

"Their first line is past you," McAuliffe reported. "But stay put. They've got a second line moving behind the first, about twenty yards behind you, moving forward. Just hang tight."

*Easy enough for you to say,* Alfie thought. He wiggled his nose. The smell of the ashes made him want to sneeze. Once the thought came, he had to concentrate to keep from actually sneezing. *One line past, one more to go. I hope the second lot doesn't decide to kip out right on top of us.*

This time it was Alfie who heard a Feddie walking past. Alfie was too deep under his tree for it, but he thought that he might have been able to reach out and trip the nearest enemy. *Loud bloke. I bet he's got socking huge feet.*

"The second line is past you, but not far enough," McAuliffe said. "You'll need to give them a few more minutes. We're pulling back, so I won't be able to tell you when it's safe. Kepner, you'll have to make that call. Good luck."

*Ten minutes,* Tory decided. *We'll wait that long no matter what. Then, if I can't hear anything close, I'll take a look.*

It was a long ten minutes. Discipline within the platoon was flawless. There were no whispered questions, no rustling of branches. Tory could imagine the impatience of his men. He knew his own. He could almost hear the voice in his head saying, "Do something; do *anything.*" But he would not listen to that, watching the time line on his visor instead. He had made his decision. He would give it exactly ten minutes, not a second more or less—unless he heard movement nearby.

He listened. As far as he could without moving, he also looked, but there was little that he could see beyond the confines of his hiding place. *It could all end in a hurry,* he reminded himself. *Maybe the Feddies are playing it even cuter than we are.* There might be a squad, a platoon, even a company of soldiers with their guns training on the I&R

platoon's hiding places, just waiting for the men to emerge.

Five minutes passed. The sounds of gunfire were still moving away from Tory, but not by so much that he was tempted to cut short the time he had allotted for waiting. There would still be Federation soldiers close enough to require stealth from his men when they did emerge. But there were no sounds close, nothing that might suggest a trap.

When only two minutes remained, Tory started flexing the muscles in his arms and legs, gingerly so that he would not disturb his camouflage. He didn't want to try to move and find that he was too stiff to accomplish anything easily. *Tense and relax, do it one arm or leg at a time, over and over. Make sure you're limber.*

Tory stared at the time line as the last seconds of his ten minutes elapsed. Then he moved carefully. He shifted his position from half on his side to prone, then started to slide toward the edge of the branches that hid him, moving an inch or so at a time, looking out under the hanging foliage in front of him, searching for any trace of an enemy.

Before he exposed more than his head, he scanned as much of his surroundings as possible. Finally, his field of vision was more than a few degrees wide. There was no one in sight. He moved farther out and lifted his head to get a better view.

"Okay, come on out, but be dead quiet about it," Tory whispered on the platoon channel. "There's no one right in our faces, but they're not all that far off."

Tory moved into a solid shooting position, kneeling, still mostly concealed by the tree he had been hiding under before. A quick glance around showed no Federation soldiers behind him. Both skirmish lines had moved south, chasing the rest of H&S Company and the other two companies.

*Just keep looking that way,* Tory thought. He saw the first of his men, Alfie, and the other squad leaders getting into defensive positions ahead of any of their men. Black against black. There was little hint of the designed camouflage pattern visible on any of the battle dress uniforms that Tory could see, or on the helmets.

"Keep low and quiet," Tory whispered. "We don't want

to start this lark quite yet. Give us a chance to pick our ground. We're going to slide to the left and move farther back from the Feddies first. Alfie, take your team out first. We're heading for the edge of this park area, into the wild growth.''

"On our way."

Alfie gestured to his men to follow him. For the first thirty yards they moved on hands and knees, keeping cover between them and the Feddies. Then Alfie got up, choosing a good vantage point behind a tree. He made a come-along gesture, then started moving at a slow trot, crouched over, less concerned about being spotted. He went from tree to tree, pausing briefly at each. He could see the goal Tory had mentioned, where the woodlands stopped looking manicured and grew wild. There was a path into that wilder area almost directly in front of him.

One squad at a time, the rest of the platoon followed. As soon as Alfie and his fire team were in the relative security of the wild growth, they took up firing positions so they would be able to cover the others if that became necessary.

Tory brought his fire team across last.

"I never thought we'd pull that off," Alfie whispered when Tory crouched next to him. "Not a glimmer of them seeing us."

"We'll give them their chances soon enough," Tory replied. "We've only done the easy half of our job."

"How do you figure to work it?"

"Hang on. I want the others in on this." He switched channels to talk with all of the squad and fire team leaders.

"We're going to slide along near the edge of this stuff and try to get within fifty or sixty yards of the Feddies before we open up," Tory said. "Grenades first, then everything we've got."

"We're running short on grenades," Will Cordamon said. "We used damn near all of them before."

"So we'll use the rest now, just to give us a few seconds of confusion and cut down the odds. We'll hit hard, then fade into the woods before they can counter. It's not just grenades we're getting short of."

"That was my next point," Cordamon said.

"We'll hit them, then slide off and get as far down the line as we can before we hit again, if we have to. If we can make the Feddies think that they didn't box all of us in, it'll be that much easier for the rest of our blokes to break free. They're going to try to punch a hole through the Feddie lines as soon as we hit the first time."

"How soon?" Alfie asked.

"I'm waiting for Captain McAuliffe to give the word. Not long, I think. Just get your men ready, all of you. Alfie, start your fire team moving. Remember, we want to get close before we start anything."

Moving was better than sitting, and worlds better than lying around hoping for a chance to get up again. Despite the wild nature of the wood where the I&R platoon was now, there were paths. Alfie set a fast pace.

"The rest are in position, waiting for us," Tory told Alfie after three minutes. "How close are you?"

"About ninety yards from the nearest," Alfie replied. "That's why we slowed down. We're getting close enough that they might see us if we're not careful."

"How much longer do you need?"

"Two minutes ought to do it. That soon enough?"

There was a delay while Tory checked with Captain McAuliffe. "Two minutes from right now, Alfie," Tory said. "Mark the time. We're coming up now."

There was no time for careful preparation. The last fire team had scarcely moved into position before the two minutes were gone. Grenades were launched. Rifles started to speak. Tory had his men firing single shots, except for those with the needle guns, which could not be fired that way. The needlers were moderate-range weapons, most effective under sixty yards.

No more than ten seconds elapsed between the start of I&R's attack and Alpha Company's surge forward. The other two companies followed close behind, widening the wedge that Alpha threw into the Federation lines as the

Feddies started to worry about the "new" force entering the fray from the north.

I&R broke contact and hurried to their next positions, fifty yards east and south, before stopping to take the Federation line under fire again. After that it was strictly fire and maneuver, stopping only long enough to let go a shot or two. Alpha had punched its hole.

"We're not done yet," Tory said when they had very nearly reached the line that the others were retreating along. "We've got to slow the Feddies down until the rest can establish a new defensive line."

"We'd best get done fast," Alfie said. "Another three minutes and all we'll have left is spit and bayonets. And that three minutes is optimistic."

"One more set-to," Tory said. "Pick your spots carefully. The captain doesn't want the Feddies to flank him too soon."

Off to the left, they could see and hear Alpha as it moved past them, eighty yards off. H&S and Delta were farther back. Delta was fighting rearguard, and some of that fighting was intense, and close. The Federation soldiers pushed in after, trying to keep the Commonwealth Marines from escaping, or from having the leisure to establish strong defensive positions.

There was also at least a company of Feddies moving along the flank of the Commonwealth withdrawal, a narrow skirmish line moving between the waiting I&R platoon and the main Commonwealth force. Few of these Feddies seemed to be watching for the sort of ambush that Tory and his men had prepared.

"Steady," Tory whispered. "We hit fast, then get the hell out of here before they catch on. Right? Wait for my command."

He did not wait long. As soon as the nearest Federation soldiers were within seventy yards, he gave the order. Twenty-nine rifles opened up at once. That brought the flanking company of Feddies to a quick halt. Some fell, casualties. The rest dropped for cover. Before more than a few could start shooting back—mostly without seeing what they were shooting at—Tory had his men running again, racing for a rendezvous with the rest of their company. There was nothing else they could do until they got more ammunition.

"Dig in the best you can," McAuliffe told his platoon leaders and sergeants. "We can't go any farther without rest."

The fighting retreat had lasted an hour, although the pressure from the Federation forces had eased after the first twenty minutes. The site McAuliffe had chosen did offer some advantages. A narrow gully ran along the west side, the side that would face any immediate Federation assault. Behind that, there were trees and dense underbrush that offered some protection.

Men nearly ready to drop from exhaustion and the decline of protracted adrenaline highs turned to preparing defensive positions. Some needed to scrape out holes as best they could, around the two thirds of the perimeter that did not have the gully. Each of the companies worked to reorganize, to treat casualties . . . and to take count of the men who had been lost.

Some Federation fire continued, but there was no immediate assault. The Feddies were strung out and had also suffered losses. Both sides needed a respite before they could think about resuming the fight at full tilt.

David Spencer went from one platoon to the next in H&S Company. That meant scurrying along on his stomach half of the time, even though H&S had been put on the east side of the perimeter, farthest from the Feddies. H&S had nearly half of the circumference to watch, with the other two companies concentrated to the west, facing the Federation troops.

"We're still trying to get through to CIC," David told Tory when they came face-to-face. "The fleet's been in and out of Q-space a couple of times, I guess. The old man's trying to arrange air cover and a supply drop. We're waiting on that now."

*More waiting!* Tory thought. He closed his eyes for a

moment. He wasn't certain how much more waiting he could take.

Ian Shrikes knew that it was not a great plan. He wasn't even certain that it was a good one. But it was all that CIC had been able to come up with, and Admiral Greene had given the orders. The fleet had already made one fighting pass through Coventry's near space, taking six enemy frigates under fire briefly before cycling back into Q-space. That foray had brought more bad news though. Two Federation battlecruisers had appeared, an obvious second wave. That meant that the Second Commonwealth fleet was now outgunned.

"We still have to get what we can to the Marines," Greene had said. "No matter the risk." The fleet had spent forty-five minutes at the far end of its circuit, making preparations. Everything had to be ready before the ships reentered Q-space. There would be no time afterward for anything but the final execution of the orders. The fleet would run back into Q-space immediately after the launch, unable to see if the plan worked.

"Coming up on time, sir," the OD told Shrikes.

Ian nodded. "Signal the launch officers. We've got to get everybody out and on their way in one minute, give them time to get clear of the interference zone before we return to Q-space."

The task force entered Q-space. Ninety seconds later it emerged, as low over Coventry as the ships could safely go, no more than 150 miles above sea level. A flight of Spacehawks was launched from *Hull*. A dozen shuttles were launched by *Victoria*. The shuttles were loaded with supplies, mostly ammunition. At least two shuttles were targeted toward each group of Marines in the hopes that at least one would reach each unit. The odds offered by CIC's computers were less than one in three.

# 16

**The question between** the Bailey and Knowles families had changed from "How soon can we move?" to "Should we bother to move at all?" For a week after the Brix family had joined the group, the three families had lived an uneventful existence. Anna Knowles started to get her strength back. Each day the improvement was more noticeable. And the baby was doing well. No other people had come by the camp, refugees or invaders.

"We should be safe here now," someone would say as the discussion returned inevitably to the topic of staying or moving. "We know what we have available here. As long as there's game, why chance moving? It would be hard to find anywhere better, and more likely all we'd find is worse conditions."

No specific decision was ever made, but was put off again and again. "Let's see what tomorrow brings."

Finally, "tomorrow" did bring strangers, but not what any of the group had expected. It was late in the morning of the eighth day after the Brixes had arrived. When everyone finally heard the new sounds, they realized that the noise had been there for some time, starting so gradually that they simply had not noticed.

"A floater," Al said. He clambered to the top of the rock outcropping that they had built their shelters against, trying to see what was making the noise. His father went for his shotgun. Eric already had his rifle, having just finished cleaning it.

"It can't be too far off," Eric whispered, "or we wouldn't hear it at all."

"The Feddies didn't let any of us keep a floater." Reggie made certain that there was a shell in the chamber of his shotgun. He and Eric exchanged glances. Reggie shook his head. "Ridiculous, isn't it? Thinking about fighting off an army."

Eric shrugged. Ted Brix looked back and forth between the two, not certain what to think. The idea of even *thinking* about fighting soldiers knotted up his stomach. He did not offer an opinion though. *Not my place. We're here on their sufferance.*

"We'd best get the guns out of sight until we know for sure what's out there," Eric said. "If it is Feddies, if they don't see guns, they might leave us alone. If they do see them . . ."

"Out of sight but close enough to get to them in case it's something else," Reggie said.

"Hey, Dad!" Al called in a stage whisper. "There's more than one floater, and people. Off that way." He pointed toward the south. "Not coming quite at us."

"Get down here," Reggie said. He and Eric put their weapons inside the shelters, under blankets. The women and younger children were all inside. It had rained earlier that morning.

"With floaters?" Ted Brix asked.

"Maybe they had them stashed, or maybe they took a chance to go back for them after the Feddies left," Al said. "But I saw two cars, and I think there may be more."

"What do we do?" Reggie asked, looking at Ted and Eric.

"If they're our people, I'd sure like to know if anyone knows anything we don't," Eric said.

"Go over and sound them out?"

"We can take a look anyway," Eric said. "If we don't like what we see, we can try to make sure that they don't see us."

"I'll show you where they are," Al said.

"No. You stay here."

"Aw, Dad."

"You stay here," Reggie repeated. "The three of us will

go." He looked at Brix and raised an eyebrow. With only the slightest hesitation, Ted nodded. Since he was being invited, he would go—whether or not he wanted to.

Reggie led the way, with Ted bringing up the rear. Before they had gone thirty yards, the sounds of the vehicles, and the sounds of people trudging along through the woods, were much clearer. It was obvious that there had to be a considerable number of people, whatever the procession was. They were making no effort to be inconspicuous, or quiet. Reggie slowed his pace. The more people, the greater the danger, and danger was something he was eager to avoid. He even stopped for a moment, suddenly uncertain whether he wanted to continue.

"We might as well," Eric whispered, guessing the reason for the stop. "We'll keep ourselves awake nights wondering what we might have missed if we don't."

Reggie's smile was rueful. He shook his head but started walking again. It was only a minute more before he saw movement ahead, going from his right to left, through the trees. A large floater, a lorry, went past. A smaller floater, painted a light green, stopped, almost directly in front of Reggie, perhaps sixty yards away.

*Somebody spot us?* Reggie wondered. He stopped again and pointed. Eric came up next to him.

"No one's doing any shouting," Eric whispered. "Maybe they haven't seen us."

"If somebody does see us and gives any reaction, we all freeze at once." Reggie glanced back to make certain that Brix also heard. "Just stand stock-still until we know what kind of reaction we're going to get. No matter who these people are, we don't want to spook them into doing anything rash."

"You'll get no argument from me," Brix said. "I'd sooner not know what they might have to tell than make anyone do anything the least bit rash."

Ted spoke with such deep earnestness that Reggie had difficulty suppressing a smile. "We'll do our best to satisfy our curiosity without ending up like the cat," he said.

Brix's obvious nervousness made it easier for Reggie to

bear his own. He started forward again. The others stayed close to him now, moving slowly, carefully, trying not to make any sudden noises. The damp ground helped, and the noise of the floaters was enough to cover any slight sounds they might have made.

The one floater remained motionless. When Reggie thought that he was within twenty yards of it, he stopped again. If he went any closer, they would certainly be spotted, and not being seen at a greater distance might make these people too nervous.

"Hey, over there!" Reggie called out, moving away from a tree trunk.

Noel Wittington sat on the step on the driver's side of his floater, watching the procession move past him. Over the last several days, the number of people had more than doubled. A few additional people from South York had joined up during the first day of the trek overland. The later arrivals had all come from Hawthorne though. Their reports had been as bleak as those from South York. Nearly everything was being destroyed by the Feddies. Everyone was being driven out of their homes. The smoke of the fires could still be seen, so Noel assumed that not everything had been burned yet. But there were Federation soldiers in and around Hawthorne. That was depressing. It had crushed the one hope that Noel had been nurturing since leading his band away from South York.

*What do we do now?* was the constant question. With more than four hundred people together, movement had become essential. They couldn't just find a place and stay put. The game animals moved away too quickly. One hunt was all that they could count on without wandering far afield. They had to move on to eat. For the last two days, they had gradually worked a semicircle around Hawthorne, staying far enough out to avoid any soldiers. Noel had sent scouts out in front of the column. Twice, those scouts had brought back word of Feddies ahead in time to allow the convoy to change direction to stay away from them.

*Halfway around Hawthorne. Where do we go from here?*

There were several towns to the north, intermediate steps between Hawthorne and The Dales, but Noel had no hope now that any of those towns would be free of the invaders, and The Dales certainly would have been hit the first night, along with Coventry City and South York. *Where else is there to go?* He knew the answer, nowhere, but that didn't offer any solutions. *We can't go back, and there's nowhere else to go. And the farther we wander, the more people we're likely to attract. We can't handle many more.*

There were already too many. It strained resources too quickly. Hunt and move. Take an hour or two and send people out to gather nuts, berries, and anything else that might be even vaguely nourishing that could be found. The daily gathering was beginning to be less successful. Finding an area that had not already been picked over by others was becoming difficult.

*We ought to break up into smaller groups, maybe a group to go off with each floater.* That seemed eminently logical, but Noel could not persuade himself to make the suggestion, and he was even more doubtful that the majority would separate willingly.

"Hey, over there!"

Noel jumped to his feet, startled by the shout. He looked around, trying to figure out where the call had come from. The people from his column who were close were all looking off to the left. Noel scanned that way, then saw the three men. One of them waved both hands over his head.

"Can we come over to talk?"

"Come on in," Noel called back. "There just the three of you?"

"Just us."

The line of refugees on the track came to a halt. Even up ahead people heard that something was going on and stopped. Without command, the entire line was soon halted. People up front started to move back, anxious to see what was going on. People from the rear of the column moved closer as well. By the time the three men emerged from the forest north of the track, more than a third of Noel's "command'' was close enough to see and hear whatever happened.

Reggie did the talking for himself and his companions. After the introductions, he said, "We lived in Hawthorne. Eric and I lived on Sherwood Pike. That would have been the last road you crossed."

"A few of us came from Hawthorne," Noel said after he had introduced himself. "But most of us are from South York."

"You've come that far?"

Noel nodded. "We had hoped that maybe Hawthorne was small enough that the Feddies wouldn't have bothered it. We know now that we were wrong."

"They burned South York too?" Reggie asked.

"They were still burning when we left."

"You come across any *good* news?"

"Possibly. Five days back, some of us thought we heard shuttles that sounded different than the Feddie landers. Nobody actually saw anything, but . . . it gives us some hope."

"You think there are Commonwealth soldiers here?"

"That's the hope. But even if they aren't here now, they'll come sooner or later. I think they'll come just as fast as they can find the men and ships." He looked both ways along the track his people had been following. "We've been listening for any hint that there are Commonwealth forces around. We have a few battle helmets from the HDF. But we haven't heard anything yet."

"So they're not here after all?"

"We don't know. They'd probably use different channels than we've got. Unless we had the latest codes, which I'm sure we don't, we wouldn't hear anything but noise, if that."

"If there are Commonwealth troops on Coventry, you might have been better off staying around South York. It might be ages before they work their way out to small towns like Hawthorne."

"It's too late for that. Anyhow, we didn't have much choice. All we can do now is keep moving, follow the game and try to keep everyone fed. What about you three?" It was time, and past, he felt, to ask a few pointed questions himself.

"We have our families camped not too far from here," Reggie said. "We didn't go out as far as most of the others from our part of town." He gestured toward the east. "I imagine you'll run into the rest, hundreds of them, before much longer."

*That's all we need,* Noel thought. "You have any idea where they might be?"

"Not the foggiest. We haven't seen anybody in a week. It's been two weeks since we got pushed out of our homes. The others could be just about anywhere. They might be having the same problems you are, finding enough meat to keep everybody fed."

Michael Polyard came walking back along the line of refugees. He had been out ahead, scouting, and had returned to find that everyone had stopped. In as few words as possible, Noel told him what had passed, and introduced the strangers.

"Some of those people probably aren't too far ahead of us now," Polyard said. "I came across the signs of a large camp, abandoned, about two miles east of here. It looks like they moved off to the northeast then."

"I suppose we'll have to move in the opposite direction then." Noel barely suppressed a sigh. "Southeast, toward the ridges. We might even have to cross the mountains before long."

Reggie almost instinctively said, "It'll be colder south of the mountains than on this side soon," but stopped himself. If these people didn't know that quirk of the climate, it was better for his family and the others with them that these hundreds of people didn't learn about it and stay north of the slopes.

"You might want to head due south," Reggie said instead. "I think that most of the people from around here went east. A few miles south you should find untouched land."

Noel nodded slowly. "What about you and your families?"

Reggie glanced at his companions before he replied. "As long as we don't have to compete with you lot for our food, I think we'll stay where we are for now. We've got a woman with a baby born after we were chased out of our homes. We'd like to avoid any traveling if we can."

Noel turned toward Michael. "What do you think? Head south? Try to avoid the crowds?"

"It's worth a try. We might find enough to keep us going for a few days before we have to worry about another major move." He looked to the sky. "We can still make another few miles before we stop to hunt, anyway."

Reggie closed his eyes for an instant while the two were looking at each other. *They're going to move on!* Short of certain word on the arrival of a Commonwealth liberation force, it was the best possible news he could think of.

"How far out are the scouts?" Noel asked.

"I was the only one out," Michael said. "I didn't send anyone else when I came back. I wanted to see what was going on back here first."

*That simplifies matters,* Noel thought. "Mr. Bailey, do you know of anyplace we'd have trouble getting our floaters across south from here?"

"I don't have any idea. Sorry. I'm already as far from home, from where my home used to be, as I've ever been." As far into the wild, in any case. He had visited some of the other towns over the years, and made it to The Dales or Coventry City at least once each year, but that wasn't the same. "I doubt that there's anything you can't at least find a way around between here and the first ridge of the mountains." *If you're willing to go far enough, anyway.*

"We'll manage, I guess. Michael, let's get everybody turned." Noel turned away from the strangers. "Everyone's had a chance to rest. We'll want a bit of good daylight left to put our hunters out when we find a place to camp."

Reggie and his companions watched for a few moments. There were no words of farewell, no parting pleasantries. Once the column had started moving south, Reggie, Eric, and Ted moved away from the track. They backed off a few steps into the forest first, then turned to walk away.

• • •

By the time he got back to camp, Reggie's hands were trembling almost out of control. He held them out and stared at them, frowning. It seemed to be some sort of fear reaction, but had he really been as frightened as that? It didn't seem possible. He needed time to get the trembling under control. He drank a cup of tea—the weak brew they had been making to help their tiny stock last longer—while he told the women and children about the meeting. Occasionally, Eric added some detail. Ted merely listened, as if he had not even been present.

"If they have HDF helmets, some of them must have been in the HDF," Al observed. "Why are they running away and not fighting the Feddies?" No one had a good answer for that. Neither Reggie nor Eric bothered to try.

"Do you really think that they'll go off and leave us alone?" Ida asked. "Go far enough away that we won't have to move to find food?"

"I think so," Reggie said. "They started south straightaway. They're no more eager to be around other folks than we are. As many people as they have, they have to keep moving to eat. They'll probably keep going until they have some overriding reason to either come back this way or head home toward South York."

"What the man said about Commonwealth troops—you think that's right?" Al asked. "You think maybe they've already come to save us?"

"Your guess is precisely as good as mine, son. We don't have any way to know. They heard something that sounded like a shuttle, but not like the Federation shuttles they had already heard. But no one saw anything. That's terribly vague."

"It is something, though," Anna said. "It's more than we had even a couple of hours ago." Her voice sounded strained. She wanted so much to believe that the ordeal might be nearing its end, but she feared disappointment.

They talked it to death and through resurrection, returning to the topic throughout the day, and into the evening. Just to get away from it for a time, Reggie took another walk.

He followed the new track south for a few hundred yards. There was no sign of the "horde" from South York. They had really gone.

There was mist before dawn, just enough to thoroughly dampen everything. Reggie stayed out on watch until it started to get light. The weather gave him something to think about other than what had happened the day before. Ida woke then, and several of the children started to stir. When the Knowles baby woke and cried loudly, everyone else woke. Lorna Brix helped Ida with breakfast. It wasn't much, of course, but breakfast always seemed to taste better than the other meals. There was meat and the broth it had been stewing in, tea, and a few crackers served in place of bread. The little of that they had brought along had only lasted three days. Crackers stayed fresh longer and took up much less space for the weight.

Morning rituals were attended to, a little more hurriedly because of the mist that was just ending and the extra chill it had brought. Everyone ate sitting inside the shelters, hunched over their bowls and mugs as if to protect them from . . . whatever.

Afterward, no one was in any hurry to go outside, even when the sky started to clear. The morning was chilly. What finally started to move the adults outside was a general reluctance to start talking. No one felt much like conversation. Reggie's impulse was to go hunting. That would take him away from camp and give him time alone. But he and Eric had each brought down large deer the morning before. There would be no need to hunt for at least one more day.

Reggie walked around the camp, trying to loosen stiff muscles. Al came out of the shelter and climbed to the top of the rock outcropping to look back toward Hawthorne. The others came and went. The younger children played, running and laughing. After two weeks, this life seemed almost normal to them—most of the time.

A sudden screeching noise some two hours after breakfast, loud and insistent, stopped Reggie's pacing. The sound came from the northwest, back toward home. Then the noise was gone. He hadn't seen a thing. He looked to the top of the mound. Al was still up there, staring off in the direction of the noises.

"Some shuttles came in, back toward town, maybe in the center!" Al shouted. "Two or three of them. They didn't look like the Feddie shuttles."

The other adults were all outside and looking northwest by then. Even the smaller children looked that way. Reggie felt a catch in his throat. *Can it really be?* He didn't want to hope, afraid that his hopes would be crushed all too quickly, but . . .

"I'm coming up there," he told Al. "Give me a little room."

Ten minutes, twenty, maybe even thirty, passed. Reggie had no idea how long he had stared, hoping to see or hear something that would confirm his hope that Commonwealth forces had arrived. It wasn't until he heard shooting, and the flat *thrump-crump* sound of grenades (although he wasn't certain what those noises were) that he decided that help really had come to Hawthorne, to Coventry. There was a battle under way, and even though the fighting had to be three or more miles away, there was enough of it going on that he could hear the sounds.

"It all sounds so tinny," Al said, almost a complaint. "Are those really gunshots?"

"I'm sure of it," Reggie said. "A lot of guns by the sound of it." Eric was also on top of the rock outcropping. Even Ted had come part of the way up. But there was nothing that any of them could see, except for the smoke of more fires.

"Shouldn't we go see what's happening?" Al asked. "Maybe we can help."

"There's nothing we could do but get ourselves killed," Reggie said. "It's after the shooting stops that we'll need to go see what happened."

"You mean who won?"

Reggie looked his son straight in the eyes. "Yes, that's what I mean."

• • •

There were ebbs and flows to the sounds of battle. For a considerable time, the noises seemed to remain stationary. Then, abruptly, they started to move.

"That's coming toward us," Reggie said, looking around—suddenly concerned at being so exposed. "It's time we get back down on the ground."

"We won't be able to see anything down there," Al protested.

"You can't see anything from here," Reggie said. "And there could be stray shots coming this way if they get much closer. Down."

Al was the first down, all but shoved by his father. The men followed. Below, the sounds of the fighting were muted a little. The younger children were herded inside the center shelter. The entrance was guarded by Ida and Lorna. Anna was inside with her baby. The three men and Al stayed outside, but even they took some care about where they stood, and after a time they moved close to the stone shelter.

"That's getting terribly close," Ted said.

Reggie and Eric exchanged glances. The sounds had quit moving again. "They're probably not more than a mile off, if that," Reggie said.

"Back by the gully where the first caches were?" Eric said.

"That's the right direction. Could be the right distance." Reggie nodded. "The gully would be a good place to put up a fight from."

The sounds seemed to remain stationary for a time, and then the volume of shooting died off to no more than a quarter of what it had been before.

"They're settling in for a long fight," Al guessed. He had seen a lot of video adventures, and there was nothing deficient about his imagination.

"That means neither side has won outright," Reggie said, a more practical consideration.

For the next quarter hour they heard only isolated shots, then there was another intense exchange that lasted for several minutes before another period of almost quiet came.

"What the hell's going on?" Eric said, almost shouting in frustration. "Who's winning?"

No one tried to answer his questions. Almost before the second was out of his mouth, they heard shuttle noises again, louder than before, shattering the air. Two landers came in from the southeast, almost directly overhead, and no more than two hundred feet off of the ground. The sound of the passage was almost physically painful.

"Commonwealth markings!" Al shouted. "I saw the emblem!"

Reggie got so light-headed that he feared he would faint. He leaned against the wall of the shelter and sank to a sitting position. *They've come! They've come at last!*

**Part 5**

# 17

**The battalion's quartermaster** sergeant was also H&S Company's service platoon sergeant. Malcolm Macdowel had held the position more than four years, the company's most senior platoon sergeant by eighteen months. Even in peacetime he might have been able to start thinking of promotion to company lead sergeant or an equivalent staff position. With wartime attrition, his promotion was long overdue, as Macdowel was quick to point out when David Spencer gave him the new assignment.

"Tell it to the chaplain, Mac," David said. "For now, you're still our QM sergeant, and that means your lads get to hustle everything out of the shuttles when they arrive."

"If they arrive," Macdowel said. "In any case, we'll need help. My supply squad can't get everything out fast enough."

"Use the whole platoon. The mechanics don't have any vehicles to repair at the moment. Anyway, your lads won't have to tote anything very far. There'll be men from every platoon in three companies waiting to grab the ammunition as quickly as you can toss it to them."

Macdowel let the habitual scowl on his face ease a little. "I just hope both shuttles make it. We're going to need everything they can carry."

"You can set that in bronze."

"Just get them in, David. We'll get them unloaded."

Spencer nodded. "It should just be a couple of minutes now, if all goes well. The last word we had was that the shuttles had all separated from the ships and were on their way in before the fleet jumped back to Q-space."

Malcolm's scowl returned, deeper than ever. "That's another thing I don't like, them kipping off to Q-space and leaving us behind all the time."

David laughed. "Save it for after you retire. You can spend twenty years writing out everything you don't like about the CSF, then ship it off to the Admiralty for immediate action."

Macdowel turned and walked away. H&S Company was still on the far side of the Commonwealth position from the Federation troops, with dense forest and a slight rise to the ground between them. So far, there had been no shooting near enough to make anyone duck on the eastern section of the perimeter. Out in front of the H&S positions there was a clearing—almost impossibly small for an LZ. The landers would come in hot, vertically, with only a few yards between them. If Federation soldiers got around to the east side first, they could make it very hot for the shuttle pilots, and for the Marines who would be rushing to unload the landers.

Tory Kepner and his men were waiting again, outside the Commonwealth lines. They were one last line of defense for the shuttles, in case the Feddies did try to come around and interfere with the landings. Carrying captured weapons, the I&R platoon was covering the most likely approaches, waiting to ambush any Feddies who came along. Two squads were concealed to the north, the other two to the south of the main Commonwealth force.

First and second squads had the southern approach, arranged in a shallow V. Any Feddies coming in would funnel straight into the notch of that V. The squads had planted a half dozen mines along the trail leading into their position and off to either side, most on the side, also to help funnel any enemy right into the center of the ambush.

Tory took his place at the apex. He was concealed under a tangle of vines with only the last two inches of the Federation rifle's barrel protruding. Using an enemy rifle held no particular challenges for I&R men. They had used captured rifles in training, enough for familiarization. Tory's only concern was the amount of ammunition available. He had a full magazine, twenty-seven rounds, in the rifle, and another full magazine stuck into his belt. His own rifle, and those of his men, were back inside the perimeter, out of ammunition. The few rounds the platoon had been able to scrape together had been parceled out to men in other platoons.

"Keep the Feddies away until the shuttles get down and we have time to unload them," Spencer had told Tory. "Ten minutes after they're on the ground should do it. Then you can start pulling your men in and we'll get you back to your own rifles."

*So far, so good,* Tory thought. After fifteen minutes there had been no hint of enemy activity along either approach. The shuttles were on their way down. Within seconds he expected to hear the sonic boom as they came in hot.

He had a clear view down an open trail, sixty yards before it bent left. *Unless they show up in the next two minutes, we should be home free.* Once the shuttles were on the ground, they should be able to hold the enemy off for ten minutes.

Forty yards away, Alfie Edwards held down the left end of the ambush. His view of the track was not as good as Tory's, but it would do. The path crossed his field of fire at an angle. He could sweep a twenty-yard stretch of it without much movement at all. Between Alfie and Tory, the rest of first squad waited.

Patrick Baker was three yards left of Tory. Kepner usually kept Baker close, where he could keep an eye on him. Baker lifted his visor just enough to slide a hand through the gap. He wiped sweat away from his eyes. As soon as he dropped the faceplate back into position, he glanced to his right to see if the platoon sergeant had seen the breach. It didn't really matter to Baker. The need to get the stinging perspiration away from his eyes had been too great for him to blink and bear it.

*You're scared half out of your wits,* Baker thought. It got worse every day, every time the prospect of fighting got close. After six days on Coventry, Patrick found himself wondering how much longer it would be before he simply could not function any longer. He squeezed his eyes shut. *I don't want to freeze up and get the other blokes killed. Better if I get it fast, before I can screw up.* He opened his eyes and looked out. There was no sign of the enemy. *Maybe they won't come. Maybe we'll get off easy this time.* That hope died almost as soon as it was born. Just as Baker became aware of the noise of the approaching shuttles, he saw movement on the trail, just a hint of motion through the trees, not yet directly in front of the ambush.

"Let them get close enough so we have them all in our sights," Tory cautioned on the platoon channel. Then he switched to the noncoms' channel. "Cordamon, you have any on your side?"

"Negative," Will Cordamon replied.

"Then just stay down. Maybe you'll catch a break. Alfie, can you see how many there are here?"

"I've counted six so far, but I can't see how far back the line goes. Could be a squad or a company, for all I can tell."

"Hang tight, Alfie."

"They come much farther, they'll see us, and they'll have time to target those shuttles."

"Wait." Tory glanced upward but could not see the incoming landers. The sound level told him they were close though. Silently, he counted to three, the muzzle of his rifle tracking the Feddie point man. "Fire!"

The two squads started shooting. The Federation soldiers who were visible all went down. Gunfire came from behind them, though, blind fire, heavy but uncoordinated. It shredded leaves and chopped branches.

*A couple of platoons, at least,* Tory thought. He heard the shuttles come in then, passing very close overhead as they dropped into the clearing and out of range of the Feddies.

"The shuttles are on the ground," Spencer told Kepner by radio. "Now, give us ten minutes."

"We'll try, but I won't guarantee that we'll have a single round of ammo left in half that." Tory went back to the other channel to tell his men to save ammunition now that the shuttles were in. "Wait until you have targets and stick to single shots as much as you can. We just need to keep them from getting close now. Another nine minutes and we can pull back."

A few seconds later, Tory had another thought. "Alfie, shut your fire team down. Make them think the ambush is narrower. If they try to flank us, be ready for them." He gave the fire team on the end of the right wing the same instructions.

For the next few minutes, Tory contented himself with an occasional glance at the time line on his visor. There was more than enough to engage his full attention out in front. There was a pause in the firing from the Feddies. Tory guessed that the Feddies would be looking for a way around the ambush, or trying to determine exactly where it was so that they could lob in grenades. Once half of the ten minutes had passed, Tory told the fire teams on each end of the V to start pulling back.

"Try to do it without letting the Feddies know what you're doing," he added.

Alfie's derisive snort was too soft for Tory to hear. *Do it without letting them hear me? I could get close enough to see the color of their eyes without them hearing me.* "We're pulling back, soft and easy," he told his men. "Not a sound, not a rustle of leaves. Give me thirty seconds to move first."

He needed less than thirty seconds to get to a new position five yards back from where he had been. He then waited for his men to make their moves. Alfie and his privates took turns, withdrawing a few yards at a time, covering each other, pulling back until they were back near the apex of the ambush.

"Okay, Kep, we're back," Alfie reported.

"I see you. Pull around behind me. Another two minutes and we should be heading back in."

"No argument from me."

*That's a relief,* Tory thought. He shifted his position just enough to ease a sudden cramp in his right leg.

"Okay, Tory, bring them on in," David whispered over the radio. "We've got the goods out."

"Are the shuttles going to try to make it back out?"

"Not just now," Spencer replied. "It seems we've picked up a few extra riflemen."

"We're on our way." Kepner gave the platoon their orders and started withdrawing his own fire team with the rest. *Extra riflemen?* That brought the mental equivalent of a snort. *Fat lot of good a couple of navy blokes'll be in a fight.*

By the time that I&R crossed the lines, they were moving at close to a run. There was no pursuit behind them, but there was also no longer any need for stealth. Once they got in, they found that men from headquarters platoon had already loaded their rifles and arranged spare magazines for them.

"Now that's service," Alfie said as he ran the bolt on his rifle to put a round in the chamber.

"Just don't ask the clerks to brew your tea," Tory advised. "They make it strong enough to dissolve a field skin."

"Speaking of tea, is there any chance for a meal?"

"Field rations and canteen water," Tory said. "They brought down extra meal packs as well. But don't take all day about it. Ten minutes and we go into the line. The captain's afraid the Feddies might try to crash the party again."

Ian Shrikes kept his hands on the armrests of his chair on the bridge of HMS *Hull*. Holding his pose of casual confidence was becoming a chore. It took conscious attention to not demonstrate relief when the ship ducked into the safety of Q-space, or to keep from showing white knuckles caused by gripping the armrests too firmly.

"I'll want those casualty reports as quickly as possible, Lieutenant Smythe," he told the officer of the deck. *Hull* had taken two hits from one of the Federation battlecruisers after launching its Spacehawks on this last excursion into the hostile space over Coventry. That ship had simply overloaded *Hull*'s defenses with a spread of missiles and mines that—combined—had contained enough explosives to fragment a dozen capital ships if they had all hit.

Lieutenant Ruby Smythe had an open line to the damage control party working the section where the missiles had hit, near the bow. She had been listening to a running report.

"One rating dead, sir," Smythe reported. "It appears that there are three wounded, two of them officers. The DCO"—Damage Control Officer—"says that none of the injuries appear life-threatening. Medical help is already on the scene."

*I don't care if they're officers or ratings,* Ian thought, tempted to tell Smythe that. *They're people. They're* my *people.* But he would not criticize an OD over that, not in front of the rest of the bridge watch, who might see it as a sign that he was as nervous as anyone else.

"What about the damage?" he asked.

"Power has been lost to three gastight sections in the number one tube. Equipment in two rooms is ... gone. That's the word the DCO used, sir. Backups are all on-line. Ship's functions have not been interrupted or compromised."

Ian nodded. The level of redundancy built into Cardiff-class ships was remarkable. For every critical system there were at least two, and often more, backup systems. The ship could even lose two of its three Nilssen generators without suffering any critical degradation of function.

"Comm, relay the damage estimate to the flagship as soon as we emerge from Q-space," Ian said. It was almost time for that, on the far end of the transit from Coventry. "Navigation, what will the light delay be when we emerge?"

The navigator, on a holographic link from his station a hundred yards from the bridge, had that answer ready. "We'll need thirty-two seconds before our exit from Coventry catches us up."

They would not be able to see anything that had happened over Coventry following their departure for at least thirty-two seconds after they came back out of Q-space.

∙    ∙    ∙

Admiral Greene stared at the large screen set into the top of his chart table aboard *Sheffield*. A larger and more sophisticated version of the mapboards that the Marines carried, it gave him the opportunity to view any section of Coventry. By switching to a three-dimensional projection, he could view holographic charts of any section of space. He had been viewing the space around Coventry, a chart showing the last known positions and courses of all of the ships and fighters on both sides. But that view, important as it was, changed too quickly, too drastically, for it to provide much guidance when the light distance was more than a few seconds.

*It all happens too bloody fast these days,* he thought. *It's too ruddy bad we ever got away from the slow ballet, taking days between Q-space transits. Even hours would be welcome. This in-and-out-and-back-in is murder. Turns my brain to jelly.* He shook his head and sighed. Alone in the outer room of his day cabin, he could afford the luxury of showing his feelings.

The new tactics had come since the start of the war. Paul Greene had been present at the creation of the new tactical manual, but he had been in uniform for more than thirty years before that, training diligently at the old, more sedate, tactics, honing those with each year's fleet war games. The new tactics had allowed the fleet to salvage a bad situation, cheat defeat, and score the first real victory of the war for the Combined Space Forces and the Second Commonwealth.

But the Confederation of Human Worlds had been quick to copy the new tactics, which nullified the advantage in all subsequent encounters. With both sides ducking in and out of Q-space as quickly as their Nilssens could cycle, space combat had become a cat-and-mouse game. The problem was that no one could be certain who was the cat and who was the mouse until it ended. The game continued until one side gave up the arena, or was destroyed.

*A game of chance, if the sides are anywhere near evenly matched,* Greene thought, not able to get his mind completely off the subject even while studying the surface map with its overlays showing troop positions. *Come out in front of an enemy who's ready for you and, pop, you're gone.*

He frowned and tried to force himself to concentrate on the problems faced by the Marines on the ground. One battalion was still aboard *Victoria*, the heavy weapons battalion. There had been no call for the tanks and artillery. Now the admiral considered putting them on the ground without their heavy weapons, as infantrymen, but two problems kept him from issuing the order. The first was that he wasn't certain where they might do the most good. The second was that, as long as the fleet was playing hide and seek with the Federation ships, it might be impossible to get that battalion to the ground without incurring prohibitive casualty rates. A landing craft was too inviting a target, too soft. Now that the Federation had battlecruisers in the system, there would be fighters to go after shuttles.

There were Marines at Coventry City, The Dales, and a half dozen other places. Without air superiority, there was little chance of even consolidating the forces that were already on the ground, putting the five battalions back together.

*The only good news is that the Feddies are spread around even more, in at least a dozen different spots. And their fleet has as much trouble trying to do anything for them as we do for ours.* Both sides were equally vulnerable. *If most of our landers got through with the supplies, we might have a slight advantage, even if the Feddies outnumber us three to one on the ground.* The last was a guess, the best estimate that CIC had been able to make.

"They snookered us for fair," Greene allowed to himself. "Kept at least half of their assets on the ground hidden, waiting for just the right moment to strike—waited six *days* without making a move, without giving us a clue." He shook his head. It had been an incredible show of patience on the part of the Federation commander, and a demonstration of no mean skill by his troops. Greene and all of his advisors had been taken in by the ruse. There had only been enough transports in system for a regiment and a half when they arrived, and those had fled. "We never asked ourselves if there might have been others, already gone.''

He continued to stare at the map, calling up columns of data on the side for each of the troop concentrations. No magical solutions sprang to mind.

''I can't do anything substantial to help the poor sods on the ground without putting the entire battle group at risk. Extreme risk.'' Even then his steps might be futile. If the task force, or a significant portion of it, were destroyed, the Federation would have a freer rein, able to reinforce and resupply their troops at will, able to concentrate fighters to provide close air support.

''I just don't have the forces to work with,'' Greene complained to the empty room. ''Until the Fourth Regiment gets here with whatever ships Stasys found to support them, we have to keep playing this damn-fool game.'' Admiral Stasys Truscott, chief of naval operations, had not been certain what ships would be available to escort the other Marine regiment.

''They should have been here already. Or they should be arriving now,'' was Greene's final comment before he switched the view back to the holographic depiction of the system. But there had been nothing so far, not even an MR from the Admiralty telling him when he could expect the reinforcements he had been shouting for.

Greene touched a key at the side of his chart table. ''Captain Hardesty, would you come to my day cabin for a moment?''

''Right away, sir.'' Mort Hardesty had been skipper of *Sheffield* for nearly three years. ''About two minutes to get to you from here.''

''Don't break your neck, Mort. I'm setting up a holo conference with the other captains.'' He pressed another key to talk to his aide, to get him to make the arrangements for the immediate conference. Then he sat down to wait. It appeared that they would all have a lot of that to do.

# 18

**It was dark** when Tory Kepner was wakened by a call from Captain McAuliffe. The sudden voice startled Tory. "Yes, sir, I'm here," he said as soon as he recovered.

"Get your skates on, lad. I've got to send your lot out for a recce. Give you a chance to plant some mischief as well."

"We've had our bit of sleep, sir. What do you want us to do?" Tory said over a yawn.

"Spencer's on his way to you. He'll give you the details."

"Aye, sir. Seems quiet enough."

"The longer it stays that way, the better I'll like it," McAuliffe said before he clicked off.

Tory switched to his platoon channel to rouse everyone. It came as no surprise to anyone that they were going to be sent out. The fact that the entire platoon had been told to bed down well before sunset had been warning enough of that.

"Get a quick meal and drink in while you can," Tory told his men. Then Spencer slipped into the foxhole with him.

"You'd best get some food down yourself," David said. "I'll talk, you listen while you eat."

Tory didn't argue. He pulled out a meal pack and pulled the strip that opened it and heated the contents. David waited until Tory started eating before he gave him the orders.

"The captain wants you to do a full tour, circle completely around the Feddies. Mark their positions and try to estimate their numbers. Plant a few mines on the approaches to our positions. Make it more costly for them to circle us in.''

''You mean they haven't closed in around us yet?'' Tory asked after quickly washing down a mouthful of food.

''Not in any strength. There may be the odd patrol, but nothing major. That's part of what the captain wants you to check. Once you make your circuit, the captain wants you to move off to the southwest, at least a mile, well out of the way. You'll be the reserve if things get touchy here in the morning.''

''Come up behind and kick them in the arse?''

David smiled. ''Just a little forward of that, I'd say, where it will slow them down a bit. Take rations and ammunition for two days. As soon as you locate a spot to go to ground, radio your report back to me or the captain. That'll give us a fix on your location as well.''

''What if we run into Feddies on the prowl?''

''Better if you don't. But if you can't avoid them, try to do them quickly. If the Feddies know we've got a force roaming around out beyond our lines, it could sour the whole deal.''

''Will we be the only ones out, or will there be others?''

''If Alpha or Delta put out patrols, they'll stay close, just to tidy up their fronts and plant a few mines. The captain wants you lot well back, t'other side of the Feddies.''

''We assume anyone we stumble over is the enemy?''

''Unless you can see differently. Now shove the rest of that meal down your throat and get moving. You'll go out on the east, where you came in this afternoon.''

The platoon crossed the perimeter one fire team at a time. Once they were all outside, Tory started them counterclockwise around the perimeter, moving farther out before they turned west. Tory kept first squad up front, intending to do most of the surveying personally. Second squad followed fifty yards back as a covering force. Third and fourth squads were put out on the wing. They would lay most of the land mines and set a few additional booby traps if they could.

''Time to play ghosts,'' Tory whispered over the platoon channel. ''We want to see any Feddies, but we don't want them to see us. If we cause a ruckus, it'll spoil the captain's sleep.''

First squad's fire teams moved single file along parallel tracks about twenty yards apart. When they moved from the wild growth back into the parklike woods, the paths disappeared, but the fire teams maintained their separation. Alfie Edwards's fire team was on the outside of Tory's going around the circle, trying to move just a little faster so that they would stay roughly even with the other team.

The order was for radio silence, for minimal use of any electronics. Even though the communications channels were secure against eavesdroppers, transmissions scrambled so that they would sound like random noise to anyone not equipped with the proper codes, the fact of transmission could be detected. Two angles could give an exact location. Commonwealth detectors could determine position to within eighteen inches. The Marines assumed that the enemy's capabilities would be roughly comparable. Being pinpointed that closely by the enemy was not healthy.

Squad and fire team leaders maintained passive scans for enemy electronics, helmets and any snoops that might have been planted to give warning of Commonwealth movements. Moving slowly might give the I&R men time to avoid setting off a snoop's alarm.

Not spotting any enemy snoops, mines, or other surprises made both Tory and Alfie nervous. They rested their men for a couple of minutes before starting to loop around to the southwest. The platoon had been out for an hour and had covered slightly more than a mile of ground without detecting a single enemy snoop or mine.

*They can't be that careless, and I know* we're *not,* Alfie thought. *Unless they're shorter on supplies than we are, they should have taken routine precautions.* That the Feddies might be critically low on supplies sounded plausible, but Alfie determined to be even more careful, to be absolutely certain that he was not missing anything.

Alfie looked around, spotting his men. Just because the team was taking a break did not mean that they had clustered together or let down their guard. Everyone was looking out, covering all directions, rifles at the ready as they squatted or sat, each man next to a tree trunk, exposing as little of himself as possible. At night, they were not easy to spot. Field skins and helmets minimized any infrared signature. Unless they moved, they were very nearly invisible, even at fairly short range.

The night-vision elements in Commonwealth battle helmets painted the darkness in shades of green and gray. The infrared half of the system assigned brighter greens to warmer objects. The available-light half gave no false colors but was not as precise in definition. Blending two systems gave the wearer a better view than either system would alone, but at a cost. The hybrid images took time to get used to: the eyes had to learn how to bring the composite into sharp focus, and the brain had to be trained to interpret the images correctly. Still, once a Marine had experience using the systems, the combination gave him an advantage over Federation gear, which used only a single system.

Any advantage in combat meant fewer casualties.

Alfie did not give his men long to rest. It wouldn't do to get too far behind the others. He signaled his men up, then started off in a low crouch again. Each step was a deliberate process. He looked at the ground and the space just above it before he placed his foot, scanning for trip wires or any hint of a land mine or snoop. Then he looked around, his gaze higher, searching the forest for movement. The pace was slow, but not impossibly so. Even with all of his caution, Alfie could travel more than a mile in an hour, sometimes considerably more. Occasional periods of standing still, or squatting, broke the rhythm of the movement, made it less likely that an enemy would spot the motion and detect the patrol. *Break the pattern as often as possible* was drilled into recruits from the start.

A soft whistle on the radio stopped the platoon. The men froze in position, then slowly lowered themselves to the ground to wait for additional information or a signal to move again.

*Tory must have found Feddies to count,* Alfie thought. There was neither gunfire nor sentry challenge. The platoon was moving south now, about halfway through their circuit. *It's about time we found Feddies.* Alfie scanned the woods around him again. *Where the devil are they all?* he wondered. *We should be doing everything but tripping over the bastards.*

"Alfie." Even over the radio it was the barest whisper.

"Yeah?"

"Hold where you are. We may have a problem."

"You mean like where are the Feddies?"

"Yes. All I've seen are a few pickets, a thin line watching our blokes. Not more than a platoon altogether."

*They can't have pulled out,* Alfie thought. *A rear guard would be making noise to keep us from figuring it out.*

"Where do we look for them?" Alfie asked. The rest of the Federation troops, perhaps as much as a battalion of them, had to be somewhere in the vicinity, undoubtedly up to no good.

"I'm sending Will's squad farther out on the flank. The rest of us will wait where we are until they get in position."

"Just tell us when to start moving again."

Alfie used hand signs to tell the others in his fire team to find cover and wait. Their formation looked like a four-point star, the muzzle of a rifle marking each apex. Forty yards away, Kepner's fire team settled into a similar formation. They were close enough to see the nearest of the Federation pickets that were watching the rest of the Commonwealth Marines.

*Lying doggo and waiting again,* Geoffrey Dayle thought with something akin to disgust. *I could kill three of those Feddies before they even knew where I was coming from.* He was looking through his sights with an assist from his helmet electronics. The crosshairs were on the neck of one of the three Federation soldiers he could see, just below the rear lip of the man's helmet. Dayle was certain that he could at least sever the man's spinal cord with a single shot. At the slight angle available, the bullet might even bore up into his brain.

*Be a crime to let these bastards go,* Dayle thought, itching to pull the trigger. Even a four-man ambush might be enough to rout this lot, those who didn't fall in the first volleys. *They'd be looking the wrong way at first, and pretty soon, the rest of our blokes would have to join in from the other side. That would tell us where the rest of the Feddie bastards are hiding, in one big hurry.* The smile that spread over his face was grim, teeth bared, almost a death's-head look.

*Let's take them, Kep.* He projected the suggestion as if he believed that he might get Kepner to issue the order by telepathy. But Dayle knew better than to say anything, to actually mention it.

Sergeant Will Cordamon had hesitated before leading his squad out on the detour that Kepner had ordered, trying to puzzle out where the Feddies were most likely to be hiding. There was a limit to how much ground his squad could cover without holding up the rest of the patrol too long. He looked at his mapboard and held a brief, whispered conversation with his assistant squad leader. But the decision still came down to something not much more reasoned than a mental toss of a coin. It was all guesswork, with virtually nothing to suggest that they were even vaguely "intelligent" guesses. *Odds and evens.*

He looked at his assistant, shrugged, then pointed. The squad's fire teams separated, but stayed close enough to see—and support—each other. Cordamon's guess was that the bulk of the enemy might be camped near the next set of buildings that had not yet been destroyed. *Maybe the officers want a roof over their heads for the night,* was how he reasoned it.

He led his men to the edge of the clearing where the earlier fight had been, staying back in the trees.

"Bingo!" he whispered. He moved more behind a tree trunk. The Federation soldiers had moved rubble to form a low rampart between two of the buildings. Perhaps there was a similar barricade on the far side. He couldn't be certain. "Kep, we've got them. They've set up a defensive perimeter of their own. Spot my location on your mapboard, then look south-southwest, about 120 yards from us. Two buildings, maybe a third, with low ramparts set up connecting them. I can't see people, but they must be inside.''

''Hang on while I check with the captain,'' Tory said. It took two minutes before he came back on the channel. ''Plant your calling cards around the edge of the clearing, back toward our lines. We'll finish the circuit and make certain that there aren't any other surprises, then finish our job.''

Tory led his fire team well south, beyond the last Federation pickets, before they resumed their movement around the circle. The squads came closer together once they turned east, hurrying now that the main concentration of enemy troops had been spotted, but still careful, wary of the chance that there might be other outposts around. By the time they crossed the gully that held part of their own lines—the near end of the Commonwealth positions almost a half mile north of them—they had been out for nearly four hours. It was time for a rest.

''When we start up again, we'll strike off east-southeast,'' Tory told his noncoms. ''We'll go out a mile or so and find a place to hide until we're needed. We'll look for a place where we can get a little sleep while we're waiting.''

''Sounds good to me,'' Alfie said. ''Did the captain say what we're going to do about the Feddies?''

Tory shook his head. ''Until they get things straight skyside, let's just hope that they're content to let well enough be, on both sides.''

Second and third squads moved along the flanks when the platoon started moving again. Tory kept first squad in the lead. Fourth squad pulled rearguard duty. But Tory kept the squads closer together than he had before.

Alfie was on point, just in front of the others from his fire team. The platoon was back in wild growth, following animal trails through forest that sometimes closed in on both sides with tangled vines under trees whose lowest branches drooped near head level. After going about seven hundred yards, Alfie stopped suddenly and whistled softly over the platoon channel, freezing the rest of the men in position.

"Tory, I see a small fire up ahead. Looks like a camp-fire."

"Hang on. I'm coming up for a look."

Alfie melted into the underbrush off to his side. He kept the point of fire under observation. Distance was difficult to gauge without some reference point. He thought that it might be a hundred yards off, perhaps a little farther. After a minute, Tory slid into position next to Alfie, a hand on the shoulder Edwards's only warning.

"Not much of a fire," Tory whispered.

"Like I said, it looks like a campfire."

"Probably civilians, refugees."

"It's sure not something a pro would do around here," Alfie said. "Not unless he was out of his flippin' mind."

"Or he had a good reason to draw somebody's atten-tion."

"A trap?"

"The Feddies have tried just about everything else," Tory said. "Why not start a small fire to draw in any curious folks like us? They could pop us off out of the dark around it."

"So we don't just walk up and ask for a spot of tea. We wouldn't have done in any case."

"I'll send third and fourth squads around for a look-see while we wait here."

"At least we've got plenty of dark to work with," Alfie said after Tory had given the other squads their new orders. "Two, close to three hours."

"Let's hope we don't have to use it all here. I want us bundled up for the day well before first light."

The two men went silent, watching while third and fourth squads moved to flank the light and investigate. It was an-other thirty minutes before Tory received a call from Will Cordamon. The two squads had met on the far side of the fire.

"Civilians," Will reported. "No more than two or three families. Looks as if they've been here since the beginning. They've got a single sentry out. He's not very good."

"Stay where you are. We'll go in from this side first,

gradually. Wait for me to call you in. And stay put if I don't call,'' Tory said. He turned to Alfie. "I figure two of us go in first to make sure that their sentry doesn't panic and start shooting. Once we've had a chance to talk with them, we'll know whether or not to bring in the rest of the platoon.''

"You and me?''

Tory hesitated—that would not be proper procedure—but then he nodded. "You might get your chance to ask about that spot of tea after all.''

Alfie's frown was invisible, but the change in his voice was obvious. "More likely, they'll be asking what we can spare.''

Eric woke Reggie, then went straight to bed, exhausted. None of them had managed much sleep all night, even though the sounds of battle had faded away well before sunset. Salvation was finally near, *if* the Commonwealth forces won.

Reggie came out of the shelter stretching and yawning. He felt as if he hadn't slept at all, which was not too far from the truth. He seldom slept while Al was on watch, and now that Ted Brix was taking part in the rotation, Reggie seldom slept while Brix was their sentry either. Ted seemed to be completely out of his element, and neither Reggie nor Eric trusted the other man's ability to stand a watch without panicking unnecessarily, or missing something important. He tried, but simply did not have it in him.

After rubbing vigorously at his face for a time, Reggie felt as if he were at least halfway alert. He continued to stretch, walking around, trying to ease sore muscles and stiff joints. Gradually, he worked his way out farther from the small fire.

The fire had been a matter of debate the evening before. The group had kept at least one small fire alight continuously since first setting up camp, but they had considered dousing it the night before. With fighting going on little more than a mile away, they doubted the wisdom of drawing attention to themselves in such a bold manner. It wasn't as if they didn't have the means to light another fire after the danger went away. The fire, however, had become an important symbol to them. After a discussion that lasted for more than an hour, they had decided to keep it going. Reggie and Eric had been uncomfortable with that decision, but had given in to the rest.

*How much longer?* Reggie wondered as he moved out of the circle of firelight. He was on the south side of the camp, in the shadow of the rock outcropping and the shelters. He leaned back against the rock. He knew that their problems would not disappear magically just because the Commonwealth won the fight—if they did. There would be months, perhaps even years, of hardship and difficulty getting everything back to normal in Hawthorne, on Coventry. None of that seemed particularly critical at the moment.

*When the Commonwealth wins* was what Reggie thought of as crossing the major hurdle. Then they could move back home, back to where their homes had been, and start rebuilding. There might be a little left in the rubble that they could salvage. They could clear away the debris and start to build new homes. Surely the Commonwealth would help. They must have some kind of disaster relief program in place, or being put together. And once the government of Coventry was back in operation, they too should have ways to help, ways to help people help themselves.

He refused to consider the possibility that the Commonwealth might lose the fight for Coventry. *If this lot can't do the job, the king will send more men next time—more men, more ships, more weapons.* Sooner or later they would succeed. Coventry was too near the center of the Second Commonwealth for any alternative to success.

Reggie rested his head on the stone behind him. *I'm so bloody tired,* he thought, closing his eyes for just an instant. *The sooner this nightmare is over, the better it will be for all of us.* He took a deep breath, then suddenly opened his eyes and stood up, moving away from the stone. It would be far too easy to fall asleep that way, and it would be criminally foolish to fall asleep on watch now, with two armies so close.

*Get up, move around. Stir your stumps. Go splash some*

*water in your face.* Reggie growled at himself and walked to the little creek that supplied them with water. He knelt next to it and lay his shotgun aside, then started to splash water against his face with both hands. The water was frigid, but so much the better; it would keep him awake that much longer. Reggie shivered, then started to get back up.

He didn't make it to his feet. A knee was thrust into the middle of his back and a hand clamped itself over his mouth, pulling his head back so roughly that Reggie feared that his neck might snap. Out of the corner of his eye, he saw a dark boot step on the barrel of his shotgun, and he saw the muzzle of a rifle move toward his face.

# 19

**Reggie Bailey felt** an instant of utter terror that seemed to last for ages. Afterward, he told himself that it couldn't have taken more than ten seconds, but while it was happening, time had stretched out unbelievably for him. He was unable to move, scarcely able to breathe. His heart raced. It was not until that first moment of shock passed that he realized that there were two men, one behind him and another in front, off to the side. The second man, the one who had stepped on Reggie's shotgun, shifted position. He leaned closer. Reggie saw the blank mask of a helmet visor.

"It's okay," the anonymous face whispered. "We're Royal Marines." The pressure on Reggie's neck and back eased. The hand came away from his mouth. The weight came off of his back. The man standing behind even helped Reggie to his feet.

"Sorry about the rough treatment," the second man whispered. "We had to do this quietly."

Reggie moved his head gingerly from side to side, as if to assure himself that his neck had not been broken. At first, he felt no reaction to what the men had said. His fading terror insisted on precedence. Only as the adrenaline rush started to ebb could he comprehend what they had said: *Royal Marines.*

"You gave me a turn," he whispered, his voice hoarse, grating. Reggie cleared his throat, then swallowed. "I didn't hear you coming."

The Marines looked at each other. Reggie couldn't even guess what their expressions might be under those faceplates. Then one of them turned back toward Reggie. This time he raised his visor before he spoke.

"My name's Tory Kepner. There are still a lot of Feddies about. You folks haven't been very careful. That fire's a beacon, and a company of us—or Feddies—could have walked in on you without being seen or heard. Sorry, you're just not very good at this."

"I never thought I'd have to be, until those bastards came here." Reggie's voice came up a little, enough to make Kepner hold up a hand to shush him.

"Ease off, mate. Let's not tell the bastards that we're talking about them."

Reggie managed a thin smile. "The fight's not over then, is it?"

"Not by a long shot," Tory said. "Look, we need to talk with you, but first things first. I've got more of my lads spread out around your camp. I need to set up a few details. First off, how many of you are there here?"

Reggie hardly hesitated at all. New caution made him reluctant to reveal vital information, even to allies, but these men could find out for themselves easily enough. He told them, the names of the families, and the number of adults and children.

"We thought there might be more folks hanging close to town," the second Marine, Alfie Edwards, said.

"Most of the people from our neighborhood went farther east," Reggie said. "We only stayed this close because we had a woman ready to give birth. And there are several hundred more people a few miles off to the south. Most of those are from South York. They might be no more than four or five miles from here. The ones who went on east, I don't have any idea how far away they might be by now, or how many might be together."

"Time enough to worry about that later," Tory said. "Right now, I've got to get my lads situated before dawn."

"Just a second. You mean you're going to come in here with us?" Reggie asked.

"We'll be around you, but not right in your laps, I think.

Keep your camp as is. We'll stay out in the trees around you.''

"But if there's any fighting here . . .''

"Any fighting will be farther off. The whole point is that the Feddies don't know that we're out here, away from the rest of our chaps. Any fighting will be where we choose it to be, if the Feddies try to get cute and close in on the rest of our mates.''

"I'm still not so sure about this." Reggie frowned. "We've got women and children here.''

"We'll do everything we can to keep you safe," Tory promised. "If things do get to looking dicey, we'll move away, but I doubt that things will come to that. Listen, I've a wife and son of my own. I know how you feel, but, frankly, you're worrying at the wrong straw.''

Reggie hesitated a moment longer, then let out a long breath and nodded. "Maybe I can quit worrying about somebody sneaking up on me, at least. Fat lot of good it did to keep watch.''

"We're professionals. We spend a lot of time training for what we do.''

Tory got his people situated around the camp and set his half-and-half watches: half stayed on watch while the other half slept. Everyone got in a quick meal, the Marines sharing their field rations with the three families of refugees. Once the I&R men moved out to their positions, they virtually disappeared from the sight of the civilians, even though they did not move too far from the camp. During the meal, and for a short time afterward, Tory questioned the civilians, trying to learn everything he could about their experiences since the invasion, and anything they could tell him about Federation operations.

"Once we get a chance to get back to the rest of our blokes, and get some sort of organization working, we'll have a medical orderly check out you and the infant," Tory promised Anna. "Seems you're both doing right well for the circumstances.''

•   •   •

"I wish I could go out and fight with them," Al Bailey told his parents and the others after Tory Kepner left to take his place in the perimeter. All thirteen civilians were crowded into the center shelter. That could not last. It was impossibly crowded, but they had to talk before they separated.

"Don't even think about it," Reggie said. "They're so good you wouldn't believe it." It did rankle that they had caught him so easily, that he had not even suspected that there was anyone around before he was gripped from behind and found himself helpless.

"I'm worried," Ida said. "All of those Marines around us. They still might draw trouble. We could get caught in the middle of something horrible."

"If trouble comes, I'd rather have thirty Royal Marines around than have to deal with it just by ourselves," Eric said. "Besides, this is our contact with the outside. Proof that there's someone here to help us."

Ted Brix held his wife's hand tightly. Marines close or far away, he was still frightened. But he had learned to try to conceal his constant fear. He did not think that he was especially successful with that deceit though. He had never managed to fool himself.

Lorna looked only briefly at her husband. She was frightened as well, but not nearly so patently as Ted. Keeping Helene from being totally terrified every waking and sleeping minute had been her mother's primary concern these past weeks. The girl had nightmares. At least she no longer woke up screaming in the night, not since they had been allowed to join these other families.

"These shelters will offer some protection if there is fighting nearby," Lorna said softly. They had all taken to speaking in little more than whispers since the Marines had come to surround them. "I mean, it would take explosives to bring them down, and those Marine chaps aren't likely to let Feddies get close enough for that."

"I'm more concerned about how long this, ah, situation might continue," Eric said. "If it wasn't for the Marines, and the Feddies as well, we'd go out hunting this morning.

We've still got meat enough to last through today, but . . ."

"With all that fighting yesterday, we'd likely have to go too far to find game anyway," Reggie said, dismissing that worry. "If we can't go back into town soon, I'm afraid we'll have to move our camp anyway—unless the Marines have enough provisions to keep us going."

"One day at a time," Ida urged. "There are Commonwealth people here now. They won't let us starve." *I hope,* she thought.

Captain McAuliffe forced himself to eat a meal pack. It wasn't that he wasn't hungry. His stomach had been growling for hours. He had even dreamed of food, during the brief intervals when he had managed to doze. But despite his hunger, he had no appetite. The field rations tasted like soggy cardboard, with no taste at all, difficult to swallow. But it was fuel. He sat in the bottom of the gully and ate methodically. He could at least show his men that he was not off his feed.

The Feddies showed no signs of coming out of their defensive perimeter. The few pickets who had been left to harass the Commonwealth Marines had pulled back before dawn. McAuliffe had sent a platoon from Delta company to take out those Feddies and found them missing.

News from the fleet remained spotty, and not at all reassuring. The opposing battle groups were still playing their game of hide-and-seek, ducking in and out of Q-space, staying around no longer than they had to in order to keep the other side from doing anything decisive.

*We need to do something on the ground to break the stalemate,* McAuliffe told himself. He had slept poorly, waking—or so it seemed—every ten minutes. There had been good reasons for some of those interruptions. The reports from the I&R platoon had been vital, and the news from Delta's platoon, the one looking for the Feddie pickets.

*They evidently don't want to attack us, and we're not all that keen on attacking them until we can get air cover or more men on the scene.* McAuliffe finished his food and set the empty carton aside. Neither side wanted to take the risks of attacking good defensive positions without some compelling edge.

*What would make me leave a good defensive position?* He thought through as many possibilities as he could come up with quickly. The basic answer was obvious. *If my defensive position suddenly looked less safe than the alternatives. So how can I make the Feddies come out in the open?*

There were ways that might work—if not an infinite number, still more than any competent commander should need to choose from. But most of those possibilities relied on resources that were not available to McAuliffe. None of the regiment's heavy guns were on the ground. The small stock of antiaircraft missiles would be unlikely to suffice, and expending them would leave the companies vulnerable to air attack. The chances of getting Spacehawks in to attack the buildings and the breastworks the Feddies had erected seemed almost as remote as the fleet in Q-space. Almost, but not quite. It would take quite a bit of arguing to convince CIC to provide them.

An hour later David Spencer was ordered to the command post. When he arrived, he found Captain Asa Ewing of Delta Company and his lead sergeant, Bandar Jawad, already with McAuliffe. Ewing and Jawad had come over to First Battalion from Fourth sixteen months earlier, while the regiment was being rebuilt after a costly campaign on the frontier world of Buchanan.

"You wanted me, sir?" David asked.

"Actually, Bandar wants you," McAuliffe said. "Sit down."

Spencer sat on the ledge that had been hacked out of the side of the gully.

"Normally, what we're doing would belong to the I&R lads, but they're already out, and I don't want to use them for anything but what they're already assigned to do," McAuliffe said, obviously for Spencer's benefit. "I asked Captain Ewing to cut loose two platoons for a special operation. He decided that Jawad should command that operation, and

Bandar asked for you to come along—ah, as a sort of technical advisor.''

"Your kind of ropey-do, David," Bandar said with a nod.

"What do you have in mind, sir?" Spencer asked, concentrating on McAuliffe yet.

"We're going to get a quick in-and-out by a pair of Spacehawks. They're going to target our group of Feddies, try to make things too hot for them to stay in that redoubt they've fashioned. I want to add to the confusion from the ground as well, do what we can to cut down their numbers without dragging all three companies out of our positions here."

"So you want sixty blokes to make the Feddies think we're the whole lot?"

"More or less," McAuliffe admitted. "If the bird-boys do their job smartly, the Feddies should be too damn busy for head counts. Make sure they can't regroup easily. You and the bird-boys get them reeling, I'll cut loose reinforcements to help finish the job, but I'll be relying on reports from you and Bandar. It will be a sticky place for mistakes."

David finally looked at Bandar, stared at him for a moment. The two nodded and smiled. They had known each other through most of their careers in the Royal Marines. Bandar had several years time-in-grade over David—seniority as a company lead sergeant.

"We'll give it a proper go, sir," Spencer said when he looked at the captain again. "When does the Navy strike up the band for us?"

"You've got forty-seven minutes to get into position. Now, here's what I want you to do . . ."

"You've been out of I&R so long, I thought you might like a taste of old times," Bandar said as he and David followed Captain Ewing back to Delta.

David snorted. "I've had more than a taste of old times here, but since you obviously think you need a specialist to keep your knickers out of the fire, glad to oblige."

"We're not so bad as all that. About half the squad leaders in first and second platoon have been through the two-week I&R familiarization course. They know the basics.''

"Two weeks is just enough time for them to recognize what mistakes they've just made while they're getting the chop.''

The two platoons chosen already knew that they were going out. The platoon sergeants, squad and assistant squad leaders gathered around Bandar and David to hear what few details they had for the operation.

"We're going to play it by ear," Jawad said. "What we do depends on how successful the lads in the birds are, and how the Feddies respond to that. Lead Sergeant Spencer here has bags of experience at this kind of go.''

"We want to make the Feddies think we're all three companies. That means we expend a lot of ammunition, and we don't let them see enough of us to get an accurate count. That means keep your flaming heads down and stay off the radio except when it's absolutely necessary. It means fire and maneuver, and it means being ready to take advantage of any break that comes our way," David said. "We raise what hell we can and try to confuse the devil out of them so that we can fry the whole lot, or serve 'em up for the rest of our lads to finish them off.''

"Do we tie them up in pretty bows?" one of the assistant squad leaders asked, earning a hearty laugh from his comrades.

"The admiral forgot to send the ribbon down for that," David said before Bandar could reprimand the wag. "Besides, I haven't the time to teach you lot how to tie a pretty bow.''

Bandar growled, then said, "The closest any of this lot is likely to come to a pretty bow is the hangman's noose. Now, we've got no more time to waste. We have a right piece of ground to cover before the birds make their run.''

Jawad traveled with first platoon, Spencer with second. By the time they reached their positions, the two platoons were spread across a five-hundred-yard front, curving slightly around the Federation perimeter, and two hundred yards out from the walls. If they got any closer, line Marines would be too apt to give themselves away. They settled in, excavating shallow trenches behind tree trunks or bushes. The line stretched from the wild growth into the more park-like area of trees.

"We got here just in time," Bandar said over a private link to David. "Captain Ewing says the birds are on their way down now."

"Good enough," David replied. "I hate long waits."

# 20

**The animal rose** so close, and moved so quickly, that Patrick Baker nearly fired from pure reflex, from fear. He pushed over on his side and brought his rifle up before he realized that it was only some small antelope or deer, not more than two feet tall. Baker slumped forward and closed his eyes. His heart was pounding so riotously that he thought it must be audible to the men on either side of him. While the animal bounded off toward the camp of the civilians, Baker could do nothing but clutch at his chest and try to get his heart rate back down. He kept his eyes closed for more than a minute. The thick feeling in his throat might have been his heart. He felt himself shaking.

"Keep your eyes front!" Tory Kepner slapped the side of Baker's helmet. With Patrick's visor down, Tory couldn't see that his eyes had even been closed. "It was just a deer. Don't fall apart. Look for what startled it."

Baker was just starting to roll back into his proper position when there was a single shot behind him, and he jumped so spastically that he might have been the target.

Tory didn't say anything about that reaction. He just got up and scurried toward the camp in the center of the I&R perimeter. He had recognized the sound of a shotgun, and had a good idea what had happened—confirmed as soon as he got to the clearing. Reggie Bailey was standing over the dead deer. He looked at the Marine with a sheepish expression on his face.

"Sorry. I got carried away. I saw meat and didn't think about the noise until I heard the shot. We were worried that having you around would drive the game away."

It wasn't so much what Reggie said that calmed Tory, but just the time he took saying it. "Okay, maybe no harm done, except to our nerves. We're far enough away from the Feddies that maybe they didn't even hear it. Just . . . no more, please?"

"I'll try to remember." Reggie felt very foolish. "It's just that the sight of dinner popping straight into camp . . ."

"Maybe I should have told you this already, but things should be popping over that way in a few minutes. We've got a couple of aircraft coming in to attack the Feddies, then our blokes will try to finish them off. It's going to get noisy, and we'll have to be ready for anything that might happen."

Reggie's expression turned worried. In the shelter doorways, several of the others mirrored that look. They had peeked out to see what the shooting was about, and had stayed to listen to Kepner.

"You think the fighting might come this way?" Reggie asked.

"Probably not, but I can't guarantee that it won't," Tory said. "If the Feddies start in this direction, we'll be off out to turn them back toward the rest of our lot. That's why we're here. But, for now . . ." He stopped and raised a hand to keep any of the others from speaking while he listened to Alfie on the radio. Alfie's report took only a few seconds.

"There are civilians coming in from the south, maybe a half dozen, all men," Tory said.

"Must be from that South York lot," Reggie said. "If they heard any of the shooting yesterday, they might well have sent a few men up to check it out."

"My lads have them now. We'll know soon enough." After just a few more seconds, and another quick report from Alfie, Tory nodded. "You had it right, Mr. Bailey. At least, that's who they say they are. Will you be able to identify them?"

"There were only the two we talked with I could be sure of, but if they're Coventrians, what difference does it make? I doubt any of those Feddie blokes could mask their accents and pass for locals."

Tory smiled. "I guess it's not likely they'd try. Anyway,

we'll see in a moment. We're bringing them here.''

Two I&R men brought the newcomers into camp. Reggie relaxed almost at once. The first of them was Noel Wittington. Noel and his companions came to a stop facing Reggie and Tory. Wittington seemed much tenser than he had been the day before.

"I know him. He did most of the talking."

"We heard fighting and figured that it had to mean that there were Commonwealth people here," Noel said. "We had to know what was going on. I tried to get out alone, but that didn't work." He gestured to his companions.

"You'd have been better off staying away until the fighting is over, and it's going to resume very shortly now," Tory said.

Noel shook his head. "It's a miracle anyone would stay behind. Everyone thinks this means we'll get to go back to our homes—or to what's left of them—right away. If I hadn't come with a few others, you might have had a hundred wandering around up here in small groups."

"A hundred? I understood you had four hundred with you," Tory said.

"A bit over four hundred, I think," Noel agreed. "I can't give you an exact count. We picked up a few more after we turned south yesterday, people who were heading back in toward Hawthorne from the east. I gather that things are getting pretty rough for the lot who went out that way."

"There might well be several thousand out there, somewhere close," Reggie said when Tory looked to him. "That's just from this end of town. The population of Hawthorne was over 25,000. I guess they've pretty much all been chased out."

"Not all," Tory said. "There were still some around when we arrived yesterday. There are still some areas of your town that haven't been torched. We're trying to save what we can."

"It won't be long before we get action, Kep," Alfie Edwards said. "What do we do with these blokes?"

"You'll have to stay here for now," Tory said, looking at Wittington. "We can't have you roaming about while the

fighting is going on. You'll be safer here. After that . . ."
He shrugged, then gestured for Alfie and his companion,
Willie Hathaway, to get back to their positions.

"Just keep down, stay put, and keep out of the way until
this is over," Tory said before he left the civilians. "We
don't want any avoidable casualties." *My lads or you lot,*
he thought as he started back toward his own position in the
perimeter.

The two Spacehawks came in directly from space, on a
hot course that kept both planes at hypersonic speeds
throughout their attack and recovery. The leading edges of
their wings, and all of the forward surfaces, glowed from
the heat. On this kind of sortie, the skin of a Spacehawk
would approach critical temperatures, but the vectors had
been chosen so that these two would not surpass design
tolerances.

Their target acquisition radar locked onto the buildings
and ramparts while the fighters were still more than a hundred miles away—most of that distance vertical. The pilots
armed and programmed their missiles. The fighters were
coming in much too fast to use their cannon for strafing. If
they fired soon enough to hit the targets, they might tear
themselves apart, running into their own bullets. But the
missiles were expected to suffice. Each Spacehawk would
launch six, coordinated for time on target. Barring malfunction, all twelve should hit within a tenth of a second. Three
would be aimed at each of the two larger buildings, two at
the smallest, and the other four would seek the ramparts that
connected the buildings.

As soon as the missiles had been launched, with the
Spacehawks still more than twenty miles from the target,
the pilots started to pull their craft back up, going through
the tightest curve that they could stand without passing out
from the g-load. The missiles continued on their own, each
locked onto its target, needing no further guidance from outside. Buildings could not take evasive actions to escape the
weapons. Cameras in the noses of the missiles relayed what
they were seeing to CIC aboard *Sheffield*. CIC in turn re-

layed some of that video to Captain McAuliffe on the ground.

The sound of the two hypersonic fighters reached Spencer and the men from the two Delta company platoons virtually at the same time as the missile explosions. The Federation troops in the target zone had no more warning. The explosions came too close together for human ears to separate the individual strikes or tote up the numbers. To Spencer and the men with him, the entire Federation compound seemed to erupt at once. The two taller buildings appeared to rise off the ground and then collapse. The Marines could not see the third building, since it was lower and concealed from their view by the other two. And the hits against the stone and plascrete breastworks that the Feddies had thrown up passed almost without notice in the greater destruction in the center of the compound.

*How could anyone survive that kind of hell?* David asked himself, though he did not doubt that there would be significant numbers of survivors, perhaps even inside the collapsed buildings. He had seen men come out of impossible situations too often before.

"Looks as if the fly-guys did the job proper for us," Bandar Jawad said on a link to David and the platoon sergeants. "Let's see if we can take care of the leftovers."

"We can't do that from this far out," David said. "After the first shock passes, they'll be back behind whatever cover they can find."

"You want to lead your platoon around on the left?" Bandar asked. "You should be able to get within seventy yards of the end over that way without exposing yourselves overmuch."

"We're on our way." David got his men moving as the first Federation soldiers started to stumble out of the smoke and dust. Many appeared to be staggering blindly, unaware of where they were going, or where they were coming from, too anxious to get away from what was behind them to worry about what might be in front. When Jawad's platoon started firing at the easy targets, the Feddies kept moving about for a time. None seemed to notice that they were under fire, unable to hear much because of the shock of the explosions, their wits not back to anything near functional levels. Many were wounded, dripping blood or worse. At least a half dozen of the Feddies were missing hands or arms.

David led Delta's second platoon at something near an all-out run, taking advantage of the Feddie confusion to get into position as quickly as possible. A few of the men tried to fire on the run, wanting part of the action. David stopped that. "Don't let them know we're here!" he snapped. "You're just giving them a trail to follow once they start thinking again."

Two minutes of running put the platoon in the nearest good cover. Some of the Federation soldiers were starting to show some awareness of where they were and what was happening. Those who could moved back into the rubble, looking for protection from the rifle fire coming from Bandar's platoon. The smoke and dust of the explosions were settling. David had a clear view into the remains of the target zone.

"Grenades, then rifle fire. Hit them hard." By the time he got the second sentence out, the grenadiers were already at work, and the rifle fire started before the first of the RPGs dropped in among the Feddies. David started firing as well, trying to pick individual targets rather than simply spray the compound. At the same time, he linked to Captain McAuliffe.

"I think they're where you want them, sir. Those birdmen did a real job, and the Feddies haven't got themselves together."

"I just heard the same thing from Jawad," McAuliffe said. "We're ready to move here. I'm going to commit everyone."

It took another twenty minutes before the rest of the three companies got into position. By then, the Federation survivors were giving a much better account of themselves. Their numbers might be seriously diminished, but those who were left fought on with determination.

After several minutes of long-range fire, Captain McAuliffe decided that it was time to move in and take the Feddies head-on. The three Marine companies advanced along half of the Feddie perimeter, fire and maneuver, by platoon, squad, and fire team—one fourth of the men moving while the rest provided covering fire to suppress Feddie gunfire and make it less accurate.

Spencer had no opportunity to get back to his own company. He moved with Delta's second platoon. They pushed forward into the open, into the most deadly variety of infantry combat, a frontal assault on strong defensive positions. Men fell around David. Medical orderlies came up from behind, as quickly as they could, to tend the wounded. The dead would have to wait.

As the Commonwealth Marines approached the Federation perimeter, the defenders pulled back from the line, first to the rubble of the three buildings, and then to the far side of the compound, the side that was not being attacked. At the far wall, they stopped again, concentrating their fire, forcing the Commonwealth force to stop as well.

During that brief halt, Spencer worked his way back to his own company and went to Captain McAuliffe.

"I didn't think they'd be able to muster up this much fight, sir," David said, almost an apology.

"I didn't expect a walkover," McAuliffe said. It was only then that Spencer noticed that the captain had been hit. There was blood on his left leg.

"I'll get a medical orderly for you, sir," David said.

"It's not all that urgent. I've already slapped a patch on it. There are too many lads hurt worse than I am. Have you been able to estimate how many Feddies are left?"

"I'd have to say at least two companies, maybe more, and they haven't shown any hint of being short of ammunition."

McAuliffe grunted. "I wish we could get those Spacehawks back for another run, but we can't, not anytime soon."

"If the Feddies keep pulling back, there are houses that haven't been burned along the road. They could keep us busy, wear us down."

"You think Kepner's lads could make the difference, coming in from behind?"

David hesitated, wanting to make certain that he gave his best opinion. "They'd have to hit from the flank, sir, not from behind. If they came up in back, it's more likely that the Feddies would roll straight over them and still get free of us. And I&R must be a good two miles off. It will take them time to get in position to do any good at all."

"That's what I thought. We'll move them in halfway, then try to push the Feddies ourselves."

"Toward our I&R platoon?"

"Past them, anyway. It would still be best to have Kepner hit them from the side."

Tory whistled over the platoon channel, then got everyone up and moving. There was no time to go back and explain to the refugees what was going on, not even time to tell them, again, to stay put. *Just have to hope they've got the sense to stay clear of this,* he thought, not with any great optimism.

The I&R platoon moved smartly covering the first two thirds of its route. The chances of coming across enemy soldiers in that stretch were minimal. It was only when the platoon approached the position where the captain wanted them to set up their ambush that Tory slowed the pace and spread the platoon out in a double skirmish line.

They were beyond the last area of larger, public buildings. Rows of houses stretched out along both sides of a road, starting just to the left of the positions the I&R platoon took. They moved to the verge between forest and the back garden of the nearest houses, along a low stone wall a hundred yards from the road. They would have a clear field of fire if the Feddies came along that road or through the tended yards behind the houses.

"There might still be civilians in these houses," Alfie said. "Remember what the Baileys said? The Feddies were only chasing people out just before they torched the houses."

"We can't do anything about it if there are," Tory replied. "Even if we had time, we couldn't take the chance of trying to warn them. There might as easily be Feddies hiding in the houses. As long as any civilians stay inside and keep down, they should do okay."

"How long do we have before it starts?" Alfie asked.

"We might have Feddies in our laps in three or four minutes. Our lads have started pressing them again. See to your fire team. You'll be closest when they do show up. Don't let the Feddies see you before we start shooting."

All of the men could hear the increase in the volume of gunfire. Soon, most could tell that the noise was moving closer. The Feddies might be retreating, but it was no rout. They were withdrawing under discipline. Tory heard the same message from Spencer. The Feddies were making a fighting retreat and doing a professional job of it. Spencer's estimate of the number of Feddies increased as well, from two companies to perhaps three.

*That could mean odds of fifteen to one, three companies against one platoon,* Tory thought. Those odds disregarded the rest of the Marines chasing the enemy, but for a few minutes, those other Marines wouldn't count—not for Tory and his men. For those minutes, it would be the I&R platoon against all of the Feddies who could take them under fire. *Alfie might say those are the right odds, but I'd rather they were turned around.*

"We'll hold off as long as we possibly can before we start our fireworks," Tory told his platoon. "I don't want this to be our last stand, and if the Feddies turn on us before the rest of our lads are close enough to get a piece of it, that's just what it could be."

*We'll make it their last stand, not ours,* Geoffrey Dayle promised himself. His position was at the left end of the fire team. He had two spare magazines for his rifle laid out at his side, within easy reach. That way he wouldn't lose more than a second each time he had to reload. While there was time to waste with idle thought, he wished that he had a grenade launcher. That could inflict so many more casualties at once. A rifle limited him to one per shot, at best. A grenade could drop Feddies by the squad with a little luck. *I'll do what I can, make every bullet do its duty.*

Ramsey Duncan was at the other end of the fire team, just to the right of Tory Kepner. The Ram was the pivot. The squad's second fire team was beyond him in line. Duncan checked to make certain that his needler was charged and had a first can of needles loaded. Even without orders, he had his bayonet fixed. Ramsey liked the balance of his needler with the extra weight on the muzzle end.

Between Dayle and Kepner, Patrick Baker lay behind his section of the garden wall clutching his rifle in both hands, so tightly that he might have been trying to strangle the weapon. After sliding, almost falling, into position, Baker had had no conscious thoughts at all. Fear had gripped him so tightly that he could scarcely have claimed to be conscious of anything, even the fear. His fear was paralytic, and this time he did not retain even enough awareness to try to fight it.

"Baker!" Patrick did not hear Kepner's shout in his ear, even amplified by his helmet. Voices simply could not penetrate the wall that terror had erected around his mind.

"Baker!" This time Kepner put a boot against Baker's shoulder and gave a rough shove. "Damn it, Baker, look at me!" Tory moved closer, set his rifle aside, rolled Baker over onto his back, and lifted his visor. Patrick's eyes were open, locked into a fixed stare that showed no emotion, no awareness at all.

Softly, Tory whispered, "Damn," under his breath. He pulled Baker's helmet off. Patrick showed no reaction at all. He might have been dead, but Tory knew that he wasn't. It was Baker's vital signs that had caused Kepner to call him. His pulse had been racing erratically, and his breathing had gone very shallow and slow, less than half of what it should have been.

Tory switched channels on his radio. "Alfie, we've got a problem here." Edwards looked along the fence toward Kepner. "Baker's frozen solid. Can't get a damn thing out of him."

Alfie crawled back from the wall, just enough to let him

see Baker's supine form down the line. *Poor sod. I knew he was scared, but I never thought he'd go like this.* "Not much we can do just now, is there?" he asked.

"Not if I can't make him snap out before the shooting starts," Tory said. "What worries me is that we might have to leave him behind if we have to move fast once the Feddies get close to us."

Alfie didn't respond. If Baker had to be left behind, so be it. There might not be any choice.

"I know," Tory said, as if he could read Alfie's thoughts. "Get ready. We've run out of time." He slid the helmet back on Baker's head and slapped the visor into place before he grabbed his rifle and moved back to his position at the wall.

The first Feddies had come into view. They were too far away to be an immediate threat, and there was no indication that the first group, about a platoon in strength, had spotted the ambush. Their attention was directed the other way, at the Marines who were pursuing them.

"Kepner? McAuliffe. You see them yet?"

"Aye, sir. The first are still more than two hundred yards from our location, moving slowly. They haven't spotted us yet."

"How many?"

"I can only see about thirty. They're off the road, but in front of the houses, on our side."

"Let that lot go past if you can. We're more interested in the main body. Don't spring your trap too early."

"As long as the first lot doesn't see us, no problem, sir."

Tory switched channels to warn his men to lay low and let the first group of Feddies pass unmolested. He pulled down lower behind the wall. While he waited, Tory stared at Patrick Baker, on the ground a couple of feet away. Baker did not look as if he had moved a muscle during the interval. Tory couldn't see Baker's eyes through the tinted shield of the visor, but there was certainly no overt sign that the private had come out of his catatonic state.

*I've lost a man and the fight hasn't even begun yet,* Tory thought. He felt an edge of annoyance that he couldn't completely suppress. He knew that fear like Baker's was beyond questions of bravery and cowardice, but sometimes it took hard thinking to remember that. If they got off of Coventry alive, Baker would be invalided out of the Royal Marines. He would receive whatever treatment he required, but he would never be trusted in a combat unit again. *The question is, will we get off of Coventry?* Tory thought.

Alfie whistled softly over his private link to Tory. "Here come the rest," he said when Kepner glanced his way. "Spread clean across, both sides of the road, and leapfrogging themselves."

Tory raised up just enough to look for himself. A two-second scan gave him enough information. He pulled his head down. The Feddies were moving in three sections, one centered on the road but spilling off into the front yards on either side. The other sections were moving behind the houses, one section on this side of the road, the last on the other. Each section was moving in two lines. One covered the other as it retreated ten to fifteen yards, then they switched roles.

"We'll take them just before the lead elements get level with us," Tory told the platoon. "We want to be shooting at their backs the first volley. When they get fifty yards from Alfie, I'll give the order to fire. Concentrate on the blokes who are closest to us. They're the ones we have to worry about first."

On the private channel, he told Alfie, "Give me the word when you've got them fifty yards off. Use your range finder."

"The nearest are seventy yards now, Kep," Alfie replied. "It won't be long. Two more jumps."

"Just tell me when." Tory switched channels to tell Captain McAuliffe that they were about to open fire.

"Fine," McAuliffe said. "We're close enough to make sure they don't have time to think about dancing on you for long."

*Dancing on our bodies, you mean,* Tory thought. He raised up to look. It was time. He brought his rifle into position. He had scarcely settled in when Alfie said, "Fifty yards."

Tory gave the order.

Geoffrey Dayle could claim the first shot, if by no more than two or three one hundredths of a second. He had been waiting, finger on trigger, for more than a minute before the order came. He had been tracking his first target for half of that time. Totally focused on what he was doing, Dayle felt no more tension than he would have on the practice range on Buckingham. The figures going down might have been cutout silhouettes instead of human beings. Dayle was not really conscious that he was counting shots, or just how closely his shots and hits matched. Nor was he really aware of what the Feddies were doing. He was through his first magazine before any of them seemed to figure out that they had been taken under fire from the flank, from up close, as well as the fire they had been receiving from the north. Even then, there wasn't a lot that the Federation soldiers could do, those who were closest, those who did not have houses to duck behind. They were caught out in the open with no cover but mown grass.

Most of those Feddies caught went prone and tried to return fire. A few tried to run for the cover of the nearest houses. One man charged directly at the I&R platoon, firing his rifle at full automatic. He took six running steps before several bullets and a spray from a needle gun brought him down.

The Feddies had little time to respond, but Tory was surprised at how quickly they did adapt. The response was not one of the possibilities he had imagined. The middle section of troops stopped long enough to provide covering fire for those who were trapped in the open east of the road. Those who could make it out of the close-in killing zone did. Then all of the Feddies changed course, moving obliquely, retreating from both threats, southeast, pulling away from the road and going behind the houses on the west side.

Tory reported that news to Captain McAuliffe.

"Make sure they keep moving," the captain said. "Don't worry about fighting them, just move along your side of the road and watch them. We'll push in behind for a bit yet. We want to get them clear of the houses that are still standing, far enough off that they can't start burning again.''

"I've got one serious casualty here, sir. He went catatonic several minutes before the Feddies showed.''

There was a slight pause before McAuliffe replied. "I'll get a medical orderly over as quickly as possible. Put a green flag on his position marker. You'll have to leave him behind. I want you close enough to those Feddies to nudge them along if they start coming back toward the road.''

"Aye, sir. We're moving out now.''

# 21

**For perhaps three** minutes, alone in the privacy of his day cabin aboard *Sheffield*, Admiral Paul Greene allowed himself to feel unbounded optimism—a most unfamiliar emotion for him. The half dozen firefights in progress on the surface of Coventry were no worse than standoffs, and in two skirmishes his Marines were clearly having the better of it. Evasive fleet maneuvers were continuing over Coventry without any great damage to any of his ships. Casualties among the Marines on the ground and the shuttle and fighter pilots were . . . statistically acceptable. But the real reason for the brief surge of confidence was the message rocket that had arrived twenty minutes before.

Greene had read through the one action message among the data that the MR had carried. He still had that message on the complink screen set in his chart table. The Fourth Regiment of Royal Marines and its transport's escort ships were finally on their way to Coventry. Their estimated time of arrival was less than six hours away.

*We can maintain the status quo for six hours,* Greene thought. With the boost in firepower the incoming ships would add, the combined fleets should be able to land the Fourth Regiment without unacceptable casualties, and maybe even force the Federation battle group to flee the system. *That* would spell the end of the Federation ground forces. Together, the Second and Fourth Regiments could mop up any residual opposition, even if the enemy still had numerical superiority. The Feddies might even surrender quickly once they knew that they had been abandoned.

*Two or three days for the mop-up. Then we can concen-*

*trate on collecting the locals who have been made homeless. Start the ball rolling on their relief.* Thinking of the problems that lay ahead for Coventry started the erosion of Greene's optimism. CIC's latest estimate was that seventy percent of the homes and vehicles had been destroyed, and more than eighty-five percent of the public buildings. It would take massive help from Buckingham and the other major worlds of the Commonwealth to repair all of the damage—an expensive and time-consuming operation, one that the government was ill-equipped to handle in addition to the military expenses of the war.

Greene leaned back in his seat and stared at the overhead. Fire had—somehow—become the Federation's weapon of choice of late. On Reunion, a world with only a few tens of thousands of residents and a quarter million soldiers in for training, fire had been launched by missiles shot in from near space, setting off a firestorm the likes of which had never been seen before.

The admiral closed his eyes. *At least they didn't try that here. They might have killed most of the residents.* That sort of catastrophe would almost certainly have been more than the Commonwealth could survive politically. There would have been massive defections, and that would have forced surrender, and the end of the Second Commonwealth. Even without widespread civilian deaths on Coventry, there might still be major repercussions.

The full extent of damages on Coventry was hard to imagine. Seventy percent of the homes destroyed translated to perhaps thirty-five million people left homeless, with winter coming and many of them already fighting off starvation any way that they could.

*First steps.* Greene straightened up in his chair and tried to concentrate on the most immediate concerns. CIC and his own staff had started putting together provisional plans for the interim relief needed on Coventry. Every surviving food replicator on the planet would have to be put into constant use, and all of the refugees would have to be guided to areas where relief could be accomplished most efficiently.

Buckingham was already trying to organize the second

stage, the transfer of industrial replicators, not just for food but also for building materials, clothing, furniture, and everything else that the Coventrians would not be able to make for themselves until the reconstruction was well under way. Months, years, would pass before everything could be finished, and the local residents would still have to do most of the work. The Marines certainly couldn't stay to do it all.

Greene stretched and closed his eyes again. The battle group was forty-five light-minutes from Coventry, safely hidden from the Federation ships by the bulk and emissions of Coventry's sun. He could afford to relax for a few minutes. *First things first. We have to win the battle before the rebuilding starts.* The battle won, prisoners lifted off-planet, the refugees fed and given what services the fleet and two regiments of Marines could provide to get them through the first days and weeks.

Greene yawned. Relaxation was one thing, but he had been critically short of sleep ever since arriving over Coventry. He had managed no more than the occasional catnap, never more than an hour or so at a time. He hadn't been out of his clothes in six days, except for the few minutes needed for a quick shower and a change to a fresh uniform once or twice a day.

"I can't sleep now." He got to his feet to stretch and pace around his chart table. It would be another six hours before the Fourth's battle group arrived. The smart thing to do would be to get well away from Coventry for at least five of those hours, hide in Q-space long enough to let his crews get some sleep. Get everyone up to a slightly higher level of alertness and efficiency before the big fight came.

"Zombies don't fight smart," he muttered.

He took another lap around the chart table while he thought through his options. Knowing that he was tired and not completely on form, he forced himself to look closely at each possibility. When he finally sat down again, he felt moderately refreshed and slightly more alert. He signaled for the flag operations officer and gave him new orders for the battle group.

"We'll jump six light-hours farther out on this side of

the system to wait. To make sure we don't miss anything, we'll use the two supply ships for observation. Split the time between them. If they see anything, or learn anything that we need to know, they beat it out to the rendezvous point. My major concern is that the Feddies might bring their battlecruisers in and launch air strikes against our lads on the ground. Other than that, we'll stand down as far as possible, rest up for the big push when our reinforcements arrive.''

The operations officer repeated what the admiral had said to make certain that he had everything correct, then left to transmit the orders to all of the ships in the task force.

Greene allowed himself to relax again. As soon as the battle group made the Q-space transit, he would see if he could get a few consecutive hours of sleep.

After the Marines broke off their pursuit of the Federation soldiers south of Hawthorne, the I&R platoon kept pace with the retreating Feddies while staying out of sight. The Feddies picked up their speed as soon as they were able to stop looking rearward every second and fighting as they moved. After an hour, they took a short break. It appeared that the rest was more to give them time to treat casualties than anything else. The break only lasted ten minutes. Then they started moving again, southwest, away from the last houses along the road.

''This is far enough for us,'' Tory said. ''The captain just wanted us to make sure they moved on to where they've got no houses to burn.''

''Are we in any hurry to get back?'' Alfie asked.

''We've got Baker back there,'' Tory said. ''But I guess we're due a few more minutes to rest.''

Alfie got down and stretched out on his stomach in the grass. He would have preferred to lie on his back, but that would have meant stripping off his field pack, and that was simply too much bother.

''Any idea what comes next?'' he asked.

Tory sat down next to Alfie. ''Not a glimmer. We don't know what the Feddies will do. I rather think we'll get put to work helping the locals if the fighting's over for us.'' He hesitated. "Not that I really think we've finished with the Feddies, even in this town. There are too many of them left, and a fleet overhead to boot. And more towns we haven't got to yet."

"If they can't bring shuttles down to move us around, how are we going to get at the rest? We sure can't walk from here to wherever. Not like that lot from South York who walked here."

"Don't say 'can't,' " Tory advised. "Some sod with more gold braid than brains might take that as a challenge."

Edwards started to say something else, but Kepner held up a hand to stop him, then lowered his visor. Alfie shut up, knowing that Tory had received a call.

"Yes, Captain, we've broken off our surveillance," Tory told McAuliffe. "They were a good half mile past the last house we saw, and heading farther away, moving southwest at a good clip. You want us to head back or should we set up a surveillance line somewhere near the last houses?"

"Bring it back in," McAuliffe said. "You might march your lads right down the center of the road, let any locals who are still in their homes know that we're around."

"What do we tell them if anybody asks what they should do?"

"Tell them we're here and we're not leaving until we've taken care of the Feddies. Tell them they'd best stick close to their houses for now, and suggest that they should offer whatever help they can to any of the refugees who come along."

"I'd hope they'd do that without anybody telling them, sir, but will do." Tory got slowly to his feet, then got his platoon up. "We're going back in. Time to put on a little parade for the locals on the way."

Al Bailey had been the only one of the civilians to notice that the Marines were leaving their positions around the camp. He had been watching them carefully all morning, going around the edge of the clearing and trying to spot where each of the men was concealed farther out. He had only been certain of the positions of seventeen of them, though; the rest had been hidden too well to be seen even from behind.

He waited for a few minutes after the Marines rushed off before he said anything, wanting to see if they were moving because of trouble nearby. When he decided that whatever was going on was too far away for him to see, he said, "The Marines have left," loud enough that the others in camp heard him.

Al remained where he was, staring off after the Marines even though he could no longer see them. His father and several others came to him, asking questions. The only one that Al could answer was, "Are you sure?"

"I'm sure. They all got up and started running off that way." He pointed.

"Is the fighting going so badly that they need every last man?" Ted asked. The battle had been audible for some time.

"They were here to provide a surprise for the Feddies if it was needed," Reggie said. "Maybe it was needed."

"We'll know soon enough, I think," Noel said. "If our chaps win, they'll be back. If not . . ." He shrugged.

"One way or another, the Commonwealth will be back," Reggie said, frowning at Wittington. "If not this lot, then another. They came quickly. They won't give us up for lost no matter what happens today."

"They might not have anyone else to send, not in the near future." Noel was unable to step free of his sudden flood of pessimism. "If they had bags of troops available, wouldn't they have sent enough to make an easy go of it?"

"They came. They'll finish the job," Reggie insisted. "What are you going to do? Are you going back to the rest of your people to let them know what's going on?"

Noel looked around at the others who had come with him. They stared at him, obviously waiting to hear his choice.

"Not just yet, I think. What have I learned? Just that there *are* Commonwealth troops here. It's better to wait until I have something more, what we should do, where we should go."

"If we stay away too long, we're liable to have everyone

else trooping after us, wondering why we haven't returned,'' one of Noel's companions said.

"We haven't been gone long enough for that. I doubt anyone will work up to that kind of choice before tomorrow morning at the earliest. It wouldn't surprise me a bit if it took that lot two or three days.''

Eric nudged Reggie's arm, then gestured with his head and moved away from the others. Reggie followed.

"I think it's time we start thinking about moving ourselves, just in case,'' Eric whispered, looking over Reggie's shoulder to make certain that none of the group from South York was paying any attention. "If things go badly for the Marines, moving may be our only option. Too many people know where we're at.''

Reggie nodded. "We have to think about it, at least.''

"It's hard telling which way would be safest for us to go,'' Eric said. "We know this lot is south of us, and there's no telling how many thousand people are off to the east.''

"We'll likely find mobs of our people no matter which direction we go, unless we head back in toward our homes. The Feddies have been pushed on past them now.''

"There won't be any game to hunt in where it's all been burned over.''

"Maybe, maybe not. But with the Commonwealth here, I'd hate to think about going farther away from town.''

Captain McAuliffe led H&S company out along the road to rendezvous with the I&R platoon, meeting them near the midpoint between the last burned out houses and the last houses at the end of the lane. After the shooting had stopped, civilians started to emerge from their homes. I&R's progress slowed to almost nothing. The rest of the company was equally slow moving out to meet them. McAuliffe left people, mostly lieutenants, to explain what was going on— as far as possible—to groups of families along the way.

Despite requests to the contrary, some of those people followed the company as it moved south, hoping to hear more, looking for assurances that the danger to their homes was past, that the Feddies would not be back. The Marines could not offer that assurance. There was still a Federation fleet overhead; there were still Federation soldiers on the ground. Neither had been decisively beaten. The Marines reminded the local residents that the real ordeal—taking care of the millions who had been left homeless, and rebuilding their world—had not even begun.

McAuliffe turned one group of Coventrians over to David Spencer when they finally met the I&R platoon. The captain wanted to talk with Tory Kepner.

"You did good," the captain said when Tory reported.

"Any word on my man Baker yet, sir?"

"All I know is that the medical orderlies got him. They'll do what they can, but any serious help will have to wait until there's a chance to evacuate casualties to *Victoria*."

"Yes, sir, I know. It's just . . . well, I worry about him."

"He'll get the best care we can give. Now, it's time we start helping these people. That lot you found out in the woods. Send half your platoon to fetch them in, with whatever they've got with them. I'll make arrangements to get them settled in with families along here temporarily." He shrugged. "It's not much, but it is a first step."

Al Bailey was still watching when the Marines returned. He had not left his post for more than five minutes at a time since the platoon had hurried off earlier. When he saw them coming back, Al went to the center of camp to tell the others. Most of them came back with him to watch the two squads approach.

Reggie felt a chill when he saw that there were only half as many as before. *Did they lose that many so fast?* he wondered. Unable to restrain himself, he moved out toward the Marines. He could not see the faces hidden behind helmet visors, could get no clue from the way they moved. For a moment, he held his breath.

"What happened?" he asked when the first Marines were still ten feet away.

Tory Kepner raised his visor. "We chased the Feddies away. There are still several hundred on the loose, but they're no immediate threat.'' The Marines came right into the camp area.

"There were more of you before,'' Reggie said, uncertain how the statement would be received.

"The captain thought we'd be enough. He sent us to bring you lot along with us. There are still families in their houses, out toward the edge of town.'' Tory made a vague gesture toward the southwest. "He's going to make arrangements for folks to take you in. It's a start, until you can get yourselves back in homes of your own.''

"Back?''

"We won't be able to find places for everyone who's been left homeless, but you're the closest in. I guess that makes you part of the lucky few.''

"Back home?'' Anna asked, clutching her baby more tightly.

"To friends' homes anyway,'' Tory said. "We'll help you carry your things back.''

"We were thinking of maybe heading back toward our own homes,'' Reggie said. "Look around, see if there's anything we can salvage. Rig shelters there, or something like that.''

"I imagine you'll have a chance to look over what's left of your homes, maybe start some of the work, but you'll be better off staying with folks who still have intact houses, and food, at least for the immediate future. As soon as we get these Feddies sorted out proper, we'll be setting up centers, I think. We won't be able to go chasing off up and down every road to provide for individual families. We'll need to have everyone in a few centralized locations.'' It was an unusually long speech for Tory, but the captain wanted the civilians brought in to where there were still houses intact, not wandering off up and down half the shire digging through the rubble.

Spencer shared the good news with the I&R platoon's third and fourth squads. "We've had word from CIC. The Fourth Regiment will be here this evening, along with another Navy battle group to help spaceside.''

There were no cheers. After chasing about most of this day, and all of the preceding days and nights of little sleep and too much danger, few of the men had energy to spare, even for good news. They were lounging around, sprawled out in the grass. Some were still eating. The rest had opted to try to get a few minutes of sleep.

"Once we've got the Fourth on the ground, things should go a lot smoother," David continued. He was sitting on a low rock wall that ran along the side of the road. The couple who lived in the nearest house had carted out several pitchers of fruit drinks for the two squads, and a selection of foods to augment the ration packs. "We might even manage a full night's sleep."

Even that wasn't enough to get any noticeable response.

"I know. You've heard that drill before," David said. "Go ahead, kip out while you can. I don't know that we've got anything up in the next few hours, but that's subject to change."

He got up and headed farther down the road to where the next platoon was resting. He would have liked nothing better than the chance to find a place and get some sleep of his own, but the men had to come first.

The duty orderly's knock was soft. He knew that it was unnecessary to pound on the captain's door, and that Captain Shrikes did not appreciate that sort of ruckus.

"I'm awake. Thank you," the captain said, and the orderly turned and headed back toward the bridge.

Inside the cabin, Ian sat up and turned to perch on the edge of his berth. Feeling unusually lethargic, he stared at the crystal clock that his wife had given him on their last anniversary. The hands of the clock blurred into invisibility. Ian continued to stare at the shifting patterns of light in the crystal. It was several minutes before he started blinking furiously, then yawned and stretched.

"It's even getting to me." He stood and glanced at the clock again. There were ninety minutes left before the battle group was due to move back toward Coventry. Within a margin of five or ten minutes either way, they hoped to appear just as the reinforcements arrived in-system. If they were late, one or the other of the supply ships would be on hand near Coventry to assure the newcomers that *Sheffield*'s task force had not left or been destroyed.

In thirty minutes, an hour before the fleet move, Admiral Greene had a conference scheduled with all of the skippers and operations officers. He would have several scenarios scripted, trying to prepare for any eventuality.

Ian moved into the head to look at himself in the mirror. "Shave, shower, and a fresh uniform," he decided—inevitably. Then he would eat—if there were time. *Hull* would likely be in combat in two hours or less.

He called the wardroom to have a tray—breakfast, even though it was late afternoon by ship's time—brought to his cabin. Then he returned to the head to make himself presentable. The "morning" ritual helped bring Ian out of his doldrums. His movements were practiced, always the same, aboard ship or at home. He took two minutes to shave, then permitted himself five minutes in the shower. The last minute was the final touch, forty seconds of water as hot as he could stand it, followed by twenty seconds of water as cold as the system could provide.

That chill lent energy to his toweling off, and it brought his mind up to speed. When he left the bathroom, with just a robe on, he found that his meal had already been delivered. There was the temptation to eat first, while the food was hot, and dress after, but Ian was too disciplined for that. If an emergency arose, he could head to the bridge without food in his stomach, but it would be undignified to go running about in only a bathrobe. He dressed more quickly than he normally did, all of the way to lacing his shoes, then sat at the table and removed the cover from the serving tray. The cooks all knew his preferences, and whoever had prepared this meal had made certain that there were extra portions of everything.

Ian inhaled deeply. The aromas kindled his appetite. He set the cover aside and moved the tray a fraction closer to the edge of the table. He sliced a healthy bit off of one of the sausages. The fork hadn't yet reached his mouth when the alarm Klaxon sounded and the intercom from the bridge buzzed.

# Part 6

# 22

**Away from the** fighting, in Hawthorne as in the other towns and cities where the Second Regiment had defeated or driven off the Federation troops, refugees started returning to the remnants of their homes. At first, the numbers of people coming back were small. The most adventurous, and the most desperate, went home first, daring the possibility that there might still be Federation soldiers blocking them, or that they might get caught up in the fighting. But returning became a chain reaction, the numbers spiraling upward. Soon, the impromptu refugee camps were virtually deserted. The sounds of battle might have been a deterrent while they lasted, but when those sounds could no longer be heard, the silence was a magnet, growing in strength the longer it continued.

Around Hawthorne there had been a dozen major concentrations of refugees, with scores of smaller enclaves, sometimes no more than one or two families, scattered between and beyond the larger groups. Some of the people had traveled ten miles or more from their homes, propelled either by fear or by the need to find game to hunt. But most people had stayed far closer, often getting no more than a mile from their homes.

Those who had the shortest distances to travel were generally among the first to return to the ashes of their houses— and the ashes of their lives. People returned to where they had lived, then many of them went looking for the Commonwealth forces who had made it possible for them to come home, hoping—expecting—that the Marines would provide food and shelter.

Hawthorne Center, the core of the town, had been completely gutted. Piles of rubble and ashes were all that remained, with vast stretches of grass and trees burned out as well. Occasionally, a lone tree stood, still living, still green, an improbable survivor of the devastation.

Along the six roads leading out of town, the limits of destruction varied. On a couple of those routes, the Federation soldiers had barely started to burn past the inner ring. On others, they had made it almost to the end of the settlement. Where the invaders had passed, the destruction was complete. They had left no exceptions in their methodical scorched-earth program.

In every city and town that the Federation had touched the story was the same. The Confederation of Human Worlds had allotted more soldiers to the larger population centers, but not in strict proportion. Coventry City, South York, and The Dales had seen significant destruction, but all retained large areas that had not yet been burned. Only a very few of the smallest and most remote towns and villages had completely escaped the devastation.

Where the Federation troops had not been stopped by the Commonwealth Marines, the burning continued, often at a faster pace than before, as if the Feddies feared that they would not complete their mission in time. Even in some areas where there was fighting going on, the Federation managed to keep some troops working at their arson while the rest fought. Pillars of smoke continued to mark the skyline in the three major cities and in the towns that had not yet been liberated.

"We're going to have the whole town right here in our laps the way things are going, Captain," David Spencer said.

The fighting locally had been over for nearly four hours, and several large groups of refugees had already come in. The first had been the band that had started in South York, with its handful of floaters. They had numbered close to five hundred by the time they came into Hawthorne. Not long after their arrival, an even larger group had come in from the east. Others were trickling in from the north, coming out from the direction of the town's center, seeking not just home but their liberators. They clustered near the Marines for protection, and for the hoped-for assistance.

"There's not much more we can do until we get help down from the fleet," McAuliffe said. "Once the Fourth Regiment gets here, we should be able to get things organized. For now, all we can do is try to keep all of the home food replicators working full-time, haul in raw materials and help distribute what comes out."

"What worries me most right now is what are we going to do with all these civilians if the Feddies come back," David said. "I know it looks like we can feed everyone today, but if we get back to fighting, it could end up a slaughter."

"It worries me too, David." McAuliffe looked around. He had set up his command post near the center of the stretch of undamaged homes, about where the three companies had rendezvoused with the I&R platoon. He could see most of the refugees. They were gathered on front lawns and along the road, possibly more than 1,500 already, with word of more coming.

"As soon as the Fourth is on the ground, the colonel says we're going to regroup, get our battalions back intact, if we can," the captain said. "And they'll ship down all of the portable food replicators they can. We'll have to set up refugee camps."

"Yes, sir," David said. "It's going to be a real job of work, especially while we've got to worry about Feddies."

"Even after. Until Buckingham can send out specialists to handle the situation. All we can do is try to muddle through."

"Kepner's got his platoon spread out off to the southwest. I told them to move back out to the end of the houses and set up a picket line. They've planted snoops as well. There's no sign of those Feddies."

"Alpha and Delta have patrols out, and we've got squads making contact with the other locals who haven't lost their homes, making sure everyone's ready to help with the refugees.'' McAuliffe hoped to break the logjam right around his force. If the entire population of Hawthorne tried to collect along the one road, the situation would quickly become unmanageable.

It had been a hectic four hours for McAuliffe. Cut off from guidance from *Sheffield*, he had been forced to make his own choices, do what he could with what was available. He did not dare fragment his command too much. His three companies, after casualties, did not offer that much of an edge over the known number of Feddies who had escaped after the morning's fight. If they returned, he had to have a large enough force in one place to meet the enemy and at least hold them until help arrived.

Sometime that night, if all went well.

All was not going well.

Aboard *Hull*, Ian Shrikes ran from his cabin to the bridge. That was faster than answering the call from the officer of the deck and then making the trip.

''What is it?'' he demanded as he entered the bridge.

''*Avon* just came out, sir,'' the OD reported. HMS *Avon* was one of the supply ships that had been monitoring Coventry while the rest of the task force took its respite. ''It looks as if a new Feddie force has arrived. *Avon* spotted troop ships and escorts. The rest of their battle group came out of Q-space as well. It looks as if they intend to land reinforcements.''

''What have we had from the admiral?''

''Just 'Call to Quarters' so far. CIC said to stand ready, that orders will be coming.''

*As soon as they figure out what the bloody hell we're going to do,* Ian thought. ''All right, I have the con.''

He went to his seat at the command console and started scrolling through reports coming in from the various stations around the ship. The pilots of the fighter squadron were in their ready room, their Spacehawks being readied for launch. Weapons divisions reported ready. Engineering. Damage control. The rest. All gastight hatches had been closed. Secondary life-support systems were functional, ready if needed. HMS *Hull* was prepared for combat.

A new message came through from CIC aboard *Sheffield*. It was not orders but a listing of the ships that *Avon* had spotted before ducking into Q-space. Ian read through the list with a sinking feeling in his chest, or stomach: two Cutter-class transports that could each carry a battalion of soldiers, one of the larger Empire-class transports that could carry an entire regiment, two battlecruisers, eight frigates, and several auxiliaries. The most depressing news was that there were two dreadnoughts—the largest ships in space, dwarfing Commonwealth battlecruisers such as *Hull* and *Sheffield*—in the new Federation task force. Those were just the ships that *Avon* had seen. Its captain was not certain that they had scanned all of the Federation ships before jumping out of harm's way.

*Even when the Fourth gets here with its task force, the Feddies will have us outgunned,* Shrikes thought. *And if those transports are filled to capacity, they might still have the Marines outnumbered as well.*

He glanced at the time on one of the monitors in front of him. He had been on the bridge for five minutes. There was still no word from the admiral. That was no surprise to Ian. All of the contingency plans that Greene had discussed earlier were suddenly obsolete. They were confronted with an entirely new situation—much more dangerous, even desperate.

*He should have* some *word for us soon, even if he hasn't figured out what to do yet.* Paul Greene was good at that. He tried to keep his captains informed. After the intelligence about the size of the enemy force had gone out, the skippers needed some assurance from their boss, or at least confirmation of the bad news. Despite this, it was another ten minutes before the admiral came on to talk with the captains.

"CIC is still trying to come up with something that isn't patently suicidal," Greene said. "It looks bleak, but we're going to have to take action. The one thing I am certain of is that we don't dare let *our* reinforcements pop in over Coventry before we get back on station there to meet them. If they emerge from Q-space in the middle of that Feddie fleet with no warning, and without us there to keep the Feddies occupied, it could be a real disaster.'' And there was no way to warn off the new Commonwealth force.

"We'll time it as closely as we can," Greene continued. "Getting out there too soon could be too sticky to contemplate. We're going to have to mix it up with the Feddies, try to keep them from landing all of their soldiers, if we're not too late for that already, and try to occupy their escorts without getting ourselves blown out of the galaxy in the process. That is not, I realize, the easiest of tasks. As soon as we've solidified a plan, I'll get it to you straightaway.''

HMS *Avon* had managed to broadcast a warning to the men on the ground before she slipped into Q-space to warn the task force. The emergency override on the transmission had insured that every officer on the ground would hear the message, as long as he had his helmet on.

Captain McAuliffe wasted ten seconds swearing before he switched to his all-hands channel and passed the news. "Try to get the civilians to cover. Then I want everyone down, out of sight, in case the Feddies come straight in." There could be fighters and shuttles, and it might not take them long to arrive.

McAuliffe linked on with the commanders of Alpha and Delta, arranging for the disposition of their men. They might not have much time to assemble defensive positions.

"We'll move back into the burned out section north of here," McAuliffe decided. "If there is fighting, we'll try to keep it away from the houses that haven't been destroyed. That might limit civilian casualties as well." Alpha and Delta would recall their patrols. McAuliffe told Spencer to get the I&R platoon back in as well.

The captain stood and looked around as Marines and civilians went into action. No more than ten percent of the refugees who had gathered could possibly be crowded into the houses along this stretch of road. The rest would have to be dispersed, preferably into the forest to the east, where they would be out of sight of any aircraft, and as far as possible from the enemy troops who had moved to the southwest. McAuliffe passed the word to tell the civilians that, and to tell them that they should move as quickly as they could, that enemy fighters or shuttles could be down in less than twenty minutes.

"Captain!" McAuliffe turned back toward Spencer. "Kepner's lads have spotted those Feddies we chased off. They're headed this way, at the double. Kep says there's at least three hundred and fifty."

"Bloody hell. That means they're in communication with their fleet, and it means we're going to get hit fast."

"Yes, sir. That's what I figured too."

"We can't let the Feddies back into this area, Spencer. They'll start torching houses again, and this time they might not bother to make sure they're empty first."

McAuliffe got on the radio to stop Alpha and Delta from moving in the other direction. Then he lifted his visor to talk with Spencer again. "We'll set up west of the houses, and across the end of the line, try to either hold the Feddies or make them slide along our front toward the areas they've already burned. If we can get them moving north, we'll leap-frog units from one end of our line to the other, try to stay ahead of them."

"Yes, sir. What about I&R?"

"How far from the Feddies are they?"

"No more than a hundred yards when I talked to Kep. Behind them now, I suspect."

"Tell Kepner . . . no, I'll tell him myself. Hold on."

Tory listened to the captain's instructions with something approaching disbelief. Blood seemed to drain from his head. *He doesn't want Marines, he wants bloody cartoon super-heroes,* Tory thought. But when the captain finished, all Tory said was, "Yes, sir. We'll do our best."

He pulled in the fire teams. The platoon had been spread over more than a half mile, so it took a few minutes.

"We've got to slow those sods down long enough to let the rest of our blokes get in position. *And* worry that there might be more Feddies dropping in our laps any minute."

"One shot-up platoon to stop two companies?" Alfie asked. "That's bloody suicide."

"Let's hope not," Tory said. "We'll hit them from behind, at maximum range, then do our best to stay out of their way. We'll nip along the side and hit them again while they're still looking where we used to be. Move and fight, then move again, at the double. Let's go before they find more houses to burn."

Even at a run in a forest, I&R men could move relatively silently. When they had closed to within 150 yards of the rear elements of the Feddie formation, Kepner brought his platoon to a stop and got them down.

"Fire!" he ordered. His own trigger was the first squeezed.

Through the first ten seconds, there was no return fire. Only a couple of Feddies appeared to go down hit, but more took cover. When the return fire did start, it was uncoordinated at first, aimed around a full semicircle. It took a moment more before the Feddies spotted where the ambush had come from and concentrated their response.

"They didn't all stop," Alfie said from his position at the extreme right end of the platoon. "Most kept moving."

"Right. Then that's what we've got to do," Tory said. "Up and off to the north. Stop firing before you start moving."

First squad was the last out, covering the rest until they had put more distance between themselves and the enemy. "Okay, Alfie-lad," Tory said. "Time for us to catch them up. Take your team. We'll be three seconds behind you."

Tory's fire team increased its rate of fire, then started moving after the others. They had only gone a few steps when Ramsey Duncan pitched forward, smashing his shoulder into a tree trunk. Kepner and Dayle went down on either side of Duncan. His left leg was bleeding. A bullet had gone through the meat behind the bone. While Dayle turned to make certain that no Feddies sneaked up on them, Kepner slapped med-patches over both of Duncan's wounds, then wrapped an elastic around the leg to help stop the bleeding.

"I think my shoulder's broken too," Duncan whispered

through gritted teeth. "Broken or dislocated. You'll have to go on without me, Sarge."

"Not a chance." Tory lowered his visor long enough to call Will Cordamon. "You've got the platoon for now, Will. The Ram's hurt bad. It'll take Dayle and me both to get him in." While he was talking, he slapped an anesthetic patch on Duncan's shoulder. There wasn't time to do any more, and it was going to hurt like hell when they moved him.

Most of the Marines under Captain McAuliffe's command had taken cover in the woods west of the road, a hundred yards from the nearest houses. A few platoons were still moving toward their positions, off to the left, the south, to block that end of the road. When McAuliffe heard the first sonic booms, he looked back toward the road and houses. There were still far too many civilians visible. Many, perhaps most, had been slow to take the advice to get into the woods on the far side of the road. Many hadn't even started to move until they heard the sounds of aircraft coming in hot. Then they ran, either for whatever protection they might find at the sides of houses, or for the woods. There were hundreds of refugees, perhaps close to a thousand, between those houses and the forest.

The first aircraft in were fighters, a pair of them. They made a run from south to north, firing rockets and then cannon—after they had reduced their speed enough to make cannon fire safe for themselves. Two houses were hit by missiles, but mostly the pilots aimed for the people who were running across the fields behind the houses, strafing through them before they pulled up to turn and come back.

Any civilians who could still move hurried to make it to the tree line before the fighters came back, strafing again. A lot of the refugees did not make it back to their feet.

The dozen shuttles that came in right after the fighters made their second pass landed farther south, beyond the last houses on the road.

# 23

**Reggie Bailey watched** from an upstairs window in the house where his family had been taken in while the Federation aircraft strafed the refugees outside. He felt sick to his stomach, but was unable to pull himself away from the window. It wasn't until Reggie heard the first missile explosions, two houses to the south, that he felt any immediate fear for himself and for his family.

"We'd better get downstairs," he said, a tight throat making his voice squeaky. He and Al were with Joseph Evans, their host.

Evans nodded. "Once this ruckus eases off a mite, we'll have to see if we can help any of those folks out there." Having been spared the destruction of his house and weeks as a refugee in the forest, the invasion had not felt completely real to Evans before. It had touched him only peripherally, a minor annoyance. But watching people die made the blood drain from his face. His voice remained under control, but just barely.

"The Marines must be better equipped for that than we are," Reggie said, swallowing heavily, as they moved out to the hallway and the stairs leading down to the main floor.

"We can still do our part," Evans said. "We need to do for ourselves as much as we can."

One of the two windows along the stairway had been starred by a bullet from one of the aircrafts' cannon, leaving a spiderweb pattern that made it almost impossible to see through the pane. Joseph Evans stopped next to that window, arrested by the sight. He touched the inner surface. It still felt smooth, but no longer flat. The damage was all on the outer layer. For a moment, Joseph seemed to forget that there were people behind him on the stairs. He stared at the window and shook his head.

"It nearly penetrated," he said finally, speaking softly, to himself. That starred window made more of an impression than the scores, perhaps hundreds, of people he had just seen killed by the same cannon fire.

"And those missiles will penetrate anything we have," Reggie said. "One of your neighbors just found that out."

Reggie's voice snapped Joseph from his reverie. He blinked, then resumed his course down the stairs. But Al paused at the window, not to wonder at the damage to the pane, but to try to see through it.

"Dad!" Al shouted. "There are shuttles coming down. Federation shuttles."

The I&R platoon had stopped its movement paralleling the Federation soldiers on the ground as soon as the enemy shuttles were spotted. Captain McAuliffe had new instructions for them. They were to get into position to see how many soldiers came off of the landers and what direction they took.

"A dozen shuttles, those could carry four full companies," Alfie commented when Tory passed the word to his noncoms. "Seven hundred men or more."

"All the more reason to find out for sure," Tory said.

The landing zone was a half mile south of the last houses on the road. Tory had to take his platoon about the same distance to get into position. It appeared that the shuttles had landed right in the road. There was forest to either side. The I&R platoon moved by fire team, spread out in a double skirmish line. There was enough distance between the two lines that even if the new Feddie troops hit the lead line hard, the second line would be able to get word back to the captain.

Alfie pushed his men. The sooner they could get the information they needed, the sooner they would be able to head back to the rest of their mates. With so many Feddies on the ground, Alfie did not fancy mucking around with just a few men, out where capture—or worse—was an immediate threat. Federation troops were not noted for their humanity in dealing with prisoners. Captured enemies were likely to be killed out of hand to save their captors the bother of guarding them.

By the time that Alfie and a few of the others reached the edge of the wooded area, off to the west of the road, and could see the Federation LZ, the shuttles had already been emptied. But there was no clear perimeter around the shuttles. Squads had been posted near the corners of the zone, with the rest of the troops held in a group near the center, where the bulk of the shuttles gave them some protection from ground attack.

"Slide off to that side," Alfie whispered, gesturing right. "I need a better hole to look through." After a few more seconds of looking, Alfie switched channels. "Tory, do you see? Those shuttles didn't come in full. There can't be more than three hundred Feddies out there, two short companies."

"Unless the rest are still inside the landers," Tory said. "We can't see up those ramps from here."

"Even Feddies can't be that stupid. Stay inside a shuttle on the ground where there's enemy troops close?"

"They might have brought supplies for the ones already here, the way we had supplies landed."

"Maybe," Alfie conceded. "But there's another possibility. Maybe they came in to get the other sods out."

"Don't get your hopes too high. Hang on a minute. I've got to report to the captain." Tory switched channels to tell Captain McAuliffe what they had seen, and he mentioned all three of the possible explanations for half-empty shuttles—including the one he himself thought least likely, that half of the Feddies were still inside them. "I don't know if it's important or not, Captain," Tory said, "but that's what we've got."

"You see any sign that they're getting ready to move away from the shuttles?" McAuliffe asked.

"Not so far. But they're formed up for something, not in defensive positions."

"Keep watching. If they show any sign that they're moving away from the shuttles, give me a shout. Make sure you're far enough under cover that they don't spot you first, but stay close enough to see what's going on."

"They'd be sitting ducks if one or two Spacehawks came along," Alfie said after the platoon had moved back from the edge. "A couple of birds could wipe out the lot of them in a single pass."

"Save your breath, Alfie," Tory advised. "We don't get miracles like that. The Spacehawks will all be busy upstairs. There's not much chance we'll see one soon enough to help."

Alfie had no chance to reply to that. Three men made the same call at once on the platoon channel. "They're moving!"

Tory looked for himself, then called the captain. "They're heading right down the road toward you."

"All right," McAuliffe said. "Get your lads back as quickly as you can. If the two lots of Feddies meet before you get past them, you may have to invent a new route in."

A hundred yards south of the last houses, the forest took over, leaning in close on both sides of the road. In places, the underbrush was impossibly thick. The lane was the only possible route for a large formation of soldiers to use if they wanted to move at any speed.

Captain McAuliffe had shifted his men as far as he could in the available time. The defensive line resembled a shepherd's crook, with the longer section of the staff along the west side of the houses, hooking around the south end and going only a hundred yards north on the east side. H&S Company was on the east and manned part of the hook. Delta was next in line, with Alpha stretched back as far as possible on the west.

No civilians had come out of their houses yet. After seeing what had happened to those who had been caught in the open by the Feddie aircraft, few would have obeyed a direct order to leave their homes, not that McAuliffe ever considered that. The civilians were safer now where they were.

The Marines had little time to dig in or erect barricades. The line was in the edge of the forest, all around. Only across the road itself was it possible to set up physical barriers. Those were lightly manned. The possibility of Feddie aircraft returning was too great.

The original Federation force, the one that had been on the ground from the beginning and had already fought the Marines of the First Battalion, had stopped moving. They were waiting, four hundred yards west of the road, approximately opposite the junction between Alpha and Delta companies.

Paul Greene felt physically ill. Only by sheer willpower, and considerable acting, was he able to keep his discomfort from showing to the men and women around him. He walked slowly onto the flag bridge just before ordering the task force to transit to Q-space. It was essential that he be at his duty post, where people could see that he was not panicked by the thought of what might lie ahead. But the personal history he had to live up to was not too difficult. Greene had never been noted as a jovial commander. He was not given to jokes or charades the way some officers— such as Admiral Stasys Truscott, his onetime commander— were. Greene always maintained a serious demeanor on duty. The pose of dignity could cover a lot, especially when that was what the men and women under his command expected.

His initial deployment for the coming battle had been selected, and everyone knew what was expected of them. Only the first few minutes could be fully scripted in advance, of course. They would not know precisely what they would be able to do, or what they might be *forced* to do, until they emerged from Q-space over Coventry and discovered the latest positions and courses of the Federation ships.

Greene leaned back in his chair at the rear of the flag bridge. The console in front of him duplicated the captain's console on *Sheffield*'s bridge, but also offered additional functions to facilitate communication with the other ships under his command, and six extra monitors. As was his habit, he keyed in the automatic diagnostics for the system. Fifteen seconds later, he had confirmation that everything was working properly.

"Transmit the execute order to the fleet," Greene said. The crews of all the ships were already at battle stations. When the task force came out of Q-space in several minutes, it would be instantly ready for action.

The automatic warning for Q-space insertion sounded. Greene took a deep breath, then expelled it slowly as *Sheffield*'s Nilssen generators slid the ship into a private universe.

Collision warnings sounded aboard HMS *Hull* less than two seconds after it emerged from Q-space over Coventry. Red lights flashed to accompany the Klaxon. Arriving in normal space traveling at nearly 26,000 miles per hour, *Hull* found itself coming up directly behind a Federation frigate, no more than sixty miles ahead. The frigate's velocity was more than 7,000 mph slower—orbital speed—which gave *Hull* less than thirty seconds to avoid collision, or prepare for it as best as she could. Thirty seconds meant that there was no chance to jump back into Q-space to escape. The minimum of ninety seconds between jumps was absolute.

Automatic collision-avoidance systems fired maneuvering thrusters at full power, working to slow *Hull* and attempt the course correction that offered the best chance for success, even if the frigate took no evasive action of its own. If the frigate ducked in the wrong direction, though, there would be no way to avert disaster.

"Fire everything we have that bears on that frigate," Ian Shrikes ordered. "Blast it out of our way."

That was highly unlikely, to say the least, but Ian kept his voice at a reasonable level. There was no hint of panic that might distract the bridge watch. On a ship the size of *Hull*, even firing all of the ship's weapons at once would produce no noticeable recoil motion, but the accumulated reactions from dozens of particle and energy beam weapons being fired continuously in the same direction would add a minute amount to the efforts to avoid collision. And a sufficient number of powerful antiship missiles hitting the frigate might at least weaken it enough structurally to mitigate the damage to *Hull* if the crash could not be averted completely.

*Even if it doesn't save us, we'll go down fighting,* Ian thought. *And we'll be damned sure we take the Feddie with us, even if it's only a frigate and not something larger.*

Ian stared at a monitor that showed the view in front of the ship. At the moment, the frigate looked as large as a dreadnought, and the gap between the ships was shrinking with appalling rapidity.

At the same time, the seconds seemed to stretch out forever, as if *Hull* were in a Q-space bubble that distorted time as well as space. There was no way that Ian could tell, just by watching that monitor, whether or not it would be possible to avoid the collision. There were updates being posted on another screen, changing constantly, showing the progress. With fifteen seconds left before impact, it was still marginal. Then the system picked up the first slight change in course by the frigate. It was working to avoid the collision as well, and it was moving in the right direction, accelerating as rapidly as it could at the same time. Their actions postponed the possible crash for an extra four seconds and indicated that—at worst—it would not be direct, but a glancing blow.

Ian blinked once. *Hull* might well survive a sideswipe, if not unscathed, then with at least most of her gastight sections intact. Crew could be saved even if the ship were too badly damaged to continue the fight.

Then the red alarm lights muted to amber. The two-note sequence of the warning horns dropped in pitch and volume. Ian let out his breath and eased his grip on the chair. Unless one of the ships altered course now, there would be no collision. As the safety margin increased, the lights went green. The audible alarm ended. And, as the two ships passed each other—with less than fifty feet clearance—even the green lights went out.

"Continue firing everything we have at the frigate," Ian

said. "CIC, where is everyone else? Give me an update now."

Data flowed onto two monitors. A third screen displayed a chart with all of the Federation and Commonwealth vessels pinpointed, showing course and speed. That monitor appeared impossibly cluttered, even to eyes accustomed to making sense of complicated displays. A voice from CIC gave Ian an oral update at the same time, pointing out salient features.

*Sheffield* had already launched her Spacehawks. *Hull* had been scheduled to launch immediately upon arrival as well, but the proximity of the Federation frigate had made that impossible. Apart from the danger of collision between the two ships, the Spacehawks and their launching cylinders would have been easy targets for the frigate at point-blank range.

One of Ian's monitors seemed to erupt in flames. He had been concentrating on the update from the Combat Intelligence Center, and the sudden burst of flame startled him. He needed a second to realize that it was just the image on the screen, not the monitor itself. The enemy frigate had exploded.

The voice from CIC faltered, then stopped. When it returned, the first comment was, "We're taking hits from debris, sir."

"Damage control, keep me posted," Ian said, keying a switch on the panel at his right side. There were audible echoes of the debris impacts reverberating inside the battlecruiser.

"Aye, sir. No hull penetration, no report of any damage yet," the officer manning the damage control hub reported. No more than ten seconds passed before she spoke again. "We've been breached, Captain. Two penetrations, sections C-117 and C-118."

Ian keyed in the numbers to see where they were, and what functions they served. Both compartments were in engineering, far back along the ship.

"The breach in C-118 has been plugged by the crew in that compartment," damage control reported. "No casualties there. We have no response from inside C-117.''

"How many crew in that section?" Ian asked.

"Four, sir."

"Get someone in there."

"Yes, sir. The last debris is past us now."

"Operations, get the birds launched as soon as possible, once we know there's no damage to the LRCs." (Launch and Recovery Cylinders.) "How do we stand with the rest of the enemy ships?"

There were multiple targets available, and *Hull* was under attack from most of them, one way or another. The captain of a battlecruiser was not required to make every tactical decision in combat. A battlecruiser was too large and complicated for that to be possible except under the most ideal of conditions. Combat rarely provided those. There were three primary weapons control centers, each with their own backup stations, and in many respects they could operate independently of the bridge, particularly in defensive counterfire. Incoming missiles or other weapons did not always allow time for consultation. The response had to be instantaneous or it would be too late.

Before exiting Q-space, the weapons control centers had been given the authority to take all available targets under fire. Even while the captain and much of the crew had worried about whether or not the ship would collide with the Federation frigate, and were doing their best to avert that, weapons that could be brought to bear on other targets were. Missiles were launched. Beamers were fired. The hulls of ships were hardened against lasers, but particle beam weapons could be effective within a limited range. Ship-to-ship fighting relied mostly on missiles. The fighters, the Commonwealth's Spacehawks and the Federation's equivalent, were mostly delivery systems for missiles, attempting to launch too close to the enemy for antimissile missiles or other weapons to destroy them all.

Ian scanned the available data, trying to assemble a picture of the developing battle. The fighters were launched, one flight to remain as a defensive screen, the rest sent out to attack enemy ships. One Commonwealth frigate had been damaged seriously. *Sheffield* was engaged with two enemy ships, a battlecruiser and one of the dreadnoughts. The rest of the Commonwealth frigates were trying to move to *Sheffield*'s aid.

"All of the enemy shuttles appear to have grounded," CIC reported. "The transports have moved out of effective range of our weapons, but they have not retreated to Q-space."

*Sheffield* disappeared from Ian's monitor as she ducked into Q-space to get out of harm's way. *Sheffield* was impossibly outclassed by the dreadnought—a twelve-mile-long behemoth that mounted nearly three times the weaponry. Ian glanced at the time. He doubted that *Sheffield* would be gone for much more than the few minutes her Nilssens would need to recycle—ninety seconds before leaving Q-space, and ninety seconds before each of the two jumps, in and out of Q-space, coming back. She might appear from any direction, at any point in near space. That minimal tactical surprise was her only advantage. But she would not stay away long, not while they were still waiting for the new Commonwealth task force to arrive with the Marine reinforcements.

Several Federation ships also vanished. There was no visible transition as they entered Q-space, no fancy visual effects. A ship was either in normal space or in Q-space. The transition was instantaneous.

"Keep a close watch for those Feddies," Ian said. "I don't want them popping up in our knickers."

"The second dreadnought is changing course, sir," the OD announced. "It looks as if she's trying to intercept us."

"Are our Spacehawks out far enough to be clear of the turbulence if we have to jump?"

"Aye, sir, all clear of the bubble zone."

"We'll give this Feddie plenty of time. Let her waste effort trying to get to us. Navigation, when we jump back in I'll want our exit calculated to put us well away from any intercept. We don't want another close shave. One shave a day has always been enough for me." Ian had not been consciously trying to make a joke. The words were out before he realized that he had. But the jest, poor though it might be, did relax him a little. It had the same effect on most of the bridge crew.

"Once we jump out, any Spacehawks not immediately engaged should be diverted to help the Marines, if they've called in any requests," Ian said, savoring the scattered laughs. "No, make that half of the Spacehawks. Keep the rest up here attacking ships. And for us, it'll have to be in and out and back to rendezvous with them. Navigation, you'll have to take that into account when you plot our return from Q-space."

"Aye, sir. It was already in the mix."

Ian took another quick scan of his situation monitors. It would be another three minutes before the dreadnought could get close enough to pose a threat—if *Hull* stayed around. Beyond that leviathan, there were no Federation ships within eight minutes of being a serious threat. Ian relaxed a little more. Finally, there was time to think, to make better plans.

"Operations, do you have suggestions?" he asked.

"*Sheffield* has returned," CIC announced before Ian received a reply. "Signal already coming in from the admiral, sir."

"Give it to me on my number three monitor." Ian leaned forward a little.

*"Well done, Shrikes, both the shooting and not ramming the Feddie."*

Ian enjoyed the compliment, but he was vaguely disappointed that there wasn't more to the message, specifically some new battle plan. But his disappointment faded almost at once. He had scarcely looked up from reading the admiral's words before there was another message—this one shouted—from CIC.

"The new fleet's here, sir! They've just popped in. Seven ships, including two battlecruisers."

# 24

**"The Marines aren't** going to get to our wounded out there anytime soon," Reggie Bailey said. "It looks as if you were right, Joseph. We're going to have to help them." Reggie had kept returning to the rear of the Evans house to look out at the bodies strewn between the line of houses and the forest. The couple of times he had opened the door a little, he had heard the cries of wounded people calling for help. The Federation aircraft had not returned, but there was fighting on the ground now, across the road and stretching north and south.

Joseph nodded. "We'll have to try to bring in any who are still alive. Maybe if the neighbors see us out there, some of them will get the idea and help. The two of us certainly can't get to all of them."

"You have a first aid kit, sticky plasters, anything?"

"Not more than the little we might have had for our own use, certainly not enough to make a difference now. I'll have Mary see what she can whip up with the replicator. I don't know that we've got the right raw materials for much." Mary was his wife.

"Even just cloths we can use for bandages would help."

"I'm going with you," Al said, moving toward the rear door.

"No," his father said. "You stay in here."

"I've got to do *something* to help." Al planted his feet wide as if he expected his father to try to knock him down to keep him inside. "If I can't help fight the Feddies, at least I can help take care of some of the people they've tried to murder."

"Your mother won't allow it."

"She doesn't have to know until we're out there. Look, I'm big enough to help carry people back—some of them anyway. There are a lot of people out there."

Joseph returned from talking to his wife about preparing bandages and anything else their home replicator could manage with what they had to feed it. She would be able to get recipes through the complink's database, and the replicator would tell her what it could make from the materials in its supply hoppers.

"Let's go," Joseph said. He appeared not to notice that the Bailey father and son had been arguing.

Reggie conceded. "Yes." His look included Al in the group.

As soon as Al opened the door, the sounds of battle grew considerably louder. The house was not completely sound-proof, but it had dampened most of the intrusive noise. Outside, the three stood close to the wall for a minute, looking out over the rear lawns, trying to spot people who might still be alive. There was no one too close, dead or alive. The nearest casualties were fifty yards away, and they were not moving at all.

"We should check all of them, shouldn't we?" Al asked. "We can't tell for sure about people unless we get right with them, can we?"

"I guess not," his father said.

"Start where we can and work from there?" Al suggested.

Neither of the adults had a better plan.

"Stay low," Reggie said. "When we're out there, get down on the ground until we know what we need to do."

Joseph Evans led the way by only a few steps, running toward the nearest group of casualties. Before they had covered half the distance, Al was a little in front of the adults. When he got close, Al slid to the ground.

It was only at that moment that Al really thought about what might come next. He had never been close to a dead person, had certainly never *touched* one. But if he hesitated it was so briefly that the others could not have noticed—

even if they hadn't been fully occupied with their own thoughts. Al moved next to the first person, got up on his knees, and rolled the man over on his back, getting blood on his hands as he did.

Green eyes stared sightlessly at him. Al's hand trembled, but he reached for the side of the man's neck to feel for a pulse. He had studied enough first aid to know that much. He pressed his fingers against the artery and held his breath while he waited—hoped—for evidence that the man's heart was beating. But there was no pulse. After seeing those eyes, Al had not expected to find one. He stared at the face for a moment. The man might have been someone he had seen, but he did not recognize him.

"He's dead," he whispered. His father and Joseph Evans were checking others. There were seven people close together in the group. Two of them were children, younger than Al's sisters.

Al almost crawled over the dead man to keep from getting too high off of the ground as he moved to the little girls. One of them had just stirred, and groaned. Al bent over her, his face almost touching hers. The girl's eyes were closed, but he could see that she was breathing, hard, rasping breaths that seemed to cause her pain. Al glanced at the other girl, who was even younger, perhaps no more than three or four. Both girls were covered with blood, but alive.

"Dad! I've got two little girls who are alive."

"We've got a live one here too," Reggie said. Al glanced that way. The other one was a very large man.

"If it's gonna take both of you to carry him back, I can get both of the kids," Al said. "If somebody will just hand the second one to me after I stand up with the first."

Reggie came over. Al stood, picking up the larger of the two girls as he did. Once Al had her adjusted in his left arm, her head on his shoulder, his father gave him the other girl.

"Be careful," Reggie said. "Don't fall with them."

The older girl continued to moan, louder than before. Al walked as quickly as he could, afraid that the movement was hurting the girl. He had fifty, maybe fifty-five yards to go to the rear door of the Evans house. His mother was standing in the doorway, holding the door half open, holding on to it as if she were restraining herself from running out to help.

Al was surprised at how heavy two very small girls felt after he had traveled less than a third of the way. His legs felt weak, as if he had just run a mile at top speed, and he began to worry that he might trip and fall, perhaps finishing the damage that the Feddies had done to the girls. But he stayed on his feet, though he nearly stumbled into the door at the end. His mother was there to steady him.

"Take this one, Mother," he said, turning his right side to her. "I'll bring the other in."

Mary Evans was in the kitchen. She took the other girl.

"Look at you," Ida said. "You're covered in blood."

"Their blood," Al said, looking down at his shirt. "Take care of them. I've got to get back out there."

His father and Joseph Evans reached the house, carrying the man between them. Al only hesitated for an instant. If he waited for the others to go out again, his mother might try to keep him from going. He ducked through the doorway and started running toward the next group of bodies.

"Where should we put him?" Joseph asked his wife.

"Anywhere. I guess we'll have to put them all on the floor. How many will there be?"

Joseph shook his head. "I don't have any idea. We'll just have to do what we can, for as long as possible."

*Tell us to get back inside our lines the best we can, then send us out again straightaway. Somebody ain't thinking with both halves of their brain.* But Alfie kept his complaints to himself. He didn't have energy to spare, and this wasn't the best time for levity in any case. He did know the difference—usually.

The I&R platoon had barely managed to get through before the two Feddie units linked up. They had sneaked through the narrowing gap, worried that the Feddies would open up on them from behind. There had been no time to crawl through the most dangerous stretch. The Feddies were moving toward them from both sides, and if the Marines didn't move fast, they wouldn't be able to move at all. They had to get across to their own lines before the shooting started.

They had drawn a few shots from the Feddies, but not until they had almost reached their own lines—close enough for covering fire. The I&R men had been running by that time, and once they got behind other Marines, they had all collapsed on the ground to get their wind back.

"Time for a spot of leave," Alfie had said once he had air to spare for a jest. No one had responded, not even with a groan.

Ten minutes later, they had been back with the rest of H&S Company, on the far end of the half perimeter that the three companies had established. And five minutes after that, before they really had a chance to recover from their earlier exertions, they were on their way out again, moving south, past the hook end of the Commonwealth positions.

Captain McAuliffe's orders had been simple, and vague. "Get behind them and do your thing. Keep their minds occupied as best you can without getting tied down and chewed up. Keep moving."

"Why don't we just blow up their shuttles, sir?" Tory had asked. "Make them wish they'd left more blokes to protect them."

McAuliffe had smiled. "That was my first thought too, but if they want to leave, let them. Let them *try*."

"Aye, sir. I get your meaning."

"What we want most right now is to keep them away from the civilians, stop them doing any more burning. And the more of them you put down hard, the fewer we'll have to worry about."

So, with only a few minutes to rest and grab a quick drink and an energy bar from a meal pack, Tory led his men out again. They moved east first, into the woods, then south. Tory planned to make a wide circle to get behind the Feddies who were already beginning their attack against the section of Commonwealth line being held by Alpha and Delta companies. The I&R men moved at the best pace they could manage through the forest, stopping only once, when they had to cross the road. If the Feddies had left anyone to watch that, the crossing could be difficult.

Tory sent scouts in both directions to look for any ambush. The rest of the platoon used the time to rest—four minutes, maybe five. The scouts reported that they had seen nothing. They would stay where they were to cover the rest as they crossed the road. When that was done, the I&R platoon was closer to the enemy shuttles than to any of the enemy infantry, except for the few men who had been left with the crews to guard the landers.

Once west of the road, Tory paused and looked south. He could see the upper rear corner of one of the shuttles. It was tempting: attack the shuttles, make the Feddies either send more men to guard them, or make the crews take off—if any of the landers survived the attack. Tory shook his head and moved on. *Maybe later,* he thought. The captain might change his mind.

The platoon stopped again ten minutes later. Tory took time to confer with his noncoms. "We'll hit them first right near the south end of their line, from behind. Then we'll move north and hit them again, as close to the far end as we can. If we can force them into a full defensive perimeter, the rest of our blokes can close them in proper, put them in the tin.''


Alfie crawled carefully into position, his rifle across his arms as he snaked along on his belly. He only lifted his head to look occasionally, keeping his visor almost in the dirt the rest of the time. The nearest Federation troops were eighty yards off, unless they had sentries hidden in the woods behind their main formation, and Alfie had seen nothing to suggest that that might be the case. Feddies were often a little careless about defensive measures. Their focus had always been on the attack.

But Alfie never took that carelessness for granted. *I've got to keep my head firmly planted on my shoulders,* he thought. *What would Tory do without me?* He did not bother to smile at his joke. Once he had taken his position, Alfie looked to each side to make sure that his fire team was with him, and ready. Then he reported to Tory.

"Hang on," Tory replied. "Another few seconds. Will hasn't got his people set yet."

*We should have brought more ammo,* Alfie thought. *If we get pinned down we could run short in a hurry.* "Don't get too wild with your ammo," he warned his fire team. "Use what you need to, but don't waste it."

Tory's few seconds stretched to a minute before he gave the order, "Ready . . . fire!" The entire platoon opened up at once.

The Feddies did not need long to realize that they were now under attack from behind. At first, there was only scattered return fire. Then the Feddies got more organized. Two squads turned to cover their rear.

"Put in a volley of grenades," Tory said. "Withdraw as soon as they go off."

The platoon had six grenade launchers left. Each grenadier had a clip of grenades in his launcher. The rounds went out almost simultaneously, ripping through leaves and snapping small branches on their trajectories, giving warning to the Feddies that they were coming.

As soon as the series of explosions sounded, the I&R platoon started withdrawing, moving more rapidly than they had coming in, using the few seconds they had before the Feddies could recover from the grenades and take them under fire again. After that it was fire and maneuver, a squad at a time moving, pulling back, west. It was not until they had broken contact with the Feddies that Tory turned them north and picked up the pace. They ran.

Geoffrey Dayle had forgotten his exhaustion. He felt exhilaration now, even running much too fast for the tangled terrain. Branches caught at his sleeves and roots threatened to trip him and bring him down. That didn't matter. Neither did the difficulty he was having sucking in enough air to maintain his progress. *This is the payoff,* he told himself. *This is where we take them all down.*

Dayle had moved out in front of the others. He even passed Alfie Edwards, whose fire team had been farthest north when they started the first attack. Twice, Tory Kepner told Dayle to slow down, but the admonitions never took for more than a few seconds.

"Far enough!" Tory finally said, on to the entire platoon. "Here's where we move in again." Switching from the platoon channel to his private link with Dayle, Tory said, "You slow down, damn it. This is no one-man crusade. You stick with me the way you're supposed to."

Dayle didn't speak. He couldn't have managed the air to do more than grunt. But he turned toward Tory and nodded, shallowly. Slowing down seemed like a good idea—at least until he got his wind back.

Again the platoon started to work its way cautiously toward the east, toward the enemy. At first, they stayed on their feet, crouched over, presenting the least possible exposure, and staying behind the cover of trees and bushes as much as they could as they moved in. Even in thick forest there was little chance that they would be able to get as close this time without being seen. After their first strike, the Feddies would certainly have sentries watching their rear. No commander could be so incompetent as to miss doing that after one warning.

Tory stopped his platoon while they were still more than 120 yards from where he expected to find the enemy. The woods were thicker here, the lowest branches of many of the trees almost brushing the ground. At 120 yards, it would take luck to see anything. Tory was not about to discount luck, good or bad.

"Alfie, slide your team in until you can see them, then let me know where they are," Tory said. "The rest of us will wait here."

Alfie clicked his transmitter on and off to tell Tory that he had heard and would comply. Then he used hand signals to get his fire team moving forward again. A flat palm gesturing downward told the others to stay flat. An index finger poked forward told them what direction they were going in. Alfie stayed in front of the others. While they watched for the enemy, they would also give a little attention to watching Alfie for more signals.

If Alfie had moved slowly the first time, now he managed to crab along at an even slower pace, being careful to avoid disturbing branches or leaves that might give a sharp-eyed enemy a clue to his presence. Tory had not needed to warn him that the Feddies would be more alert this time. Alfie had almost as much time in the platoon as its sergeant. And he always did his best to anticipate what the enemy might do, what *he* would do if the situation were reversed.

After he had crawled thirty yards, taking fifteen minutes to do so, Alfie gestured for his companions to stop. Then he cranked the pickups for his earphones to their maximum gain and listened for sounds in front of him. The gunfire was a distraction, but it was far enough away that it didn't threaten his hearing.

*That's way too far off,* he realized after a moment. He cranked the volume down and called Tory. "That shooting is all way over to our right. I think we've moved right past the end of the Feddie line."

"Try angling a little to the southeast then," Tory said. "We still have to know where they are."

Alfie clicked his transmitter, then started moving again, changing direction slowly. He picked up his pace a little as well. If they had gone past the end of the enemy line, this might be the one angle they would not be expected to come from. But Alfie slowed down again after just a couple of minutes. Caution overruled his assumption. He stopped and took a breath. Carefully, he stretched each arm and leg in turn to keep from cramping up. Then he started forward again, at a pace that a snail would have little trouble exceeding. There was a particularly dense tangle of undergrowth in front of him, apparently growing out of a low knob of soil. He had to move several yards to the side, east, to get around it. There was no chance of getting through it without causing more motion in the greenery than he dared to chance.

He was not all of the way around the end of the thicket when he came to a dead stop again. He had almost crawled right into the middle of the enemy. Three Federation soldiers were sheltered on the other side of the thicket, not ten feet away from him.

Alfie froze. For once, it was not just training or instinct. There was a distinct element of fear added in. It seemed impossible that he had gotten so close to the enemy in daylight without being seen, and it seemed even less likely that he would be able to withdraw without being noticed. This near the enemy, he did not even dare use the radio to warn his companions that they were almost in Feddie drawers. The slightest whisper might be heard.

He wanted to close his eyes, but he could not—*dared not*. If any of the Feddies started to make a move, he needed to be quick to respond. With his rifle across his arms for crawling, he might not be able to get it into position in time to get off a single shot.

Alfie could hear his heart beating, ticking off the seconds—perhaps his final seconds of life. He expected to hear one of his companions on the radio, asking what was keeping him, a sound that might be loud enough to reach the Feddies, draw their eyes his way. A fraction of an inch at a time, Alfie started to move his arms, trying to get into a position that would let him get his rifle up and into action. He had little room to maneuver, though, and there was the constant fear that even his very slow, very slight movements might be enough to draw the attention of one of the Feddies.

*No one ever said you'd live forever in the RM,* Alfie thought. He wished he had a hand grenade that he could pop over the hump of dirt, but he didn't. He had an urge to simply grab for the trigger and foreguard of his rifle, start shooting as he lurched forward, hoping to be enough of a surprise to survive the encounter. That sort of show was common enough in the action vids that he had watched growing up on Buckingham, but his years as a Marine had given him a more realistic opinion of the consequences that type of reckless gesture was likely to bring.

One of the enemy helmets turned a little, almost directly toward Alfie. There were no eyes visible. The visor of the Feddie helmet was tinted the same way that Commonwealth helmets were, presenting a totally nonreflective surface. Alfie froze again, and did not resume his slow shifting around until the helmet turned away again.

*This is no good,* Alfie decided. *It'd take me thirty minutes this way.* And even thirty seconds might be too long. But he kept inching around, pulling one hand back and moving the other arm a little to the side, trying to give himself the best chance of getting his rifle into action, while he desperately tried to think of a better alternative.

When a single shot sounded, fifty yards to Alfie's right and behind him, he was so startled that he almost jumped up involuntarily. Then there was a flurry of shooting, and one voice screaming almost incomprehensible epithets at the Feddies.

*That's Dayle,* Alfie thought. But he was already moving. The three Feddies he could see had turned their attention to the side and had started to shoot back. Alfie got his rifle in position and lurched up to his knees, almost falling forward as he spread a quick burst of rifle fire among the Feddies who had held him motionless for so long.

Then there was more incoming fire, but not from so close. Alfie dove in among the bodies of the three men he had just killed, and called Tory.

"They were waiting for us."

# 25

**The arrival of** a new Commonwealth fleet had caused the Federation battle group to retreat to Q-space. No one in the combined Commonwealth task forces expected the retreat to be permanent, however. As soon as the enemy devised a plan to meet the new situation, they would almost certainly be back.

"We simply can't give them any time," Admiral Greene said on a link that included all of the ships' captains and Rear Admiral Regina Osgood, who had her flag on HMS *Cornwall*, one of the two battlecruisers among the new arrivals. "The Feddies still have us outgunned. We have to get the Fourth on the ground fast, before the Feddies come back. We'll use the battlecruisers for high cover. Let the frigates go as low as they can without skimming air, and use all of the fighters to cover the landings."

"We're ready to launch the Fourth," Osgood replied. "I had the men in their shuttles when we came out of Q-space."

It was only the work of another minute to get tactical dispositions to all of the captains. In eight minutes, all of the ships would be in position to launch the Marines of the Fourth Regiment and cover them on their way down. Most of the shuttles would remain on the ground afterward, at least temporarily, available to ferry men and supplies—as conditions permitted.

"I want to get the various scattered elements of the Second Regiment back together as quickly as we can," Greene said, "subject to tactical considerations on the ground."

It was during those eight minutes while the fleet was moving into position that CIC received the first reports from the surface about the earlier Federation landings. CIC immediately relayed that news to Admiral Greene. "It looks as if their shuttles grounded half filled, as if they're trying to pick up the men they already had on the ground and make a fighting withdrawal."

Greene and Osgood, with their respective operations chiefs on line, discussed the possibilities over a holographic link.

"Do we let them withdraw?" Osgood asked. "If they abandon Coventry, we've won without risking anything more."

Paul Greene could not reject the suggestion out of hand, although that was his inclination. Even with the arrival of *Cornwall* and the other ships accompanying HMS *Charlotte*, the Fourth's transport, Greene's force was still not equal to the Federation battle group. The presence of two dreadnoughts insured that. Contesting the withdrawal meant chancing serious losses, and the Commonwealth could scarcely afford to lose capital ships. Landing Marines under combat conditions, when the enemy might be able to launch fighters to hunt shuttles, could be costly as well.

"We take them," Greene said after a moment's reflection, to convince himself that his instinctive response was the correct one. "We're talking about serious war crimes on the ground here, Regina. They have systematically attempted to destroy every foundation for human settlement on an entire world and run the entire population out into the wild. It's been a thousand years since humans treated other humans that badly. We can't let them walk away from it, certainly not on one of our core worlds."

Osgood did not argue. "I had to make the suggestion, Paul, but I don't like the idea of letting them walk either." She hesitated. "I don't think it would play well back on Buckingham either. The Admiralty left the decision to you, but there's been publicity about what the Federation has done here, and public sentiment is very strong."

Greene nodded. "Let's get the Fourth ashore before the

Feddie ships come back. We're ninety seconds from shuttle launch.''

People from a dozen homes along the east side of the road had joined in the rescue efforts started by Joseph Evans and the Bailey father and son. They hauled wounded civilians in from their backyards and the verge of the forest. Houses that had already been crowded with residents and other refugees overflowed now with the addition of casualties.

A few Marine medical orderlies had come to help treat the casualties, but there were too many wounded for any but the most seriously hurt to get immediate treatment. There were not nearly enough trauma tubes available, and the Marines could not abandon their own casualties completely. Even some individuals with life-threatening wounds had to wait and take their chances. The only good news was that no additional casualties were suffered by civilians during the rescue operation. The ground fighting was far enough away, and no Federation aircraft returned.

West of the homes, the fighting continued.

Alfie Edwards and his fire team had been unable to withdraw. They were pinned down; but with the rest of their platoon providing covering fire, the Feddies couldn't get at them.

*I wish I was a mole,* Alfie thought. Twenty minutes of hearing bullets flying by too close for comfort had taken their effect on his nerves. Twice, grenades had exploded close by, but each time the fire team had been saved by all of the wood around them. They had crawled into the dense thicket that had occasioned their predicament in the first place. Only a grenade that dropped right in among them would be certain to cause serious damage, and the profusion of tree trunks made that prospect slight.

*Just lie here and wait,* Alfie reminded himself. He had told his companions the same thing, several times. It had been ten minutes since he had even dared try a shot at the Feddies who had them pinned down. The odds against were simply too long. *Let the other blokes handle the heroics this time. Just stay alive.*

"Stalemate so far, Alfie-lad," Tory said. "They can't get at you. They can't get at us."

"But you can't get to us either."

"Soon enough, Alfie. It's not just us. The rest of our lads are doing what they can. Alpha's pushing in from your left, trying to force the Feddies south, and they're sending a platoon around to reinforce us here. Just keep your head and arse down."

*I can't get them down any farther unless somebody shovels dirt in my face,* Alfie thought. That image caused a deep shiver. Getting dirt shoveled in his face was an all-too-likely prospect.

"These aren't like the Feddies we've fought before," David Spencer told Captain McAuliffe as the rest of the company worked its way around the southern end of the Federation troops, trying to complete the encirclement. "The ones we've faced before never put up this much of a fight."

"We've never faced them when they had a fleet upstairs to back them up," McAuliffe said. "Or when they had shuttles waiting to carry them off."

McAuliffe had posted one platoon, mostly mechanics, to cover the road leading to the Federation shuttles. As long as the landers had only a few men to guard them, they were no threat, and as long as the rest of the Feddies couldn't get to those shuttles, they did not merit further attention.

H&S Company had the farthest to travel as McAuliffe tried to encircle the Feddies. Delta would bend around behind them. Alpha was working to close off the northern end and link up with the I&R platoon. The elements of both line companies that were not moving worked to keep up the pressure on the Feddies to allow the rest to get to their new positions.

"They still walked into something they shouldn't have, sir," Spencer said. "Why didn't they just pull the people they already had here back to the shuttles while they could instead of sending more men in where they might not be able to get out? They could have done that without risking anything. The one lot was close enough to get to their LZ before we could have stopped them.''

''Don't ask me to read minds,'' McAuliffe said. ''Maybe their intelligence is even worse than ours. Maybe they thought they had the numbers to do the job. Or maybe they just had ludicrous orders: 'Do the job you were sent to do, no matter the cost.' ''

For the first time since starting their move around the end, H&S came under fire then, just a scattering of rifle fire, but enough to halt the advance as everyone went to ground.

''To the left, sir,'' Spencer said. ''Either we didn't go far enough west before we turned or we've just run into a patrol.''

''Take a squad and see if you can tell,'' McAuliffe said.

''Aye, sir.'' David gritted his teeth for an instant. ''First squad, come with me,'' he said after switching channels. ''Time to see how much good all that training's done.'' The first squad of headquarters platoon consisted of clerks and the captain's driver. For eighteen months they had complained about their lead sergeant's attempts to turn them into I&R Marines.

*I wish I did have proper I&R lads for this,* David thought as he led the squad off to the left. He glanced around at the men he did have—clerks, red-tape specialists. Even if they had taken most of the combat training courses that the line companies got, they had spent less time rehearsing them. They were still just clerks. They spent more time at complinks than anything else, more time sitting on their backsides than squirming through the dirt.

The patrol had been moving for five minutes before David realized that he had not seen or heard anything to complain about in the performance of his clerks. They might look awkward trying to sneak through the forest, but they were being careful. They almost looked like proper Marines.

*Maybe,* David thought, careful approbation with no accompanying smile. He positioned himself in the middle of the squad. The corporal on point moved more slowly than an I&R point man might, but under the circumstances that was no criticism. The only alternative would have been for David to take the point himself. In some circumstances, he might have done that, but these lads—the oldest was only twenty-three, most had not seen their twenty-first birthday— needed him in the middle of the formation, where they could all see him, where they were all close enough to take some consolation from his proximity.

It was poor sound discipline, but David did not stint himself on the occasional comment or suggestion, delivered softly, either to a single individual or to the entire squad, as needed. The patrol had been out for twelve minutes when the point man stopped and sank slowly to the ground, first squatting, then going flat. The rest of the squad went to cover as well.

"Sarge, I think I've got something," Corporal Jengin Rice whispered.

"What?"

Rice hesitated. "I can't see it now, but there was movement that didn't look right, maybe camouflage moving the wrong way."

"Keep watching. I'll be up there in a moment."

David moved on elbows and knees. Eventually he slid into position next to Rice. "Where?" he asked.

Rice cautiously raised an arm a little and pointed. "I think it was like a small area of green moving one way while everything else moved more the other way."

"How far out?"

"I don't know," Rice said. "At least twenty-five yards. Maybe twice that. I just can't be sure."

"Don't worry about it," Spencer said. He thought that the distance was probably nearer the larger estimate, because at twenty-five yards there was little chance that an enemy sentry would have missed seeing Rice before he went down. David looked behind him. The next man in line had a grenade launcher. David gestured for him to come forward.

"Give me the launcher."

The private complied as quickly as he could. He had his rifle in his hands, the grenade launcher slung on his back.

When Spencer finally got the weapon, he checked to make sure that it was loaded. There was a full chain—five grenades—in it, one in the chamber, four in the awkward magazine below.

David used the squad channel. "Keep your heads down. I'm going to drop three grenades out there, in an arc. Wait for the third one to pop, then give it another four seconds before you get your heads out of the dirt. Then be ready for anything."

Three grenades: *left, right, center,* David decided. He adjusted the sights for fifty yards. That was as close as "The Book" advised dropping the rocket-propelled grenades. The kill radius was thirty yards in open terrain. Even at fifty yards, the shrapnel could do serious damage.

David lifted up to his knees, slowly, and brought the grenade launcher up the same way. *One, two, three.* He took in a breath and held it while he launched the three grenades. As soon as the third was out, he dropped forward, going flat on his face. The flames of the grenades' propellant burned out before they left the barrel, but the grenades made a tearing noise as they ripped through the greenery toward their destinations. The flight was too short for that noise to give an enemy time to recognize the sound and react. But if someone had heard them pop out of the barrel, or seen the flash of the final exhaust of flames, there might be time for a few shots before . . .

One, two, three: the grenades went off with little more than a second separating first from last. The sounds blended together, initial explosions and the ripping of wood and leaves as the shrapnel raced away. There was a sharp crack as one large branch broke and a subsequent crashing sequence as it came down through other branches.

David strained for sounds of gunfire through the echoes of the explosions, but he heard nothing close, nothing that seemed to be directed at his patrol. He lifted his head enough to look.

"Keep low now, but let's move on," he told the squad. "By low, I mean on your knees."

Knees and elbows. Spencer patted Rice on the shoulder

to tell him to start moving. They needed to get close to where the explosions had been, just in case somebody had an idea where the grenades had come from and decided to retaliate in kind. Change positions just to make it harder for the enemy to target them.

David dropped back into the third spot in line. "Unless we run into hostiles, keep going until you reach the edge of the blast areas," he told Rice. "Then pull in and wait for me."

The squad scuttled along on elbows and knees, rifles in their hands. In combat, men could move rapidly even in an awkward crawling position. Adrenaline, from fear or anticipation, kicks in. The body finds new limits, and sometimes surpasses even those. Even normally deskbound sorts such as these clerks moved at a lively pace.

When the patrol reached the edge of the grenades' major damage, the men spread out just short of it. There were no real craters, but it was easy to see where each grenade had exploded from the way the ground had been stripped bare and the surface layer of dirt and detritus pulverized. Over and around the impact spot, the heaviest damage to trees was found.

There were also four Federation soldiers to mark the locations. Only one showed any sign of life, and not for long. Multiple wounds in his chest and stomach were oozing blood, and there appeared to be serious internal damage.

"Captain?" Spencer was on a direct link to McAuliffe. "We've scratched four Feddies. Where the RPGs went off. No sign of anyone else close."

"Wait for us there. Good work."

*Allocation of resources.* The phrase itself had become overused in the councils Paul Greene held to determine how best to send in the Fourth Regiment. His first, and easiest, decision was that he would not break up individual battalions. The Second Regiment was too fragmented on the ground. As soon as possible, Greene planned to correct that, but in the meantime he would not exacerbate the problem by shipping in the reinforcements the same way. Regimental headquarters and the four line battalions would go down at once. The engineers and heavy weapons battalions would be held aboard *Charlotte*. Now Greene regretted sending the Second's engineers down in the initial assault. There would be a lot of work for engineers after the fighting was over, starting the people of Coventry on the road to recovery.

The next decision was where to send each of the Fourth's line battalions. Where would they do the most good? Where were they most needed? Those questions needed study, and there was no time to do that properly. *Concentrate on the three largest cities,* Greene decided. *Secure those first and you've accounted for three quarters of the Feddies on the ground.* The Second had battalions in each of those cities, but they had not been able to finish off the enemy forces they faced. The smaller cities and towns, those not already secured or being contested by the Second Regiment, would simply have to wait. In any case, the situation was not out of control anywhere where there were already Marines on the ground. The towns that they had not been able to get to yet . . . there was simply no help for that.

Greene's ships moved into position. The Spacehawks of all four battlecruisers were launched to cover the Fourth's landers. *At the double:* they had to try to get everyone on the ground before the Federation fleet returned to contest the landings.

There were long minutes of deep anxiety for Greene and his subordinate commanders. Every available camera and sensor was looking for the first hint of the Feddie fleet returning. Every possible eye was scanning monitors. And, aboard the shuttles carrying the Fourth, the men knew how precarious their situation might become if Feddie ships and fighters came back to attack them before they could get out of those boxes.

Remembering to breathe became a chore for Admiral Greene. There was no masking his anxiety now. It was something everyone on the flag bridge of *Sheffield* shared. Even though they were not in one of those shuttles, exposed to any enemy weapon that came within range, they felt the tension. They knew the risks.

"Here they come!" The shout, coming after ten minutes of near silence interrupted only by the whispered necessities of duty, was a shock to Greene and many of the others. Two people were pointing at video monitors. The admiral blinked and scanned his own bank, then saw the new blips, hardly identifiable images yet, of Federation ships that had returned to normal space.

Their spread and courses showed that the Federation commander had anticipated Commonwealth landings. His ships were moving to intercept. Fighters were being launched. Frigates were heading for the lowest approaches they could make without leaving the vacuum of space that was necessary for their survival. The full Federation battle group appeared to have come in for this. All of those ships seemed intent on attacking Commonwealth shuttles. None of them were on vectors that indicated designs against the Commonwealth task force. Even the two dreadnoughts were going in as low as might be safe, trying to bring their weaponry to bear on the shuttles and on the fighters accompanying them.

If they had returned from Q-space even three minutes sooner, the Federation might have caught the flotilla of landers high enough to do massive damage. It would not have been inconceivable that they might have destroyed more than half of the shuttles, more than half of the troops.

But those three minutes made a galaxy of difference. Even the last shuttles had gone atmospheric before the Feddie ships started to blink into normal space and launch fighters and missiles. By the time those weapons were launched, the shuttles were too deep in the atmosphere of Coventry for the Feddies to get at more than two or three in the air.

Once on the ground, it took the Marines only seconds to evacuate each lander and go to ground, away from the easy target. Federation fighter pilots took those easy targets, as many as they could on a single pass. By that time, though, it was almost an empty gesture.

# 26

**Alfie and his** companions could neither retreat nor go forward with any hope of surviving, but they remained untouched where they had taken refuge. Gradually, the rest of the I&R platoon moved in closer on either side, but it looked as if they might have difficulty actually linking up with Alfie's fire team. The range between the platoon and the Federation units was simply too close, even in thick forest. Gaps remained on either side, gaps that could not be crossed safely.

"Spend your ammo smart," Alfie told his men. "There's no telling how much we'll need it later." They had already fixed bayonets. If the fighting got much closer, they could be down to blades and fists in a matter of seconds.

"Tory, this is gettin' a trifle uncomfortable," Alfie said after the fight had been going on for forty minutes. He thought it was a magnificent piece of understatement.

"Just keep both ends down, Alfie," Kepner replied. "We've got these Feddies surrounded now."

"Anyone bother to tell them?"

"They'll get the message soon enough. If it's any comfort, the captain just passed the word. The Fourth Regiment is on the ground."

"I didn't hear any shuttles," Alfie complained. "Where the devil are they?"

"Ah, none close by. They're taking care of the cities first. We still have to do for ourselves for a while longer."

"The Fourth might as well be back on Buckingham then."

At almost any other time, Tory would not have indulged

in such chatter, or permitted others in his platoon to. Sound discipline was not so important at the moment, except that talk reduced concentration on the more important concerns. But . . . *I've got to keep him occupied so he doesn't get some wild notion in that red head of his to get up and charge the Feddies,* Tory thought. Alfie Edwards had a low frustration index.

"It means the lads in front of us are on their own, Alfie-lad. They can't look for any help, and if they've got any sort of communications, they'll know the end is coming for them. Maybe they'll wise up and surrender."

"And maybe the lasses from Sweet Marie's will show up to tuck us in tonight," Alfie said. Sweet Marie's was the most notorious bordello in the Cheapside district of Westminster, back on Buckingham, the strip where most of the sailors and Marines from the CSF base took their liberties.

"If they do, you'll have to cover for me," Tory said. "I'm a married man, remember?" He frowned. It was a poor time to think of his family. "Time to quit larking about, lad. It's bad form to let the mind wander too far during a show like this."

Tory looked right and left, checking on the placement of his men—those he could see. There wasn't an RPG left in the platoon. The last grenades had been launched in the first rush to keep Alfie's fire team safe. Nor was there any immediate prospect of getting even a single chain of grenades from anyone else. When the rest of H&S Company got into position, maybe. Tory had been on to David Spencer. Some of the grenadiers in the other platoons had a few grenades left. Whether or not they still would when they completed the ring around the Feddies was another question.

"How much longer, David?" Tory asked, switching channels again. "We've still got Alfie's team hanging by their chins."

"I'm not forty yards from you now," Spencer said. "Alpha's in position on the other side. We've got the Feddies encircled now. We're just waiting for the captain to decide what we do next."

"It would help if someone could drop a few grenades in

on top of the Feddies closest to Alfie, with enough warning for our lads to make like worms and burrow in. You've got their positions, don't you?''

Spencer let his gaze flicker over the head-up display on his visor that showed the positions of Commonwealth helmets. ''I see them. I don't know that any of my lads are up to anything that precise though. Alfie's almost on top of the nearest Feddies. The lads in Alpha might have a better angle. Let me check. Tell them to get down and stay down.''

David needed several minutes to arrange the diversion. Before he called Alpha's lead sergeant, he had to check with Captain McAuliffe. When everything was set, he called Tory back. ''Forty-five seconds. As soon as the volley of grenades goes off, tell Alfie to get his lads back to the rest of you. We'll give them general covering fire, all the way around the corner.''

Tory checked the time on his visor as he relayed the information to Alfie. Then they all waited.

Alfie had already squirmed as deeply into the debris on the forest floor as he could. He continued his efforts, though, virtually attempting to flatten his body out by an act of will. He knew the damage that shrapnel could do at close quarters, and he also knew just how close the nearest Feddies were. If any of those grenades went off in the air—detonating on a tree trunk or limb—instead of when they hit the ground, the shrapnel could easily rain in on Alfie and his comrades. Little bits of hot metal could not tell friend from foe.

He would worry about withdrawing from the exposed position after the grenades went off . . . if he were still able to worry then. He heard the first grenades tearing through the forest canopy on their high trajectories. Heard them plunging in. He brought his shoulders up a little, against the rim of his helmet. His teeth were gritted, his eyes closed. *Should've asked how many grenades,* he thought. It was too late now. He would just have to wait for the silence to return after the explosions, or until somebody told him to get up and move.

The chain of explosions was continuous, rocking the

trees, scattering debris, and shaking the ground that Alfie was hugging. He held his breath. Counting the blasts was impossible. He could only hold on and hope that he would still be alive—and able to move—after the last shrapnel and debris had come to rest.

*What if a tree falls on me?* That sudden fear was somehow worse than all of the rest. He could hear wood cracking. Somewhere close, trees or large branches were falling, too weakened by the shrapnel to continue holding themselves up.

"Now, Alfie!" Tory shouted over the radio. "Up and back here. While they've still got their heads down."

"Let's go!" Alfie shouted on his fire team's channel, but the others were getting up even as he started to lever himself to his feet. Alfie was only partly conscious of the fact that they were all moving in the right direction. It would have been easy to get that wrong, far too easy.

He was almost unaware of the rifle fire pouring into the Federation positions as he ran back to where the rest of the first squad was. Alfie dove over a fallen tree trunk and did an involuntary somersault before coming to rest.

Alfie could do nothing but lie on his back and stare into the forest canopy while he sucked in monstrously deep breaths. His lungs felt as if they were burning, or trying to turn themselves inside out. He could hear Tory talking to him, but he could not make out the words at first. He certainly could not begin to reply.

"Just lie there, Alfie-lad." Finally, Alfie understood the words in his earphones. "Try to relax. Your heart's beating over two hundred times a minute."

*Can't be,* Alfie thought. *It'd blow itself out.* But he could not get in enough air to even try to talk.

"I've stuck a patch on. You'll be right in a minute or two." Tory had never seen vital signs go so completely berserk before. Selectively, the platoon sergeant could view medical data on each of his men. Monitors were built into each helmet, and the telemetry could be used by officers and noncoms. Alfie's heart rate had actually gone well over 225, almost went into fibrillation, and his respiration and blood pressure had fluctuated all over the place, from deeply depressed to wildly exaggerated. Tory had known that he had to do something quickly, and he wasn't certain that the medical patch he had slapped on Alfie's neck was the right thing to do, but the relaxant patch's nanobugs ought to give Alfie time, even if they could not correct the problem on their own. It might be a half hour before a medical orderly could get to Alfie, maybe with something better suited to the problem.

"Keep you eye on him, Mac," Tory told John McGregor. "I think he'll be okay for now. I've got to get back to the rest of the platoon."

McGregor simply nodded. He didn't feel that he had all that much extra air for talk yet himself.

Tory slid off through the undergrowth, keeping the fallen tree trunk between him and the Feddie positions as possible. There was still a lot of shooting going on, but most of it was farther off now. *There must be fighting going on all around the perimeter now,* Tory thought.

He needed a moment to get to the positions the rest of the platoon held. There had been some movement in the minutes that he had been concentrating on Alfie. He was ready to call Spencer again, to find out what they were going to do, when a long series of explosions—quite some distance off—stopped him.

"Must be on the other side," he whispered. The blasts seemed to go on and on, a series of chains, some overlapping, others separate, for two minutes or more. Most he could identify as grenade explosions, maybe Commonwealth, maybe Federation, but some of the blasts were deeper-toned, and louder than grenades or small antipersonnel land mines.

*What the hell?* he wondered. Then Captain McAuliffe came on the noncoms' circuit.

"The Feddies are attempting a breakout on the east side. They've punched at least three holes through Alpha and they're pouring through. We've got to push in after them. Tell your men to watch out for any surprises the Feddies may have left behind."

• • •

Al Bailey could not recall ever working so hard, or sweating so much. No matter how many trips he made out into the fields east of the road, and no matter how many other residents came out to help, there always seemed to be more wounded people who needed to be carried in for medical help. There was scarcely room left in any of the houses on the east side of the lane to hold any more casualties. And there were scores of dead lying between the houses and the forest. More than a few of the dead were people Al had known.

At one point, after perhaps a half dozen round-trips, Al had managed to catch his reflection in a window. What he saw shocked him so badly that he went inside to look in a mirror, to get a better image of himself. His face was streaked with blood and tears and dirt. His cheeks seemed sunken, as if he were near starvation. His eyes were bloodshot and dripping tears. Seeing his eyes made Al aware that they hurt, stung. But there was no time to do anything about any of what he saw. He had to get back to work.

On his next trip out behind the Evans house, Al had found something too useful to be left with the corpse of its owner, a revolver and a full box of ammunition. Al had stuck the pistol in his belt, under his shirt, and the ammunition had gone into his rear pocket. There were still Feddies on Coventry. He might find a use for the weapon.

The searchers had finally reached almost to the woods. Al, his father, and Joseph Evans stood at the edge looking around for several minutes, even peering beyond the first ranks of trees. All three of them were breathing heavily. They had run across from the Evans house. To the north and south, other residents were still carrying wounded back to their homes, or to the shady sides of them, so that they could be treated. But there were no longer any wounded close enough for Joseph and the Baileys to go after them.

"We've done our bit, I think," Evans said, not quite gasping for breath. "Let's rest up for a minute or two, then go home. The women are going to need all the help we can provide."

Reggie was staring west, through the gap between two houses, not really listening to what Evans was saying. "It sounds as if the fighting has picked up again. Listen to it."

Joseph blinked several times. He had not been conscious of the sounds of battle. Gunfire, explosions. There seemed to be a hint of fire growing in the forest, maybe a mile away.

"It would serve them right if they got themselves burned out," Joseph whispered, talking to himself. "They burned out enough of us."

"Are my ears playing tricks on me, or does it sound like the fighting is moving this way?" Al asked.

A startled look crossed his father's face. Reggie tried to listen more closely, tried to decide if his son was right.

"I can't tell," he said after a moment. "It's all a jumble."

"If it is moving this way, we'd best get back to the house now, while we can," Joseph said. "We might not be able to make it later."

Joseph was too tired to run, but he rushed the walk as much as he could, until he was breathing so hard that he had to slow down. Reggie had already fallen behind, his chest burning from the effort. Al didn't stop until his father called for him to wait. With his back to the others, Al moved his right hand to his waist, feeling the comfortable hardness of the revolver under his shirt.

*Maybe I* will *get a chance to use it,* he thought. There was a dizzying headiness to the idea.

Al glanced over his shoulder. His father had almost caught up. That was good enough for Al; he started moving again. At first, he tried to restrain his pace; he didn't want his father to yell for him to slow down again. But soon he was moving almost at a run. Al didn't slow down until he got to the rear door. Inside, he had to step past and over wounded. They were lying on every piece of furniture that would hold them, and on the floor in every room.

"We couldn't find any more wounded," he announced, loud enough that his mother, Mary Evans, and the other adults who were helping the casualties could hear. "It sounds like the fighting's getting closer again."

His mother scarcely looked up from the young woman

she was bandaging. She did not notice that her son went straight through to the front door and out into the courtyard of the Evans house.

As soon as he opened the front door, Al was certain that the fighting was closer. It seemed to be moving toward the road again. He crossed to the stone pillar next to the gate, an almost subconscious recognition of the need for caution gripping him. He had seen too much blood, too many dead and wounded Coventrians, to be totally reckless now. There was so much blood on his clothing that it was hard to tell what colors the shirt and trousers had been before.

Al's right hand touched the butt of the pistol in his belt as he looked across the road and between two houses. He could not see any of the combatants, but he could hear the sounds—even the occasional scream of a wounded man.

*If I get a chance to do anything, I'll take it.* Then he took the revolver out from under his shirt, making sure that his back was to the door, so that neither his mother nor father would be able to see it. He checked to see that all six cylinders were loaded, then put the gun back in his belt. After his shirt had been pulled down over it, he looked back to assure himself that the gun had not been seen by anyone who might take it away.

*It's my world too. I've got every right to help kick the Feddies off.* He looked at the door again, defiantly this time. *Just give me a chance.*

# 27

"**Sir, you were** there at the beginning, weren't you?" Lieutenant Zileski asked on the bridge of HMS *Hull*.

"At the beginning of what?" Ian Shrikes asked. He had not been paying much attention to the casual conversation going on around him. *Hull* and the rest of the fleet were in Q-space, about ready to return to Coventry again. Between his worries about that return and making certain that all stations were prepared for whatever might come, he had tuned out all but the essential duty talk.

"Back when Admiral Truscott changed all of our tactical doctrine to start diving in and out of Q-space so quickly."

Ian smiled. "You make it sound as if it were a generation ago, and not . . . barely eighteen months."

"That's not what I meant, sir. What I meant was, well, I mean, didn't the admiral think that it would give us a big advantage over the Feddies?"

"It *did* give us a big advantage, Lieutenant, over-whelming even. For all of five weeks. Two engagements. And I doubt that Admiral Truscott expected the advantage to last even that long. In war, if one side comes up with an important innovation, the other side has to find some way to counter it in a hurry, or else. All that the admiral was really interested in when he started working out the new tactics was winning one battle, the one he was involved in at the moment. The rest was beer and gravy, as they say. He was improvising to meet a very immediate crisis. That shaped the way both navies operate."

"That was a decisive engagement," Zileski said.

"And now we just play hide-and-seek," Shrikes said,

sensing the frustration that had prompted the original question.

"Yes, sir. At least, that's how it seems. One side comes out of Q-space, the other ducks in, taking just a passing swipe on the way out, if that. Come back in and the other side scoots. That sort of show. It can go on forever, now, can't it?"

"Theoretically, unless one side withdraws from the system. Barring that, the first commander to make a serious mistake comes up the loser. Those are the facts of life for us now. It does place more emphasis on intelligence and training, less on the sheer size or strength of your forces." Ian went quiet for a moment. One of the responsibilities of command was helping junior officers develop professionally. Zileski had not been looking for a lecture when he asked his question, but Ian would not pass up the opportunity to make a point.

"At times like this, that makes a difference," he said. "Losses are difficult to replace. The Commonwealth can't afford to build all of the ships we'd want to have clear numerical superiority each time we meet the enemy. And, as far as I know, the Commonwealth has no plans to build anything comparable to the Feddie dreadnoughts. They are simply too expensive to build and maintain, and too easy to lose in combat."

"You mean saving *money* is more important than winning the war?" Disbelief was clear in Zileski's voice.

Ian laughed. "Money is an important consideration, even in wartime, Lieutenant. Especially in this war, I fancy. And it's more important for us than it is for the Federation. Their, ah, tax base, is much larger than ours, and they aren't so strictly limited in what they can extract from their population."

"It seems a bit of a letdown, sir," Zileski said. "I mean, fighting a war with accounting clerks rather than patriotism."

"It's the accounting clerks on Buckingham and Union who might bring this insanity to an end someday, Zileski. Don't slight them."

• • •

Noel Wittington's lips were bleeding. Over the last several hours he had bit at them so much that they were raw and extremely painful. He had been out collecting wounded for most of that time, starting almost as soon as the Baileys and their host had. The casualties, the dead and the wounded, were mostly strangers to Noel. He had only seen two people he recognized as coming from South York, and he only knew one of them by name.

After his first several trips out to help the wounded, he had started collecting weapons as well as people—weapons and ammunition, stockpiling them next to the house he was staying in. Inside, that house was quickly packed with casualties. Up and down the lane, there had to be two or three hundred injured civilians . . . and at least as many dead had been left out in the fields.

Once the wounded had all been accounted for, Noel had started going from house to house, looking for able-bodied men. "We've collected some weapons and ammunition. Those Marines might need our help. By God, Coventry is *our* world. We should be helping to kick those Federation bastards off, not just sitting around waiting for someone else to do it for us."

There was no time for him to recall the ignominious results of his previous encounter with Federation soldiers. For the first time in many days he did not rub at the fading tattoo that they had placed on his forehead. He did not even think about Captain Stanley.

"We can get together enough of us to make a difference," he told people. "Maybe make *the* difference."

For all of his arguments and cajolery, he earned only meager results. After talking to at least fifty men, he had persuaded only eight of them to join him, and few of those had shown any real eagerness for the prospect of fighting. Saying yes to Noel had simply become less distasteful than continuing to listen to him. The only really avid volunteer had been a twelve-year-old boy, one Noel had met in the camp to the east, and the boy's parents had vetoed the idea out of hand. Noel had not tried to change their minds, but he had used the example of the boy to try to attract more adult volunteers. Later, when the sounds of fighting intensified and started to move toward the houses, two more men came to accept the challenge.

"I think it's time we move out to where we can get a piece of this," Noel told his ten volunteers. "If those Feddies get to the houses, they might start burning again."

He led his men across the road. Behind cover of one of the houses on the west side, Noel listened to the gunfire and explosions for several minutes, trying to decide which way to head. *A little farther to the south,* he decided. *It sounds like that's where it's hottest.*

Eleven civilians, armed with a motley collection of mostly old weapons, few with as many as twenty rounds of ammunition, ran toward the low stone wall that separated the yard from the forest beyond. None of the men noticed the twelve-year-old boy who came running after them, clutching a revolver in his hand. Al Bailey was very determined. He wanted a part of this. And he would not be denied.


Alfie Edwards felt as if he had been put through a blender, poured out, and frozen back in shape. He still felt more than a little shaky—his hands were trembling violently—but mostly from the memory of what he had been through. It had been a novel, and entirely unpleasant, experience, one that he had no desire to ever repeat. But his vital signs were back to normal—relatively close to normal, in any case— and he was eager to get back into action.

*I sure don't want more time to think about it. I might really freeze up then, like Baker.* It hadn't been fear in Alfie's case, except perhaps a retroactive sort. He had experienced fear often enough, and he knew how to deal with that, how to use it to his advantage. He had no idea what had happened to him this time, how his body had gotten so far out of control, going berserk just when he was reaching safety after a sticky patch. He had never even heard of the like, nor had the medic who had treated him.

Alfie wasn't even certain how much time he had lost. But when he became aware of his surroundings again, when his heart and lungs were through with their nearly catastrophic race, the battle seemed to be raging even hotter than it had been while all of the covering fire was being laid down to let his fire team escape from the tight corner they had been in.

Then came the word that the Feddies were breaking through on the other side, heading east, back toward the houses and all of those civilians.

"I'm ready to go, Tory," Alfie said. "No use me hanging around back here."

Tory's arguments had been short and halfhearted. Within two minutes, Alfie was back with the rest of the squad, pushing through the area where the Feddies had been earlier, moving past the bodies of dead and wounded who had been left behind.

There was a lot of confused talk on the noncoms' channel. Alpha had been split three ways by the Federation break-through. They had heavy casualties, but were still trying to keep between the Feddies and the civilians—with less and less success. Part of Delta was pushing through behind, along with H&S, trying to catch up with the Feddies, while the rest of Delta was swinging around the end, trying to get as many men as possible between the Feddies and their shut-tles. Squads were getting separated from their platoons; platoons were getting separated from their companies. All over the place individual Marines were losing touch with their mates.

*A right bloody mess,* Alfie thought. The I&R platoon was together, at least.

A burst of gunfire made first squad take cover. The Feddies were leaving behind ambushes to slow down the pursuit. They would shoot, then withdraw, sometimes under cover of a series of grenades.

"They've broken free of the forest," an anonymous voice said on the noncoms' channel. "They're heading for the houses."

Noel and his volunteers, including the uninvited Al Bailey, saw camouflaged uniforms coming out of the forest.

The first to emerge were Commonwealth Marines, breaking to either side, withdrawing slowly, still fighting, trying to stop the Federation soldiers from breaking clear of the encirclement.

"Those are Commonwealth men!" Noel shouted as one of the men in line with him started to raise his rifle. "Hold on. It's the folks they're shooting at that we want a piece of. Wait until they come out into the open where we can get clear shots at them." It was no more than fifty yards from the thirty-inch high stone wall they were crouched behind to the edge of the trees.

A dozen Marines sprinted toward the wall and took up positions to the right of the civilians. The Marines gave Noel's group a close look, but no one said anything to the civilians. They merely got into firing positions and waited, rifles pointed into the gap between two other groups of Marines.

Neither Marines nor civilians had long to wait.

Al recognized the different camouflage pattern at once, even before he could see the outline of the Federation crest on the sides of the new helmets—the crest was also in camouflage colors and almost impossible to make out at a distance.

A wedge of Federation soldiers went into prone firing positions right at the edge of the forest, most taking cover behind trees. They opened fire together. Noel shouted a command for his civilians to return the fire. The Marines also opened up, though their orders were not heard by the civilians.

Al had knocked one rock out of the wall in front of him. That let him keep more of himself behind cover, so that the entire top of his head wasn't exposed. He rested the barrel of his revolver in the notch. He could sight and fire, and only a little of his head, and his hand, were exposed to enemy fire.

He had never fired a pistol before. The recoil of the first shot surprised him. The gun came up off of the rock ledge. It was clear that he had not hit anything with it. At fifty yards, he wasn't certain that he would be able to hit a standing target, let alone one lying on the ground exposing so little. But he kept shooting, aiming as carefully as he could, just over the helmets he could see, estimating the ballistic fall of his shots. But the only basis he had for that was the .17 caliber pellet gun that he had received for his last birthday, and the two weapons were certainly not comparable.

After emptying the revolver, Al pulled back to reload. He felt disgusted with himself. As far as he could tell, he had not scored a single hit, not even a minor wound. His hands were trembling as he reloaded, an awkward operation done for the first time.

*I've got to be more careful,* he told himself. *I know what it feels like now. I can do better.* He closed the cylinder and pulled back the hammer before he moved into position to start shooting again. He was only barely aware of a slight whooshing noise, nearly to the far end of the squad of Marines. Out of the corner of his eye, though, he did see a couple of those Marines throw themselves flat on the ground next to the wall.

It was pure reflex that made Al start to dive sideways as well, but he wasn't quite fast enough. He really did not hear the sound of the grenade exploding behind the Marines. All that he was aware of was the agony as bits of hot shrapnel tore into his unprotected body.

Noel Wittington had been marking his shots carefully. Conscious of how few rounds of ammunition he had, he was particularly determined to make them count. He was certain that he had hit at least one Feddie. The bullet had struck the man's shoulder, from the top, right next to his helmet. Noel hoped that the bullet had gone on to do massive damage inside, but he could not simply watch to see if the man moved. He looked to his next target instead.

He heard the grenade explode off to his right. Noel looked that way and saw Marines and civilians fall. Just as he looked back out toward the Feddies, he saw an object arcing through the air toward him, a thrown grenade, not one fired from a launcher.

His next actions were not the product of Home Defense Force drills or conscious thought. They came from some instinct too primal for reflection or fear. Noel tracked the grenade as he might have tracked a cricket ball. He did not try to catch it though. As it hit the ground on his side of the wall—where it would have made casualties of the rest of his volunteers, Noel threw himself over the grenade, smothered it under him.

He was not aware of the explosion.

# 28

**With Patrick Baker** permanently out of the picture, and Ramsey Duncan not yet returned to duty from his injuries, there was little point in continuing to run I&R's first squad as two fire teams. Fourth squad had also been reduced to, effectively, one fire team. Second and third had each lost a single man in the fighting.

Geoffrey Dayle set the pace for first squad now, and indirectly for the entire platoon. For once, Tory did not try to rein Dayle in. That was less because he thought it might be a waste of breath and more because speed was critical now. But the speed brought its own problems. A few men in the platoon had trouble keeping up with the Coventry native, tripping over exposed tree roots or falling into tangled underbrush.

The men took risks they might not have in other circumstances. Here and there, the Feddies had left land mines behind to stall the Commonwealth pursuit. But Dayle seemed to have a charmed life. The one time he did come within range of a mine, he spotted it before it could go off, and dove to the ground as he shouted a warning, then detonated the mine with a single rifle shot.

A sergeant from Alpha Company provided commentary on the Federation breakthrough on an open noncoms' circuit. The Feddies were heading directly for the nearest houses. There were more civilian casualties. A group of locals had come out with weapons to try to help stem the Feddie movement. Those civilians and a squad of Marines had been caught between two RPG explosions. Although no one had been able to check yet, it appeared as though there might be more dead than wounded in both groups.

Just minutes later, there was another update from the sergeant. The Feddies had not taken cover in the houses or started to torch them. They had merely grabbed as many uninjured civilians as they could find out of the houses, holding them on the side of their formation facing the woods, and out in front, using them as human shields. The Feddies were headed south, obviously trying to win through to their shuttles so they could escape from Coventry.

The Feddies moved south between the two lines of houses, not out in the road, but in front of the houses on the west side of it, using the buildings for cover as well, leapfrogging from one to the next—*fire and maneuver*—with more men providing the covering fire than were moving at any given time.

More Commonwealth Marines were emerging from the forest, or stopping just before the trees ended, keeping pace with the Feddies, and even getting a little ahead of them. But they could not stop them. There were too many civilians to permit random fire into the Feddie ranks. Everything was single shot, not fully automatic.

Tory brought his platoon out from the forest north of the Federation soldiers, behind them. He had new instructions from Captain McAuliffe. Once more, the platoon was being asked to do more than their share, a lot of hard physical effort that would be followed—almost certainly—with more difficult fighting. I&R moved across the road. For a moment, they came under fire from the Feddies, but from a range of more than two hundred yards. That fire was not especially accurate.

John McGregor fell as the platoon crossed the road. He tumbled to the ground, hard, knocking the air out of his lungs. At first, he wasn't aware that he had been hit. He thought that he had simply tripped. It was only when he tried to get back up and found that his legs would not support him that he looked and saw the blood gushing from his left thigh.

"I'm hit," he called over the platoon channel. The others had gone past him.

Alfie dove to the ground where he was, then turned to look back. ''How bad?''

''My leg. I think the artery's bust.''

The rest of first squad stopped to provide covering fire. Alfie crawled back toward McGregor while the rest of the platoon got to the low stone wall on the east side of the road and helped cover him. By the time Alfie got to McGregor, the man from Bannockburn had lost consciousness from loss of blood.

''Hang on, lad,'' Alfie said. ''I'll take care of you.'' Alfie worked frantically. The blood that McGregor had lost worried him. A man could bleed to death in a hurry from a severed artery. He stripped the sling from McGregor's rifle and tied a tourniquet around the upper thigh. That was far more urgent than getting the two of them out of the way of the gunfire.

Eugene Wegener slid to the ground on the other side of the wounded man. ''He would be the biggest man in the platoon,'' Wegener grumbled. ''It'll take the both of us to move him.''

''Let's hit it. Grab him up and let's scoot,'' Alfie said.

With their own rifles slung, Edwards and Wegener got up, hauling McGregor with them. They started to move east even before they were fully erect.

John McGregor's weight seemed to increase with each step. Before they were halfway to the cover of the low stone wall that fronted the road, Alfie found himself wondering whether they would be able to make it. *Deadweight,* he thought. *How'd he get so bloody heavy?* Then Alfie pitched over toward the left, last domino in a chain reaction as the other two fell into him. Alfie hit the ground hard. For an instant, he lost consciousness, but came awake even as the other two were being pulled off of him and dragged the rest of the way to cover.

''What happened?'' Alfie asked.

''McGregor's dead, and Wegener's in bad shape. I don't know if he's going to make it,'' Tory said once they were behind the wall. ''You're not bleeding at any rate. How do you feel?''

"Like someone dropped a bleeding tank on top of me."
But Alfie started to raise himself up.

"Don't get too high. We've only got about twenty-four
inches of wall between us and the Feddies. Give it another
moment until they're farther off."

Tory gave his men just one minute before they ran on to
the cover of the nearest house on the east side of the road,
carrying Wegener with them, and laying him with several
civilian casualties who had been lined up there.

"We've got a long haul now," Tory told his men. "The
captain wants us to go around and get in front of the Feddies, set up a cross fire so that they're stuck. We're to be
careful about the civilians, but the idea is to get guns on so
many sides of the Feddies that the hostages aren't enough
for them."

Tory knew that there would be casualties among the hostages, almost certainly. There had been already. That could
not be helped. The Federation soldiers—there appeared to
be about three hundred of them left, slightly less than the
number of effectives that the three companies of Marines
could still muster—*would* be stopped, whatever it took. That
was the order.

The I&R platoon could not race along behind the houses
at full speed for long. When they crossed the gaps between
houses, which varied between thirty and one hundred yards,
they were in full view of the enemy, within eighty yards of
them at their nearest approach, and they drew fire each time
they came in view. The platoon had to provide its own covering fire, one squad moving across the gap while the rest
did the shooting, trying to aim more carefully than they
normally did during that kind of maneuver; they had to try
to avoid hitting civilians. The Feddies were under no restric-
tions. They didn't worry about creating civilian casualties,
but used all of their weapons. Several of the houses took
hits from RPGs or antiaircraft missiles.

It took Tory and his men until the last house along the
road before they got ahead of the Feddies, and even then it
was only by a matter of a few dozen yards, scarcely enough
to matter. The platoon took up positions to fire into the

Feddies, who finally had to stop, with the last house shielding them from the west. Their cover was about to run out. There were no more buildings, and the gap before the road moved into forest was nearly two hundred yards, with more than half of the Commonwealth Marines now in position to reach them.

*This is where they've got to give it up,* Alfie thought. *They must know they can't make it across that gap. It's quit or die.* After the day he had had, Alfie desperately wanted the confrontation to end soon. But he did not need long to decide that he was wrong, that the Federation soldiers were still going to try to escape. The hostages were moved about, some put in front, others shifted to the left side. There weren't enough to provide a solid wall around the Feddies, but the hostages were spaced out as best they could be.

None of the Marines could hear the order that was given, but the Feddies came up from their firing positions and started forward again, pushing and dragging their hostages along. A few, a very few, civilians managed to pull free and run off to one side or the other before diving for cover. No attempt was made to recapture them.

"I don't believe it!" Alfie said as he started shooting again. The Feddies had not moved into the courtyard of the house behind them. That would have given them good cover on two sides and fair cover on the other two. It would have given them a chance to hold out . . . for a time. "They're still going to try for their bloody shuttles."

Soldiers and hostages fell. The formation continued to move south, closing over the gaps in its ranks as possible. Almost from the start, the Feddies were losing a dozen men or more for each pace south they made. There was no question of the outcome. By the time the group reached the midpoint between the last house and the cover of the forest, there were no more than thirty soldiers and a half dozen civilians still on their feet. The civilians were dragged to the ground, the Feddies continuing to use them as shields, as ramparts around a makeshift perimeter. They rested rifles on the backs of the hostages and used them as shooting rests. But it was only a matter of minutes before the last Federation soldiers stopped firing. They were out of ammunition. Slowly, very slowly, seven soldiers got up, their hands above their heads.

The I&R platoon was the nearest Commonwealth unit. Several of the men got up almost as soon as the Feddies did. Tory was too busy watching the last surviving enemy soldiers, too horrified at what had happened in the last few minutes to give enough thought to his own men, to think of the possibility.

Geoffrey Dayle had just slipped a fresh magazine into his rifle. He needed less than a second to empty it into the seven men who had just surrendered.

Dayle dropped his rifle just as Tory Kepner swung his own weapon to knock the gun from Geoffrey's hands. Then Tory brought his rifle butt up and across, smashing it into Dayle's helmet, knocking him to the ground.

In space, the cat-and-mouse game continued. While the Commonwealth task force was over Coventry, reports came up from the surface. Hawthorne was the first contested site to be won. Over the next eight hours, several other units reported an end to hostilities in their areas. Some Federation shuttles did get off the ground, mostly from towns where there had been no Commonwealth presence. Fewer than half of those shuttles made it back to their transports, though. Commonwealth Spacehawks went hunting, and shuttles had little chance of escaping those birds of prey.

Sunset moved across the major settlements of Coventry. Fighting continued in Coventry City, South York, and The Dales. But not for long. Before midnight, local time, the last Federation units on the ground had surrendered. Two hours earlier, the Federation battle group had retreated into Q-space. It had not returned.

On the flag bridge of HMS *Sheffield*, men and women turned to look at Admiral Greene when news of the last troop surrender was relayed by CIC. The bridge watch stared, waiting for the admiral's reaction to the news.

Paul Greene remained motionless. Not even the expression on his face changed. For nearly a minute, he didn't so much as blink. It took time for the news to register on a mind numbed by exhaustion and the tension of the past days. The blink came, finally. Then another. Greene squeezed his eyes shut for a moment and let out his breath. The fight was over, on the ground, at least. In space? He opened his eyes.

"CIC, is there any trace of that Feddie fleet yet?"

"No sign at all, Admiral, not as far out as we can scan."

"Do you think they've gone home, Admiral?" Greene's aide asked. "Is it over?"

Greene's answer was slow in coming, and was preceded by a deep sigh. "I don't know. I hope so. Maybe that's why the Feddies on the ground finally started to surrender instead of fighting on. Maybe they were told that their fleet was leaving." He paused and looked around the bridge, his glance stopping briefly on each of the people there, as if he had never seen any of them before.

"I don't know," he repeated. After another shorter pause, he said, "We'll maintain battle watches through the night. If the enemy battle group hasn't returned by local dawn in Coventry City, we'll proceed on the assumption that the Feddies aren't going to return."

He frowned. "There's still a lot of work to be done here, and it will take time before Buckingham can send in all of the specialists and materials that are going to be needed. For the time being, it will be up to us."

Greene stood, very slowly. For a second, he feared that his knees were going to buckle under him. He squeezed his eyes shut for a moment, then opened them.

"I've got to get some sleep," he mumbled as he staggered off of the bridge.

# Epilogue

**It was three** weeks later before the Second Regiment of Royal Marines left Coventry, and another month after that before the Fourth was relieved. By that time, elements of the Seventeenth Territorial Army and the 101st Air Defense Wing had been transferred to Coventry, along with an engineering battalion and nearly two hundred civilian specialists to assist the people of Coventry in rebuilding their world.

In Hawthorne, Al Bailey was one of the few survivors from the group of civilians who had tried to help fight the Federation off. His right arm had been so badly shattered by shrapnel that it had to be amputated above the elbow. That meant a long term in a trauma tube for Al while the arm was regenerated, and many months of physical therapy before the new arm was able to do everything the old one had.

Noel Wittington did not survive. Only his instinctive dive to cover the second grenade with his body had allowed any of the others with him at the wall to survive. Of the eleven men, four survived, in addition to Al Bailey.

John McGregor was buried with military honors within a mile of the place where he had died, along with the other Marines who had died in the liberation of Hawthorne. Privates Eugene Wegener and Ramsey Duncan were returned to duty following medical treatment. Private Patrick Baker was returned to Buckingham for treatment and then given medical discharge from the Royal Marines. His status as a combat veteran invalided out of His Majesty's Combined Space Forces helped him to land a civil service job in government, Ministry of Crown Lands.

• • •

Four days after the conclusion of hostilities on Coventry, Private Geoffrey Dayle, Headquarters and Service Company, First Battalion, Second Regiment of Royal Marines, was court-martialed for killing seven Federation soldiers who had already surrendered. Seven Marine officers sat in judgement. Private Dayle refused to present any defense, even though there was a possibility of a sentence of death or life imprisonment.

The inescapable verdict was guilty. The sentence delivered was forfeiture of all pay and allowances, and immediate discharge from the Royal Marines. The discharge was issued within an hour after the verdict was rendered, less than ten minutes after Colonel Arkady Laplace, as convening officer, gave it his approval.

Geoffrey Dayle did not return to Buckingham with the regiment. He remained on Coventry, the world of his birth.